THE WORLD'S CLASSICS

AN ANTHOLOGY OF ELIZABETHAN PROSE FICTION

PAUL SALZMAN has taught at Monash, Adelaide, and Melbourne Universities, and is currently a Lecturer in the English Department at La Trobe University, Melbourne, Australia. He is the author of *English Prose Fiction 1558–1700: A Critical History* (Oxford: Clarendon Press).

An Anthology of Elizabethan Prose Fiction

*Edited with an Introduction
and Notes by*

PAUL SALZMAN

Oxford   New York

OXFORD UNIVERSITY PRESS

Oxford University Press, Walton Street, Oxford OX2 6DP

Oxford New York
Athens Auckland Bangkok Bombay
Calcutta Cape Town Dar es Salaam Delhi
Florence Hong Kong Istanbul Karachi
Kuala Lumpur Madras Madrid Melbourne
Mexico City Nairobi Paris Singapore
Taipei Tokyo Toronto

and associated companies in
Berlin Ibadan

Oxford is a trade mark of Oxford University Press

Introduction, Note on the Texts, Select Bibliography,
and Explanatory Notes © Paul Salzman 1987

This selection first published 1987 as a World's Classics paperback

British Library Cataloguing in Publication Data

Data available

Library of Congress Cataloging in Publication Data
An Anthology of Elizabethan prose fiction.
(The World's classics)
Bibliography: p.
1. English fiction—Early Modern, 1500-1700.
I. Salzman, Paul.
PR1293.A58 1987   823'.3'08   87-5759
ISBN 0-19-281744-2 (pbk.)

5 7 9 10 8 6

Printed in Great Britain by
BPC Paperbacks Ltd.
Aylesbury, Bucks

CONTENTS

CONTENTS

INTRODUCTION

A GENERATION ago, an introduction to an anthology of Elizabethan fiction would probably have begun with an apology. The reader would be, perhaps, gently coaxed into conceding some merit to these 'obscure' (or 'slight', or 'quaint') works. A change has occurred. No one would be so bold as to say that a reader, even a scholarly one, would now reach for a work of Elizabethan fiction ahead of a Shakespeare play or a Donne poem. However, as modern fiction has turned away from unrelenting realism, so tastes have generally widened sufficiently to appreciate the many kinds of narrative loosely grouped under the title of this anthology.

The five works presented here illustrate the wide variety of approaches to prose narrative that flourished alongside the vigorous experiments with poetry and drama that characterize the Elizabethan period. Ranging from Gascoigne's *Master F.J.*, published in 1573, through to Deloney's *Jack of Newbury*, which probably first appeared a generation later, around 1597, this anthology also allows the reader to trace the changes that fiction underwent during a time of rapid literary, as well as social, development.

My selection has involved some difficult choices. As a generic category, 'Elizabethan Fiction' is a convenient holdall rather than a coherent classification. If we include translations, over a hundred works of prose fiction (counting collections of stories as single items) were published between 1558 and 1603. Many are of interest only to the specialist, but setting those aside, an editor forced to choose five appealing and representative texts will have to reject a number of likely candidates. John Lyly's sequel to *Euphues: The Anatomy of Wit, Euphues and His England* (1580), is a lively account of the further adventures of Euphues and more particularly of Philautus.[1] The romance form can be traced through various

[1] It can be most conveniently found in *Complete Works of John Lyly*, ed. R. W. Bond (Oxford, 1902).

metamorphoses by following the work of Robert Greene, especially in *Menaphon* (1589)[2], and the greatest and most complex work in this genre, Sir Philip Sidney's *Arcadia*, is now readily available in its original form (the *'Old' Arcadia*) as a World's Classics volume.[3] In choosing Greene's *Pandosto*, the source for Shakespeare's *The Winter's Tale*, I have had to sacrifice the source for *As You Like It*, Thomas Lodge's fascinating romance *Rosalynde* (1590).[4]

While Nashe's *Unfortunate Traveller* is in many ways a unique work, it can usefully be compared to formally disjunctive works appearing in the 1590s, such as Henry Chettle's *Piers Plainness* (1595), Greene's *The Black Book's Messenger* (1592), or even Nashe's own *Pierce Penniless* (1592).[5] A similar range of works awaits the reader who wishes to explore Deloney's style of fiction, including Deloney's own works, *The Gentle Craft* (*c*.1598) and *Thomas of Reading* (*c*.1599).[6]

Short fiction also flourished during this period, stimulated by many translations from French and Italian writers, but including numerous native productions. Starting with William Painter's large collection *The Palace of Pleasure* (1566), moving through the individual stories of George Pettie's *A Petite Palace of Pettie his Pleasure* (1576), to the stories of Greene and Barnaby Rich in the 1580s and 1590s, the Elizabethan short story was a favourite hunting ground for dramatists in search of a good tale to turn into a plot for a play.[7]

---

[2] *Menaphon* has been edited by G. B. Harrison (Oxford, 1927).

[3] Sir Philip Sidney, *The Old Arcadia*, ed. Katherine Duncan-Jones (Oxford, 1985); the revised *New Arcadia* is best consulted in Sidney's *Prose Works*, ed. A. Feuillerat (Cambridge, 1912).

[4] *Rosalynde* is printed in Geoffrey Bullough, *Narrative and Dramatic Sources of Shakespeare*, ii (London, 1958).

[5] *Piers Plainness* in *The Descent of Euphues*, ed. James Winny (Cambridge, 1957); *The Black Book's Messenger* in *Works*, ed. A. B. Grosart (London, 1881–6); *Pierce Penniless* in *Works*, ed. R. B. McKerrow, rev. F. P. Wilson (Oxford, 1958), or more conveniently in *The Unfortunate Traveller and Other Works*, ed. J. B. Steane (Harmondsworth, 1971).

[6] In *The Novels of Thomas Deloney*, ed. Merrit E. Lawlis (Bloomington, 1961).

[7] For the Elizabethan dramatists' use of fiction, see Max Bluestone, *From Story to Stage* (The Hague, 1974).

After much sifting, the five works presented here were chosen for two main reasons—first, for their intrinsic interest, not just for students and scholars, but for general readers; second, for their ability to display the wide range of fiction, aimed at an increasingly diverse audience, produced during the Elizabethan period. To appreciate Elizabethan fiction, a modern reader will, as I stated at the beginning of this introduction, probably have less trouble with its avoidance of the realism that a previous generation associated almost inextricably with the nature of the novel. This led to studies of Elizabethan fiction which engaged in an anachronistic search for glimmers of novelistic realism.[8] Indeed, we are now adjusting to forms of criticism that relentlessly remind us of the narrative as text, not mirror in the roadway. A reader who enjoys recent fiction by a wide range of writers from Lessing to Calvino to Rushdie to Borges will scarcely repine over the fact that *Pandosto* is not like *Middlemarch*. The greatest barrier that might remain, however, is that of style.

Even when it is modernized, as it is here, Elizabethan prose is often difficult. The prose used by writers of narrative in particular often seems eccentric; Lyly's style, which acquired the name of euphuism, being the most obvious example. The reason is simply that fiction played an important part in the sense of excitement and controversy that surrounded writers' use of the vernacular. Each writer represented here was engaged in an experiment: an exploration of a style suitable for narrative. We need not be as acutely aware of rhetoric and its rules as the Elizabethans to appreciate the effect of pens twisting language this way and that.[9] Lyly's balanced sentences, Nashe's new-coined words, reveal an acute stylistic self-consciousness. This is less evident in Deloney, who wrote for a different audience, but *Jack of Newbury*, while written 'in a plain and humble manner' (p. 313), is not nearly as plain in style as Deloney's disclaimer might lead one to believe. In

---

[8] A problem with Margaret Schlauch, *Antecedents of the English Novel 1400–1600* (London, 1963), and even David Margolies, *Novel and Society in Elizabethan England* (London, 1985).

[9] For Elizabethan rhetoric and Elizabethan fiction see W. G. Crane, *Wit and Rhetoric in the Renaissance* (New York, 1937).

these narratives, the nuances of style, from G.T.'s raised eyebrow 'etc.' (p. 61) in *Master F.J.* to Nashe's claustrophobically familiar bullying in the persona of Jack Wilton, must be savoured by the reader.

Between the first and last works printed here an important change can be traced. The fiction of Gascoigne, Lyly, and especially Sidney, was written by people we might characterize as amateur authors, who addressed a real or feigned audience of gentlemen (Gascoigne) or ladies (Lyly, Sidney). Greene and Nashe are important examples of a new kind of writer, more like a professional writer.[10] In *Pandosto*, Greene, in search of patronage, was still writing a dedication to a gentleman. By the second edition of *The Unfortunate Traveller*, Nashe had deleted the dedication to Henry Wriothesley, third Earl of Southampton. Deloney dedicated *Jack of Newbury* not to a noble patron, but 'To All Famous Cloth Workers in England' (p. 313). The enormous increase in the production of prose fiction right through the period covered here, and continuing on through the following century, parallels the general expansion of vernacular printed books as the population grew more literate. The result of this was a greatly expanded range of narrative; by the end of the sixteenth century many different forms of prose fiction flourished, aimed at specific audiences.

While my comments on the individual works printed here will make it clear that I lay great stress on how unique each is, it would be misleading to see Elizabethan fiction as a completely hermetic series of distinct genres. Popular works were influenced by courtly works, and vice versa. A writer like Greene could turn his hand to anything from elevated romance to cony-catching pamphlets (stories of the tricks played by Elizabethan 'con-artists'). Elizabethan fiction frequently mixed modes of narrative together; that is an essential aspect of its liveliness. Rosalie Colie has pointed out that 'literary invention . . . in the Renaissance was largely generic', and Elizabethan authors were fascinated by hybrid types (*genera mista*: mixed genres).[11] So Nashe tries his hand

[10] See Margolies, chap. 3.
[11] Rosalie Colie, *The Resources of Kind* (Berkeley and Los Angeles, 1973), p. 17, chap. 3.

at satire, travel narrative, sermon, mock-romance, historical fiction, and even more in *The Unfortunate Traveller*, to take just one example of this impulse.

One thing does hold these works together: an interest in a tale, or ways of telling a tale. In his *Defence of Poetry*, Philip Sidney, whose definition of poetry includes prose fiction, focuses on this aspect of the poet's power: 'with a tale forsooth he cometh unto you, with a tale which holdeth children from play, and old men from the chimney corner'.[12] It is not just the story that's the thing, it is also the method of telling it. That is perhaps most evident in *Euphues*, where Lyly might well seem more interested in rhetorical display than plot. Another key aspect of this is the 'repetition with variation' evident in Elizabethan narrative.[13] Elizabethan authors did not share the post-Romantic obsession with 'originality', so it comes as no surprise to find, for example, Thomas Lodge using the Middle English romance called *Gamelyn* as the basis for his *Rosalynde* (1590), which Shakespeare in turn used for his play *As You Like It*.[14] But more than this sense of unconcern about how 'new' a story should be, the authors collected here were interested in the angle of attack taken by the writer when a particular subject is tackled. In the early part of the twentieth century, Russian formalist critics expounded the useful distinction between *fabula* (the subject matter of the narrative) and *sujet* (the manner of telling the story), often labelled today 'story' and 'discourse'.[15] The exploration of *how* a story can be told, reshaped, retold, repeated with a (narrative) difference is evident in Gascoigne's second version of *Master F.J.* as an Italian story, as well as the

[12] Sir Philip Sidney, *Miscellaneous Prose*, ed. K. Duncan-Jones and J. Van Dorsten (Oxford, 1973), p. 92.

[13] A rather more complex notion of repetition in narrative than mine, but one which is still illuminating in relation to some of the issues raised here, may be found in J. Hillis Miller, *Fiction and Repetition* (Cambridge, Mass., 1982).

[14] For a much more sophisticated and important analysis of imitation in Renaissance literature, see Thomas M. Greene, *The Light in Troy* (New Haven, 1982).

[15] See, for example, Boris Tomashevsky, 'Thematics', *Russian Formalist Criticism*, trans. L. T. Lemon and M. J. Reis (Lincoln, Nebraska, 1965), Seymour Chatman, *Story and Discourse* (Ithaca, New York, 1978).

interpolated tales about love and jealousy in the narrative itself; in Lyly's sequel to *Euphues*, his constant circling around the reformed prodigal theme[16]; in Greene's doubled plot in *Pandosto* (not to mention Shakespeare's adaptation of the romance in *The Winter's Tale*); in Jack Wilton's (or Nashe's) role-playing, his re-learning of the same lesson about the follies of travel; in Deloney's relentless rags-to-riches stories, including the repeated motif in Jack's picture gallery. Elizabethan fiction is hungry for the variety of *sujet*, of discourse, of narrative *method*. But it is the individual approach to such narrative variation by the writers represented here that makes Elizabethan fiction so heterogeneous.

MASTER F. J.

THE earliest work printed in this anthology is also in many ways the most sophisticated. George Gascoigne is one of those fascinating, restless Elizabethan writers, whose life and works both involved constant change. His date of birth is unclear (probably 1539, but dates between 1525 and 1542 have been suggested).[17] Gascoigne was educated at Trinity College, Cambridge, left without taking a degree, was admitted to Gray's Inn but did not practise as a lawyer, served, as his father had done, as an MP for Bedford, tried to find preferment at court but ran into debt and fled to the country.

Gascoigne's first known literary works are two plays which he wrote for performance at Gray's Inn when he returned there in 1564: *Supposes*, a comedy based on an Italian play, and *Jocasta*, written in collaboration with Francis Kinwelmersh, a version of Euripides' *Phoenissae*. Gascoigne was involved in a series of lawsuits over various tangled family disputes, and in 1572 he joined the army in Holland, having spent some time in jail for debt. He returned to England quickly, but was forced back to the army under a cloud,

---

[16] For this theme see Richard Helgerson, *The Elizabethan Prodigals* (Berkeley, 1976).

[17] Biographical information stems from C. T. Prouty, *George Gascoigne* (New York, 1942).

accused of various crimes, just when he was about to re-enter Parliament.

It was at this dark stage of his life that he published a volume called *A Hundreth Sundry Flowers*, in 1573. This could best be described as an anthology, or miscellany. It contained Gascoigne's two plays, poems (the hundred flowers of the title), and 'A Discourse of the Adventures passed by Master F.J.' The response to this volume was harsh; as the author explained in his apologetic preface to a revised anthology, called *The Posies of George Gascoigne* (1575), objections were made to 'sundry wanton speeches and lascivious phrases, but further I hear that the same have been doubtfully construed and (therefore) scandalous'.[18] The notion that the narrative of F.J. might refer to a real incident, encouraged by remarks made in the story by the narrator, must have fuelled this response. Gascoigne revised *Master F.J.* for his edition of his *Posies*. He divided his writings into 'Flowers', 'Weeds', and 'Herbs', and among the weeds included 'The Pleasant Fable of Ferdinando Jeronimi and Leonora de Velasco, translated out of the Italian riding tales of Bartello'. The story is the same as that of the first version, printed in this anthology. Gascoigne simply gave the characters Italian names and removed the role of G.T., the intrusive narrator. He protested in the preface to *The Posies* that those who read the first version as a *roman à clef* were mistaken, and his thin disguise of it as a translation would seem to support his assertion, as a true scandal would only be averted by the complete excision of the narrative.

The first version of *Master F.J.*, printed here, is preferable because of Gascoigne's skilful use of G.T. as a narrator (although I have included the account of the fate of the leading characters, added by Gascoigne to the revised version, as an appendix).[19] G.T.'s role is emphasized, before the narrative proper starts, through the exchange with H.W. This exchange is in part a product of the Elizabethan courtly author's desire

[18] *The Posies*, ed. J. W. Cunliffe (Cambridge, 1907), p. 3, my modernization.

[19] The opposite preference is challengingly detailed by Walter R. Davis, *Idea and Act in Elizabethan Fiction* (Princeton, 1969), pp. 97–109.

to seem unwilling to appear in print, but it also prepares the reader for the recessed nature of this narrative, with its rationale disingenuously claimed by G.T. to be merely a provision of the background to F.J.'s poems.

In *Master F.J.*, Gascoigne subjects the code of courtly love to vigorous scrutiny. By 1573, the courtly pose had integrated some of the earlier courtly love stance with a new, almost flirtatious, relationship between the sexes. F.J.'s narrative begins with the hero launching himself into the courtly love pose, writing an elegant letter declaring his passion to Elinor. The affair is immediately cast in a satirical light by the doubts raised about the authenticity of Elinor's letter of reply. While on the one hand F.J. and Elinor are adopting the ceremonial roles of 'HE' and 'SHE', G.T. is determined to draw the reader's attention to the sexual opportunism and hypocrisy behind the poses. This prepares us for Elinor's soft shrieking when she willingly succumbs to F.J.'s advances.

F.J., perhaps because of G.T.'s presentation, shifts between the role of naïve lover playing out the courtly love rituals, and that of a nasty gloater, happy to send up Elinor's husband as a cuckold. The role of the third major character, Frances, is also quite ambivalent. On the one hand, Frances waits in the wings, an alternative to Elinor who is ignored by F.J., content to offer him advice and comfort. On the other hand, she is far from being the passive female onlooker; a notable example of how she avoids this role is her theft of F.J.'s sword, that glaringly obvious phallic symbol, leeringly emphasized by G.T.

For all its often coarse humour, the narrative is quite harsh in its implications. Frances and F.J. exchange the titles of 'Hope' and 'Trust'—holding out the possibility of a very different relationship from the one developed between F.J. and Elinor, 'HE' and 'SHE': merely the anonymous labels of gender. However, F.J. refuses the chance. We watch him become harsher as his affair degenerates; he engages in a virtual rape as the promise of spring slides into summer in the course of the narrative. This is, for the characters if not the reader, a 'thriftless history', to quote G.T. Lessons spelled out allegorically in the interpolated tale of Suspicion are not

learned. Frances' tale of reconciliation after infidelity stands
as a final image of lost chances in this story. *Master F.J.* could
be described as a comedy of manners with a sting in its tail.

EUPHUES

JOHN LYLY's *Euphues: The Anatomy of Wit* sets out to
provide the reader with a fruitful, rather than thriftless,
history. However, *Euphues* had an impact as a style rather
than as a story. When Lyly wrote *Euphues* he was trying to
achieve some recognition at Elizabeth's court, having cut a
figure at university as a fashionable young man. In his
important book *John Lyly: The Humanist as Courtier*
(London, 1962), G. K. Hunter has described Lyly as the
typical example of the decline of the Renaissance 'Humanist
ideal' to 'that of "the courtier" who . . . was to use his learning
as decoration, not as part of his belief' (p. 31). Lyly's
grandfather was a distinguished humanist, a friend of More
and Erasmus; Lyly himself danced the tightrope of the court
with much more success than Gascoigne, but still found his
position ultimately frustrating. Following the success of
Euphues and its sequel, he wrote a number of plays for
performance by the boy actors of St Paul's and the Chapel
Royal, but he never gained the major court favour he sought.

The elaborate prose style that Lyly achieved in *Euphues* was
an instant success, to the extent that it even became
fashionable to *speak* euphuism as well as write it. Like all
fashions, that of euphuism faded, became quaint with the
passing of time. Shakespeare mocked it in *1 Henry IV* by
having Falstaff speak it when he plays at being king: 'For
though the camomile, the more it is trodden on the faster it
grows, yet youth, the more it is wasted the sooner it wears'
(II. iv. 393 ff.). One can see the attraction of euphuism by
comparing Lyly's tightly structured sentences with the often
loose, even rambling periods of Gascoigne. Lyly's elaborate
use of antithesis and alliteration may seem monotonous now,
but it had the distinct advantage of giving prose sentences a
firm shape, in contrast to many other sloppy approaches to
prose.

As Jonas Barish points out in an excellent analysis of Lyly's style, euphuism encapsulates 'the precarious closeness of extremes'.[20] Euphuism is not just a matter of opposing clauses and alliteration, but of opposing strings of illustrative examples: 'The fine crystal is sooner crazed than the hard marble, the greenest beech burneth faster than the driest oak, the fairest silk is soonest soiled, and the sweetest wine turneth to the sharpest vinegar' (p. 94). As Lyly points out later in the narrative, 'neither is there anything but that hath his contraries' (p. 101).

Setting the importance of Lyly's prose style and his exploration of humanist ideas aside, there is no doubt that *Euphues* has less narrative interest than the other works printed here. In fact, many readers of *Euphues* have felt the way that Samuel Johnson felt about Richardson: 'If you were to read (him) for the story your impatience would be so much fretted that you would hang yourself.' Of Richardson, Johnson went on to say 'You must read him for the sentiment, and consider the story as giving occasion to the sentiment', and many critics would simply substitute 'style' for 'sentiment' in applying this remark to Lyly. But while Lyly is often interested only in rhetorical display, he does also use his style to explore the situation that Euphues, Philautus, and Lucilla find themselves in, and the soliloquies often reveal a sudden, searching insight into their characters (such as Lucilla's little Freudian slip of 'lust' for 'list', p. 112).

The most challenging attempt to meet head on the modern reader's alienation from euphuism as a style is that of Madelon Gohlke, in her article 'Reading *Euphues*'.[21] She relates the contradictory style to the nature of the narrative itself, focusing especially on the love triangle. While not agreeing entirely with the psychoanalytical basis for this approach, I think that Gohlke makes the interested reading of *Euphues* a distinct possibility for a modern audience, as her provocative closing remarks indicate:

The dominant reality of the tale is betrayal, and it is against this awareness that Euphues, Philautus and Lucilla conduct their endless

[20] Jonas Barish, 'The Prose Style of John Lyly', *ELH* 23 (1956), 21.
[21] *Criticism*, 19 (1977), 103–17.

monologues, their ceaseless search for a principle of stability outside
the self, their manic self-questioning and self-justification. Finally,
even language betrays. Relationships between men and women are
functionally impossible, between men and men only possible through
physical separation. The only security in this tale is in withdrawal,
isolation, and perhaps, silence. (p. 117)

PANDOSTO

ROBERT GREENE's career reflects the social changes I
mentioned earlier in this introduction. Greene began as a
figure who, like Lyly, set out to woo a courtly audience, but
ended as a popular writer, caught up in the expansion of the
reading public. Like his friend Nashe, whose career ran
parallel in many ways, Greene was at all stages of his varied
writing life proud of his university education, of his learning.
Born around 1560 to fairly well off parents, Greene went to
St John's College, Cambridge in 1575. His literary output
began precociously at the age of 20 with the writing of a
euphuistic work called *Mamillia* (written *c*.1580, published
1583). Before he died in 1592, Greene became an incredibly
prolific professional writer, producing a large number of
works of prose fiction, six or more plays, and numerous
ephemeral works.

Pandosto appeared in the middle of Greene's professional
life, perhaps around 1585 (the first extant edition is 1588), a
few years before Shakespeare's dramatic career is thought to
have begun with *Henry VI*. Shakespeare, however, became
interested in *Pandosto* late in his career, long after Greene was
dead. *The Winter's Tale* is generally dated 1611. By that time,
Pandosto had gone through four editions, the latest being
1607. *Pandosto* does not have a place in this anthology simply
because of Shakespeare's use of it, but one cannot deny its
fascination as an example of how Shakespeare worked with an
admired source. As J. H. P. Pafford, the editor of the Arden
Winter's Tale, explains: 'to anyone reading romance and play
consecutively . . . the picture is inescapable of a Shakespeare
who, having closely studied the story and made his plot,

had *Pandosto* at his elbow as he wrote, and as he wrote from time to time turned to the book to refresh his memory, using it sometimes almost verbatim, sometimes with little change, and sometimes with much, and sometimes departing from it altogether, but finding there the constant source for most of his material'.[22]

Pandosto is, in some ways, a more unusual romance than *The Winter's Tale*, for Shakespeare's major change was the creation of a 'happy ending' with the transformation of Greene's Bellaria, who dies after the trial scene, into Hermione, who comes to life at the end of the play. *Pandosto*, through its sour conclusion, shakes up the reader accustomed to romance conventions. In some ways *Pandosto* can be split into two. *Pandosto. The Triumph of Time* is the tragic story of Bellaria and Pandosto, who, as Greene relates at the end of the romance, 'fell in a melancholy fit, and to close up the comedy with a tragical stratagem, he slew himself' (p. 204). However, the 1636 edition took the running title, 'The History of Dorastus and Fawnia', as the main title. Emphasis was thus switched from time's triumph to what later readers were assured was the 'pleasant' history of the two lovers (Shakespeare's Florizel and Perdita), who provide the expected happy romance ending.

This tension in Greene's work adds greatly to its narrative interest (which is not, of course, to criticize what Shakespeare chose to do with the story). In the opening of the romance Greene lays particular stress on the theme of jealousy. The arbitrary nature of that passion links it with fortune, the arbitrary ruler over the romance's plot: 'for all other griefs are either to be appeased with sensible persuasions, to be cured with wholesome counsel, to be relieved in want, or by tract of time to be worn out' (p. 155). Greene's carefully worked out narrative has behind it the central image of fortune's wheel, of the contingent lives of his characters. The central pastoral section, Fawnia's upbringing among the shepherds and her wooing by Dorastus, is hedged about by a much more threatening world. It is telling that Greene's concluding, ambivalent sentence (unintentionally ambivalent, I believe), 'Dorastus,

[22] *The Winter's Tale*, ed. J. H. P. Pafford (London, 1981), p. xxxi.

taking leave of his father, went with his wife and the dead corpse into Bohemia where, after they were sumptuously entombed, Dorastus ended his days in contented quiet' (p. 204), has led some critics to believe that Greene may be implying the death of Fawnia, as well as Pandosto and Bellaria.[23] I do not believe that Greene intended the romance to end on quite so dark a note, but it is not unfitting in view of the general tenor of *Pandosto*.

THE UNFORTUNATE TRAVELLER

THOMAS NASHE began his literary career by writing a preface to Greene's *Menaphon* (1589), a romance of considerable interest in its own right. Nashe was not particularly concerned to say anything about *Menaphon*, but instead took the opportunity to launch himself into the role of *enfant terrible*, which he also displayed in his first full length work published the same year: *The Anatomy of Absurdity*. Like Greene, Nashe attended St John's College, Cambridge, which he praised in the preface to *Menaphon* as 'an university within itself'. Nashe lived for only a dozen years after he left Cambridge in 1588, but for those years he was a controversial figure in the London literary scene. He tried his hand at many genres, never concentrating on one for very long. In 1597 he was forced to run away from London and hide out in Yarmouth for his contribution to the scandalous play *The Isle of Dogs* (Ben Jonson, a co-writer, was jailed). He produced poetry, controversial polemic (taking part in the battle between the established Church and dissenting Puritans known as the Marprelate controversy—Nashe wrote for the Church party), and a variety of prose works which defy exact definition, part-satire, part social comment, one an elaborate religious meditation (*Christ's Tears Over Jerusalem*, 1593), one ostensibly written in praise of the red herring for which Yarmouth was famous (*Lenten Stuff*, 1599).

Nashe, even more than Greene, was throughout his career deeply ambivalent about his literary role. This has been

[23] Ibid., p. xxx.

usefully characterized by David Margolies, focusing on the social change that surrounded Nashe:

The contradictory character of his relationship with his audience results largely from his inability to adjust to the changes of the last quarter of the century. Caught between a disintegrating feudal-aristocratic world view and the beginning of commercialised, bourgeois social relations, he writes for a market yet tries to preserve the character of a literary world run on patronage.[24]

This is very much in evidence in *The Unfortunate Traveller*, with the dedication to Henry Wriothesley omitted from the second edition which appeared in the same year as the first (1594). Through the voice of Jack Wilton, a page, Nashe simultaneously satirizes and celebrates the aristocracy (Jack is a mere 'appendix', but also outplays Surrey in his own role as gentleman; courtly love, sonnet conventions, jousts are all mocked).

The Unfortunate Traveller is perhaps the most challenging and fascinating work of Elizabethan fiction. Much critical argument has been waged over how it might be classified. It was once fashionable to see it as a picaresque novel, but recent scholars have stressed more disjunctive characteristics, linking it to the grotesque mode,[25] to Nashe's highly self-conscious engagement with language.[26] Within this constantly changing work, Nashe displays his virtuosity at a number of genres: jest-book tricks, a sermon, satire, travel literature, historical fiction, revenge-tale, tragedy, tragi-comedy.

All this is tenuously held together by Nashe's explosive prose style, projected into the voice of Jack Wilton. Nashe has been shown to have coined an extremely large number of new words.[27] Within *The Unfortunate Traveller* Nashe displays the tension present as an oral culture becomes a print culture. He is able to pun elaborately on the whole notion of pages,

---

[24] Margolies, p. 86.

[25] Neil Rhodes, *Elizabethan Grotesque* (London, 1980), chaps. 1–4.

[26] Jonathan Crewe, *Unredeemed Rhetoric* (Baltimore, 1982), chap. 4.

[27] Jürgen Schäfer, *Documentation in the O.E.D.: Shakespeare and Nashe as Test Cases* (Oxford, 1980).

paper, and print.[28] At the same time, he is at pains to create an illusion of a speaking voice, almost parodying it: 'soft, let me drink before I go any further' (p. 210). In both senses of the word, the 'page' cannot be trusted; but neither, we find, can the voice, as we see most notably in the chain of horror extending from Heraclide's unheeded words which 'might have moved a compound heart of iron and adamant, but in his (Esdras's) heart they obtained no impression' (p. 277); to Cutwolfe's revenge over Esdras, which involves his enforced speaking of blasphemy followed by shooting him in the throat 'that he might never speak after, or repent him' (p. 307); culminating in Cutwolfe's own punishment, which is a repetition of violent silencing: 'His tongue he pulled out, lest he should blaspheme in his torment' (p. 308). This most linguistically self-conscious work eventually finds no secure resting place on the page or in the voice.

The violence that I have been describing is another feature of *The Unfortunate Traveller* that has disturbed many readers. Nashe's comedy is often witty and satirical, but it is also often linked to violence—much more so in this work than in any other he wrote, which is why I do not believe that it can be explained by some kind of psychological factor in Nashe himself. The public, almost celebratory, violence displayed in the executions of Zadok and Cutwolfe could usefully be linked to the work of Michel Foucault on punishment.[29] Throughout *The Unfortunate Traveller* Nashe makes the body and its ills the subject of extended comic treatment. The celebration of public punishment simultaneously supports its role as a method of control, and subverts that control by paralleling it with Jack's mock-dissection: his fear of dismemberment from which he is comically saved by an execution, just as he himself is saved from execution at the last moment (a moment when he is preparing to celebrate his own death with a ballad called *Wilton's Wantonness*).

This aspect of *The Unfortunate Traveller* also involves the

---

[28] See Crewe, and Margaret Ferguson, 'Nashe's *The Unfortunate Traveller*: The "Newes of the Maker" Game', *ELR* 11 (1981), 165–82.

[29] See especially Foucault's *Discipline and Punish*, trans. A. Sheridan (Harmondsworth, 1982).

whole treatment of female characters, both in Nashe and in Elizabethan fiction generally. Elizabethan fiction, in all its varied forms, generally closes out any position for a woman reader, and that may well be because there were no female authors of fiction in England until the seventeenth century. In Nashe, Heraclide's rape is depicted in a voyeuristic, male-centred manner (Jack peers down at it through a 'cranny'). *Euphues* enthusiastically endorses a popular misogyny. However much he may be undercut at times, we view Master F.J.'s adventures through the leering eyes of G.T., although Frances perhaps provides a challenging female perspective at times. *Pandosto* locks its female characters into traditional romance roles. In contrast, Deloney gives us a portrait of a number of strong-willed women. Although Jack's ultimate happiness is grounded in his second marriage with a conventionally submissive wife, his first wife has the economic and personal upper hand. There are certainly tensions present which feminist critics have yet to explore in Elizabethan fiction.

But to return to Nashe, it is worth stressing that because the tone of *The Unfortunate Traveller* is never stable, it seems to play out a variety of ambivalent attitudes, not just towards women but towards the aristocracy, mortality—even towards travel. Nashe can be seen as a transitional writer, especially at this stage of our understanding of Elizabethan society and culture. Perhaps for that reason he chose to set *The Unfortunate Traveller* in an earlier period, a nostalgic period for the Elizabethans. But even in this Nashe is self-conscious, calling Henry VIII 'the only true subject of chronicles', a phrase with considerable ironic reverberations (how true is Nashe's fictional Henry? What kind of chronicle is this pot-pourri of a book? Is Henry its real subject?).

JACK OF NEWBURY

THOMAS DELONEY also used the reign of Henry VIII as the setting for *Jack of Newbury*. His motives for this seem to have been quite complex. Late in Elizabeth's reign, at a time of economic hardship but also at a time when the power and influence of merchants had increased considerably, Deloney looked back to an earlier age for inspiration, finding it in an account of an actual clothier. Deloney was the only writer represented here who did not attend university and, in contrast to Greene, appealed to a popular audience with which he himself could be identified. Although little definite biographical information about Deloney is available, it all points to a different social situation from the other authors in this anthology. Deloney was a silk-weaver, and it seems probable that his education extended only as far as grammar school at his native town of Norwich.

By the 1590s, Deloney had attained notoriety in London as a ballad writer. In 1597, Deloney turned to fiction, producing four works in approximately three years: *Jack of Newbury*, two parts of *The Gentle Craft*, and *Thomas of Reading*. He evidently died in 1600 or 1601. All of Deloney's works were immensely popular, and *Jack of Newbury* proved to be a best-selling book through the seventeenth century.

It was once common to see Deloney's fiction as an anticipation of the novel in response to a new middle-class reading public. Now, perceptions of both the development of prose fiction and the social structure of Elizabethan England have changed quite dramatically. In *Jack of Newbury* one can see a conservative use of elements such as the jest-book tradition, as well as the more realistic dialogue and the scenes of working life seized upon by earlier historians of the novel. The most important account of Deloney in his social context is to be found in a fascinating book by the historian Laura Stevenson, *Praise and Paradox: Merchants and Craftsmen in Elizabethan Popular Literature* (Cambridge, 1984). Stevenson indicates, in a searching account, how *Jack of Newbury* reflects what could be described as an ideological impasse at the end of the sixteenth century. Merchants had gained great power and influence but no adequate social category was available for them, and frequently the literature which sought to praise them turned to anachronistic values.

Within Stevenson's account of the paradoxical effect of the merchant rise to power, *Jack of Newbury* is a key text because it encapsulates important social contradictions that Deloney powerfully depicts but cannot resolve. When Jack is seen as a lord, a powerful figure able to lead 150 men to war, Deloney backs away from the implied social challenge. Jack does not want to be considered a gentleman. In his confrontation with Wolsey, Jack is safely seen as superior because Wolsey was a man who rose to power from humble origins and abused that power. But beneath Deloney's depiction of Jack as a man content with his position in society, the Jack who refuses a knighthood, lies, as Stevenson writes, a more threatening possibility:

In describing Jack as a prince, however, Deloney raises problems which he cannot solve. It is all very well to show that Jack is a model to his monarch and a governor whose social commitment puts ambitious Wolsey to shame. But one cannot ignore the fact that Wolsey has become a prince by conventional courtly channels, while Jack has become a prince by running a clothing empire. Jack's method of attaining princely dignity puts pressure on the concept of princeliness, even though all his values are those of the elite. For if he is really a prince, then princeliness must depend not on high birth and royal favour, but on the great wealth that comes from industrial service. (p. 124)

All this should not lead one to ignore the more obvious literary appeal of *Jack of Newbury*: its sharply observed comic scenes; its wry social satire; and its brisk chapters, which might well come as some relief to the modern reader who has missed such narrative divisions in the other works printed here. Deloney's purpose seems ultimately to have been didactic, but he easily achieves what Nashe succinctly (if disingenuously) terms, in his dedication to *The Unfortunate Traveller*, 'variety of mirth'. In fact, Nashe's complete purpose could easily stand as a description of the intentions behind this anthology as a whole: 'All that in this fantastical treatise I can promise is some reasonable conveyance of history and variety of mirth.'

ACKNOWLEDGEMENTS

MERRITT E. LAWLIS's fine anthology, *Elizabethan Prose Fiction* (New York, 1967), has been extremely useful to me, and I would like to acknowledge it here as a model of editorial proficiency. A grant from the La Trobe University School of Humanities enabled me to employ the services of Jan Schumacher for some valuable research assistance at the beginning of this project. The secretarial staff of the La Trobe English Department, especially Judi Benney, fought the word processor for me. I would like to thank Gregory Kratzmann for reading and commenting on the introduction, and an anonymous reader for an important suggestion about the date of *Pandosto*. Susan Bye saved me from numerous textual, and other, errors.

NOTE ON THE TEXTS

THIS anthology is directed at a wide audience, and I have therefore modernized the texts in order to make them more accessible. While I have paid close attention to the important position on modernizing set out in Stanley Wells's monograph, *Modernizing Shakespeare's Spelling* (Oxford, 1979), I have decided that the works presented here require a more conservative process of modernization than that followed in the new Oxford Shakespeare. Thus words such as 'accompt' or 'advant' have not been changed to their modern forms of 'account' and 'avouch', but have been glossed instead. All spelling has, of course, been modernized. Direct speech has been marked by inverted commas, and punctuation has generally been added to clarify the sense. Similarly, I have paragraphed the often unbroken stretches of Elizabethan prose.

This is not a scholarly edition with full critical apparatus. However, as the details set out below indicate, each text has been edited afresh from the original printed source. I have, in the notes, indicated particularly important or interesting emendations and variant readings, but obvious errors have been silently corrected.

Master F.J.: The copy-text is a British Museum copy of *A Hundreth Sundrie Flowres* (1573); the narrative is found on sigs. A1-M3. I have compared this with C. T. Prouty's edition of *A Hundreth Sundrie Flowres* (Columbia, 1942), which also provided information for a number of the notes. The text has been checked against the revised version found in *The Posies of George Gascoigne* (1575).

Euphues: The copy-text is a British Museum copy of the 'corrected and augmented' 1579 edition of *Euphues: The Anatomy of Wit*. Only the narrative section, sigs. A1–L4^v, has been reproduced here. The text has been checked against a British Museum copy of the first edition (1578). I have referred to the texts in Lyly's *Works*, ed. R. W. Bond (Oxford, 1902); in *Euphues*, ed. M. W. Croll and W. H. Clemons (London, 1916); in R. Ashley and E. M. Moseley, eds., *Elizabethan Fiction* (New York, 1953); and in Merritt E. Lawlis, *Elizabethan Prose Fiction* (Indianapolis, 1967). All of these have provided information for a number of notes.

Pandosto: The copy-text is the British Museum copy of the first extant edition (1588). (Copies of *The Triumph of Time*, probably the first edition of *Pandosto*, are listed in a 1585 inventory of the stock of the Shrewsbury bookseller Roger Ward, noted by Alexander Rodger in *The Library*, series 5, Vol. 13 (1958), p. 264.) This has been checked against the Folger Library copy of the 1592 edition, which is also followed for the contents of signature B, missing in the BM copy of 1588. I have referred to the texts in the Arden *Winter's Tale*, ed. J. H. P. Pafford (London, 1963); in Lawlis's anthology; and in *Narrative and Dramatic Sources of Shakespeare*, ed. Geoffrey Bullough, viii (London, 1975).

The Unfortunate Traveller: The copy-text is a Huntington Library copy of the first edition (1594), checked against the 'newly corrected and augmented' second edition (also 1594). In following the first edition I am in agreement with Lawlis, as against McKerrow and most editors who have followed him. I have referred to the texts in *The Works of Thomas Nashe*, ed. R. B. McKerrow, rev. F. P. Wilson (Oxford, 1958); in Lawlis's anthology; in *Selected Writings*, ed. Stanley Wells (London, 1964); and in *The Unfortunate Traveller and Other Works*, ed. J. B. Steane (Harmondsworth, 1972). All of these, but McKerrow especially, have provided information for a number of notes.

Jack of Newbury: The copy-text is a Huntington Library copy of the first extant edition, possibly the eighth (1619). The first edition was probably in 1597. I have referred to the texts in *Works*, ed. F. O. Mann (Oxford, 1912), whose copy-text is the 1626 edition; in Ashley and Moseley's anthology; and in

The Novels of Thomas Deloney, ed. Merritt E. Lawlis (Bloomington, 1961), whose copy-text is 1619. All of these have provided information for a number of notes.

SELECT BIBLIOGRAPHY

BIBLIOGRAPHY

An excellent resource for further research is provided by James L. Harner, *English Renaissance Prose Fiction 1500–1660: An Annotated Bibliography of Criticism* (Boston, 1978), which covers the period up to 1976, with supplements available to update the material.

ANTHOLOGIES

R. Ashley and E. M. Moseley, *Elizabethan Fiction* (New York, 1953); Merritt E. Lawlis, *Elizabethan Prose Fiction* (Indianapolis, 1967); G. Saintsbury, rev. P. Henderson, *Shorter Novels: Elizabethan* (Everyman, 1969).

GENERAL STUDIES

Although much of the information is unreliable, a charming and pioneering study is J. J. Jusserand, *The English Novel in the Time of Shakespeare*, originally published in 1890, reissued with an introduction by Philip Brockbank (London, 1966). Another older study that is still useful is E. A. Baker, *The History of the English Novel*, ii (London, 1929). Sections in C. S. Lewis, *English Literature in the Sixteenth Century Excluding Drama* (Oxford, 1954) are useful. An important but somewhat anachronistic attempt to find the sources of the realistic novel in Elizabethan fiction is contained in Margaret Schlauch, *Antecedents of the English Novel 1400–1600* (London, 1963). A very stimulating and wide-ranging approach which studiously avoids such anachronism is found in Walter R. Davis, *Idea and Act in Elizabethan Fiction* (Princeton, 1969), although Davis's thematic scheme becomes rather unwieldy at times. The recent book by David Margolies, *Novel and Society in Elizabethan England* (London, 1985), reverts to some of Schlauch's anachronism and ignores a lot of recent criticism, but still argues an interesting case, albeit one which devalues the sophisticated fiction of writers like Sidney and Gascoigne. The first half of Paul Salzman, *English Prose Fiction 1558–1700* (Oxford, 1985), provides an overview of Elizabethan fiction, while the second half traces the development of fiction through the following century.

More specialized studies include: Margaret Schlauch, 'English Short Fiction in the 15th and 16th Centuries', *Studies in Short Fiction* 3 (1966), 393–434; William Nelson, *Fact or Fiction: The Dilemma of the Renaissance Storyteller* (Cambridge Mass., 1973); Max Bluestone, *From Story to Stage* (The Hague, 1974); R. S. White, 'Comedy in Elizabethan Prose Romances', *YES* 5 (1975), 46–51; Richard Helgerson, *The Elizabethan Prodigals* (Berkeley, 1976), on Gascoigne, Lyly, Greene, Lodge, and Sidney; A. C. Hamilton, 'Elizabethan Romance: The Example of Prose Fiction', *ELH* 49 (1982), 287–99, and 'Elizabethan Prose Fiction and Some Trends in Recent Criticism', *Renaissance Quarterly*, 37 (1984), 21–33.

MASTER F. J.

A scholarly edition of *Master F.J.* is available in *A Hundreth Sundrie Flowres*, ed. C. T. Prouty (Columbia, 1942), while the revised version may be found in *The Complete Works of George Gascoigne*, ed. J. W. Cunliffe (Cambridge, 1907–10), i. Prouty's biography, *George Gascoigne* (New York, 1942), is thorough and useful. The only book-length study is a competent volume in the Twayne series: Ronald C. Johnson, *George Gascoigne* (New York, 1972). Articles on *Master F.J.* have proliferated as discussion has moved from the question of its possible autobiographical content to a consideration of its structural and thematic complexity. Some of the more interesting are: Robert P. Adams, 'Gascoigne's *Master F.J.* as Original Fiction', *PMLA* 73 (1958), 315–26; Frank B. Fieler, 'Gascoigne's Use of Courtly Love Conventions in *Master F.J.*', *SSF* 1 (1963), 26–32; Richard A. Lanham, 'Narrative Structure in Gascoigne's *F.J.*', *SSF* 4 (1966), 42–50; Lynette McGrath, 'George Gascoigne's Moral Satire: The Didactic Use of Convention in *Master F.J.*', *JEGP* 70 (1971), 432–50; Paul A. Parrish, 'The Multiple Perspectives of Gascoigne's *Master F.J.*', *SSF* 10 (1973), 75–84; M. R. Rohr Philmus, 'Gascoigne's Fable of the Artist as a Young Man', *JEGP* 73 (1974), 13–31; Gordon Williams, 'Gascoigne's *Master F.J.* and the Development of the Novel', *Trivium*, 10 (1975), 137–50; George E. Rowe Jr., 'Interpretation, Sixteenth-Century Readers, and George Gascoigne's *Master F.J.*', *ELH* 48 (1981), 271–89.

EUPHUES

The most useful edition of *Euphues* is that edited by M. W. Croll and W. H. Clemons (London, 1916); it is also worth consulting the edition in the *Complete Works*, ed. R. W. Bond (Oxford, 1902).

G. K. Hunter's excellent book, *John Lyly: The Humanist as Courtier* (London, 1962), contains important material on *Euphues*. The best discussion of euphuism is Jonas A. Barish, 'The Prose Style of John Lyly', *ELH* 23 (1956), 14–35; there is also interesting material in Walter N. King, 'John Lyly and Elizabethan Rhetoric', *SP* 52 (1955), 149–61. A series of more recent studies have probed beyond Lyly's prose style, and the interpretation of *Euphues* remains far from being fixed; a selection of these are: Madelon Gohlke, 'Reading *Euphues*', *Criticism*, 19 (1977), 103–17; Theodore L. Steinberg, 'The Anatomy of *Euphues*', *SEL* 17 (1977), 27–38; Raymond Stephanson, 'John Lyly's Prose Fiction: Irony, Humour and Anti-Humanism', *ELR* 11 (1981), 3–21; Richard A. McCabe, 'Wit, Eloquence and Wisdom in *Euphues*', *SP* 81 (1984), 299–324.

PANDOSTO

The best editions of *Pandosto* are in Lawlis's anthology; Geoffrey Bullough, *Narrative and Dramatic Sources of Shakespeare*, viii (1975); and the Arden *Winter's Tale*, ed. J. H. P. Pafford (London, 1963). There is only a small amount of useful criticism available. Brief discussions occur in the general books by Davis, Margolies, and Salzman. René Pruvost's French study of Greene is useful: *Robert Greene et ses romans* (Paris, 1938). Discussions of *Pandosto* in relation to *The Winter's Tale* occur in: Kenneth Muir, *Shakespeare's Sources*, i (London, 1957); John Lawlor, '*Pandosto* and the Nature of Dramatic Romance', *PQ* 41 (1962), 96–113; Bluestone, *From Story to Stage*; and Stanley Wells, 'Shakespeare and Romance', in *Later Shakespeare*, ed. S. R. Brown and B. Harris, Stratford-upon-Avon Studies 8 (1966).

THE UNFORTUNATE TRAVELLER

The scholarly edition of Nashe's *Works*, ed. R. B. McKerrow, rev. F. P. Wilson (Oxford, 1958), is a model of its kind, and the notes on *The Unfortunate Traveller* are a mine of information. The recent biography of Nashe by Charles Nicholl, *A Cup of News* (London, 1984), is detailed, although solid biographical information about Nashe is scarce. Two important early studies of *The Unfortunate Traveller* are: Fredson Bowers, 'Thomas Nashe and the Picaresque Novel', in *Humanistic Studies in Honour of John Calvin Metcalf* (Charlottesville, 1941), and Agnes M. C. Latham, 'Satire on Literary Themes and Modes in Nashe's *The Unfortunate Traveller*', *Essays and Studies*, n.s. 1 (1948), 85–100. Nashe's style is examined in a useful article by David Kaula, 'The Low Style in Nashe's *The Unfortunate Traveller*', *SEL* 6 (1966), 43–57. Other important articles are: Richard A. Lanham, 'Tom Nashe and Jack Wilton: Personality as Structure in *The Unfortunate Traveller*', *SSF* 4 (1967), 201–16; Katherine Duncan-Jones, 'Nashe and Sidney: The Tournament in *The Unfortunate Traveller*', *MLR* 63 (1968), 3–6; Dorothy Jones, 'An Example of Anti-Petrarchan Satire in Nashe's *The Unfortunate Traveller*', *YES* 1 (1971), 48–54; Alexander Leggatt, 'Artistic Coherence in *The Unfortunate Traveller*', *SEL* 14 (1974), 31–46; Charles Larson, 'The Comedy of Violence in Nashe's *The Unfortunate Traveller*', *Cahiers Elisabéthains*, 8 (1975), 15–29; Madelon Gohlke, 'Wits Wantonness: *The Unfortunate Traveller* as Picaresque', *SP* 73 (1976), 397–413; Margaret Ferguson, 'Nashe's *The Unfortunate Traveller*: The "Newes of the Maker" Game', *ELR* 11 (1981), 165–82; Raymond Stephanson, 'The Epistemological Challenge of Nashe's *The Unfortunate Traveller*', *SEL* 23 (1983), 21–36; Ann Rosalind Jones, 'Inside the Outsider: Nashe's *The Unfortunate Traveller* and Bakhtin's Polyphonic Novel', *ELH* 50 (1981), 61–81; Robert Weimann, '*Fabula* and *Historia*: The Crisis of the "Universal Consideration" in *The Unfortunate Traveller*', *Representations*, 8 (1984), 14–29; Mihoko Suzuki, ' "Signiorie over the Pages": The Crisis of Authority in Nashe's *The Unfortunate Traveller*', *SP* 81 (1984), 348–71. There is an interesting discussion of Nashe in Neil Rhodes, *Elizabethan Grotesque* (London, 1980). Two excellent, albeit very different, books on Nashe contain stimulating analyses of *The Unfortunate Traveller*: G. R. Hibbard, *Thomas Nashe: A Critical Introduction* (London, 1962), and Jonathan V. Crewe, *Unredeemed Rhetoric: Thomas Nashe and the Scandal of Authorship* (Baltimore, 1982), the latter drawing on recent critical theory.

JACK OF NEWBURY

A scholarly edition of *Jack of Newbury* may be found in *The Novels of Thomas Deloney*, ed. Merritt E. Lawlis (Bloomington, 1961); Lawlis has also written the only book-length study of Deloney: *Apology for the Middle Class: The Dramatic Novels of Thomas Deloney* (Bloomington, 1960). Critical articles on Deloney are not numerous. The most useful are: Hyder E. Rollins, 'Thomas Deloney's Euphuistic Learning and *The Forest*', *PMLA* 50 (1935), 679–86, and 'Deloney's Sources for Euphuistic Learning', *PMLA* 51 (1936), 399–406; O. Reuter, 'Some Aspects of Thomas Deloney's Prose Style', *Neuphilologische Mitteilungen*, 40 (1939), 23–72; E. D.

Mackerness, 'Thomas Deloney and The Virtuous Proletariat', *Cambridge Journal*, 5 (1951), 34–50; David Parker, '*Jack of Newbury*: A New Source', *ELN* 10 (1973), 173–80; Max Dorsinville, 'Design in Deloney's *Jack of Newbury*', *PMLA* 88 (1973), 233–9; Constance Jordan, 'The "Art of Clothing": Role Playing in Deloney's Fiction', *ELR* 11 (1981), 183–93. An important analysis of *Jack of Newbury* occurs in Laura Caroline Stevenson, *Praise and Paradox: Merchants and Craftsmen in Elizabethan Popular Literature* (Cambridge, 1984).

GEORGE GASCOIGNE

The Adventures of Master F.J.

(1573)

A discourse of the adventures passed by Master F.J.

H.W. To the Reader

IN August last passed my familiar friend Master G.T. bestowed upon me the reading of a written book, wherein he
had collected diverse discourses and verses invented upon
sundry occasions by sundry gentlemen (in mine opinion) right
commendable for their capacity. And herewithal my said
friend charged me that I should use them only for mine own
particular commodity, and eftsoons safely deliver the original
copy to him again, wherein I must confess myself but half a
merchant, for the copy unto him I have safely redelivered; but
the work (for I thought it worthy to be published) I have
entreated my friend A.B. to print, as one that thought better
to please a number by common commodity than to feed the
humour of any private person by needless singularity. This I
have adventured for thy contentation, learned reader, and
further have presumed of myself to christen it by the name of
A Hundred Sundry Flowers, in which poetical posy are set forth
many trifling fantasies, humoral* passions, and strange affects
of a lover.

And therein, although the wiser sort would turn over the
leaf as a thing altogether fruitless, yet I myself have reaped
this commodity: to sit and smile at the fond devices of such
as have enchained themselves in the golden fetters of fantasy,
and having bewrayed themselves to the whole world do yet
conjecture that they walk unseen in a net. Some other things
you may also find in this book which are as void of vanity as
the first are lame for government; and I must confess that,
what to laugh at the one and what to learn by the other, I have,
contrary to the charge of my said friend G.T., procured for
these trifles this day of publication. Whereat if the authors
only repine, and the number of other learned minds be
thankful, I may then boast to have gained a bushel of good will
in exchange for one pint of peevish choler. But if it fall out,
contrary to expectation, that the readers' judgements agree not

with mine opinion in their commendations, I may then—
unless their courtesies supply my want of discretion—with
loss of some labour accompt also the loss of my familiar
friends; in doubt whereof I cover all our names and refer you
to the well-written letter of my friend G.T. next following,
whereby you may more at large consider of these occasions.

And so I commend the praise of other men's travails,
together with the pardon of mine own rashness, unto the well-
willing minds of discrete readers. From my lodging near the
Strand, the 20 of January, 1572.

H. W.

The letter of G.T. to his very friend H.W. concerning this
work.

Remembering the late conference passed between us in my
lodging, and how you seemed to esteem some pamphlets
which I did there show unto you far above their worth in skill,
I did straightway conclude the same your judgement to proceed of two especial causes. One, and principal, the steadfast good will which you have ever hitherto sithens our first
familiarity borne towards me. Another—of no less weight—the
exceeding zeal and favour that you bear to good letters, the
which—I agree with you—do no less bloom and appear in
pleasant ditties or compendious sonnets devised by green
youthful capacities than they do fruitfully flourish unto
perfection in the riper works of grave and greyhaired writers.
For as in the last, the younger sort may make a mirror of
perfect life, so in the first, the most frosty-bearded philosopher may take just occasion of honest recreation, not
altogether without wholesome lessons tending to the reformation of manners. For who doubteth but that poets in their
most feigned fables and imaginations have metaphorically set
forth unto us the right rewards of virtues and the due
punishments for vices?

Marry indeed I may not compare pamphlets unto poems,
neither yet may justly advant for our native countrymen that
they have in their verses hitherto, translations excepted,
delivered unto us any such notable volume as have been by

poets of antiquity left unto the posterity. And the more pity that amongst so many toward wits noone hath been hitherto encouraged to follow the trace of that worthy and famous knight Sir Geoffrey Chaucer, and after many pretty devices spent in youth for the obtaining a worthless victory might consume and consummate his age in describing the right pathway to perfect felicity, with the due preservation of the same. The which although some may judge over grave a subject to be handled in vile metrical, yet for that I have found in the verses of eloquent Latinists, learned Greeks, and pleasant Italians sundry directions whereby a man may be guided toward the attaining of that unspeakable treasure, I have thus far lamented that our countrymen have chosen rather to win a passover praise by the wanton penning of a few loving lays, than to gain immortal fame by the clerkly handling of so profitable a theme. For if quickness of invention, proper vocables, apt epithets, and store of monosyllables may help a pleasant brain to be crowned with laurel, I doubt not but both our countrymen and country language might be entronized among the old foreleaders unto the mount Helicon.

But now let me return to my first purpose, for I have wandered somewhat beside the path, and yet not clean out of the way. I have thought good, I say, to present you with this written book, wherein you shall find a number of sonnets, lays, letters, ballads, roundlets, verlays, and verses, the works of your friend and mine Master F.J. and diverse others; the which when I had with long travail confusedly gathered together I thought it then *opere precium** to reduce them into some good order. The which I have done according to my barren skill in this written book, commending it unto you to read and to peruse, and desiring you, as I only do adventure thus to participate the sight thereof unto your former good will, even so that you will by no means make the same common, but after your own recreation taken therein that you will safely redeliver unto me the original copy. For otherwise I shall not only provoke all the authors to be offended with me, but farther shall lose the opportunity of a greater matter, half and more granted unto me already, by the willing consent of one of them. And to be plain with you my friend, he hath written—which as far as I can learn, did never yet come to the reading or perusing of any man but himself—two notable works: the one called *The Sundry Lots of Love*, the other of his own invention entitled *The Climbing of an Eagle's Nest*. These things, and especially the latter, doth seem by the name to be a work worthy the reading. And the rather I judge so because his fantasy is so occupied in the same as that, contrary to his wonted use, he hath hitherto withheld it from sight of any his familiars; until it be finished you may guess him by his nature. And therefore I request your secrecy herein, lest if he hear the contrary we shall not be able by any means to procure these other at his hands. So fare you well, from my chamber this tenth of August, 1572.

Yours or not his own,
G.T.

When I had with no small entreaty obtained of Master F.J. and sundry other toward young gentlemen the sundry copies of these sundry matters, then as well for that the number of them was great, as also for that I found none of them so barren but that, in my judgement, had in it *aliquid salis*,* and especially being considered by the very proper occasion whereupon it was written (as they themselves did always with the verse rehearse unto me the cause that then moved them to write) I did with more labour gather them into some order and so placed them in this register. Wherein, as near as I could guess, I have set in the first places those which Master F.J. did compile. And to begin with this his history that ensueth, it was (as he declared unto me) written upon this occasion. The said F.J. chanced once in the north parts of this realm to fall in company of a very fair gentlewoman whose name was Mistress Elinor; unto whom, bearing a hot affection, he first adventured to write this letter following.

G.T.

Mistress I pray you understand that, being altogether a stranger in these parts, my good hap hath been to behold you to my no small contentation, and my evil hap accompanies the same with such imperfection of my deserts as that I find always a ready repulse in mine own frowardness. So that, considering the natural climate of the country, I must say that I have found fire in frost; and yet comparing the inequality of my deserts with the least part of your worthiness, I feel a continual frost in my most fervent fire. Such is, then, the extremity of my passions, the which I could never have been content to commit unto this telltale paper were it not that I am destitute of all other help. Accept, therefore, I beseech you, the earnest good will of a more trusty than worthy servant who, being thereby encouraged, may supply the defects of his ability with ready trial of dutiful loyalty. And let this poor paper, besprent with salt tears and blown over with scalding sighs, be saved of you as a safeguard for your sampler, or a bottom to wind your sewing silk, that when your last needleful is wrought you may return to reading thereof and consider the care of him who is

more yours than his own,

F.J.

This letter by her received, as I have heard him say, her answer was this. She took occasion one day at his request to dance with him, the which doing she bashfully began to declare unto him that she had read over the writing which he delivered unto her, with like protestation that, as at the delivery thereof she understood not for what cause he thrust the same into her bosom, so now she could not perceive thereby any part of his meaning; nevertheless at last seemed to take upon her the matter, and though she disabled herself, yet gave him thanks as etc.* Whereupon he broke the brawl and walking abroad devised immediately these few verses following.

G.T.

Fair Bersabe the bright once bathing in a well
With dew bedimmed King David's eyes that ruled Israel.
And Solomon himself, the source of sapience,
Against the force of such assaults could make but small defence.
To it the stoutest yield, and strongest feel like woe,
Bold Hercules and Sampson both did prove it to be so.

What wonder seemeth then, when stars stand thick in skies,
If such a blazing star have power to dim my dazzled eyes?

Lenvoi

To you these few suffice, your wits be quick and good,
You can conject by change of hue what humours feed my blood.

F.J.

I have heard the author say that these were the first verses that ever he wrote upon like occasion; the which considering the matter precedent may in my judgement be well allowed, and to judge his doings by the effects, he declared unto me that before he could put the same in legible writing, it pleased the said Mistress Elinor of her courtesy thus to deal with him. Walking in a garden among diverse other gentlemen and gentlewomen, with a little frowning smile in passing by him, she delivered unto him a paper with these words. 'For that I understand not', quoth she, 'the intent of your letters, I pray you take them here again and bestow them at your pleasure.' The which done and said, she passed by without change either of pace or countenance.

F.J., somewhat troubled with her angry look, did suddenly leave the company and, walking into a park near adjoining, in great rage began to wreak his malice on this poor paper and the same did rend and tear in pieces. When suddenly at a glance he perceived it was not of his own handwriting, and therewithal abashed upon better regard he perceived in one piece thereof written in Roman these letters: 'SHE'. Wherefore, placing all the pieces thereof as orderly as he could, he found therein written these few lines hereafter following.

G.T.

Your sudden departure from our pastime yesterday did enforce me for lack of chosen company to return unto my work,* wherein I did so long continue till at the last the bare bottom did draw unto my remembrance your strange request. And although I found therein no just cause to credit your coloured words, yet have I thought good hereby to requite you with like courtesy, so that at least you shall not condemn me for ungrateful. But as to the matter therein contained, if I could persuade myself that there were in me any coals to kindle such sparks of fire, I might yet peradventure be drawn to believe that your mind were frozen with like fear. But as no smoke ariseth where no coal is kindled, so without cause of affection the passion is easy to be cured. This is all that I understand of your dark letters. And as much as I mean to answer.

SHE

My friend F.J. hath told me diverse times that immediately upon receipt hereof he grew in jealousy that the same was not her own device. And therein I have no less allowed his judgement than commended his invention of the verses and letters before rehearsed. For as by the style this letter of hers bewrayeth that it was not penned by a woman's capacity, so the sequel of her doings may decipher that she had more ready clerks than trusty servants in store. Well, yet as the perfect hound when he hath chased the hurt deer amid the whole herd will never give over till he have singled it again, even so F.J., though somewhat abashed with this doubtful show, yet still constant in his former intention, ceased not by all possible means to bring this deer yet once again to the bows, whereby she might be the more surely stricken, and so in the end enforced to yield. Wherefore he thought not best to commit the said verses willingly into her custody, but privily lost them, in her chamber, written in counterfeit. And after on the next day thought better to reply, either upon her or upon her secretary, in this wise as here followeth.

G.T.

The much that you have answered is very much, and much more than I am able to reply unto; nevertheless in mine own defence thus much I allege: that if my sudden departure pleased not you I cannot myself therewith be pleased, as one that seeketh not to please many and more desirous to please you than any. The cause of mine affection I suppose you behold daily. For, self-love avoided, every wight may judge of themselves as much as reason persuadeth; the which if it be in your good nature suppressed with bashfulness, then mighty love grant you may once behold my wan cheeks washed in woe, that therein my salt tears may be a mirror to represent your own shadow, and that like unto Narcissus you may be constrained to kiss the cold waves wherein your countenance is so lively portrayed. For if abundance of other matters failed to draw my gazing eyes in contemplation of so rare excellency, yet might these your letters both frame in me an admiration of such divine esprit, and a confusion to my dull understanding which so rashly presumed to wander in this endless labyrinth. Such I esteem you, and thereby am become such, and even

HE.   F.J.

This letter finished and fair written over, his chance was to meet her alone in a gallery of the same house where, as I have heard him declare, his manhood in this kind of combat was first tried; and therein I can compare him to a valiant prince who, distressed with power of enemies, had committed the safeguard of his person to treaty of ambassade and suddenly, surprised with a *Camnassado* in his own trenches, was enforced to yield as prisoner. Even so my friend F.J., lately overcome by the beautiful beams of this Dame Elinor, and having now committed his most secret intent to these late rehearsed letters, was at unawares encountered with his friendly foe, and constrained either to prepare some new defence or else like a recreant to yield himself as already vanquished.

Wherefore, as in a trance, he lifted up his dazzled eyes and so continued in a certain kind of admiration, not unlike the astronomer who, having after a whole night's travail in the grey morning found his desired star, hath fixed his hungry eyes to behold the comet long looked for. Whereat this gracious dame, as one that could discern the sun before her chamber windows were wide open, did deign to embolden the fainting knight with these or like words.

'I perceive now', quod she, 'how mishap doth follow me, that having chosen this walk for a simple solace, I am here disquieted by the man that meaneth my destruction'; and therewithal, as half angry, began to turn her back, whenas my friend F.J., now awaked, gan thus to salute her.

'Mistress,' quod he, 'and I perceive now that good hap

haunts me, for being by lack of opportunity constrained to commit my welfare unto these blabbing leaves of bewraying paper,' showing that in his hand, 'I am here recomforted with [the] happy view of my desired joy,' and therewithal reverently kissing her* hand, did softly distrain her slender arm and so stayed her departure.

The first blow thus proffered and defended, they walked and talked, traversing diverse ways; wherein I doubt not but that my friend F.J. could quit himself reasonably well. And though it stood not with duty of a friend that I should therein require to know his secrets, yet of himself he declared thus much: that after long talk she was contented to accept his proffered service, but yet still disabling herself and seeming to marvel what cause had moved him to subject his liberty so wilfully, or at least in a prison—as she termed it—so unworthy. Whereunto I need not rehearse his answer but suppose now that thus they departed; saving I had forgotten this, she required of him the last rehearsed letter, saying that his first was lost and now she lacked a new bottom for her silk, the which I warrant you he granted. And so, proffering to take an humble congé by *bezo las manos*,* she graciously gave him the *zuccado dez labros*,* and so for then departed. And thereupon recompting her words he compiled these following, which he termed '*Terza sequenza** to sweet Mistress SHE'.

G.T.

> Of thee dear Dame three lessons would I learn.
> What reason first persuades the foolish fly,
> As soon as she a candle can discern,
> To play with flame till she be burnt thereby?
> Or what may move the mouse to bite the bait
> Which strikes the trap that stops her hungry breath?
> What calls the bird where snares of deep deceit
> Are closely couched to draw her to her death?
> Consider well what is the cause of this,
> And though percase thou wilt not so confess,
> Yet deep desire, to gain a heavenly bliss,
> May drown the mind in dole and dark distress:
> Oft is it seen (whereat my heart may bleed)
> Fools play so long till they be caught indeed.
> And then

It is a heaven to see them hop and skip
And seek all shifts to shake their shackles off;
It is a world to see them hang the lip
Who earst at love were wont to scorn and scoff.
But as the mouse, once caught in crafty trap,
May bounce and beat against the boorden wall
Till she have brought her head in such mis-shape
That down to death her fainting limbs must fall;
And as the fly once singed in the flame
Cannot command her wings to wave away,
But by the heel she hangeth in the same
Till cruel death her hasty journey stay;
So they that seek to break the links of love
Strive with the stream, and this by pain I prove.
                                        For when
I first beheld that heavenly hue of thine,
Thy stately stature and thy comely grace,
I must confess these dazzled eyes of mine
Did wink for fear when I first viewed thy face.
But bold desire did open them again
And bad me look, till I had looked too long.
I pitied them that did procure my pain
And loved the looks that wrought me all the wrong.
And as the bird once caught but works her woe,
That strives to leave the limed twigs behind,
Even so the more I strave to part thee fro,
The greater grief did grow within my mind.
Remediless then must I yield to thee,
And crave no more thy servant but to be.

                              Till then, and ever.   HE.   F.J.

When he had well sorted this sequence, he sought opportunity to leave it where she might find it before it were lost; and now the coals began to kindle whereof but erewhile she feigned herself altogether ignorant. The flames began to break out on every side and she, to quench them, shut up herself in her chamber solitarily. But as the smithy gathers greater heat by casting on of water, even so the more she absented herself from company, the fresher was the grief which galded her remembrance, so that at last the report was spread through the house that Mistress Elinor was sick; at which news F.J. took small comfort, nevertheless Dame

Venus with good aspect did yet thus much further his enterprise.

The Dame, whether it were by sudden change or of wonted custom, fell one day into a great bleeding at the nose,* for which accident the said F.J., amongst other pretty conceits, had* a present remedy, whereby he took occasion, when they of the house had all in vain sought many ways to stop her bleeding, to work his feat in this wise. First he pleaded ignorance as though he knew not her name, and therefore demanded the same of one other gentlewoman in the house whose name was Mistress Frances; who, when she had to him declared that her name was Elinor, he said these words, or very like in effect. 'If I thought I should not offend Mistress Elinor I would not doubt to stop her bleeding without either pain or difficulty.' This gentlewoman, somewhat tickled with his words, did incontinent make relation thereof to the said Mistress Elinor, who immediately—declaring that F.J. was her late received servant—returned the said messenger unto him with especial charge that he should employ his devoir towards the recovery of her health; with whom the same F.J. repaired to the chamber of his desired, and finding her set in a chair leaning on the one side over a silver basin.

After his due reverence, he laid his hand on her temples, and privily rounding her in her ear, desired her to command a hazel stick and a knife; the which being brought, he delivered unto her saying on this wise. 'Mistress, I will speak certain words in secret to myself, and do require no more but, when you hear me say openly this word, "Amen", that you with this knife will make a nick upon this hazel stick, and when you have made five nicks, command me also to cease.' The dame, partly of good will to the knight, and partly to be stanched of her bleeding, commanded her maid and required the other gentils somewhat to stand aside. Which done, he began his orisons, wherein he had not long muttered before he pronounced 'Amen', wherewith the lady made a nick on the stick with her knife. The said F.J. continued to another 'Amen', when the lady, having made another nick, felt her bleeding began to stanch, and so by the third 'Amen' thoroughly stanched.

F.J. then changing his prayers into private talk, said softly unto her 'Mistress, I am glad that I am hereby enabled to do you some service, and as the stanching of your own blood may some way recomfort you, so if the shedding of my blood may any way content you I beseech you command it, for it shall be evermore readily employed in your service.' And therewithal with a loud voice pronounced 'Amen'. Wherewith the good lady, making a nick, did secretly answer thus. 'Good servant,' quod she, 'I must needs think myself right happy to have gained your service and good will and be you sure that although there be in me no such desert as may draw you into this depth of affection, yet such as I am I shall be always glad to show myself thankful unto you. And now, if you think yourself assured that I shall bleed no more, do then pronounce your fifth "Amen".' The which pronounced, she made also her fifth nick, and held up her head, calling the company unto her, and declaring unto them that her bleeding was thoroughly stanched.

Well, it were long to tell what sundry opinions were pronounced upon this act, and I do dwell over-long in the discourses of this F.J., especially having taken in hand only to copy out his verses. But for the circumstance doth better declare the effect, I will return to my former tale. F.J., tarrying a while in the chamber, found opportunity to lose his sequence near to his desired mistress and, after *congé* taken, departed. After whose departure the lady arose out of her chair and, her maid going about to remove the same, espied and took up the writing; the which her mistress perceiving, gan suddenly conjecture that the same had in it some like matter to the verses once before left in like manner, and made semblant* to mistrust that the same should be some words of conjuration. And, taking it from her maid, did peruse it and immediately said to the company that she would not forgo the same for a great treasure. But to be plain, I think that—F.J. excepted—she was glad to be rid of all company until she had with sufficient leisure turned over and retossed every card in this sequence. And not long after being now tickled through all the veins with an unknown humour, adventured of herself to commit unto a like ambassador the deciphering of that which hitherto she had kept more secret, and thereupon wrote with her own hand and head in this wise.

G.T.

Good servant, I am out of all doubt much beholding unto you, and I have great comfort by your means in the stanching of my blood, and I take great comfort to read your letters, and I have found in my chamber diverse songs which I think to be of your making, and I promise you they are excellently made, and I assure you that I will be ready to do for you any pleasure that I can during my life. Wherefore I pray you come to my chamber once in a day till I come abroad again, and I will be glad of your company; and for because that you have promised to be my HE, I will take upon me this name: your SHE.

This letter I have seen, of her own handwriting, and as therein the reader may find great difference of style from her former letter, so you may now understand the cause. She had in the same house a friend, a servant, a secretary—what should I name him? Such one as she esteemed in time past more than was cause in time present, and to make my tale good I will, by report of my very good friend F.J., describe him unto you. He was in height the proportion of two pigmies, in breadth the thickness of two bacon hogs, of presumption a giant, of power a gnat, apishly witted, knavishly mannered, and crabbedly favoured. What was there in him then to draw a fair lady's liking? Marry sir, even all in all a well-lined purse wherewith he could at every call provide such pretty conceits as pleased her peevish fantasy, and by that means he had thoroughly, long before, insinuated himself with this amorous dame.

This manling, this minion, this slave, this secretary, was now by occasion ridden to London forsooth, and though his absence were unto her a disfurnishing of eloquence, it was yet unto F.J. an opportunity of good advantage, for when he perceived the change of her style, and thereby grew in some suspicion that the same proceeded by absence of her chief chancellor, he thought good now to smite while the iron was hot, and to lend his mistress such a pen in her secretary's absence as he should never be able at his return to amend the well-writing thereof. Wherefore, according to her command, he repaired once every day to her chamber, at the least, whereas he guided himself so well, and could devise such store of sundry pleasures and pastimes, that he grew in favour not only with his desired but also with the rest of the gentlewomen.

And one day passing the time amongst them, their play grew to this end, that his mistress, being Queen, demanded of him these three questions.* 'Servant,' quod she, 'I charge you, as well upon your allegiance being now my subject, as also upon your fidelity, having vowed your service unto me, that you answer me these three questions by the very truth of your secret thought. First, what thing in this universal world doth most rejoice and comfort you?' F.J., abasing his eyes towards the ground, took good advisement in his answer, when a fair gentlewoman of the company clapped him on the shoulder, saying 'How now, sir, is your hand on your halfpenny?'* To whom he answered 'No, fair lady, my hand is on my heart, and yet my heart is not in mine own hands.' Wherewithal abashed, turning towards Dame Elinor, he said 'My Sovereign and Mistress, according to the charge of your command and the duty that I owe you, my tongue shall bewray unto you the truth of mine intent. At this present, a reward given me without desert doth so rejoice me with continual remembrance thereof, that though my mind be so occupied to think thereon as that day nor night* I can be quiet from that thought, yet the joy and pleasure which I conceive in the same is such that I can neither be cloyed with continuance thereof, nor yet afraid that any mishap can countervail so great a treasure. This is to me such a heaven to dwell in, as that I feed by day and repose by night upon the fresh record of this reward.' This, as he saith, he meant by the kiss that she lent him in the gallery, and by the profession of her last letters and words.

Well, though this answer be somewhat misty, yet let my friend's excuse be that, taken upon the sudden, he thought better to answer darkly than to be mistrusted openly. Her second question was what thing in this life did most grieve his heart and disquiet his mind. Whereunto he answered that, although his late rehearsed joy were incomparable, yet the greatest enemy that disturbed the same was the privy worm of his own guilty conscience, which accused him evermore with great unworthiness, and that this was his greatest grief.

The lady, biting upon the bit at his cunning answers made unto these two questions, gan thus reply. 'Servant, I had thought to have touched you yet nearer with my third question, but I will refrain to attempt your patience; and now for my third demand, answer me directly in what manner this passion doth handle you, and how these contraries may hang together by any possibility of concord, for your words are strange.'

F.J., now rousing himself boldly, took occasion thus to handle his answer. 'Mistress,' quod he, 'my words indeed are strange, but yet my passion is much stranger, and thereupon this other day to content mine own fantasy I devised a sonnet which, although it be a piece of Cocklorell's music,* and such as I might be ashamed to publish in this company, yet because my truth in this answer may the better appear unto you, I pray you vouchsafe to receive the same in writing.' And, drawing a paper out of his pocket,* presented it unto her, wherein was written this sonnet.

G.T.

Love, hope and death do stir in me such strife
As never man but I led such a life.
First burning love doth wound my heart to death,
And when death comes at call of inward grief
Cold lingering hope doth feed my fainting breath
Against my will, and yields my wound relief:
So that I live, but yet my life is such,
As death would never grieve me half so much.
No comfort then but only this I taste,
To salve such sore, such hope will never want,
And with such hope, such life will ever last,
And with such life, such sorrows are not scant.
Oh strange desire, oh life with torments tossed,
Through too much hope mine only hope is lost.

Even HE   F.J.

This sonnet was highly commended, and in my judgement it deserveth no less. I have heard F.J. say that he borrowed the invention of an Italian,* but were it a translation or invention, if I be judge, it is both pretty and pithy. His duty thus performed, their pastimes ended, and at their departure for a watchword he counselled his mistress by little and little to walk abroad, saying that the gallery near adjoining was so pleasant as if he were half dead he thought that by walking therein he might be half and more revived. 'Think you so servant?' quod she, 'and the last time that I walked there I suppose I took the cause of my malady. But by your advice, and for you have so clerkly stanched my bleeding, I will assay to walk there tomorrow.' 'Mistress,' quod he, 'and in more full accomplishment of my duty towards you, and in sure hope that you will use the same only to your own private commodity, I* will there await upon you and between you and me will teach you the full order how to stanch the bleeding of any creature, whereby you shall be as cunning as myself.' 'Gramercy good servant,' quod she, 'I think you lost the same in writing here yesterday, but I cannot understand it, and therefore tomorrow, if I feel myself anything amended, I will send for you thither to instruct me thoroughly.'

Thus they departed, and at suppertime, the knight of the castle finding fault that his guest's stomach served him no better, began to accuse the grossness of his viands, to whom one of the gentlewomen which had passed the afternoon in his company answered. 'Nay sir,' quod she, 'this gentleman hath a passion, the which once in a day at the least doth kill his appetite.' 'Are you so well acquainted with the disposition of his body?' quod the lord of the house. 'By his own saying,' quod she, 'and not otherwise.' 'Fair lady,' quod F.J., 'you either mistook me or overheard me then, for I told of a comfortable humour which so fed me with continual re-membrance of joy as that my stomach being full thereof doth desire in manner none other vittles.' 'Why sir,' quod the host, do you then live by love?' 'God forbid sir,' quod F.J., 'for then my cheeks would be much thinner than they be, but there are diverse other greater causes of joy than the doubtful lots of love, and for mine own part, to be plain, I cannot love, and I dare not hate.' 'I would I thought so,' quod the gentlewoman.

And thus with pretty nips they passed over their supper, which ended, the lord of the house required F.J. to dance and pass the time with the gentlewomen, which he refused not to do. But suddenly, before the music was well tuned, came out Dame Elinor in her night attire, and said to the lord that, supposing the solitariness of her chamber had increased her malady, she came out for her better recreation to see them dance. 'Well done daughter,' quod the lord. 'And I, Mistress,' quod F.J., 'would gladly bestow the leading of you about this great chamber, to drive away the faintness of your fever.' 'No, good servant,' quod the lady, 'but in my stead I pray you dance with this fair gentlewoman,' pointing him to the lady that had so taken him up at supper. F.J., to avoid mistrust, did agree to her request without further entreaty.

The dance begun, this knight marched on with the image of St Frances in his hand, and St Elinor in his heart. The violands at end of the pavion stayed a while, in which time this dame said to F.J. on this wise. 'I am right sorry for you in two respects, although the familiarity have hitherto had no great continuance between us. And as I do lament your case, so do I rejoice for mine own contentation that I shall now see a due trial of the experiment which I have long desired.' This said, she kept silence. When F.J., somewhat astonied with her strange speech, thus answered. 'Mistress, although I cannot conceive the meaning of your words, yet by courtesy I am constrained to yield you thanks for your good will, the which appeareth no less in lamenting of mishaps, than in rejoicing at good fortune. What experiment you mean to try by me I know not, but I dare assure you that my skill in experiments is very simple.' Herewith the instruments sounded a new measure and they passed forthwards, leaving to talk until the noise ceased.

Which done, the gentlewoman replied 'I am sorry, sir, that you did erewhile deny love and all his laws, and that in so open audience.' 'Not so,' quod F.J., 'but as the word was roundly taken, so can I readily answer it by good reason.' 'Well,' quod she, 'how if the hearers will admit no reasonable answer?' 'My reason shall yet be nevertheless', quod he, 'in reasonable judgement.' Herewith she smiled, and he cast a

glance towards Dame Elinor askances* art thou pleased?
Again the viols called them forthwards, and again at the end
of the brawl said F.J. to this gentlewoman 'I pray you,
Mistress, and what may be the second cause of your sorrow
sustained in my behalf?' 'Nay soft,' quod she, 'percase I have
not yet told you the first; but content yourself, for the second
cause you shall never know at my hands until I see due trial
of the experiment which I have long desired.' 'Why then,'
quod he, 'I can but wish a present occasion to bring the same
to effect, to the end that I might also understand the mystery
of your meaning.' 'And so might you fail of your purpose,'
quod she, 'for I mean to be better assured of him that shall
know the depth of mine intent in such a secret than I do
suppose that any creature—one except—may be of you.'
'Gentlewoman,' quod he, 'you speak Greek, the which I have
now forgotten, and mine instructors are too far from me at this
present to expound your words.' 'Or else too near,' quod she,
and so smiling stayed her talk, when the music called them to
another dance.

Which ended, F.J. half afraid of false suspect, and more
amazed at this strange talk, gave over, and bringing Mistress
Frances to her place, was thus saluted by his mistress.
'Servant,' quod she, 'I had done you great wrong to have
danced with you, considering that this gentlewoman and you
had former occasion of so weighty conference.' 'Mistress,' said
F.J., 'you had done me great pleasure, for by our conference
I have but brought my brains in a busy conjecture.' 'I doubt
not', said his mistress, 'but you will end that business easily.'
'It is hard', said F.J., 'to end the thing whereof yet I have
found no beginning.'

His mistress, with change of countenance, kept silence,
whereat Dame Frances, rejoicing, cast out this bone to gnaw
on. 'I perceive', quod she, 'it is evil to halt before a cripple.'
F.J., perceiving now that his mistress waxed angry, thought
good on her behalf thus to answer: 'And it is evil to hop before
them that run for the bell.'* His mistress replied 'And it is evil
to hang the bell at their heels which are always running.' The
lord of the castle, overhearing these proper quips, rose out of
his chair and coming towards F.J., required him to dance a

galliard. 'Sir,' said F.J., 'I have hitherto at your appointment but walked about the house, now if you be desirous to see one tumble a turn or twain, it is like enough that I might provoke you to laugh at me. But in good faith, my dancing days are almost done, and therefore sir,' quod he, 'I pray you speak to them that are more nimble at tripping on the toe.'

Whilst he was thus saying, Dame Elinor had made her *congé*, and was now entering the door of her chamber, when F.J. all amazed at her sudden departure followed to take leave of his mistress. But she, more than angry, refused to hear his good-night, and entering her chamber caused her maid to clap the door. F.J., with heavy cheer, returned to his company and Mistress Frances, to touch his sore with a corrosive, said to him softly in this wise. 'Sir, you may now perceive that this our country cannot allow the French manner of dancing for they, as I have heard tell, do more commonly dance to talk, than entreat to dance.'

F.J., hoping to drive out one nail with another, and thinking this a mean most convenient to suppress all jealous supposes, took Mistress Frances by the hand and with a heavy smile answered. 'Mistress, and I, because I have seen the French manner of dancing, will eftsoons entreat you to dance a bargynet.' 'What mean you by this?' quod Mistress Frances. 'If it please you to follow,' quod he, 'you shall see that I can jest without joy, and laugh without lust,' and calling the musicians, caused them softly to sound the Tyntarnell, when he, clearing his voice, did *alla Napolitana*, apply these verses following unto the measure.

G.T.

In prime of lusty years, when Cupid caught me in
And nature taught the way to love, how I might best begin:
To please my wandering eye, in beauty's tickle trade,
To gaze on each that passed by, a careless sport I made.

With sweet enticing bait I fished for many a dame,
And warmed me by many a fire, yet felt I not the flame:
But when at last I spied the face that pleased me most,
The coals were quick, the wood was dry, and I began to toast.

And smiling yet full oft, I have beheld that face,
When in my heart I might bewail mine own unlucky case:

And oft again with looks that might bewray my grief,
I pleaded hard for just reward and sought to find relief.

What will you more? So oft my gazing eyes did seek
To see the rose and lily strive upon that lively cheek:
Till at the last I spied, and by good proof I found,
That in that face was painted plain the piercer of my wound.

Then (all too late) aghast, I did my foot retire,
And sought with secret sighs to quench my greedy scalding fire:
But lo, I did prevail as much to guide my will,
As he that seeks with halting heel to hop against the hill.

Or as the feeble sight would search the sunny beam,
Even so I found but labour lost to strive against the stream.
Then gan I thus resolve, since liking forced love,
Should I mislike my happy choice, before I did it prove?

And since none other joy I had but her to see,
Should I retire my deep desire? No no it would not be:
Though great the duty were, that she did well deserve,
And I poor man unworthy am so worthy a wight to serve.

Yet hope my comfort stayed, that she would have regard
To my good will, that nothing craved, but like for just reward:
I see the falcon gent sometimes will take delight,
To seek the solace of her wing, and dally with a kite.

The fairest wolf will choose the foulest for her make,
And why? Because he doth endure most sorrow for her sake:
Even so had I like hope, when doleful days were spent
When weary words were wasted well, to open true intent.

When floods of flowing tears had washed my weeping eyes,
When trembling tongue had troubled her with loud lamenting cries:
At last her worthy will would pity this my plaint,
And comfort me her own poor slave, whom fear had made so faint.

Wherefore I made a vow, the stony rock should start,
Ere I presume to let her slip out of my faithful heart.

Lenvoi

And when she saw by proof, the pith of my good will,
She took in worth this simple song, for want of better skill:
And as my just deserts, her gentle heart did move,
She was content to answer thus: I am content to love.

These verses are more in number than do stand with contentation of some judgements, and yet the occasion thoroughly considered, I can commend them with the rest, for it is (as may be well termed) *continua oratio*,* declaring a full discourse of his first love; wherein, over and besides that the epithets are aptly applied and the verse of itself pleasant enough, I note that by it he meant in clouds to decipher unto Mistress Frances such matter as she would snatch at, and yet could take no good hold of the same. Furthermore, it answered very aptly to the note which the music sounded, as the skilful reader by due trial may approve.

This singing dance or dancing song ended, Mistress Frances, giving due thanks, seemed weary also of the company and proffering to depart, gave yet this farewell to F.J. not vexed by choler, but pleased with contentation and called away by heavy sleep. 'I am constrained', quod she, 'to bid you good night,' and so turning to the rest of the company, took her leave. Then the master of the house commanded a torch to light F.J. to his lodging where, as I have heard him say, the sudden change of his mistress's countenance, together with the strangeness of Mistress Frances's talk, made such an encounter in his mind that he could take no rest that night. Wherefore in the morning rising very early, although it were far before his mistress's hour, he cooled his choler by walking in the gallery near to her lodging, and there in this passion compiled these verses following.

G.T.

A cloud of care hath covered all my coast,
And storms of strife do threaten to appear:
The waves of woe, which I mistrusted most,
Have broke the banks wherein my life lay clear:
Chips of ill-chance are fallen amid my choice,
To mar the mind that meant for to rejoice.

Before I sought, I found the haven of hap,
Wherein (once found) I sought to shroud my ship,
But lowering love hath lift me from her lap,
And crabbed lot begins to hang the lip:
The drops of dark mistrust do fall so thick,
They pierce my coat, and touch my skin at quick.

What may be said, where truth cannot prevail?
What plea may serve, where will itself is judge?
What reason rules, where right and reason fail?
Remediless then must the guiltless trudge,
And seek out care, to be the carving knife
To cut the thread that lingereth such a life.

F.J.

This is but a rough metre, and reason, for it was devised in great disquiet of mind and written in rage, yet have I seen much worse pass the musters, yea and where both the lieutenant and provost marshal were men of ripe judgement; and as it is, I pray you let it pass here, for the truth is that F.J. himself had so slender liking thereof, or at least of one word escaped therein, that he never presented it—but to the matter.

When he had long, and all in vain, looked for the coming of his mistress into her appointed walk, he wandered into the park near adjoining to the castle wall, where his chance was to meet Mistress Frances, accompanied with one other gentlewoman, by whom he passed with a reverence of courtesy; and so walking on, came into the side of a thicket, where he sat down under a tree to allay his sadness with solitariness. Mistress Frances, partly of courtesy and affection, and partly to content her mind by continuance of such talk as they had commenced over night, entreated her companion to go with her unto this tree of reformation, whereas they found the knight with his arms folded in a heavy kind of contemplation, unto whom Mistress Frances stepped apace (right softly) and at unawares gave this salutation. 'I little thought sir knight,' quod she, 'by your evensong yesternight to have found you presently at such a morrow mass, but I perceive you serve your saint with double devotion, and I pray God grant you treble meed for your true intent.'

F.J. taken thus upon the sudden could none otherwise answer but thus: 'I told you Mistress,' quod he, 'that I could laugh without lust, and jest without joy,' and therewithal starting up, with a more bold countenance came towards the dames, proffering unto them his service to wait upon them homewards. 'I have heard say oft times', quod Mistress Frances, 'that is it hard to serve two masters at one time, but we will be right glad of your company.' 'I thank you', quod F.J., and so walking on with them fell into sundry discourses, still refusing to touch any part of their former communication, until Mistress Frances said unto him 'By my troth,' quod she, 'I would be your debtor these two days to answer me truly but unto one question that I will propound.' 'Fair gentlewoman,' quod he, 'you shall not need to become my debtor, but if it please you to quit question by question I will be more ready to gratify you in this request than either reason requireth or than you would be willing to work my contentation.' 'Master F.J.,' quod she, and that sadly, 'peradventure you know but a little how willing I would be to procure your contentation, but you know that hitherto familiarity hath taken no deep root betwixt us twain. And though I find in you no manner of cause whereby I might doubt to commit this or greater matter unto you, yet have I stayed hitherto so to do, in doubt lest you might thereby justly condemn me both of arrogancy and lack of discretion. Wherewith I must yet foolishly affirm that I have with great pain bridled my tongue from disclosing the same unto you. Such is then the good will that I bear towards you, the which if you rather judge to be impudency than a friendly meaning I may then curse the hour that I first concluded thus to deal with you.'

Herewithal, being now red for chaste bashfulness, she abased her eyes and stayed her talk, to whom F.J. thus answered. 'Mistress Frances, if I should with so exceeding villainy requite such and so exceeding courtesy, I might not only seem to degenerate from all gentry, but also to differ in behaviour from all the rest of my life spent; wherefore to be plain with you in few words, I think myself so much bound unto you for diverse respects as, if ability do not fail me, you shall find me mindful in requital of the same, and for disclosing your mind to me, you may if so please you adventure it without adventure. For by this sun,' quod he, 'I will not deceive such trust as you shall lay upon me, and furthermore, so far forth as I may, I will be yours in any respect, wherefore I beseech you accept me for your faithful friend, and so shall you surely find me.'

'Not so,' quod she, 'but you shall be my *Trust*, if you vouchsafe the name, and I will be to you as you shall please to term me.' 'My *Hope*,' quod he, 'if you so be pleased'; and thus agreed, they two walked apart from the other gentle-woman, and fell into sad talk, wherein Mistress Frances did very courteously declare unto him that indeed one cause of her sorrow sustained in his behalf was that he had said so openly overnight that he could not love, for she perceived very well the affection between him and Madame Elinor, and she was also advertised that Dame Elinor stood in the portal of her chamber hearkening to the talk that they had at supper that night, wherefore she seemed to be sorry that such a word, rashly escaped, might become great hindrance unto his desire. But a greater cause of her grief was, as she declared, that his hap was to bestow his liking so unworthily, for she seemed to accuse Dame Elinor for the most unconstant woman living; in full proof whereof she bewrayed unto F.J. how she, the same Dame Elinor, had of long time been yielded to the minion secretary whom I have before described. 'In whom though there be', quod she, 'no one point of worthiness, yet shameth she not to use him as her dearest friend, or rather her holiest idol'; and that this notwithstanding, Dame Elinor had been also sundry times won to choice of change, as she named unto F.J. two gentlemen whereof the one was named H.D. and that other H.K., by whom she was during sundry times of their several abode in those parts* entreated to like courtesy.

For these causes the Dame Frances seemed to mislike F.J.'s choice, and to lament that she doubted in process of time to see him abused. The experiment she meant was this: for that she thought F.J.—I use her words—a man in every respect very worthy to have the several use of a more commodious common, she hoped now to see if his enclosure thereof might be defensible against her said secretary, and such like. These things and diverse other of great importance this courteous Lady Frances did friendly disclose unto F.J., and furthermore did both instruct and advise him how to proceed in his enterprise.

Now to make my talk good, and lest the reader might be drawn in a jealous suppose of this Lady Frances, I must let you understand that she was unto F.J. a kinswoman, a virgin of rare chastity, singular capacity, notable modesty, and excellent beauty; and though F.J. had cast his affection on the other (being a married woman), yet was there in their beauties no great difference, but in all other good gifts a wonderful diversity, as much as might be between constancy and flitting fantasy, between womanly countenance and girlish garishness, between hot dissimulation and temperate fidelity. Now if any man will curiously ask the question why F.J. should choose the one and leave the other, over and besides the common proverb 'So many men, so many minds', thus may be answered. We see by common experience that the highest flying falcon doth more commonly prey upon the corn-fed crow and the simple, shiftless dove than on the mounting kite—and why? Because the one is overcome with less difficulty than that other.

Thus much in defence of this Lady Frances, and to excuse the choice of my friend F.J., who thought himself now no less beholding to good fortune to have found such a trusty friend, than bounden to Dame Venus to have won such a mistress. And to return unto my pretence, understand you that F.J., being now with these two fair ladies come very near the castle, grew in some jealous doubt (as on his own behalf) whether he were best to break company or not. When his assured *Hope*, perceiving the same, gan thus recomfort him. 'Good sir,' quod she, 'if you trusted your trusty friends, you should not need thus cowardly to stand in dread of your friendly enemies.' 'Well said in faith,' quod F.J., 'and I must confess you were in my bosom before I wist, but yet I have heard said often that in *Trust* is treason.' 'Well spoken for yourself,' quod his *Hope*.

F.J. now remembering that he had but erewhile taken upon him the name of her *Trust* came home *per misericordiam*,* when his *Hope*, entering the castle gate, caught hold of his lap* and half by force led him by the gallery into his mistress's chamber; whereas, after a little dissembling disdain, he was at last by the good help of his *Hope* right thankfully received. And for his mistress was now ready to dine, he was therefore for that time arrested there, and a *supersedias** sent into the great chamber unto the lord of the house, who expected his coming out of the park.

The dinner ended, and he thoroughly contented both with welfare and welcome, they fell into sundry devices of pastime. At last F.J., taking into his hand a lute that lay on his mistress's bed, did unto the note of the Venetian galliard apply the Italian ditty written by the worthy Bradamant unto the noble Rugier as Ariosto hath it: '*Rugier qual semper fui etc.*'* But his mistress could not be quiet until she heard him repeat the tyntarnell which he used overnight, the which F.J. refused not; at end whereof his mistress, thinking now she had showed herself too earnest to use any further dissimulation, especially perceiving the toward inclination of her servant's *Hope*, fell to flat plain dealing, and walking to the window, called her servant apart unto her, of whom she demanded secretly and in sad earnest who devised this tyntarnell. 'My father's sister's brother's son,' quod F.J. His mistress, laughing right heartily, demanded yet again by whom the same was figured.* 'By a niece to an aunt of yours, Mistress,' quod he. 'Well then servant,' quod she, 'I swear unto you here by my father's soul, that my mother's youngest daughter doth love your father's eldest son above any creature living.'

F.J. hereby recomforted gan thus reply. 'Mistress, though my father's eldest son be far unworthy of so noble a match, yet since it pleaseth her so well to accept him, I would thus much say behind his back: that your mother's daughter hath done him some wrong.' 'And wherein, servant?' quod she. 'By my troth Mistress,' quod he, 'it is not yet twenty hours since without touch of breast she gave him such a nip by the heart as did altogether bereave him his night's rest with the bruise thereof.' 'Well servant,' quod she, 'content yourself, and for your sake I will speak to her to provide him a plaster the which I myself will apply to his hurt. And to the end it may work the better with him, I will purvey a lodging for him where hereafter he may sleep at more quiet.'

This said, the rosy hue distained* her sickly cheeks, and she returned to the company, leaving F.J. ravished between hope and dread, as one that could neither conjecture the meaning of her mystical words, nor assuredly trust unto the knot of her sliding affections. When the Lady Frances, coming to him, demanded 'What? Dream you sir?' 'Yea marry do I fair lady,' quod he. 'And what was your dream sir?' quod she. 'I dreamt', quod F.J., 'that walking in a pleasant garden garnished with sundry delights, my hap was to espy hanging in the air a hope wherein I might well behold the aspects and face of the heavens, and calling to remembrance the day and hour of my nativity, I did thereby, according to my small skill in astronomy, try the conclusions of mine adventures.' 'And what found you therein?' quod Dame Frances. 'You awaked me out of my dream,' quod he, 'or else peradventure you should not have known.' 'I believe you well,' quod the Lady Frances, and laughing at his quick answer, brought him by the hand unto the rest of his company, where he tarried not long before his gracious mistress bade him to farewell and to keep his hour there again when he should by her be summoned.

Hereby F.J. passed the rest of that day in hope awaiting the happy time when his mistress should send for him. Supper time came and passed over, and not long after came the handmaid of the Lady Elinor into the great chamber, desiring F.J. to repair unto their mistress, the which he willingly accomplished. And being now entered into her chamber, he might perceive his mistress in her night's attire, preparing herself towards bed, to whom F.J. said 'Why how now mistress? I had thought this night to have seen you dance, at least or at last, amongst us.' 'By my troth good servant,' quod she, '[I] adventured so soon into the great chamber yesternight that I find myself somewhat sickly disposed, and therefore do strain courtesy, as you see, to go the sooner to my bed this night. But before I sleep', quod she, 'I am to charge you with a matter of weight,' and taking him apart from the rest, declared that at* that present night she would talk with him more at large in the gallery near adjoining to her chamber.

Hereupon F.J., discretely dissimulating his joy, took his leave and returned into the great chamber, where he had not long continued before the lord of the castle commanded a torch to light him unto his lodging, whereas he prepared himself and went to bed, commanding his servant also to go to his rest. And when he thought as well his servant as the rest of the household to be safe, he arose again and, taking his nightgown, did under the same convey his naked sword, and so walked to the gallery where he found his good mistress walking in her nightgown and attending his coming.

The moon was now at the full, the skies clear, and the weather temperate, by reason whereof he might the more plainly and with the greater contentation behold his long-desired joys, and spreading his arms abroad to embrace his loving mistress, he said 'Oh my dear lady, when shall I be able with any desert to countervail the least part of this your bountiful goodness?' The dame, whether it were of fear indeed, or that the wiliness of womanhood had taught her to cover her conceits with some fine dissimulation, stert back from the knight, and shrieking (but softly) said unto him 'Alas servant, what have I deserved that you come against me with naked sword as against an open enemy?' F.J., perceiving her intent, excused himself, declaring that he brought the same for their defence and not to offend her in any wise. The lady being therewith somewhat appeased, they began with more comfortable gesture to expel the dread of the said late affright, and sithens to become bolder of behaviour, more familiar in speech, and most kind in accomplishing of common comfort.

But why hold I so long discourse in describing the joys which, for lack of like experience, I cannot set out to the full? Were it not that I know to whom I write, I would the more beware what I write. F.J. was a man, and neither of us are senseless, and therefore I should slander him, over and besides a greater obloquy to the whole genealogy of Aeneas, if I should imagine that of tender heart he would forbear to express her more tender limbs against the hard floor. Sufficed that of her courteous nature she was content to accept boards for a bed of down, mats for camerike sheets, and the nightgown of F.J. for a counterpoint to cover them. And thus with calm content, instead of quiet sleep, they beguiled the night until the proudest star began to abandon the firmament, when F.J. and his mistress were constrained also to abandon their delights, and with ten thousand sweet kisses and straight embracings did frame themselves to play loath to depart.

Well, remedy was there none, but Dame Elinor must return unto her chamber, and F.J. must also convey himself as closely as might be into his chamber, the which was hard to do, the day being so far sprung, and he having a large base court to pass over before he could recover his stair-foot door. And though he were not much perceived, yet the Lady Frances, being no less desirous to see an issue of these enterprises than F.J. was willing to cover them in secrecy, did watch and even at the entering of his chamber door perceived the point of his naked sword glistering under the skirt of his nightgown; whereat she smiled and said to herself 'This gear goeth well about.'

Well, F.J. having now recovered his chamber he went to bed, and there let him sleep, as his mistress did on that other side. Although the Lady Frances, being thoroughly tickled now in all the veins, could not enjoy such quiet rest, but arising, took another gentlewoman of the house with her, and walked into the park to take the fresh air of the morning. They had not long walked there but they returned, and though F.J. had not yet slept sufficiently for one which had so far travailed* in the night past, yet they went into his chamber to raise him, and coming to his bedside found him fast asleep.

'Alas,' quod that other gentlewoman, 'it were pity to awake him.' 'Even so it were,' quod Dame Frances, 'but we will take away somewhat of his whereby he may perceive that we were here.' And looking about the chamber, his naked sword presented itself to the hands of Dame Frances, who took it with her and, softly shutting his chamber door again, went down the stairs and recovered her own lodging in good order and unperceived of anybody, saving only that other gentlewoman which accompanied her. At the last F.J. awaked and, apparelling himself, walked out also to take the air and, being thoroughly recomforted as well with the remembrance of his joys forepassed as also with the pleasant harmony which the birds made on every side, and the fragrant smell of the redolent flowers and blossoms which budded on every branch, he did in these delights compile these verses following. (The occasion, as I have heard him rehearse, was by encounter that

he had with his lady by light of the moon; and forasmuch as
the moon in midst of their delights did vanish away, or was
overspread with a cloud, thereupon he took the subject of his
theme. And thus it ensueth, called 'A Moonshine Banquet'.)

G.T.

Dame Cynthia herself (that shines so bright,
And deigneth not to leave her lofty place
But only then when Phoebus shows his face
Which is her brother born and lends her light),
Disdained not yet to do my lady right:
To prove that in such heavenly wights as she
It sitteth best that right and reason be.
For when she spied my lady's golden rays,
Into the clouds
Her head she shrouds,
And shamed to shine where she her beams displays.

Good reason yet that to my simple skill
I should the name of Cynthia adore:
By whose high help I might behold the more
My lady's lovely looks at mine own will,
With deep content to gaze* and gaze my fill:
Of courtesy and not of dark disdain,
Dame Cynthia disclosed my lady plain,
She did but lend her light (as for a light)
With friendly grace,
To show her face,
That else would show and shine in her despite.

Dan Phoebus he with many a lowering look,
Had her beheld of yore in angry wise:
And when he could none other mean devise
To stain her name, this deep deceit he took
To be the bait that best might hide his hook:
Into her eyes his parching beams he cast,
To scorch their skins that gazed on her full fast:
Whereby when many a man was sunburnt so
They thought my Queen
The sun had been
With scalding flames, which wrought them all that woe.

And thus when many a look had looked so long,
As that their eyes were dim and dazzled both:

Some fainting hearts that were both lewd and loath
To look again from whence the error sprung,
Gan close their eye for fear of further wrong:
And some again once drawn into the maze
Gan lewdly blame the beams of beauty's blaze:
But I with deep foresight did soon espy
How Phoebus meant,
By false intent,
To slander so her name with cruelty.

Wherefore at better leisure thought I best
To try the treason of his treachery:
And to exhalt my lady's dignity
When Phoebus fled and drew him down to rest
Amid the waves that walter in the west.
I gan behold this lovely lady's face,
Whereon dame nature spent her gifts of grace:
And found therein no parching heat at all,
But such bright hue
As might renew
An angel's joys in reign celestial.

The courteous moon that wished to do me good
Did shine to show my dame more perfectly,
But when she saw her passing jollity
The moon for shame did blush as red as blood,
And shrunk aside and kept her horns in hood:
So that now when Dame Cynthia was gone,
I might enjoy my lady's looks alone,
Yet honoured still the moon with true intent:
Who taught us skill
To work our will
And gave us place till all the night was spent.

F.J.

This ballad, or howsoever I shall term it, percase you will
not like, and yet in my judgement it hath great good store of
deep invention, and for the order of the verse, it is not
common, I have not heard many of like proportion. Some will
accompt it but a diddledum, but who so had heard F.J. sing
it to the lute, by a note of his own device, I suppose he would
esteem it to be a pleasant diddledum; and for my part, if I were
not partial, I would say more in commendation of it than now
I mean to do, leaving it to your and like judgements.

And now to return to my tale. By that time that F.J. returned out of the park it was dinner time, and at dinner they all met—I mean both Dame Elinor, Dame Frances, and F.J. I leave to describe that the Lady Frances was gorgeously attired and set forth with very brave apparel, and Madam Elinor only in her night gown girt to her, with a coif trimmed *alla Piedmonteze*,* on the which she wore a little cap crossed over the crown with two bands of yellow sarsenet or cypress, in the midst whereof she had placed of her own handwriting in paper this word: 'Contented'. This attire pleased her then to use, and could not have displeased Mistress Frances, had she not been more privy to the cause than to the thing itself; at least the lord of the castle of ignorance, and Dame Frances of great temperance, let it pass without offence.

At dinner, because the one was pleased with all former reckonings, and the other made privy to the accompt, there passed no word of taunt or grudge, but *omnia bene*.* After dinner Dame Elinor, being no less desirous to have F.J.['s] company, than Dame Frances was to take him in some pretty trip, they began to question how they might best pass the day. The Lady Elinor seemed desirous to keep her chamber, but Mistress Frances for another purpose seemed desirous to ride abroad and thereby to take the open air. They agreed to ride a mile or twain for solace, and requested F.J. to accompany them, the which willingly granted. Each one parted from other to prepare themselves, and now began the sport, for when F.J. was booted, his horses saddled, and he ready to ride, he gan miss his rapier, whereat all astonied he began to blame his man, but blame whom he would, found it could not be.

At last the ladies, going towards horseback, called for him in the base court, and demanded if he were ready, to whom F.J. answered 'Madames, I am more than ready, and yet not so ready as I would be'; and immediately taking himself in trip,* he thought best to utter no more of his conceit, but in haste more than good speed mounted his horse and, coming towards the dames, presented himself, turning, bounding, and taking up his courser to the uttermost of his power in bravery. After suffering his horse to breathe himself, he gan also allay his own choler, and to the dames he said 'Fair ladies, I am ready when it pleaseth you to ride whereso you command.' 'How ready soever you be servant,' quod Dame Elinor, 'it seemeth your horse is readier at your command than at ours.' 'If he be at my command, Mistress,' quod he, 'he shall be at yours.' 'Gramercy good servant,' quod she, 'but my meaning is that I fear he be too stirring for our company.' 'If he prove so, Mistress,' quod F.J., 'I have here a soberer palfrey to serve you on.'

The dames being mounted, they rode forthwards by the space of a mile or very near, and F.J., whether it were of his horse's courage or his own choler, came not so near them as they wished. At last the Lady Frances said unto him 'Master F.J., you said that you had a soberer horse, which if it be so, we would be glad of your company, but I believe by your countenance your horse and you are agreed.' F.J., alighting, called his servant, changed horses with him and, overtaking the dames, said to Mistress Frances 'And why do you think, fair lady, that my horse and I are agreed?' 'Because by your countenance', quod she, 'it seemeth your patience is stirred.' 'In good faith,' quod F.J., 'you have guessed aright, but not with any of you.' 'Then we care the less servant,' quod Dame Elinor. 'By my troth Mistress,' quod F.J. (looking well about him that none might hear but they two) 'it is with my servant, who hath lost my sword out of my chamber.'

Dame Elinor, little remembering the occasion, replied. 'It is no matter servant,' quod she, 'you shall hear of it again, I warrant you, and presently we ride in God's peace, and I trust shall have no need of it.' 'Yet Mistress,' quod he, 'a weapon serveth both uses, as well to defend as to offend.' 'Now by my troth,' quod Dame Frances, 'I have now my dream, for I dreamt this night that I was in a pleasant meadow alone, where I met with a tall gentleman, apparelled in a nightgown of silk all embroidered about with a guard of naked swords, and when he came towards me I seemed to be afraid of him, but he recomforted me saying "Be not afraid fair lady, for I use this garment only for mine own defence, and in this sort went that warlike God Mars what time he taught Dame Venus to make Vulcan a hammer of the new fashion."

Notwithstanding these comfortable words, the fright of the dream awaked me, and sithens unto this hour I have not slept at all.' 'And what time of the night dreamt you this?' quod F.J. 'In the grey morning about dawning of the day—but why ask you?' quod Dame Frances. F.J. with a great sigh answered 'Because that dreams are to be marked more at some hour of the night than at some other.' 'Why, are you so cunning at the interpretation of dreams servant?' quod the Lady Elinor. 'Not very cunning Mistress,' quod F.J., 'but guess, like a young scholar.'

The dames continued in these and like pleasant talks, but F.J. could not be merry, as one that esteemed the preservation of his mistress's honour no less than the obtaining of his own delights; and yet to avoid further suspicion he repressed his passions as much as he could. The Lady Elinor, more careless than considerative of her own case, pricking forwards said softly to F.J. 'I had thought you had received small cause, servant, to be thus dumpish when I would be merry.' 'Alas dear Mistress,' quod F.J., 'it is altogether for your sake that I am pensive.'

Dame Frances with courtesy withdrew herself and gave them leave, whenas F.J. declared unto his mistress that his sword was taken out of his chamber, and that he dreaded much by the words of the Lady Frances that she had some understanding of the matter. Dame Elinor, now calling to remembrance what had passed the same night, at the first was abashed, but immediately (for these women be readily witted) cheered her servant and willed him to commit unto her the salving of that sore.

Thus they passed the rest of the way in pleasant talk with Dame Frances, and so returned towards the castle, where F.J. suffered the two dames to go together and he alone unto his chamber to bewail his own misgovernment. But Dame Elinor, whether it were according to old custom or by wily policy, found mean that night that the sword was conveyed out of Mistress Frances's chamber and brought unto hers, and after redelivery of it unto F.J. she warned him to be more wary from that time forwards.

Well, I dwell too long upon these particular points in

discoursing this trifling history, but that the same is the more apt mean of introduction to the verses which I mean to rehearse unto you, and I think you will not disdain to read my conceit with his invention about declaration* of his comedy. The next that ever F.J. wrote then upon any adventure happened between him and this fair lady was this, as I have heard him say, and upon this occasion. After he grew more bold and better acquainted with his mistress's disposition, he adventured one Friday in the morning to go unto her chamber and thereupon wrote as followeth, which he termed 'A Friday's Breakfast'.

G.T.

That self-same day, and of that day that hour,
When she doth reign that mocked Vulcan the smith:
And thought it meet to harbour in her bower
Some gallant guest for her to dally with.
That blessed hour, that blist and happy day,
I thought it meet with hasty steps to go
Unto the lodge wherein my lady lay,
To laugh for joy, or else to weep for woe.
And lo, my lady of her wonted grace,
First lent her lips to me (as for a kiss),
And after that her body to embrace,
Wherein dame nature wrought nothing amiss.
What followed next guess you that know the trade,
For in this sort my Friday's feast I made.

F.J.

This sonnet is short and sweet, reasonably well, according to the occasion etc. Many days passed these two lovers with great delight, their affairs being no less politicly governed than happily achieved. And surely I have heard F.J. affirm in sad earnest that he did not only love her, but was furthermore so ravished in ecstasies with continual remembrance of his delights that he made an idol of her in his inward conceit. So seemeth it by this challenge to beauty which he wrote in her praise and upon her name.

G.T.

Beauty shut up thy shop, and truss up all thy trash,
My Nell hath stolen thy finest stuff, and left thee in the lash:
Thy market now is marred, thy gains are gone God wot,
Thou hast no ware that may compare with this that I have got.
As for thy painted pale, and wrinkles surfled up:
Are dear enough for such as lust to drink of every cup:
Thy bodies bolstered out with bumbast and with bags,
Thy rolls, thy ruffs, thy cauls, thy coifs, thy jerkins and thy jags.*
Thy curling and thy cost, thy frisling and thy fare,
To court, to court with all those toys, and there set forth such ware
Before their hungry eyes that gaze on every guest:
And choose the cheapest chaffer still to please their fancy best.
But I whose steadfast eyes could never cast a glance,
With wandering look amid the press to take my choice by chance,
Have won by due desert a piece that hath no peer,
And left the rest as refuse all to serve the market there.
There let him choose that list, there catch the best who can:
A painted blazing bait may serve to choke a gazing man.
But I have slipped* the flower that freshest is of hue,
I have thy corn, go sell thy chaff, I list to seek no new:
The windows of mine eyes are glazed with such delight
As each new face seems full of faults that blazeth in my sight.
And not without just cause, I can compare her so,
Lo here my glove: I challenge him that can, or dare, say no.
Let Theseus come with club, or Paris brag with brand,
To prove how fair their Helen was that scourged the Grecian land,
Let mighty Mars himself come armed to the field,
And vaunt Dame Venus to defend with helmet, spear and shield,
This hand that had good hap, my Helen to embrace,
Shall have like luck to foil her foes and daunt them with disgrace.
And cause them to confess by verdict and by oath,
How far her lovely looks do stain the beauties of them both.
And that my Helen is more fair than Paris' wife,
And doth deserve more famous praise than Venus for her life.
Which if I not perform, my life then let me leese,
Or else be bound in chains of change to beg for beauty's fees.

F.J.

By this challenge I guess that either he was then in an
ecstasy, or else sure I am now in a lunacy, for it is a proud
challenge made to beauty herself and all her companions, and
imagining that beauty, having a shop where she uttered her

wares of all sundry sorts, his lady had stolen the finest away, leaving none behind her but painting, bolstering, forcing and such like, the which in his rage he judgeth good enough to serve the court, and thereupon grew a great quarrel when these verses were by the negligence of his mistress dispersed into sundry hands, and so at last to the reading of a courtier. Well, F.J. had his desire if his mistress liked them but, as I have heard him declare, she grew in jealousy that the same were not written by her,* because her name was Elinor and not Helen. And about this point have been diverse and sundry opinions, for this and diverse other of his most notable poems have come to view of the world, although altogether without his consent. And some have attributed this praise unto a Helen, who deserved not so well as this Dame Elinor should seem to deserve by the relation of F.J., and yet never a barrel of good herring between them both. But that other Helen, because she was and is of so base condition as may deserve no manner commendation in any honest judgement, therefore I will excuse my friend F.J. and adventure my pen in his behalf, that he would never bestow verse of so mean a subject. And yet some of his acquaintance, being also acquainted, better than I, that F.J. was sometimes acquainted with Helen, have stood in argument with me, that it was written by Helen and not by Elinor.

Well, F.J. told me himself that it was written by this Dame Elinor, and that unto her he thus alleged, that he took it all for one name, or at least he never read of any Elinor such matter as might sound worthy like commendation for beauty. And indeed, considering that it was in the first beginning of his writings, as then he was no writer of any long continuance, comparing also the time that such reports do spread of his acquaintance with Helen, it cannot be written less than six or seven years before he knew Helen; marry peradventure if there were any acquaintance between F.J. and that Helen afterwards, the which I dare not confess, he might adapt it to her name, and so make it serve both their turns, as elder lovers have done before and still do and will do world without end Amen.

Well, by whom he wrote it I know not, but once* I am sure

that he wrote it, for he is no borrower of inventions, and this
is all that I mean to prove, as one that send you his verses by
stealth, and do him double wrong, to disclose unto any man
the secret causes why they were devised. But this for your
delight I do adventure, and to return to the purpose, he sought
more certainly to please his mistress Elinor with this sonnet
written in her praise as followeth.

G.T.

> The stately dames of Rome their pearls did wear
> About their necks to beautify their name,
> But she whom I do serve her pearls doth bear
> Close in her mouth, and smiling shows the same.
> No wonder then, though every word she speaks
> A jewel seems in judgement of the wise,
> Since that her sugared tongue the passage breaks
> Between two rocks bedecked with pearls of price.
> Her hair of gold, her front of ivory,
> (A bloody heart within so white a breast)
> Her teeth of pearl, lips ruby, crystal eye,
> Needs must I honour her above the rest,
> Since she is formed of none other mould
> But ruby, crystal, ivory, pearl, and gold.

F.J.

Of this sonnet I am assured that it is but a translation,* for
I myself have seen the invention of an Italian, and Master J.
hath a little dilated the same, but not much besides the sense
of the first, and the addition very aptly applied, wherefore I
cannot condemn his doing therein, and for the sonnet were it
not a little too much praise, as the Italians do most commonly
offend in the superlative, I could the more commend it. But
I hope the party to whom it was dedicated had rather it were
much more, than anything less.

Well, thus these two lovers passed many days in exceeding
contentation and more than speakable pleasures, in which
time F.J. did compile very many verses according to sundry
occasions proffered, whereof I have not obtained the most at
his hands, and the reason that he denied me the same was that
(as he alleged) they were for the most part sauced with a taste
of glory; as you know that in such cases a lover being charged

with inexprimable joys, and therewith enjoined both by duty and discretion to keep the same covert, can by no means devise a greater consolation than to commit it into some ciphered words and figured speeches in verse, whereby he feeleth his heart half, or more than half, eased of swelling. For as sighs are some present ease to the pensive mind, even so we find by experience that such secret intercommoning of joys doth increase delight. I would not have you conster my words to this effect, that I think a man cannot sufficiently rejoice in the lucky lots of love unless he impart the same to others. God forbid that ever I should enter into such an heresy, for I have always been of this opinion, that as to be fortunate in love is one of the most inward contentations to man's mind of all earthly joys, even so if he do but once bewray the same to any living creature immediately either dread of discovering doth bruise his breast with an intolerable burden, or else he leeseth the principal virtue which gave effect to his gladness, not unlike to a 'pothecary's pot which being filled with sweet ointments or perfumes doth retain in itself some scent of the same, and being poured out doth return to the former state, hard, harsh, and of small savour, so the mind being fraught with delights, as long as it can keep them secretly enclosed, may continually feed upon the pleasant record thereof as the well-willing and ready horse biteth on the bridle, but having once disclosed them to any other, straightway we lose the hidden treasure of the same, and are oppressed with sundry doubtful opinions and dreadful conceits. And yet for a man to record unto himself in the inward contemplation of his mind the often remembrance of his late received joys doth as it were ease the heart of burden and add unto the mind a fresh supply of delight, yea and in verse principally, as I conceive, a man may best contrive this way of comfort in himself. Therefore, as I have said, F.J. swimming now in delights did nothing but write such verse as might accumulate his joys to the extremity of pleasure, the which for that purpose he kept from me, as one more desirous to seem obscure and defective than overmuch to glory in his adventures, especially for that in the end his hap was as heavy as hitherto he had been fortunate; amongst other I remembered one happened upon this occasion.

The husband of the Lady Elinor being all this while absent

from her gan now return, and kept cut* at home, with whom
F.J. found means so to insinuate himself that familiarity took
deep root between them, and seldom but by stealth you could
find the one out of the other's company. On a time, the knight
riding on hunting desired F.J. to accompany him, the which
he could not refuse to do, but like a lusty younker ready
at all assays, apparelled himself in green and about his neck
[hung]* a bugle, pricking and galloping amongst the foremost
according to the manner of that country. And it chanced that
the married knight thus galloping lost his horn,* which some
divines might have interpreted to be but moulting, and that
by God's grace he might have a new come up again shortly
instead of that.

Well, he came to F.J. requiring him to lend him his bugle,
'For', said the knight, 'I heard you not blow this day, and I
would fain encourage the hounds if I had a horn.' Quod F.J.:
'Although I have not been over-lavish of my coming hitherto,
I would you should not doubt but that I can tell how to use
a horn well enough, and yet I may little do if I may not lend
you a horn,' and therewithal took his bugle from his neck and
lent it to the knight who, making in unto the hounds, gan
assay to rechat, but the horn was too hard for him to wind,
whereat F.J. took pleasure, and said to himself 'Blow till thy
break that, I made thee one within these few days that thou
wilt never crack whiles thou livest.' And hereupon, before the
fall of the buck, devised this sonnet following, which at his
homecoming he presented unto his mistress.

G.T.

As some men say there is a kind of seed
Will grow to horns if it be sowed thick:
Wherewith I thought to try if I could breed
A brood of buds well sharped on the prick,
And by good proof of learned skill I found
(As on some special soil all seeds best frame)
So jealous brains do breed the battleground
That best of all might serve to bear the same.
Then sought I forth to find such supple soil,
And called to mind thy husband had a brain,
So that percase by travail and by toil

His fruitful front might turn my seed to gain:
And as I groped in that ground to sow it,
Start up a horn, thy husband could not blow it.

F.J.

This sonnet treateth of a strange seed, but it tasteth most of
rye,* which is more common amongst men nowadays. Well,
let it pass amongst the rest, and he that liketh it not turn over
the leaf to another, I doubt not but in this register he may find
some to content him, unless he be too curious. And here I will
surcease to rehearse any more of his verses until I have
expressed how that his joys, being now exalted to the highest
degree, began to bend towards declination. For now the
unhappy secretary, whom I have before remembered, was
returned from London, on whom F.J. had no sooner cast his
eyes but immediately he fell into a great passion of mind
which might be compared unto a fever. This fruit grew of the
good instructions that his *Hope* had planted in his mind,
whereby I might take just occasion to forwarn every lover how
they suffer this venomous serpent jealousy to creep into their
conceits; for surely of all other diseases in love I suppose that
to be uncurable, and would hold longer discourse therein were
it not that both this tale and the verses of F.J. himself hereafter to be recited shall be sufficient to speak for me in this
behalf.

The lover, as I say, upon the sudden was droven into such
a malady as no meat might nourish his body, no delights
please his mind, no remembrance of joys forepassed content
him, nor any hope of the like to come might recomfort him.
Hereat some unto whom I have imparted this tale have taken
occasion to discommend his fainting heart, yet surely, the
cause inwardly and deeply considered, I cannot so lightly
condemn him, for an old saying is that every man can give
counsel better than follow it, and needs must the conflicts of
his thoughts be strange between the remembrance of his
forepassed pleasure and the present sight of this monster
whom before, for lack of like instruction, he had not so
thoroughly marked and beheld.

Well, such was the grief unto him that he became sickly and

kept his chamber. The ladies, having received the news thereof, gan all at once lament his misfortune, and of common consent agreed to visit him. They marched thither in good equipage, I warrant you, and found F.J. lying upon his bed languishing, whom they all saluted generally and sought to recomfort, but especially his mistress, having in her hand a branch of willow wherewith she defended her from the hot air, gan thus say unto him. 'Servant,' quod she, 'for that I suppose your malady to proceed of none other cause but only sloth-fulness, I have brought this pretty rod to beat you a little, nothing doubting but when you feel the smart of a twig or twain you will, like a tractable young scholar, pluck up your quickened spirits and cast this drowsiness apart.' F.J., with a great sigh, answered 'Alas good Mistress,' quod he, 'if any like chastisement might quicken me, how much more might the presence of all you lovely dames recomfort my dulled mind, whom to behold were sufficient to revive an eye now dazzled with the dread of death, and that not only for the heavenly aspects which you represent, but also much the more for your exceeding courtesy, in that you have deigned to visit me, so unworthy a servant. But good Mistress,' quod he, 'as it were shame for me to confess that ever my heart could yield for fear, so I assure you that my mind cannot be content to induce infirmity by sluggish conceit. But in truth Mistress I am sick,' quod he, and therewithal the trembling of his heart had sent up such throbbing into his throat as that his voice, now deprived of breath, commanded the tongue to be still.

When Dame Elinor for compassion distilled into tears, and drew towards the window, leaving the other gentlewomen about his bed, who being no less sorry for his grief, yet for that they were none of them so touched in their secret thoughts they had bolder spirits and freer speech to recomfort him; amongst the rest the Lady Frances, who indeed loved him deeply and could best conjecture the cause of his conceits, said unto him: 'Good *Trust*,' quod she, 'if any help of physic may cure your malady, I would not have you hurt yourself with these doubts which you seem to retain. If choice of diet may help, behold us here, your cooks, ready to minister all things needful; if company may drive away your annoy, we mean not to leave you solitary. If grief of mind be cause of your infirmity, we all here will offer our devoir to turn it into joy. If mishap have given you cause to fear or dread anything, remember *Hope*, which never faileth to recomfort an afflicted mind. And good *Trust*,' quod she, distraining his hand right heartily, 'let this simple proof of our poor good wills be so accepted of you as that it may work thereby the effect of our desires.'

F.J., as one in a trance, had marked very little of her courteous talk, and yet gave her thanks and so held his peace; whereat, the ladies being all amazed, there became a silence in the chamber on all sides. Dame Elinor, fearing thereby that she might the more easily be espied, and having now dried up her tears, returned to F.J., recomforting him by all possible means of common courtesy, promising that since in her sickness he had not only stanched her bleeding, but also by his gentle company and sundry devices of honest pastime had driven away the pensiveness of her mind, she thought herself bound with like willingness to do her best in anything that might restore his health. And taking him by the hand said further: 'Good servant, if thou bear indeed any true affection to thy poor mistress, start upon thy feet again, and let her enjoy thine accustomed service to her comfort. For sure', quod she, 'I will never leave to visit this chamber once in a day until I may have thee down with me.'

F.J., hearing the hearty words of his mistress, and perceiving the earnest manner of her pronunciation, began to receive unspeakable comfort in the same, and said 'Mistress, your exceeding courtesy were able to revive a man half dead, and to me it is both great comfort and it doth also gald my remembrance with a continual smart of mine own unworthiness; but as I would desire no longer life than till I might be able to deserve some part of your bounty, so I will endeavour myself to live, were it but only unto that end that I might merit some part of your favour with acceptable service, and requite some deal the courtesy of all these other fair ladies, who have so far above my deserts deigned to do me good.'

Thus said, the ladies tarried not long before they were called to Evensong, when his mistress, taking his hand, kissed it, saying 'Farewell good servant, and I pray thee suffer not the malice of thy sickness to overcome the gentleness of thy good heart.' F.J., ravished with joy, suffered them all to depart, and was not able to pronounce one word.

After their departure he gan cast in his mind the exceeding courtesy used towards him by them all, but above all other the bounty of his mistress, and therewithal took a sound and firm opinion that it was not possible for her to counterfeit so deeply (as indeed I believe that she then did not) whereby he suddenly felt his heart greatly eased, and began in himself thus to reason. 'Was ever man of so wretched a heart? I am the most bounden to love', quod he, 'of all them that ever professed his service. I enjoy one, the fairest that ever was found, and I find her the kindest that ever was heard of; yet in mine own wicked heart I could villainously conceive that of her which, being compared with the rest of her virtues, is not possible to harbour in so noble a mind. Hereby I have brought myself without cause into this feebleness, and good reason that for so high an offence I should be punished with great infirmity. What shall I then do? Yield to the same? No, but according to my late protestation I will recomfort this languishing mind of mine to the end I may live but only to do penance for this so notable a crime so rashly committed.'

And thus saying, he start from his bed and gan to walk towards the window, but the venomous serpent which, as before I rehearsed, had stung him, could not be content that these medicines applied by the mouth of his gentle mistress should so soon restore him to guerison. And although indeed they were such mithridate to F.J. as that they had now expelled the rancour of the poison, yet that ugly hellish monster had left behind her in the most secret of his bosom, even between the mind and the man, one of her familiars named *Suspect*, which gan work in the weak spirits of F.J. effects of no less peril than before he had conceived. His head swelling with these troublesome toys, and his heart swimming in the tempests of tossing fantasy, he felt his legs so feeble that he was constrained to lie down on his bed again, and repeating in his own remembrance every word that his mistress had spoken unto him, he gan to dread that she had brought the willow branch to beat him with in token that he was of her forsaken, for so lovers do most commonly expound the willow garland, and this to think did cut his heart in twain.

A wonderful change! And here a little to stay you, I will describe, for I think you have not read it in Ariosto,* the beginning, the fall, the return and the dying of this hellish bird who indeed may well be counted a very limb of the devil. Many years since, one of the most dreadful dastards in the world, and one of them that first devised to wear his beard at length lest the barber might do him a good turn sooner than he looked for it, and yet not so soon as he deserved, had builded for his security a pile on the highest and most inaccessible mount of all his territories; the which being fortified with strong walls and environed with deep ditches had no place of entry but one only door so strait and narrow as might by any possibility receive the body of one living man, from which he ascended up a ladder, and so creeping through a marvellous strait hole, attained to his lodging, the which was so dark and obscure as scarcely either sun or air could enter into it.

Thus he devised to lodge in safety, and for the more surety gan trust none other letting down this ladder but only his wife, and at the foot thereof kept always by daylight a fierce mastiff close enkennelled, which never saw nor heard the face or voice of any other creature but only of them two. Him by night he trusted with the scout of this pretty passage, having nevertheless between him and this dog a double door with treble locks, quadruple bars, and before all a port coulez of iron. Neither yet could he be so hardy as to sleep until he had caused a guard of servants, whom he kept abroad for that purpose, to search all the corners adjoining to his fortress, and then between fearful sweat and shivering cold, with one eye open and the other closed, he stole sometimes a broken sleep divided with many terrible dreams.

In this sort the wretch lived all too long, until at last his wife being not able any longer to support this hellish life grew so hardy as with his own knife to dispatch his carcass out of this earthly purgatory; the which being done, his soul (and good reason) was quickly conveyed by Charon unto hell. There Rhadamanthus, judge of that bench, commanded him quickly to be thrust into a boiling pool, and being therein plunged very often, he never shrieked or cried 'I scald!', as his other companions there cried, but seemed so lightly to esteem it that the judge thought meet to condemn him unto the most terrible place, where are such torments as neither pen can write, tongue express, or thought conceive. But the miser even there seemed to smile and to make small accompt of his punishment. Rhadamanthus, hereof informed, sent for him and demanded the cause why he made so light of his durance. He answered that whiles he lived on earth he was so continually afflicted and oppressed with suspicion as that now only to think that he was out of those meditations was sufficient armour to defend him from all other torments.

Rhadamanthus, astonied hereat, gan call together the senators of that kingdom, and propounded this question: how and by what punishment they might devise to touch him according to his deserts. And hereupon fell great disputation. At last, being considered that he had already been plunged in the most unspeakable torments, and thereat little or nothing had changed countenance, therewithal that no soul was sent unto them to be relieved of his smart, but rather to be punished for his former delights, it was concluded by the general council that he should be eftsoons sent into the world and restored to the same body wherein he first had his resiance, so to remain for perpetuity and never to depart nor to perish.

Thus his* body and soul being once again united, and now eftsoons with the same pestilence infected, he became of a suspicious man *Suspicion* itself; and now the wretch remembering the treason of his wife, who had so willingly dispatched him once before, gan utterly abhor her and fled her company, searching in all countries some place of better assurance. And when he had in vain trod on the most part of the earth, he embarked himself to find some unknown island wherein he might frame some new habitation, and finding none so commodious as he desired, he fortuned, sailing along by the shore, to espy a rock more than six-hundreth cubits high, which hung so suspiciously over the seas as though it would threaten to fall at every little blast. This did *Suspicion* imagine to be a fit foundation whereon he might build his second bower. He forsook his boat and travelled by land to espy what entry or access might be made unto the same, and found from land no manner of entry or access unless it were that some courteous bird of the air would be ambassador, or convey some engines, as whilom the eagle did carry Ganymede* into heaven.

He then returned to seas and, approaching near to his rock, found a small stream of fresh water issuing out of the same into the seas, the which, although it were so little and so strait, as might uneaths receive a boat of bigness to carry one living creature at once, yet in his conceit he thought it more large and spacious than that broad way called of our forefathers *Via Appia*, or than that other named *Flaminia*.* He abandoned his bark and, putting off his clothes, adventured—for he was now assured not to drown—to wade and swim against the stream of this unknown brook, the which (a wondrous thing to tell and scarcely to be believed) came down from the very top and height of this rock. And by the way he found six strait and dangerous places where the water seemed to stay his course, passing under six strait and low bridges, and hard by every of those places a pile raised up in manner of a bulwark the which were hollow in such sort as lodgings and other places necessary might in them commodiously be devised by such one as could endure the hellishness of the place.

Passing by these, he attained with much pain unto the top of the rock, the which he found hollowed as the rest, and far more fit for his security than otherwise apt for any commodity. There gan *Suspicion* determine to nestle himself and having now placed six chosen porters, to wit Dread, Mistrust, Wrath, Desperation, Frenzy, and Fury, at these six strange bulwarks, he lodged himself in the seventh all alone, for he trusted no company. But ever mistrusting that his wife should eftsoons find him out, therein he shrieketh continually like to a shriek owl to keep the watch waking, never content to sleep by day or by night. But to be sure that he should not oversleep himself gan stuff his couch with porpentine's quills, to the end that when heavy sleep overcame him and he thereby should be constrained to charge his pallet* with more heavy burden, those plumes might then prick through and so awake him.

His garments were steel upon iron, and that iron upon iron, and iron again, and the more he was armed the less he trusted to be out of danger. He chopped and changed continually, now this now that: new keys, new locks, ditches new scoured and walls newly fortified, and thus always uncontented liveth this wretched hellhound *Suspicion* in this hellish dungeon of habitation, from whence he never removeth his foot, but only in the dead and silent nights when he may be assured that all creatures but himself are whelmed in sound sleep. And then with stealing steps he stalketh about the earth, infecting, tormenting, and vexing all kinds of people with some part of his afflictions, but especially such as either do sit in chair of greatest dignity and estimation, or else such as have achieved some dear and rare emprise. Those above all others he continually galleth with fresh wounds of dread, lest they might lose and forgo the rooms whereunto with such long travail and good haps they had attained, and by this means percase he had crept into the bosom of F.J. who, as is before declared, did erst swim in the deepest seas of earthly delights.

Now then, I must think it high time to return unto him who, being now through feebleness eftsoons cast down upon his bed, gan cast in his inward meditations all things passed, and as one thoroughly puffed up and filled with one peevish conceit, could think upon nothing else, and yet accusing his own guilty conscience to be infected with jealousy, did compile this translation of Ariosto's thirty-first song* as followeth.

What state to man, so sweet and pleasant were,
As to be tied in links of worthy love?
What life so blist and happy might appear
As for to serve Cupid, that God above?
If that our minds were not sometimes infect
With dread, with fear, with care, with cold suspect:
With deep despair, with furious frenzy,
Handmaids to her whom we call jealousy.

For ev'ry other sop of sour chance,
Which lovers taste amid their sweet delight,
Increaseth joy, and doth their love advance
In pleasure's place, to have more perfect plight.
The thirsty mouth thinks water hath good taste,
The hungry jaws are pleased with each repast;
Who hath not proved what dearth by wars doth grow
Cannot of peace the pleasant plenties know.

And though with eye we see not every joy,
Yet may the mind full well support the same,
An absent life long led in great annoy,
When presence comes, doth turn from grief to game,
To serve without reward is thought great pain,
But if despair do not therewith remain
It may be borne, for right rewards at last
Follow true service, though they come not fast.

Disdains, repulses, finally each ill,
Each smart, each pain, of love each bitter taste,
To think on them gan frame the lover's will
To like each joy the more that comes at last;
But this infernal plague if once it touch
Or venom once the lover's mind with grutch,
All feasts and joys that afterwards befall
The lover compts them light or nought at all.

This is that sore, this is that poisoned wound,
The which to heal nor salve nor ointments serve,
Nor charm of words nor image can be found,
Nor observance of stars can it preserve,
Nor all the art of magic can prevail
Which Zoroastes found for our avail.
Oh cruel plague, above all sorrow's smart,
With desperate death thou slay'st the lover's heart.

And me even now thy gall hath so infect
As all the joys which ever lover found,
And all good haps that ever Troilus' sect
Achieved yet above the luckless ground
Can never sweeten once my mouth with mel,
Nor bring my thoughts again in rest to dwell.
Of thy mad moods and of nought else I think,
In such like seas, fair Bradamant did sink.

                                                    F.J.

This is the translation of Ariosto his thirty-first song, all but the last staff, which seemeth as an allegory applied to the rest. It will please none but learned ears: he was tied to the invention, troubled in mind, etc. So I leave it to your judgement and return to F.J., who continued on his bed until his bountiful mistress, with the company of the other courteous dames, returned after supper to his chamber. At their first entry, 'Why how now servant,' quod Dame Elinor, 'we hoped to have found you on foot.' 'Mistress,' quod F.J., 'I have assayed my feet since your departure, but I find them yet unable to support my heavy body, and therefore am constrained, as you see, to acquaint myself with these pillows.' 'Servant,' said she, 'I am right sorry thereof, but since it is of necessity to bear sickness, I will employ my devoir to allay some part of your pains, and to refresh your weary limbs with some comfortable matter.' And therewithal calling her handmaid, delivered unto her a bunch of pretty little keys and, whispering in her ear, dispatched her towards her chamber.

The maid tarried not long, but returned with a little casket, the which her mistress took, opened, and drew out of the same much fine linen, amongst the which she took a pillowbere very fine and sweet, which although it were of itself as sweet as might be, being of long time kept in that odoriferous chest, yet did she with damask water (and that the best that might be, I warrant you) all to sprinkle it with her own hands—which in my conceit might much amend the matter. Then calling for a fresh pillow, sent her maid to air the same, and at her return put on this thus perfumed pillowbere.

In meantime also she had with her own hands attired her servant's head in a fair wrought kerchief taken out of the same casket, then laid him down upon this fresh and pleasant place and prettily, as it were in sport, bedewed his temples with sweet water which she had ready in a casting bottle of gold, kissing his cheek and saying 'Good servant be whole, for I might not long endure thus to attend thee, and yet the love that I bear towards thee cannot be content to see thee languish.' 'Mistress,' said F.J., and that with a trembling voice, 'assure yourself that if there remain in me any spark of life or possibility of recovery, then may this excellent bounty of yours be sufficient to revive me without any further travail or pain unto your person, for whom I am highly to blame, in that I do not spare to put you unto this trouble: and better it were that such a wretch as I had died unknown than that by your exceeding courtesy you should fall into any malady, either by resorting unto me, or by these your pains taken about me.'

'Servant,' quod she, 'all pleasures seem painful to them that take no delight therein, and likewise all toil seemeth pleasant to such as set their felicity in the same, but for me be you sure I do it with so good a will that I can take no hurt thereby, unless I shall perceive that it be rejected or neglected as unprofitable or uncomfortable unto you.' 'To me Mistress,' quod F.J., 'it is such pleasure as neither my feeble tongue can express nor my troubled mind conceive.' 'Why, are you troubled in mind then servant?' quod Dame Elinor. F.J. now blushing answered 'But even as all sick men be, Mistress.'

Herewith they stayed their talk awhile, and the first that break silence was the Lady Frances, who said 'And to drive away the troubles of your mind, good *Trust*, I would be glad if we could devise some pastime amongst us to keep you company, for I remember that with such devices you did greatly recomfort this fair lady when she languished in like sort.' 'She languished indeed gentle *Hope*,' quod F.J., 'but God forbid that she had languished in like sort.' 'Everybody thinketh their grief greatest,' quod Dame Elinor, 'but indeed whether my grief were the more or the less, I am right sorry that yours is such as it is. And to assay whether our passions proceeded of like cause or not, I would we could, according to this lady's saying, devise some like pastimes to try if your malady would be cured with like medicines.'

A gentlewoman of the company, whom I have not hitherto named, and that for good respects lest her name might altogether disclose the rest, gan thus propound. 'We have accustomed', quod she, 'heretofore in most of our games to choose a king or queen, and he or she during their government have charged every of us either with commandments or questions as best seemed to their majesty, wherein to speak mine opinion we have given over-large a scope, neither seemeth it reasonable that one should have the power to discover the thoughts, or at least to bridle the effects, of all the rest. And though indeed in questioning, which doth of the twain more nearly touch the mind, everyone is at free liberty to answer what they list, yet oft have I heard a question demanded in such sort and upon such sudden that it hath been hardly answered without moving matter of contention. And in commands also sometimes it happeneth one to be commanded unto such service as either they are unfit to accomplish, and then the party's weakness is thereby detected, or else to do something that they would not, whereof ensueth more grutch than game. Wherefore in mine opinion we shall do well to choose by lot amongst us a governor who, for that it shall be sufficient preeminence to use the chair of majesty, shall be bound to give sentence upon all such arguments and questions as we shall orderly propound unto them, and from him or her, as from an oracle, we will receive answer and deciding of our litigious causes.'

This dame had stuff in her—an old courtier and a wily wench, whom for this discourse I will name Pergo, lest her name natural were too broad before, and might not drink of all waters.* Well, this proportion* of Pergo pleased them well, and by lot it happened that F.J. must be moderator of these matters, and collector of these causes; the which being so constituted, the Lady Elinor said unto this Dame Pergo 'You have devised this pastime,' quod she, 'and because we think you to be most expert in the handling thereof, do you propound the first question, and we shall be both the more ready and able to follow your example.'

The Lady Pergo refused not, and began on this wise. 'Noble governor,' quod she, 'amongst the adventures that have befallen me I remember especially this one, that in youth it was my chance to be beloved of a very courtlike young gentleman, who abode near the place wherein my parents had their resiance. This gentleman, whether it were for beauty or for any other respect that he saw in me I know not, but he was enamoured of me, and that with an exceeding vehement passion, and of such force were his affects that notwithstanding many repulses which he had received at my hands, he seemed daily to grow in the renewing of his desires.

I on the other side, although I could by no means mislike of him by any good reason, considering that he was of birth no way inferior unto me, of possessions not to be disdained, of person right comely, of behaviour courtly, of manners modest, of mind liberal, and of virtuous disposition, yet such was the gaiety of my mind as that I could not be content to lend him over large thongs of my love,* but always dangerously behaved myself towards him, and in such sort as he could neither take comfort of mine answers nor yet once find himself requited with one good look for all his travail.

'This notwithstanding, the worthy knight continued his suit with no less vehement affection than erst he had begun it, even by the space of seven years. At the last, whether discomfited by my dealings or tired by long travail, or that he had percase light upon the lake that is in the forest of Ardena,* and so in haste and all thirsty had drunk some drops of disdain whereby his hot flames were quenched, or that he had undertaken to serve no longer but his just term of apprenticehood, or that the teeth of time had gnawn and tired his dulled spirits in such sort as that all benumbed he was constrained to use some other artificial balm for the quickening of his senses, or by what cause moved I know not, he did not only leave his long continued suit, but (as I have since perceived) grew to hate me more deadly than before I had disdained him.

'At the first beginning of his retire I perceived not his hatred, but imagined that, being over-wearied, he had withdrawn himself for a time. And considering his worthiness, therewithal his constancy of long time proved, I thought that I could not in the whole world find out a fitter match to bestow myself than on so worthy a person, wherefore I did by all possible means procure that he might eftsoons use his accustomed repair unto my parents; and further, in all places where I happened to meet him, I used all the courtesies towards him that might be contained within the bonds of modesty. But all was in vain, for he was now become more dangerous to be won than the haggard falcon.

'Our lots being thus unluckily changed, I grew to burn in desire, and the more dangerous that he showed himself unto me, the more earnest I was by all means to procure his consent of love. At the last I might perceive that not only he disdained me but, as me thought, boiled in hatred against me, and the time that I thus continued tormented with these thoughts was also just the space of seven years. Finally, when I perceived no remedy for my perplexities, I assayed by absence to wear away this malady, and therefore utterly refused to come in his presence, yea or almost in any other company, whereby I have consumed in lost time the flower of my youth, and am become as you see (what with years and what with the tormenting passions of love) pale, wan, and full of wrinkles. Nevertheless, I have thereby gained thus much, that at last I have wound myself clear out of Cupid's chains, and remain careless at liberty.

'Now mark to what end I tell you this. First seven years passed in the which I could never be content to yield unto his just desires; next other seven years I spent in seeking to recover his lost love; and sithens both those seven years there are even now on Saint Valentine's day last other seven years passed, in the which neither I have desired to see him nor he hath coveted to hear of me. My parents now perceiving how the crow's foot is crept under mine eye, and remembering the long suit that this gentleman had in youth spent on me, considering therewithal that green youth is well mellowed in us both, have of late sought to persuade a marriage between us, the which the knight hath not refused to hear of and I have not disdained to think on. By their mediation we have been eftsoons brought to parly, wherein over and besides the ripping up of many old griefs this hath been chiefly rehearsed and objected between us: what wrong and injury each of us hath done to other; and hereabouts we have fallen to sharp contention. He alleged that much greater is the wrong which I have done unto him, than that repulse which he hath sithens used to me; and I have affirmed the contrary—the matter yet hangeth in variance. Now of you, worthy governor, I would be most glad to hear this question decided, remembering that there was no difference in the times between us; and surely, unless your judgement help me, I am afraid my marriage will be marred and I may go lead apes in hell.*'

F.J. answered 'Good Pergo, I am sorry to hear so lamentable a discourse of your luckless love, and much the sorrier in that

I must needs give sentence against you. For surely great was the wrong that either of you have done to other; and greater was the needless grief which, causeless, each of you hath conceived in this long time; but greatest in my judgement hath been both the wrong and the grief of the knight in that, notwithstanding his deserts, which yourself confess, he never enjoyed any guerdon of love at your hands. And you, as you allege, did enjoy his love of long time together, so that by the reckoning it will fall out—although being blinded in your own conceit you see it not—that of the one and twenty years you enjoyed his love seven at the least, but that ever he enjoyed yours we cannot perceive. And much greater is the wrong that rewardeth evil for good than that which requireth tip for tap. Further, it seemed that whereas you went about in time to try him you did altogether lose time which can never be recovered, and not only lost your own time, whereof you would seem now to lament, but also compelled him to leese his time which he might, be it spoken without offence to you, have bestowed in some other worthy place. And therefore, as that grief is much greater which hath no kind of comfort to allay it, so much more is that wrong which altogether without cause is offered.'

'And I', said Pergo, 'must needs think that much easier is it for them to endure grief which never tasted of joy, and much less is that wrong which is so willingly proffered to be by recompense restored; for if this knight will confess that he never had cause to rejoice in all the time of his service, then with better contentation might he abide grief than I who, having tasted of the delight which I did secretly conceive of his deserts, do think each grief a present death by the remembrance of those forepassed thoughts. And less wrong seemeth it to be destitute of the thing which was never obtained than to be deprived of a jewel whereof we have been already possessed, so that under your correction I might conclude that greater hath been my grief and injury sustained than that of the knight.'

To whom F.J. replied 'As touching delight, it may not be denied but that every lover doth take delight in the inward contemplation of his mind to think of the worthiness of his beloved, and therefore you may not allege that the knight had never cause to rejoice, unless you will altogether condemn yourself of unworthiness. Marry, if you will say that he tasted not the delights that lovers seek, then mark who was the cause but yourself? And if you would accuse him of like ingratitude for that he disdained you in the latter seven years, whenas he might by accepting your love have recompensed himself of all former wrongs, you must remember therewithal that the cruelty by you showed towards him was such that he could by no means perceive that your change proceeded of good will, but rather eftsoons to hold him enchained in unknown links of subtle dealings, and therefore not without cause he doubted you, and yet without cause you rejected him.

'He had often sought occasion, but by your refusals he could never find him; you having occasion fast by the foretop did dally with him so long, till at last he slipped his head from you, and then catching at the bald noddle you found yourself the cause, and yet you would accuse another. To conclude, greater is the grief that is sustained without desert, and much more is the wrong that is offered without cause.'

Thus F.J. decided the question propounded by Pergo, and expected that some other dame should propound another. But his mistress, having her hand on another halfpenny, gan thus say unto him. 'Servant, this pastime is good, and such as I must needs like of, to drive away your pensive thoughts, but sleeping time approacheth, and I fear we disquiet you, wherefore the rest of this time we will, if so like you, bestow in trimming up your bed, and tomorrow we shall meet here and renew this new begun game with Madame Pergo.' 'Mistress,' quod F.J., 'I must obey your will, and most humbly thank you of your great goodness, and all these ladies for their courtesy; even so, requiring you that you will no further trouble yourselves about me, but let my servant alone with conducting me to bed.' 'Yes servant,' quod she, 'I will see if you can sleep any better in my sheets'; and therewith commanded her handmaid to fetch a pair of clean sheets, the which being brought (marvellous fine and sweet) the Ladies Frances and Elinor did courteously unfold them, and laid them on the bed, which done they also entreated F.J. to unclothe him and go to bed. Being laid, his mistress dressed and couched the clothes about him, sithens moistened his temples with rosewater, gave him handkerchiefs and other fresh linen about him, in doing whereof she whispered in his ear, saying 'Servant, this night I will be with thee,' and after with the rest of the dames gave him goodnight and departed, leaving F.J. in a trance between hope and despair, trust and mistrust.

Thus he lay ravished, commanding his servant to go to bed and feigning that himself would assay if he could sleep. About ten or eleven of the clock came his mistress in her nightgown who, knowing all privy ways in that house very perfectly, had conveyed herself into F.J.'s chamber unseen and unperceived and, being now come unto his bedside, kneeled down and, laying her arm over him, said these or like words. 'My good servant, if thou knewest what perplexities I suffer in beholding of thine infirmities, it might then suffice either utterly to drive away thy malady or much more to augment thy griefs, for I know thou lovest me, and I think also that thou hast had sufficient proof of mine unfeigned good will, in remembrance whereof I fall into sundry passions. First I compt the happy lots of our first acquaintance, and therein I call to mind the equality of our affections, for I think that there were never two lovers conjoined with freer consent on both parties; and if my over-hasty delivery of yielding words be not wrested hereafter to my condemnation, I can then assure myself to escape forever without desert of any reproof. Herewithal I cannot forget the sundry adventures happened since we became one heart divided in two bodies, all which have been both happily achieved and delectably enjoyed. What resteth then to consider but this thy present state? The first corrosive that I have felt, and the last cordial that I look for, the end of my joys and the beginning of my torments'— and hereat her salt tears gan bathe the dying lips of her servant who, hearing these words and well considering her demeanour, began now to accuse himself of such and so heinous treason as that his guilty heart was constrained to yield unto a just scourge for the same.

He swooned under her arm; the which, when she perceived,

it were hard to tell what fears did most affright her. But I have heard my friend F.J. confess that he was in a happy trance, and thought himself for diverse causes unhappily revived. For surely I have heard him affirm that to die in such a passion had been rather pleasant than like to pangs of death. It were hard now to rehearse how he was revived, since there were none present but he dying (who could not declare), and she living (who would not disclose so much as I mean to bewray). For my friend F.J. hath to me imported that, returning to life, the first thing which he felt was that his good mistress lay pressing his breast with the whole weight of her body, and biting his lips with her friendly teeth; and peradventure she refrained, either of courtesy towards him or for womanish fear to hurt her tender hand, to strike him on the cheeks in such sort as they do that strive to call again a dying creature, and therefore thought this the aptest mean to reduce him unto remembrance.

F.J., now awaked, could no less do than of his courteous nature receive his mistress into his bed; who, as one that knew that way better than how to help his swooning, gan gently strip off her clothes and, lovingly embracing him, gan demand of him in this sort. 'Alas good servant,' quod she, 'what kind of malady is this that so extremely doth torment thee?' F.J., with fainting speech, answered 'Mistress, as for my malady, it hath been easily cured by your bountiful medicines applied. But I must confess that in receiving that guerison at your hands I have been constrained to fall into an ecstasy through the galding remembrance of mine own unworthiness. Nevertheless good Mistress, since I perceive such fidelity remaining between us as that few words will persuade such trust as lovers ought to embrace, let these few words suffice to crave your pardon, and do eftsoons pour upon me, your unworthy servant, the abundant waves of your accustomed clemency; for I must confess that I have so highly offended you as, but your goodness surpass the malice of my conceits, I must remain (and that right worthily) to the severe punishment of my deserts, and so should you but lose him who hath cast away himself, and neither can accuse you nor dare excuse himself of the crime.'

Dame Elinor, who had rather have found her servant perfectly revived than thus with strange conceits encumbered, and musing much at his dark speech, became importunate to know the certainty of his thoughts. And F.J., as one not master of himself, gan at the last plainly confess how he had mistrusted the change of her vowed affections. Yea, and that more was, he plainly expressed with whom, of whom, by whom, and to whom she bent her better liking.

Now here I would demand of you and such other as are expert: is there any greater impediment to the fruition of a lover's delights than to be mistrusted? Or rather, is it not the ready way to raze all love and former good will out of remembrance to tell a guilty mind that you do mistrust it? It should seem yes by Dame Elinor, who began now to take the matter hotly, and of such vehemency were her fancies that she now fell into flat defiance with F.J. who, although he sought by many fair words to temper her choleric passions, and by yielding himself to get the conquest of another, yet could he by no means determine the quarrel.

The soft pillows being present at all these hot words put forth themselves as mediators for a truce between these enemies, and desired that if they would needs fight it might be in their presence but only one push of the pike, and so from thenceforth to become friends again forever. But the dame denied flatly, alleging that she found no cause at all to use such courtesy unto such a recreant, adding further many words of great reproach, the which did so enrage* F.J. as that, having now forgotten all former courtesies, he drew upon his new-professed enemy and bare her up with such a violence against the bolster that, before she could prepare the ward, he thrust her through both hands and etc.; whereby the dame, swooning for fear, was constrained for a time to abandon her body to the enemy's courtesy.

At last, when she came to herself, she rose suddenly and determined to save herself by flight, leaving F.J. with many despiteful words, and swearing that he should never eftsoons take her at the like advantage, the which oath she kept better than her former professed good will; and having now recovered her chamber, because she found her hurt to be nothing dangerous, I doubt not but she slept quietly the rest of the night—as F.J. also, persuading himself that he should with convenient leisure recover her from this haggard* conceit, took some better rest towards the morning than he had done in many nights forepast.

So let them both sleep whiles I turn my pen unto the beforenamed secretary, who being, as I said, come lately from London, had made many proffers to renew his accustomed consultations, but the sorrow which his mistress had conceived in F.J. his sickness, together with her continual repair to him during the same, had been such lets unto his attempts as it was long time before he could obtain audience. At the last these new accidents fell so favourably for the furtherance of his cause that he came to his mistress's presence and there pleaded for himself.

Now if I should at large write his allegations, together with her subtle answers, I should but cumber your ears with unpleasant rehearsal of feminine frailty. To be short, the late disdainful mood which she had conceived against F.J., together with a scruple which lay in her conscience touching the eleventh article of her belief,* moved her presently with better will to consult with this secretary as well upon a speedy revenge of her late received wrongs as also upon the reformation of her religion. And in very deed it fell out that the secretary, having been of long time absent and thereby his quills and pens not worn so near as they were wont to be, did now prick such fair large notes that his mistress liked better to sing faburden under him than to descant any longer upon F.J.'s plainsong.

And thus they continued in good accord until it fortuned that Dame Frances came into her chamber upon such sudden as she had like to have marred all the music. Well, they conveyed their clefs as closely as they could, but yet not altogether without some suspicion given to the said Dame Frances who, although she could have been content to take any pain in F.J.'s behalf, yet otherwise she would never have bestowed the watching about so worthless a prize. After womanly salutations they fell into sundry discourses, the secretary still abiding in the chamber with them. At last two or three other gentlewomen of the castle came into Madame Elinor's chamber who, after their *bonjour*, did all *una voce*[*] seem to lament the sickness of F.J., and called upon the Dames Elinor and Frances to go visit him again.

The Lady Frances courteously consented, but Madame Elinor first alleged that she herself was also sickly, the which she attributed to her late pains taken about F.J., and said that only for that cause she was constrained to keep her bed longer than her accustomed hour. The dames, but especially the Lady Frances, gan straighways conjecture some great cause of sudden change, and so leaving Dame Elinor, walked together into the park to take the air of the morning.

And as they thus walked, it chanced that Dame Pergo heard a cuckoo chant, who (because the pride of the spring was now past) cried 'cuck cuck cuckoo' in her stammering voice. 'Aha,' quod Pergo, 'this foul bird begins to fly the country, and yet before her departure see how spitefully she can devise to salute us.' 'Not us,' quod Dame Frances, 'but some other whom she hath espied'; wherewith Dame Pergo, looking round about her and espying none other company, said 'Why, here is nobody but we few women,' quod she. 'Thanks be to God, the house is not far from us,' quod Dame Frances.

Hereat the wily Pergo, partly perceiving Dame Frances's meaning, replied on this sort. 'I understand you not,' quod she, 'but to leap out of this matter, shall we go visit Master F.J. and see how he doth this morning?' 'Why,' quod Dame Frances, 'do you suppose that the cuckoo called unto him?' 'Nay marry,' quod Dame Pergo, 'for, as far as I know, he is not married.*' 'As who should say', quod Dame Frances, 'that the cuckoo envieth none but married folks?' 'I take it so,' said Pergo. The Lady Frances answered 'Yes sure, I have noted as evil luck in love, after the cuckoo's call, to have happened unto diverse unmarried folks, as ever I did unto the married; but I can be well content that we go unto Master J., for I promised on the behalf of us all that we would use our best devoir to recomfort him until he had recovered health, and I do much marvel that the Lady Elinor is now become so unwilling to take any travail in his behalf, especially remembering that but yesternight she was so diligent to bring him to bed; but I perceive that all earthly things are subject unto change.' 'Even so they be,' quod Pergo, 'for you may behold the trees which but even this other day were clad in gladsome green, and now their leaves begin to fade and change colour.'

Thus they passed talking and walking until they returned unto the castle, whereas they went straight unto F.J.'s chamber, and found him in bed. 'Why how now *Trust*,' quod Dame Frances, 'will it be no better?' 'Yes, shortly I hope,' quod F.J. The ladies all saluted him, and he gave them the gramercy. At the last, Pergo popped this question unto him. 'And how have you slept in your mistress's sheets, Master F.J.?' quod she. 'Reasonable well,' quod F.J., 'but I pray you, where is my mistress this morning?' 'Marry,' said Pergo, 'we left her in bed scarce well at ease.' 'I am the more sorry,' quod F.J. 'Why *Trust*,' said Mistress Frances, 'be of good comfort, and assure yourself that here are others who would be as glad of your well-doing as your mistress in any respect.' 'I ought not to doubt thereof,' quod F.J., 'having the proof that I have had of your great courtesies, but I thought it my duty to ask for my mistress, being absent.'

Thus they passed some time with him until they were called away unto prayers, and that being finished, they went to dinner, where they met Dame Elinor attired in a night kerchief after the soolenest (the solemnest fashion, I should have said), who looked very drowsily upon all folks, unless it were her secretary, unto whom she deigned sometime to lend a friendly glance. The lord of the castle demanded of her how F.J. did this morning. She answered that she knew not, for she had not seen him that day. 'You may do well then, daughter,' quod the lord, 'to go now unto him, and to assay if he will eat anything, and if here be no meats that like him, I pray you command for him anything that is in my house.' 'You must pardon me sir,' quod she, 'I am sickly disposed, and would be loath to take the air.' 'Why then, go you Mistress Frances,' quod he, 'and take somebody with you; and I charge you see that he lack nothing.'

Mistress Frances was glad of the ambassade and, arising from the table with one other gentlewoman, took with her a dish of chickens boiled in white broth, saying to her father 'I think this meat meetest for Master J. of any that is here.' 'It is so,' quod he, 'daughter, and if he like not that, cause somewhat else to be dressed for him according to his appetite.'

Thus she departed and came to F.J. who, being plunged in sundry woes and thrilled with restless thoughts, was now beginning to arise; but seeing the dames, couched down again, and said unto them 'Alas fair ladies, you put yourselves to more pains than either I do desire or can deserve.' 'Good *Trust*,' quod Dame Frances, 'our pains are no greater than duty requireth, nor yet so great as we could vouchsafe in your behalf, and presently my father hath sent us unto you', quod she, 'with this pittance, and if your appetite desire any one thing more than other, we are to desire likewise that you will not refrain to call for it.' 'Oh my good *Hope*,' quod he, 'I perceive that I shall not die as long as you may make me live.' And being now some deal recomforted with the remembrance of his mistress's words which she had used overnight at her first coming, and also thinking that although she parted in choler it was but justly provoked by himself, and that at leisure he should find some salve for that sore also, he determined to take the comfort of his assured *Hope*, and so to expel all venoms of mistrust before received.

Wherefore, raising himself in his bed, he cast a nightgown about his shoulders, saying 'It shall never be said that my fainting heart can reject the comfortable cordials of so friendly physicians.' 'Now by my troth well said gentle *Trust*,' quod Dame Frances, 'and in so doing assure yourself of guerison with speed.' This thus said, the courteous dame became his carver, and he with a bold spirit gan taste of her cookery. But the late conflicts of his conceits had so disacquainted his stomach from repasts, that he could not well away with meat; and yet nevertheless by little and little received some nouriture.

When his *Hope* had crammed him as long as she could make him feed, they delivered the rest to the other gentlewoman who, having not dined, fell to her provender. In which meanwhile the Lady Frances had much comfortable speech with F.J., and declared that she perceived very well the cause of his malady. 'But my *Trust*,' quod she, 'be all whole, and remember what I foretold you in the beginning; nevertheless you must think that there are remedies for all mischiefs, and if you will be ruled by mine advice we will soon find the mean to ease you of this mishap.' F.J. took comfort in her discretion, and friendly kissing her hand, gave her a cartload of thanks for her great good will, promising to put to his uttermost force and evermore to be ruled by her advice.

Thus they passed the dinner while, the Lady Frances always refusing to declare her conceit of the late change which she perceived in his mistress, for she thought best first to win his will unto conformity by little and little, and then in the end to persuade him with necessity. When the other gentlewoman had vittled her, they departed, requiring F.J. to arise and boldly to resist the faintness of his fever, the which he promised and so bad them *a dio*.*

The ladies, at their return, found the court in Dame Elinor's chamber, who had there assembled her secretary, Dame Pergo and the rest. There they passed an hour or twain in sundry discourses, wherein Dame Pergo did always cast out some bone for Mistress Frances to gnaw upon, for that indeed she perceived her hearty affection towards F.J.; whereat Mistress Frances changed no countenance, but reserved her revenge until a better opportunity. At last quod Dame Frances unto Mistress Elinor 'And when will you go unto your servant, fair lady?' 'When he is sick and I am whole,' quod Dame Elinor. 'That is even now,' quod the other, 'for how sick he is yourself can witness, and how well you are we must bear record.' 'You may as well be deceived in my disposition', quod Dame Elinor, 'as I was overseen in his sudden alteration, and if he be sick you are meetest to be his physician, for you saw yesterday that my pains did little profit towards his recomfort.' 'Yes surely', said the other, 'not only I but all the rest had occasion to judge that your courtesy was his chief comfort.' 'Well,' quod Dame Elinor, 'you know not what I know.' 'Nor you what I think,' quod Dame Frances. 'Think what you list,' quod Elinor. 'Indeed,' quod Frances, 'I may not think that you care, neither will I die for your displeasure,' and so half angry she departed.

At supper they met again, and the master of the house demanded of his daughter Frances how F.J. did. 'Sir,' quod she, 'he did eat somewhat at dinner, and sithens I saw him not.' 'The more to blame,' quod he, 'and now I would have all you gentlewomen take of the best meats and go sup with him, for company driveth away carefulness, and leave you me here with your leavings alone.' 'Nay sir,' quod Mistress Elinor, 'I pray you give me leave to bear you company, for I dare not adventure thither.'

The lord of the castle was contented, and dispatched away the rest who, taking with them such viands as they thought meetest, went unto F.J.'s chamber, finding him up and walking about to recover strength; whereat Dame Frances rejoiced, and declared how her father had sent that company to attend him at supper. F.J. gave great thanks and, missing now nothing but his mistress, thought not good yet to ask for her, but because he partly guessed the cause of her absence he contented himself, hoping that when his lure was new garnished he should easily reclaim her from those coy conceits.

They passed over their supper all in quiet, and soon after Mistress Frances, being desirous to requite Dame Pergo's quips, requested that they might continue the pastime which Dame Pergo had begun overnight; whereunto they all consented, and the lot fell unto Dame Frances to propound the second question who, addressing her speech unto F.J., said in this wise.

'Noble governor, I will rehearse unto you a strange history, not feigned, neither borrowed out of any old authority, but a thing done indeed of late days, and not far distant from this place where we now remain. It chanced that a gentleman our neighbour, being married to a very fair gentlewoman, lived with her by the space of four or five years in great contentation, trusting her no less than he loved her, and yet loving her as much as any man could love a woman. On that other side the gentlewoman had won unto her beauty a singular commendation for her chaste and modest behaviour. Yet it happened in time that a lusty young gentleman, who very often resorted to them, obtained that at her hands which never any man could before him attain; and to be plain, he won so much in her affections that, forgetting both her own duty and her husband's kindness, she yielded her body at the commandment of this lover, in which pastime they passed long time by their politic government.

'At last, the friends of this lady, and especially three sisters which she had, espied overmuch familiarity between the two lovers and, dreading lest it might break out to their common reproach, took their sister apart and declared that the world did judge scarce well of the repair of that gentleman unto her house, and that if she did not foresee it in time she should not only leese the good credit which she herself had hitherto possessed, but furthermore should distain their whole race with common obloquy and reproach.

'These and sundry other godly admonitions of these sisters could not sink in the mind of this gentlewoman, for she did not only stand in defiance what any man could think of her, but also seemed to accuse them that, because they saw her estimation (being their younger) to grow above their own, they had therefore devised this mean to set variance between her husband and her. The sisters, seeing their wholesome counsel so rejected, and her continue still in her obstinate opinion, addressed their speech unto her husband, declaring that the world judged not the best, neither they themselves did very well like of the familiarity between their sister and that gentleman, and therefore advised him to forecast all perils and in time to forbid him his house.

'The husband, on that otherside, had also conceived such a good opinion of his guest, and had grown into such a strict familiarity with him, that you might with more ease have removed a stone wall than once to make him think amiss either of his wife or of her lover. Yea, and immediately after this conference he would not stick thus to say unto his wife. "Bess," for so indeed was her name, "thou has three such busy-brained sisters as I think shortly their heads will break. They would have me to be jealous of thee—no, no, Bess and etc." So that he was not only far from any such belief, but furthermore did every day increase his courtesies towards the lover.

'The sisters being thus on all sides rejected, and yet perceiving more and more an unseemly behaviour between their sister and her minion, began to melt in their own grease; and such was their enraged pretence of revenge that they suborned diverse servants in the house to watch so diligently as that this treason might be discovered. Amongst the rest, one maid of subtle spirit had so long watched them that at last she espied them go into a chamber together and lock the door to them, whereupon she ran with all haste possible to her master and told him that if he would come with her she would show him a very strange sight. The gentleman, suspecting nothing, went with her until he came into a chamber near unto that wherein they had shut themselves and she, pointing her master to the keyhole, bad him look through, where he saw the thing which most might mislike him to behold. Whereat he suddenly drew his dagger and turned towards the maid, who fled from him for fear of mischief. But when he could not overtake her, in the heat of his choler he commanded that she should forthwith truss up that little which she had and to depart his service; and before her departure he found means to talk with her, threatening that if ever she spake any word of this mystery in any place where she should come it should cost her life.

'The maid, for fear, departed in silence, and the master never changed countenance either to his wife or to her paramour, but feigned unto his wife that he had turned away the maid upon that sudden for that she had thrown a kitchen knife at him whiles he went about to correct a fault in her and etc. Thus the good gentleman drank up his own sweat unseen every day, increasing courtesy to the lover, and never changing countenance to his wife in anything, but only that he refrained to have such knowledge of her carnally as he in times past had, and other men have of their wives.

'In this sort he continued by the space almost of half a year, nevertheless lamenting his mishap in solitary places. At last (what moved him I know not) he fell again to company with his wife as other men do, and as I have heard it said, he used this policy. Every time that he had knowledge of her he would leave, either in the bed, or in her cushion-cloth, or by her looking-glass, or in some place where she must needs find it, a piece of money which then was fallen to three halfpence, and I remember they called them slips.

'Thus he dealt with her continually by the space of four or five months, using her nevertheless very kindly in all other respects, and providing for her all things necessary at the first call. But unto his guest he still augmented his courtesy in such sort that you would have thought them to be sworn brothers. All this notwithstanding, his wife, much musing at these three halfpenny pieces which she found in this sort, and furthermore having sundry times found her husband in solitary places making great lamentation, she grew inquisitive what should be the secret cause of these alterations; unto whom he would none otherwise answer but that any man should find occasion to be more pensive at one time than at another. The wife, notwithstanding, increasing her suspect, imparted the same unto her lover, alleging therewithal that she doubted very much lest her husband had some vehement suspicion of their affairs. The lover encouraged her, and likewise declared that if she would be importunate to enquire the cause her husband would not be able to keep it from her; and having now thoroughly instructed her, she dealt with her husband in this sort.

'One day, when she knew him to be in his study alone, she came in to him and, having fast locked the door after her and conveyed the key into her pocket, she began first with earnest entreaty and then with tears to crave that he would no longer keep from her the cause of his sudden alteration. The husband dissimuled the matter still; at last she was so earnest to know for what cause he left money in such sort at sundry times that he answered on this wise. "Wife," quod he, "thou knowest how long we have been married together, and how long I made so dear accompt of thee as ever man made of his wife, since which days thou knowest also how long I refrained thy company, and how long again I have used thy company leaving the money in this sort; and the cause is this. So long as thou didst behave thyself faithfully towards me I never loathed thy company, but sithens I have perceived thee to be a harlot, and therefore did I for a time refrain and forbear to lie with thee; and now I can no longer forbear it, I do give thee every time that I lie with thee a slip, which is to make thee understand thine own whoredom, and this reward is sufficient for a whore."

'The wife began very stoutly to stand at defiance, but the husband cut off her speech and declared when, where, and how he had seen it. Hereat the woman, being abashed, and finding her conscience guilty of as much as he had alleged, fell down on her knees and with most bitter tears craved pardon, confessing her offence. Whereat her husband, moved with pity and melting likewise in floods of lamentation, recomforted her, promising that if from that day forwards she would be true unto him he would not only forgive all that was past but become more tender and loving unto her than ever he was.

'What do I tarry so long? They became of accord, and in full accomplishment thereof the gentlewoman did altogether eschew the company, the speech, and, as much as in her lay, the sight of her lover, although her husband did continue his courtesy towards him, and often charged his wife to make him fair semblant. The lover was now only left in perplexity, who knew nothing what might be the cause of all these changes, and that most grieved him, he could by no means obtain again the speech of his desired. He watched all opportunities, he suborned messengers, he wrote letters, but all in vain. In the end, she caused to be declared unto him a time and place where she would meet him and speak with him.

'Being met, she put him in remembrance of all that had passed between them; she layed also before him how trusty she had been unto him in all professions. She confessed also how faithfully he had discharged the duty of a friend in all respects, and therewithal she declared that her late alteration and pensiveness of mind was not without great cause, for that she had of late such a mishap as might change the disposition of any living creature; yea, and that the cause was such as, unless she found present remedy, her death must needs ensue and that speedily, for the preventing whereof she alleged that she had beaten her brains with all devices possible and that in the end she could think of no redress but one, the which lay only in him to accomplish. Wherefore she besought him for all the love and good will which passed between them now to show the fruits of true friendship, and to gratify her with a free grant to this request.

'The lover, who had always been desirous to pleasure her in anything, but now especially to recover her wonted kindness, gan frankly promise to accomplish anything that might be to him possible; yea, though it were to his great detriment, and therewithal did deeply blame her in that she would so long torment herself with any grief, considering that it lay in him to help it. The lady answered that she had so long kept it from his knowledge because she doubted whether he would be contented to perform it or not, although it was such a thing as he might easily grant without any manner of hurt to himself, and yet that now in the end she was forced to adventure upon his courtesy, being no longer able to bear the burden of her grief.

'The lover solicited her most earnestly to disclose it, and she as fast seemed to mistrust that he would not accomplish it. In the end she took out a book, which she had brought for the nonce, and bound him by oath to accomplish it. The lover, mistrusting nothing less than that ensued, took the oath willingly. Which done, she declared all that had passed between her and her husband: his grief, her repentance, his pardon, her vow, and in the end of her tale enjoined the lover that from thenceforthwards he should never attempt to break her constant determination. The lover replied that this was impossible, but she plainly assured him that if he granted her that request she would be his friend in all honest and godly wise; if not, she put him out of doubt that she would eschew his company and fly from his sight as from a scorpion.

'The lover, considering that her request was but just, accusing his own guilty conscience, remembering the great courtesies always used by her husband, and therewithal seeing the case now brought to such an issue as that by none other means than by this it could be concealed from knowledge of the world, but most of all being urged by his oath, did at last give an unwilling consent, and yet a faithful promise to yield unto her will in all things. And thus being become of one assent, he remaineth the dearest friend and most welcome guest that may be, both to the lady and her husband, and the man and wife so kind, each to other, as if there never had been such a breach between them.

'Now of you, noble governor, I would fain learn whether the perplexity of the husband when he looked in at the keyhole, or of the wife when she knew the cause why the slips were so scattered, or of the lover when he knew what was his mistress's charge, was greater of the three. I might have put in also the troubled thoughts of the sisters and the maid when they saw their good will rejected, but let these three suffice.'

'Gentle *Hope*,' quod F.J., 'you have rehearsed, and that right eloquently, a notable tale, or rather a notable history, because you seem to affirm that it was done indeed of late and not far hence. Wherein I note five especial points. That is, a marvellous patience in the husband; no less repentance in the wife; no small boldness of the maid; but much more rashness in the sisters; and last of all a rare tractability in the lover. Nevertheless, to return unto your question, I think the husband's perplexity greatest, because his losses abounded above the rest, and his injuries were uncomparable.'

The Lady Frances did not seem to contrary him, but rather smiled in her sleeve at Dame Pergo, who had no less patience to hear the tale recited than the Lady Frances had pleasure in telling of it—but I may not rehearse the cause why, unless I should tell all. By this time, the sleeping hour approached, and the ladies prepared their departure, whenas Mistress Frances said unto F.J. 'Although percase I shall not do it so handsomely as your mistress, yet good *Trust*,' quod she, 'if you vouchsafe it I can be content to trim up your bed in the best manner that I may, as one who would be as glad as she to procure your quiet rest.' F.J. gave her great thanks, desiring her not to trouble herself, but to let his man alone with that charge.

Thus they departed, and how all parties took rest that night I know not, but in the morning F.J. began to consider with himself that he might lie long enough in his bed before his mistress would be appeased in her peevish conceits. Wherefore he arose and, being apparelled in his nightgown, took occasion to walk in the gallery near adjoining unto his mistress's chamber. But there might he walk long enough ere his mistress would come to walk with him.

When dinner time came he went into the great chamber, whereas the lord of the castle saluted him, being joyful of his recovery. F.J., giving due thanks, declared that his friendly entertainment, together with the great courtesy of the gentlewomen, was such as might revive a man although he were half dead. 'I would be loath', quod the host, 'that any gentleman coming to me for good will should want any courtesy of entertainment that lieth in my power.'

When the meat was served to the table, the gentlewomen came in, all but Dame Elinor and Mistress Pergo, the which F.J. marked very well, and it did somewhat abate his appetite. After dinner, his *Hope* came unto him and demanded of him how he would pass the day for his recreation, to whom he answered even as it best pleased her. She devised to walk into the park, and so by little and little to acquaint himself with the air. He agreed, and they walked together, being accompanied with one or two other gentlewomen. Here, lest you should grow in some wrong conceit of F.J., I must put you out of doubt that, although there were now more cause that he should mistrust his mistress than ever he had before received, yet the vehement passions which he saw in her when she first came to visit him, and moreover the earnest words which she pronounced in his extremity, were such a refreshing to his mind as that he determined no more to trouble himself with like conceits; concluding further that if his mistress were not faulty, then had he committed a foul offence in needless jealousy, and that if she were faulty, especially with the secretary, then no persuasion could amend her, nor any passion help him. And this was the cause that enabled him, after such passing pangs, to abide the doubtful conclusion, thus manfully and valiantly to repress faintness of his mind, nothing doubting but that he should have won his mistress to pardon his presumption and lovingly to embrace his service in wonted manner.

But he was far deceived, for she was now in another tune, the which Mistress Frances began partly to discover unto him as they walked together, for she burdened him that his malady proceeded only of a disquiet mind. 'And if it did so, my gentle *Hope*,' quod he, 'what remedy?' 'My good *Trust*,' quod she, 'none other but to plant quiet where disquiet began to grow.' 'I have determined so,' quod he, 'but I must crave the help of your assured friendship.' 'Thereof you may make accompt,' quod she, 'but wherein?'

F.J., walking apart with her, began to declare that there was some contention happened between his mistress and him. The lady told him that she was not ignorant thereof. Then he desired her to treat so much in the cause as they might eftsoons come to parley. 'Thereof I dare assure you,' quod Mistress Frances, and at their return she led F.J. into his mistress's chamber, whom they found lying on her bed, whether galded with any grief or weary of the thing which you wot of I know not, but there she lay, unto whom F.J. gave two or three salutations before she seemed to mark him.

At last, said the Lady Frances unto her 'Your servant, hearing of your sickness, hath adventured thus far into the air to see you.' 'I thank him,' quod Dame Elinor, and so lay still, refusing to give him any countenance. Whereat F.J., perceiving all the other gentlewomen fall to whispering, thought good boldly to plead his own case and, approaching the bed, began to enforce his unwilling mistress unto courtesy, wherein he used such vehemence as she could not well by any means refuse to talk with him. But what their talk was I may not take upon me to tell you, unless you would have me fill up a whole volume only with his matters, and I have dilated them over-largely already. Sufficeth this to be known: that in the end she pretended to pass over all old grudges, and thenceforth to pleasure him as occasion might serve, the which occasion was so long in happening that in the end F.J., being now eftsoons troubled with unquiet fantasies, and forced to use his pen again as an ambassador between them, one day amongst the rest found opportunity to thrust a letter into her bosom, wherein he had earnestly requested another moonshine banquet or Friday's breakfast to recomfort his dulled spirits; whereunto the dame yielded this answer in writing, but of whose enditing judge you.

G.T.

I can but smile at your simplicity, who burden your friends with an impossibility. The case so stood as I could not, though I would. Wherefore from henceforth either learn to frame your request more reasonably, or else stand content with a flat repulse.

SHE

F.J. liked this letter but a little, and being thereby driven into his accustomed vein, he compiled in verse this answer following, upon these words contained in her letter: *I could not though I would.*

G.T.

'I could not though I would': good lady say not so,
Since one good word of your good will might soon redress my woe.
Where would is free before, there could can never fail:
For proof you see how galleys pass where ships can bear no sail.
The weary mariner when skies are overcast
By ready will doth guide his skill and wins the haven at last.
The pretty bird that sings with prick against her breast*
Doth make a virtue of her need to watch when others rest.
And true the proverb is, which you have laid apart,
There is no hap can seem so hard unto a willing heart.
Then lovely lady mine, you say not as you should,
In doubtful terms to answer thus: 'I could not though I would.'
Yes, yes, full well you know your can is quick and good,
And wilful will is eke too swift to shed my guiltless blood.
But if good will were bent as pressed as power is,
Such will would quickly find the skill to mend that is amiss.
Wherefore if you desire to see my true love spilt,
Command and I will slay myself, that yours may be the guilt.
But if you have no power to say your servant nay
Write thus: 'I may not as I would, yet must I as I may.'

F.J.

Thus F.J. replied upon his mistress's answer, hoping thereby to recover some favour at her hands, but it would not be. So that now he had been as likely as at the first to have fretted in fantasies had not the Lady Frances continually comforted him, and by little and little she drove such reason ¦nto his mind that now he began to subdue his humours with discretion, and to determine that if he might espy evident proof of his mistress's frailty, he would then stand content with patience perforce, and give his mistress the *bezo los manos*.

And it happened one day amongst others that he resorted to his mistress's chamber and found her *allo solito** lying upon her bed, and the secretary with Dame Pergo and her handmaid keeping of her company. Whereat F.J., somewhat repining, came to her and fell to dalliance, as one that had now rather adventure to be thought presumptuous than yield to be accompted bashful. He cast his arm over his mistress and began to accuse her of sluggishness, using some other bold parts, as well to provoke her as also to grieve the other. The lady seemed little to delight in his dallying, but cast a glance at her secretary and therewith smiled, whenas the secretary and Dame Pergo burst out into open laughter. The which F.J. perceiving, and disdaining her ingratitude, was forced to depart and in that fantasy compiled this sonnet.

G.T.

> With her in arms that had my heart in hold,
> I stood of late to plead for pity so,
> And as I did her lovely looks behold,
> She cast a glance upon my rival foe,
> His fleering face provoked her to smile,
> When my salt tears were drowned in disdain:
> He glad, I sad, he laughed (alas the while),
> I wept for woe, I pined for deadly pain.
> And when I saw none other boot prevail,
> But reason's rule must guide my skilful mind:
> 'Why then,' quod I, 'old proverbs never fail,
> For yet was never good cat out of kind,*
> Nor woman true but even as stories tell,
> Won with an egg, and lost again with shell.'*

F.J.

This sonnet declareth that he began now to accompt of her as she deserved, for it hath a sharp conclusion, and it is somewhat too general. Well, as it is he lost it where his mistress found it, and she immediately imparted the same unto Dame Pergo, and Dame Pergo unto others, so that it quickly became common in the house. Amongst others Mistress Frances, having recovered a copy of it, did seem to pardon the generality and to be well pleased with the particularity thereof, the which she bewrayed one day unto F.J. in this wise. 'Of all the joys that ever I had, my good *Trust*,' quod she, 'there is none wherein I take more comfort than in your conformity, and although your present rage is such that you can be content to condemn a number unknown for the transgression of one too well known, yet I do rather rejoice that you should judge your pleasure over many than to be abused by any.'

'My good *Hope*,' quod he, 'it were not reason that after such manifold proofs of your exceeding courtesies I should use strange or contentious speech with so dear a friend, and indeed I must confess that the opinion which I have conceived of my mistress hath stirred my pen to write very hardly against all the feminine gender, but I pray you pardon me,' quod he, 'and if it please you I will recant it, as also, percase, I was but cloyed with surquedry, and presumed to think more than may be proved.'

'Yea, but how if it were proved?' quod Dame Frances. 'If it were so, which God forbid,' quod he, 'then could you not blame me to conceive that opinion.' 'Howsoever I might blame you,' quod she, 'I mean not to blame you, but I demand further, if it be as I think and you suspect, what will you then do?' 'Surely', quod F.J., 'I have determined to drink up mine own sorrow secretly, and to bid them both *adieu*.' 'I like your farewell better than your fantasy,' quod she, 'and whensoever you can be content to take so much pains as the knight which had a nightgown guarded with naked swords did take, I think you may put yourself out of doubt of all these things.'

By these words, and other speech which she uttered unto him, F.J. smelt how the world went about, and therefore did one day in the grey morning adventure to pass through the gallery towards his mistress's chamber, hoping to have found the door open. But he found the contrary, and there attending in good devotion heard the parting of his mistress and her secretary with many kind words, whereby it appeared that the one was very loath to depart from the other. F.J. was enforced to bear this burden, and after he had attended there as long as the light would give him leave, he departed also to his chamber and, apparelling himself, could not be quiet until he had spoken with his mistress, whom he burdened flatly with this despiteful treachery, and she as fast denied it, until at last, being still urged with such evident tokens as he alleged, she gave him this bone to gnaw upon. 'And if I did so,' quod she, 'what then?'

Whereunto F.J. made none answer, but departed with this farewell. 'My loss is mine own, and your gain is none of yours, and sooner can I recover my loss than you enjoy the gain which you gape after.' And when he was in place solitary, he compiled these following for a final end of the matter.

G.T.

'And if I did what then?
Are you aggrieved therefore?
The sea hath fish for every man,
And what would you have more?'

Thus did my mistress once
Amaze my mind with doubt,
And popped a question for the nonce
To beat my brains about.

Whereto I thus replied:
'Each fisherman can wish
That all the sea at every tide
Were his alone to fish.

And so did I (in vain),
But since it may not be,
Let such fish there as find the gain
And leave the loss for me.

And with such luck and loss
I will content myself,
Till tides of turning time may toss
Such fishers on the shelf.

And when they stick on sands,
That every man may see,
Then will I laugh and clap my hands,
As they do now at me.'

F.J

It is time now to make an end of this thriftless history wherein, although I could wade much further, as to declare his departure, what thanks he gave to his *Hope* and etc., yet I will cease, as one that had rather leave it unperfect than make it too plain. I have passed it over with 'quod he' and 'quod she' after my homely manner of writing, using sundry names for one person, as 'the Dame', 'the Lady', 'Mistress' and etc., 'the lord of the castle', 'the master of the house', and 'the host'. Nevertheless, for that I have seen good authors term every gentlewoman a Lady, and every gentleman *domine*, I have thought it no greater fault than petty treason thus to intermingle them, nothing doubting but you will easily understand my meaning, and that is as much as I desire.

Now henceforwards I will trouble you no more with such a barbarous style in prose, but will only recite unto you sundry verses written by sundry gentlemen, adding nothing of mine own but only a title to every poem*. . .

APPENDIX:* Conclusion of the revised version of F.J.: *The Pleasant Fable of Ferdinando Jeronomi and Leonora de Valasco, translated out of the Italian riding tales of Bartello* (1575)

Thus Ferdinando [F.J.], being no longer able to bear these extreme despights, resolved to absent himself, as well for his own further quiet as also to avoid the occasion of greater mischiefs that might ensue. And although the exceeding courtesies and approved fidelity of Dame Frances had been sufficient to allure the fast liking of any man, especially considering that she was reasonably fair, and descended of a worthy father, who now fell flatly to move and solicit the same, yet such sinister conceits had he taken by the frailty of Dame Elinor as that, rejecting all proffers and condemning all courtesies, he took his leave, and without pretence of return departed to his house in Venice, spending there the rest of his days in a dissolute kind of life, and abandoning the worthy Lady Frances [china], who daily being galled with the grief of his great ingratitude did shortly bring herself into a miserable consumption, whereof, after three years' languishing, she died.

Notwithstanding all which occurrents, the Lady Elinor

lived long in the continuance of her accustomed change, and thus we see that where wicked lust doth bear the name of love, it doth not only infect the light-minded, but it may also become confusion to others which are vowed to constancy. And to that end I have recited this fable, which may serve as ensample to warn the youthful reader from attempting the like worthless enterprise. . . .

JOHN LYLY

Euphues: The Anatomy of Wit
(1578)

*Euphues:** The Anatomy of Wit*. Very pleasant for all gentle-men to read, and most necessary to remember. Wherein are contained the delights that wit followeth in his youth, by the pleasantness of love, and the happiness he reapeth in age, by the perfectness of wisdom. By John Lyly, Master of Art. Corrected and augmented.*

The Epistle Dedicatory: To the Right Honourable my very good lord and master Sir William West, Knight, Lord de la Warre,* John Lyly wisheth long life with increase of honour.

PARRHASIUS, drawing the counterfeit of Helen, right honourable, made the attire of her head loose, who being demanded why he did so, he answered she was loose. Vulcan was painted curiously, yet with a polt foot. Leda cunningly, yet with her black hair. Alexander, having a scar in his cheek, held his finger upon it that Appelles might not paint it; Appelles painted him with his finger cleaving to his face. 'Why,' quod Alexander, 'I laid my finger on my scar because I would not have thee see it.' 'Yea,' said Appelles, 'and I drew it there because none else should perceive it, for if thy finger had been away, either thy scar would have been seen or my art misliked.' Whereby I gather that in all perfect works as well the fault as the face is to be shown.

The fairest leopard is made with his spots, the finest cloth with his list, the smoothest shoe with his last.* Seeing then that in every counterfeit as well the blemish as the beauty is coloured, I hope I shall not incur the displeasure of the wise in that in the discourse of Euphues I have as well touched the vanities of his love as the virtues of his life. The Persians, who above all their kings most honoured Cyrus, caused him to be engraven as well with his hooked nose as his high forehead. He that loved Homer best concealed not his flattering, and he that praised Alexander most bewrayed his quaffing. Demonides must have a crooked shoe for his wry foot, Damocles a smooth glove for his straight hand.* For as every painter that shadoweth a man in all parts giveth every piece his just proportion, so he that deciphereth the qualities of the mind ought as well to show every humour in his kind as the other doth every part in his colour. The surgeon that maketh the anatomy showeth as well the muscles in the heel as the veins of the heart.

If then the first sight of Euphues shall seem too light to be read of the wise, or too foolish to be regarded of the learned, they ought not to impute it to the iniquity of the author, but to the necessity of the history. Euphues beginneth with love as allured by wit, but endeth not with lust as bereft of wisdom. He wooeth women provoked by youth, but weddeth not himself to wantonness as pricked by pleasure. I have set down the follies of his wit without breach of modesty, and the sparks of his wisdom without suspicion of dishonesty. And certes I think there be mo speeches which for gravity will mislike the foolish, than unseemly terms which for vanity may offend the wise. Which discourse, right honourable, I hope you will the rather pardon for the rudeness in that it is the first, and protect it the more willingly if it offend in that it may be the last.

It may be that fine wits will descant upon him that having no wit goeth about to make the anatomy of wit; and certainly their jesting in my mind is tolerable. For if the butcher should take upon him to cut the anatomy of a man because he hath skill in opening an ox, he would prove himself a calf, or if the horseleech would adventure to minister a potion to a sick patient, in that he hath knowledge to give a drench to a diseased horse, he would make himself an ass. The shoemaker must not go above his latchet, nor the hedger meddle with anything but his bill. It is unseemly for the painter to feather a shaft, or the fletcher to handle the pencil. All which things make most against me, in that a fool hath intruded himself to discourse of wit. But as I was willing to commit the fault, so am I content to make amends.

Howsoever the case standeth, I look for no praise for my labour, but pardon for my good will; it is the greatest reward that I dare ask, and the least that they can offer. I desire no more, I deserve no less. Though the style nothing delight the dainty ear of the curious sifter, yet will the matter recreate the mind of the courteous reader. The variety of the one will abate the harshness of the other. Things of greatest profit are set forth with least price. Where the wine is neat there needeth no ivy bush. The right coral needeth no colouring. Where the matter itself bringeth credit the man with his gloss winneth small commendation. It is therefore, me thinketh, a greater show of a pregnant wit than perfect wisdom in a thing of sufficient excellency to use superfluous eloquence. We commonly see that a black ground doth best beseem a white counterfeit. And Venus, according to the judgement of Mars, was then most amiable when she sate close by Vulcan.

If these things be true, which experience trieth—that a naked tale doth most truly set forth the naked truth, that where the countenance is fair there need no colours, that painting is meeter for ragged walls than fine marble, that verity then shineth most bright when she is in least bravery—I shall satisfy mine own mind though I cannot feed their humours which greatly seek after those that sift the finest meal, and bear the whitest mouths.* It is a world to see how Englishmen desire to hear finer speech than the language will allow, to eat finer bread than is made of wheat, to wear finer cloth than is wrought of wool. But I let pass their fineness, which can no way excuse my folly.

If your lordship shall accept my good will, which I have always desired, I will patiently bear the ill will of the malicious, which I never deserved.

Thus committing this simple pamphlet to your lordship's patronage, and your Honour to the Almighty's protection, for the preservation of the which, as most bounden, I will pray continually, I end,

your lordship's servant to command,

J. LYLY

To the Gentleman readers

I was driven into a quandary, Gentlemen, whether I might send this my pamphlet to the printer or to the pedlar; I thought it too bad for the press and too good for the pack. But seeing my folly in writing to be as great as others', I was willing my fortune should be as ill as any's. We commonly see the book that at Christmas* lieth bound on the stationer's stall, at Easter to be broken in the haberdasher's shop; which sith it is the order of proceeding I am content this winter to have my doings read for a toy that in summer they may be ready for trash. It is not strange whenas the greatest wonder lasteth but nine days that a new work should not endure but three months. Gentlemen use books as gentlewomen handle their flowers, who in the morning stick them in their heads and at night straw them at their heels. Cherries be fulsome when they be through ripe, because they be plenty, and books be stale when they be printed in that they be common. In my mind printers and tailors are bound chiefly to pray for gentlemen, the one hath so many fantasies to print, the other such diverse fashions to make, that the pressing iron of the one is never out of the fire, nor the printing press of the other any time lieth still.

But a fashion is but a day's wearing, and a book but an hour's reading; which seeing it is so I am of the shoemaker's mind, who careth not so the shoe hold the plucking on, nor I so my labours last the running over. He that cometh in print because he would be known is like the fool that cometh into the market because he would be seen. I am not he that seeketh praise for his labour, but pardon for his offence, neither do I set this forth for any devotion in print, but for duty which I owe to my patron.

If one write never so well he cannot please all, and write he never so ill he shall please some. Fine heads will pick a quarrel with me if all be not curious, and flatterers a thank* if anything be current. But this is my mind, let him that findeth fault amend it, and him that liketh it use it. Envy braggeth but draweth no blood, the malicious have more mind to quip than might to cut. I submit myself to the judgement of the wise and little esteem the censure of fools; the one will be satisfied with reason, the other are to be answered with silence. I know gentlemen will find no fault without cause, and bear with those that deserve blame; as for others, I care not for their jests, for I never meant to make them my judges.

Farewell.*

EUPHUES

THERE dwelt in Athens a young gentleman of great patrimony, and of so comely a personage, that it was doubted whether he were more bound to nature for the lineaments of his person, or to fortune for the increase of his possessions. But nature, impatient of comparisons, and as it were disdaining a companion or copartner in her working, added to this comeliness of his body such a sharp capacity of mind that not only she proved fortune counterfeit, but was half of that opinion that she herself was only current. This young gallant of more wit than wealth, and yet of more wealth than wisdom, seeing himself inferior to none in pleasant conceits thought himself superior to all in honest conditions, in so much that he thought himself so apt to all things that he gave himself almost to nothing but practising of those things commonly which are incident to these sharp wits: fine phrases, smooth quips, merry taunts, jesting without mean and abusing mirth without measure.

As therefore the sweetest rose hath his prickle, the finest velvet his brack, the fairest flower his bran, so the sharpest wit hath his wanton will, and the holiest head his wicked way. And true it is that some men write and most men believe, that in all perfect shapes a blemish bringeth rather a liking every way to the eyes than a loathing any way to the mind. Venus had her mole in her cheek which made her more amiable; Helen her scar in her chin which Paris called *Cos Amoris*, the whetstone of love. Aristippus his wart, Lycurgus his wen; so likewise in the disposition of the mind either virtue is overshadowed with some vice or vice overcast with some virtue.

Alexander valiant in war yet given to wine. Tully* eloquent in his glozes yet vainglorious. Solomon wise yet too too wanton. David holy, but yet an homicide. None more witty than Euphues, yet at the first none more wicked. The freshest colours soonest fade, the teenest* razor soonest turneth his edge, the finest cloth is soonest eaten with moths, and the cambric sooner stained than the coarse canvas; which appeared well in this Euphues, whose wit being like wax apt to receive any impression, and bearing the head in his own hand, either to use the rein or the spur, disdaining counsel, leaving his country, loathing his old acquaintance, thought either by wit to obtain some conquest, or by shame to abide some conflict; who, preferring fancy before friends and his present humour before honour to come, laid reason in water, being too salt for his taste, and followed unbridled affection, most pleasant for his tooth.

When parents have more care how to leave their children wealthy than wise, and are more desirous to have them maintain the name than the nature of a gentleman; when they put gold into the hands of youth, where they should put a rod under their girdle; when instead of awe they make them past grace, and leave them rich executors of goods and poor executors of godliness—then is it no marvel that the son, being left rich by his father's will, become retchless by his own will. But it hath been an old said saw, and not of less truth than antiquity, that wit is the better if it be the dearer bought, as in the sequel of this history shall most manifestly appear.

It happened this young imp to arrive at Naples (a place of more pleasure than profit, and yet of more profit than piety), the very walls and windows whereof showed it rather to be the tabernacle of Venus than the temple of Vesta. There was all things necessary and in readiness that might either allure the mind to lust or entice the heart to folly: a court more meet for an atheist than for one of Athens; for Ovid than for Aristotle; for a graceless lover than for a godly liver; more fitter for Paris than Hector; and meeter for Flora than Diana.

Here my youth (whether for weariness he could not, or for wantonness would not go any farther) determined to make his abode, whereby it is evidently seen that the fleetest fish swalloweth the delicatest bait, that the highest soaring hawk traineth to the lure, and that the wittiest brain is inveigled with the sudden view of alluring vanities. Here he wanted no companions which courted him continually with sundry kinds of devices whereby they might either soak his purse to reap commodity or sooth his person to win credit, for he had guests and companions of all sorts.

There frequented to his lodging as well the spider to suck poison of his fine wit as the bee to gather honey; as well the drone as the dove; the fox as the lamb; as well Damocles to betray him as Damon to be true to him. Yet he behaved himself so warily that he singled his game* wisely. He could easily discern Apollo's music from Pan his pipe, and Venus' beauty from Juno's bravery, and the faith of Laelius from the flattery of Aristippus. He welcomed all but trusted none; he was merry but yet so wary that neither the flatterer could take advantage to entrap him in his talk, nor the wisest any assurance of his friendship. Who, being demanded of one what countryman he was, he answered 'What countryman am I not? If I be in Crete I can lie, if in Greece I can shift, if in Italy I can court it. If thou ask whose son I am also I ask thee whose son I am not. I can carouse with Alexander, abstain with Romulus, eat with the Epicure, fast with the Stoic, sleep with Endimion, watch with Chrisippus'—using these speeches and other like.

An old gentleman in Naples, seeing his pregnant wit, his eloquent tongue somewhat taunting yet with delight, his mirth without measure yet not without wit, his sayings vainglorious yet pithy, began to bewail his nurture, and to muse at his nature, being incensed against the one as most pernicious, and inflamed with the other as most precious. For he well knew that so rare a wit would in time either breed an intolerable trouble, or bring an incomparable treasure to the commonweal. At the one he greatly pitied, at the other he rejoiced. Having therefore gotten opportunity to communicate with him his mind, with watery eyes, as one lamenting his wantonness, and smiling face, as one loving his wittiness, encountered him on this manner.

'Young gentleman, although my acquaintance be small to entreat you, and my authority less to command you, yet my good will in giving you good counsel should induce you to believe me, and my hoary hairs, ambassadors of experience, enforce you to follow me. For by how much the more I am a stranger to you, by so much the more you are beholding to me. Having therefore opportunity to utter my mind I mean to be importunate with you to follow my meaning. As thy birth doth show the express and lively image of gentle blood, so thy bringing up seemeth to me to be a great blot to the lineage of so noble a brute, so that I am enforced to think that either thou didst want one to give thee good instructions, or that thy parents made thee a wanton with too much cockering; either they were too foolish in using no discipline, or thou too froward in rejecting their doctrine; either they willing to have thee idle or thou wilful to be ill employed.

'Did they not remember that which no man ought to forget: that the tender youth of a child is like the tempering of new wax, apt to receive any form? He that will carry a bull with Milo must use to carry him a calf also; he that coveteth to have a straight tree must not bow him being a twig. The potter fashioneth his clay when it is soft and the sparrow is taught to come when he is young. As therefore the iron, being hot, receiveth any form with the stroke of the hammer and keepeth it, being cold, forever, so the tender wit of a child, if with diligence it be instructed in youth, will with industry use those qualities in his age.

'They might also have taken example of the wise husbandmen who in their fattest and most fertile ground sow hemp before wheat, a grain that drieth up the superfluous moisture and maketh the soil more apt for corn; or of good gardeners who in their curious knots* mix hyssop with thyme as aiders the one to the growth of the other, the one being dry, the other moist; or of cunning painters who for the whitest work cast the blackest ground to make the picture more amiable. If therefore thy father had been as wise an husbandman as he was a fortunate husband, or thy mother as good a huswife as she was a happy wife, if they had been both as good gardeners to keep their knot as they were grafters to bring forth such fruit, or as cunning painters as they were happy parents, no doubt they had sowed hemp before wheat, that is discipline before affection; they had set hyssop with thyme, that is manners with wit, the one to aid the other; and to make thy dexterity more, they had cast a black ground for their white work, that is they had mixed threats with fair looks.

'But things past are past calling again; it is too late to shut the stable door when the steed is stolen. The Trojans repented too late when their town was spoiled; yet the remembrance of thy former follies might breed in thee a remorse of conscience and be a remedy against further concupiscence. But now to the present time. The Lacedemonians were wont to show their children drunken men and other wicked men that by seeing their filth they might shun the like fault, and avoid the like vices when they were at the like state. The Persians, to make their youth abhor gluttony, would paint an epicure sleeping with meat in his mouth and most horribly overladen with wine, that by the view of such monstrous sights they might eschew the means of the like excess. The Parthians, to cause their youth to loathe the alluring trains of women's wiles and deceitful enticements, had most curiously carved in their houses a young man blind, besides whom was adjoined a woman so exquisite that in some men's judgement Pygmalion's image was not half so excellent, having one hand in his pocket as noting her theft, and holding a knife in the other hand to cut his throat.

'If the sight of such ugly shapes caused a loathing of the like sins, then my good Euphues consider their plight, and beware of thine own peril. Thou art here in Naples a young sojourner, I an old senior; thou a stranger, I a citizen; thou secure doubting no mishap, I sorrowful dreading thy misfortune. Here mayest thou see that which I sigh to see: drunken sots wallowing in every house, in every chamber, yea in every channel. Here mayest thou behold that which I cannot without blushing behold, nor without blubbering utter: those whose bellies be their gods, who offer their goods as sacrifice to their guts, who sleep with meat in their mouths, with sin in their hearts, and with shame in their houses. Here, yea here Euphues, mayest thou see not the carved vizard of a lewd woman, but the incarnate visage of a lascivious wanton; not the shadow of love but the substance of lust.

'My heart melteth in drops of blood to see a harlot with the one hand rob so many coffers and with the other to rip so many corses. Thou art here amidst the pikes between Scylla and Charybdis, ready if thou shun Syrtis to sink into

Symplegades.* Let the Lacedemonian, the Persian, the Parthian, yea the Neapolitan cause thee rather to detest such villainy at the sight and view of their vanity. Is it not far better to abhor sins by the remembrance of others' faults than by repentance of thine own follies? Is not he accompted most wise whom other men's harms do make most wary?

'But thou wilt haply say that although there be many things in Naples to be justly condemned, yet there are some things of necessity to be commended; and as thy will doth lean unto the one, so thy wit would also embrace the other. Alas Euphues, by how much the more I love the high climbing of thy capacity by so much the more I fear thy fall. The fine crystal is sooner crazed than the hard marble, the greenest beech burneth faster than the driest oak, the fairest silk is soonest soiled, and the sweetest wine turneth to the sharpest vinegar. The pestilence doth most rifest infect the clearest complexion, and the caterpillar cleaveth unto the ripest fruit. The most delicate wit is allured with small enticement unto vice and most subject to yield unto vanity. If therefore thou do but hearken to the Sirens thou wilt be enamoured; if thou haunt their houses and places thou shalt be enchanted. One drop of poison infecteth the whole tun of wine; one leaf of colloquintida mareth and spoileth the whole pot of porridge; one iron mole defaceth the whole piece of lawn.*

'Descend into thine own conscience and consider with thyself the great difference between staring and stark blind, wit and wisdom, love and lust. Be merry but with modesty, be sober but not too sullen, be valiant but not too venturous. Let thy attire be comely but not costly, thy diet wholesome but not excessive. Use pastime as the word importeth—to pass the time in honest recreation. Mistrust no man without cause, neither be thou credulous without proof. Be not light to follow every man's opinion, nor obstinate to stand in thine own conceit. Serve God, love God, fear God, and God will so bless thee as either heart can wish or thy friends desire. And so I end my counsel, beseeching thee to begin to follow it.'

This old gentleman having finished his discourse, Euphues began to shape him an answer in this sort. 'Father and friend—your age showeth the one, your honesty the other—I am neither so suspicious to mistrust your good will, nor so sottish to mislike your good counsel. As I am therefore to thank you for the first, so it stands me upon to think better on the latter. I mean not to cavil with you as one loving sophistry, neither to control you as one having superiority; the one would bring my talk into the suspicion of fraud, the other convince* me of folly.

'Whereas you argue, I know not upon what probabilities but sure I am upon no proof, that my bringing up should be a blemish to my birth, I answer and swear too, that you were not therein a little overshot. Either you gave too much credit to the report of others or too much liberty to your own judgement. You convince my parents of peevishness in making me a wanton, and me of lewdness in rejecting correction. But so many men, so many minds; that may seem in your eye odious which in another's eye may be gracious. Aristippus a philosopher yet who more courtly? Diogenes a philosopher yet who more carterly? Who more popular than Plato, retaining always good company? Who more envious than Timon, denouncing all human society? Who so severe as the Stoics, which like stocks were moved with no melody? Who so secure as the Epicures, which wallowed in all kind of licentiousness?

'Though all men be made of one metal, yet they be not cast all in one mould. There is framed of the self same clay as well the tile to keep out water as the pot to contain liquor, the sun doth harden the dirt and melt the wax, fire maketh the gold to shine and the straw to smother, perfumes doth refresh the dove and kill the beetle, and the nature of the man disposeth that consent of the manners.

'Now whereas you seem to love my nature and loathe my nurture, you bewray your own weakness in thinking that nature may any ways be altered by education, and as you have ensamples to confirm your pretence, so I have most evident and infallible arguments to serve for my purpose. It is natural for the vine to spread: the more you seek by art to alter it, the more in the end you shall augment it. It is proper for the palm tree to mount: the heavier you load it the higher it sprouteth.

Though iron be made soft with fire it returneth to his hardness. Though the falcon be reclaimed to the fist she retireth to her haggardness.* The whelp of a mastiff will never be taught to retrieve the partridge; education can have no show where the excellency of nature doth bear sway. The silly mouse will by no manner of means be tamed; the subtle fox may well be beaten but never broken from stealing his prey; if you pound spices they smell the sweeter; season the wood never so well, the wine will taste of the cask; plant and translate the crab tree where and whensoever it please you and it will never bear sweet apple, unless you graft by art which nothing toucheth nature.

'Infinite and innumerable were the examples I could allege and declare to confirm the force of nature and confute these your vain and false forgeries, were not the repetition of them needless, having showed sufficient, or bootless, seeing those alleged will not persuade you. And can you be so unnatural, whom Dame Nature hath nourished and brought up so many years, to repine as it were against nature?

'The similitude you rehearse of the wax argueth your waxing and melting brain, and your example of the hot and hard iron showeth in you but cold and weak disposition. Do you not know that which all men do affirm and know, that black will take no other colour? That the stone abeston being once made hot will never be made cold? That fire cannot be forced downward? That nature will have course after kind? That everything will dispose itself according to nature? Can the Aethiop change or alter his skin, or the leopard his hue? Is it possible to gather grapes of thorns, or figs of thistles, or to cause anything to strive against nature?

'But why go I about to praise nature, the which as yet was never any imp so wicked and barbarous, any Turk so vile and brutish, any beast so dull and senseless, that could, or would, or durst dispraise or contemn? Doth not Cicero conclude and allow that if we follow and obey nature we shall never err? Doth not Aristotle allege and confirm that nature frameth or maketh nothing in any point rude, vain, or unperfect?

'Nature was had in such estimation and admiration among the heathen people that she was reputed for the only Goddess in heaven; if nature then have largely and bountifully endued me with her gifts, why deem you me so untoward and graceless? If she have dealt hardly with me, why extol you so much my birth? If nature bear no sway, why use you this adulation? If nature work the effect, what booteth any education? If nature be of strength or force, what availeth discipline or nurture? If of none, what helpeth nature? But let these sayings pass as known evidently, and granted to be true which none can or may deny unless he be false, or that he be an enemy to humanity.

'As touching my residence and abiding here in Naples, my youthly affections, my sports and pleasures, my pastimes, my common dalliance, my delights, my resort and company, which daily use to visit me, although to you they breed more sorrow and care than solace and comfort because of your crabbed age, yet to me they bring more comfort and joy than care and grief, more bliss than bale, more happiness than heaviness, because of my youthful gentleness. Either you would have all men old as you are, or else you have quite forgotten that you yourself were young, or ever knew young days. Either in your youth you were a very vicious and ungodly man, or now being aged, very superstitious and devout above measure.

'Put you no difference between the young flourishing bay tree and the old withered beech? No kind of distinction between the waxing and the waning of the moon; and between the rising and the setting of the sun? Do you measure the hot assaults of youth by the cold skirmishes of age, whose years are subject to more infirmities than our youth? We merry, you melancholy; we zealous in affection, you jealous in all your doings; you testy without cause, we hasty for no quarrel; you careful, we careless; we bold, you fearful; we in all points contrary unto you, and ye in all points unlike unto us.

'Seeing therefore we be repugnant each to the other in nature, would you have us alike in qualities? Would you have one potion ministered to the burning fever and to the cold palsy? One plaster to an old issue and a fresh wound; one salve for all sores; one sauce for all meats? No, no, Eubulus*—but

I will yield to more than either I am bound to grant either*
thou able to prove. Suppose that which I never will believe:
that Naples is a cankered storehouse of all strife, a common
stews for all strumpets, the sink of shame and the very nurse
of all sin. Shall it therefore follow of necessity that all that are
wooed of love should be wedded to lust? Will you conclude,
as it were *ex consequenti*,* that whosoever arriveth here shall
be enticed to folly, and being enticed of force shall be
entangled? No, no, it is the disposition of the thought that
altereth the nature of the thing.

'The sun shineth upon the dunghill and is not corrupted,
the diamond lieth in the fire and is not consumed, the crystal
toucheth the toad and is not poisoned, the bird Trochilus*
liveth by the mouth of the crocodile and is not spoiled, a
perfect wit is never bewitched with lewdness, neither enticed
with lasciviousness. Is it not common that the holm tree
springeth amidst the beech? That the ivy spreadeth upon the
hard stones? That the soft featherbed breaketh the hard blade?
If experience have not taught you this you have lived long and
learned little; or if your moist brain have forgot it you have
learned much and profited nothing. But it may be that you
measure my affections by your own fancies, and knowing
yourself either too simple to raise the siege by policy or too
weak to resist the assault by prowess, you deem me of as little
wit as yourself or of less force, either of small capacity or of
no courage.

'In my judgement, Eubulus, you shall as soon catch a hare
with a tabor* as you shall persuade youth with your aged and
overworn eloquence to such severity of life which as yet there
was never Stoic in precepts so strict, neither any in life so
precise, but would rather allow it in words than follow it in
works, rather talk of it than try it. Neither were you such
a saint in your youth that, abandoning all pleasures, all
pastimes, and delights, you would choose rather to sacrifice
the first fruits of your life to vain holiness than to youthly
affections. But as, to the stomach quatted with dainties, all
delicates seem queasy, and as he that surfeiteth with wine
useth afterward to allay with water, so these old huddles,
having overcharged their gorges with fancy, accompt all

honest recreation mere folly and, having taken a surfeit of delight, seem now to savour it with despite.

'Seeing therefore it is labour lost for me to persuade you, and wind vainly wasted for you to exhort me, here I found you and here I leave you, having neither bought nor sold with you, but changed ware for ware. If you have taken little pleasure in my reply, sure I am that by your counsel I have reaped less profit. They that use to steal honey burn hemlock to smoke the bees from their hives, and it may be that to get some advantage of me you have used these smoky arguments, thinking thereby to smother me with the conceit of strong imagination. But as the chameleon though he have most guts draweth least breath, or as the elder tree though he be fullest of pith is farthest from strength, so though your reasons seem inwardly to yourself somewhat substantial, and your persuasions pithy in your own conceit, yet being well-weighed without, they be shadows without substance and weak without force. The bird Taurus hath a great voice but a small body, the thunder a great clap yet but a little stone, the empty vessel giveth a greater sound than the full barrel. I mean not to apply it, but look into yourself and you shall certainly find it, and thus I leave you seeking it; but were it not that my company stay my coming I would surely help you to look it,* but I am called hence by my acquaintance.'

Euphues, having thus ended his talk, departed, leaving this old gentleman in a great quandary; who perceiving that he was more inclined to wantonness than to wisdom, with a deep sigh, the tears trickling down his cheeks, said 'Seeing thou wilt not buy counsel at the first hand good cheap, thou shalt buy repentance at the second hand, at such an unreasonable rate that thou wilt curse thy hard pennyworth, and ban thy hard heart. Ah Euphues, little dost thou know that if thy wealth waste, thy wit will give but small warmth, and if thy wit incline to wilfulness, that thy wealth will do thee no great good. If the one had been employed to thrift, the other to learning, it had been hard to conjecture whether thou shouldst have been more fortunate by riches or happy by wisdom, whether more esteemed in the commonweal for wealth to maintain war or for counsel to conclude peace. But alas, why

do I pity that in thee which thou seemest to praise in thyself?'
And so saying, he immediately went to his own house, heavily
bewailing the young man's unhappiness.

Here ye may behold, gentlemen, how lewdly wit standeth in
his own light, how he deemeth no penny good silver but his
own, preferring the blossom before the fruit, the bud before the
flower, the green blade before the ripe ear of corn, his own wit
before all men's wisdoms. Neither is that geason, seeing for
the most part it is proper to all those of sharp capacity to
esteem of themselves as most proper. If one be hard in
conceiving* they pronounce him a dolt, if given to study they
proclaim him a dunce, if merry a jester, if sad a saint, if full
of words a sot, if without speech a cipher. If one argue with
them boldly then is he impudent, if coldly an innocent. If
there be reasoning of divinity they cry '*Quae supra nos nihil
ad nos*',* if of humanity '*Sententias loquitur carnifex*'.*

Hereof cometh such great familiarity between the ripest
wits when they shall see the disposition the one of the other,
the *sympathia* of affections and, as it were, but a pair of sheets
to go between their natures. One flattereth another in his own
folly, and layeth cushions under the elbow of his fellow when
he seeth him take a nap with fancy, and as their wit wresteth
them to vice so it forgeth them some feat excuse to cloak their
vanity.

Too much study doth intoxicate their brains for (say they)
although iron the more it is used the brighter it is, yet silver
with much wearing doth waste to nothing. Though the
cammock the more it is bowed the better it serveth, yet the
bow the more it is bent and occupied the weaker it waxeth.
Though the camomile the more it is trodden and pressed
down the more it spreadeth, yet the violet the oftener it is
handled and touched the sooner it withereth and decayeth.
Besides this, a fine wit, a sharp sense, a quick understanding, is able to attain to more in a moment or a very little
space than a dull and blockish head in a month. The scythe
cutteth far better and smoother than the saw, the wax yieldeth
better and sooner to the seal than the steel to the stamp, the
smooth and plain beech is easier to be carved than the knotty
box.

For neither is there anything but that hath his contraries. Such is the nature of these novices that think to have learning without labour and treasure without travail; either not understanding or else not remembering that the finest edge is made with the blunt whetstone and the fairest jewel fashioned with the hard hammer. I go not about, gentlemen, to inveigh against wit, for then I were witless, but frankly to confess mine own little wit. I have ever thought so superstitiously of wit that I fear I have committed idolatry against wisdom, and if nature had dealt so beneficially with me to have given me any wit I should have been readier in the defence of it to have made an apology than any way to turn to apostasy. But this I note, that for the most part they stand so on their pantofles* that they be secure of perils, obstinate in their own opinions, impatient of labour, apt to conceive wrong, credulous to believe the worst, ready to shake off their old acquaintance without cause and to condemn them without colour. All which humours are by so much the more easier to be purged by how much the less they have fettered the sinews. But return we again to Euphues.

Euphues, having sojourned by the space of two months in Naples, whether he were moved by the courtesy of a young gentleman named Philautus,* or enforced by destiny, whether his pregnant wit or his pleasant conceits wrought the greater liking in the mind of Euphues, I know not for certain, but Euphues showed such entire love towards him that he seemed to make small accompt of any others, determining to enter into such an inviolable league of friendship with him as neither time by piecemeal should impair, neither fancy utterly dissolve, nor any suspicion infringe. 'I have read,' saith he, 'and well I believe it, that a friend is in prosperity a pleasure, a solace in adversity, in grief a comfort, in joy a merry companion, at all times another I, in all places the express image of mine own person, insomuch that I cannot tell whether the immortal Gods have bestowed any gift upon mortal men either more noble or more necessary than friendship.

'Is there anything in the world to be reputed, I will not say compared, to friendship? Can any treasure in this transitory pilgrimage be of more value than a friend, in whose bosom thou mayest sleep secure without fear, whom thou mayest make partner of all thy secrets without suspicion of fraud, and partaker of all thy misfortune without mistrust of fleeting, who will accompt thy bale his bane, thy mishap his misery, the pricking of thy finger the piercing of his heart? But whither am I carried? Have I not also learned that one should eat a bushel of salt* with him whom he meaneth to make his friend? That trial maketh trust, that there is falsehood in fellowship? And what then? Doth not the sympathy of manners make the conjunction of minds? Is it not a byword like will to like? Not so common as commendable it is to see young gentlemen choose them such friends with whom they may seem, being absent, to be present; being asunder, to be conversant; being dead, to be alive. I will therefore have Philautus for my fere, and by so much the more I make myself sure to have Philautus, by how much the more I view in him the lively image of Euphues.'

Although there be none so ignorant that doth not know, neither any so impudent that will not confess friendship to be the jewel of human joy, yet whosoever shall see this amity grounded upon a little affection will soon conjecture that it shall be dissolved upon a light occasion; as in the sequel of Euphues and Philautus you shall see, whose hot love waxed soon cold. For, as the best wine doth make the sharpest vinegar, so the deepest love turneth to the deadliest hate. Who deserved the most blame, in mine opinion it is doubtful and so difficult that I dare not presume to give verdict. For love being the cause for which so many mischiefs have been attempted, I am not yet persuaded whether* of them was most to be blamed, but certainly neither of them was blameless. I appeal to your judgement, gentlemen, not that I think any of you of the like disposition able to decide the question, but being of deeper discretion than I am are more fit to debate the quarrel. Though the discourse of their friendship and falling out be somewhat long, yet being somewhat strange, I hope the delightfulness of the one will attenuate the tediousness of the other.

Euphues had continual access to the place of Philautus, and

no little familiarity with him, and finding him at convenient leisure, in these short terms unfolded his mind unto him. 'Gentleman and friend, the trial I have had of thy manners cutteth off diverse terms which to another I would have used in the like matter. And sithens a long discourse argueth folly, and delicate words incur the suspicion of flattery, I am determined to use neither of them, knowing either of them to breed offence. Weighing with myself the force of friendship by the effects, I studied ever since my first coming to Naples to enter league with such a one as might direct my steps, being a stranger, and resemble my manners, being a scholar, the which two qualities as I find in you able to satisfy my desire, so I hope I shall find a heart in you willing to accomplish my request. Which, if I may obtain, assure yourself that Damon to his Pythias, Pilades to his Orestes, Titus to his Gysippus, Theseus to his Pirithous, Scipio to his Laelius, was never found more faithful than Euphues will be to Philautus.'

Philautus, by how much the less he looked for this discourse, by so much the more he liked it, for he saw all qualities both of body and mind in Euphues, unto whom he replied as followeth. 'Friend Euphues (for so your talk warranteth me to term you), I dare neither use a long process, neither a loving speech, lest unwittingly I should cause you to convince me of those things which you have already condemned. And verily I am bold to presume upon your courtesy, since you yourself have used so little curiosity, persuading myself that my short answer will work as great an effect in you as your few words did in me. And seeing we resemble, as you say, each other in qualities, it cannot be that the one should differ from the other in courtesy; seeing the sincere affection of the mind cannot be expressed by the mouth, and that no art can unfold the entire love of the heart, I am earnestly to beseech you not to measure the firmness of my faith by the fewness of my words, but rather think that the overflowing waves of good will leave no passage for many words. Trial shall prove trust—here is my hand, my heart, my lands and my life at thy commandment. Thou mayest well perceive that I did believe thee, that* so soon I did love thee, and I hope thou wilt the rather love me in that I did believe thee.'

Either Euphues and Philautus stood in need of friendship or were ordained to be friends. Upon so short warning to make so soon a conclusion might seem in mine opinion, if it continued, miraculous, if shaken off, ridiculous. But after many embracings and protestations one to another they walked to dinner, where they wanted neither meat, neither music, neither any other pastime; and having banqueted, to digest their sweet confections, they danced all that afternoon. They used not only one board but one bed, one book (if so be it they thought not one too many). Their friendship augmented every day, insomuch that the one could not refrain the company of the other one minute; all things went in common between them, which all men accompted commendable.

Philautus being a town-born child, both for his own countenance and the great countenance which his father had while he lived, crept into credit with Don Ferardo, one of the chief governors of the city who, although he had a courtly crew of gentlewomen sojourning in his palace, yet his daughter, heir to his whole revenues, stained the beauty of them all, whose modest bashfulness caused the other* to look wan for envy, whose lily cheeks dyed with a vermilion red made the rest blush for shame. For as the finest ruby staineth the colour of the rest that be in place, or as the sun dimmeth the moon that she cannot be discerned, so this gallant girl more fair than fortunate and yet more fortunate than faithful, eclipsed the beauty of them all and changed their colours. Unto her had Philautus access, who won her by right of love, and should have worn her by right of law had not Euphues by strange destiny broken the bonds of marriage and forbidden the bans of matrimony.

It happened that Don Ferardo had occasion to go to Venice about certain his own affairs, leaving his daughter the only steward of his household, who spared not to feast Philautus her friend with all kinds of delights and delicates, reserving only her honesty as the chief stay of her honour. Her father being gone she sent for her friend to supper, who came not as he was accustomed, solitarily alone, but accompanied with his friend Euphues. The gentlewoman, whether it were for niceness or for niggardness of courtesy, gave him such a cold welcome that he repented that he was come.

Euphues, though he knew himself worthy every way to have a good countenance, yet could he not perceive her willing any way to lend him a friendly look. Yet lest he should seem to want gestures, or to be dashed out of conceit with her coy countenance, he addressed him to a gentlewoman called Livia, unto whom he uttered this speech. 'Fair lady, if it be the guise of Italy to welcome strangers with strangeness I must needs say the custom is strange and the country barbarous, if the manner of ladies to salute gentlemen with coyness then I am enforced to think the women without courtesy to use such welcome and the men past shame that will come. But hereafter I will either bring a stool on mine arm for an unbidden guest or a vizard on my face for a shameless gossip.'

Livia replied 'Sir, our country is civil, and our gentlewomen are courteous, but in Naples it is compted a jest at every word to say "In faith you are welcome." ' As she was yet talking supper was set on the board. Then Philautus spake thus unto Lucilla: 'Yet gentlewoman, I was the bolder to bring my shadow with me', meaning Euphues, 'knowing that he should be the better welcome for my sake.' Unto whom the gentlewoman replied 'Sir, as I never when I saw you thought that you came without your shadow, so now I cannot a little marvel to see you so overshot in bringing a new shadow with you.'

Euphues, though he perceived her coy nip, seemed not to care for it, but taking her by the hand said 'Fair lady, seeing the shade doth often shield your beauty from the parching sun, I hope you will the better esteem of the shadow, and by so much the less it ought to be offensive by how much the less it is able to offend you, and by so much the more you ought to like it by how much the more you use to lie in it.'

'Well gentleman,' answered Lucilla, 'in arguing of the shadow we forego the substance. Pleaseth it you therefore to sit down to supper.' And so they all sat down, but Euphues fed of one dish, which ever stood before him: the beauty of Lucilla.

Here Euphues at the first sight was so kindled with desire that almost he was like to burn to coals. Supper being ended, the order was in Naples that the gentlewomen would desire to hear some discourse, either concerning love or learning. And although Philautus was requested, yet he posted it over to Euphues, whom he knew most fit for that purpose. Euphues being thus tied to the stake by their importunate entreaty began as followeth.

'He that worst may is always enforced to hold the candle, the weakest must still to the wall, where none will the Devil himself must bear the cross. But were it not, gentlewomen, that your lust* stands for law, I would borrow so much leave as to resign mine office to one of you, whose experience in love hath made you learned, and whose learning hath made you so lovely. For me to entreat of the one, being a novice, or to discourse of the other, being a truant, I may well make you weary but never the wiser, and give you occasion rather to laugh at my rashness than to like my reasons. Yet I care the less to excuse my boldness to you, who were the cause of my blindness. And since I am at mine own choice either to talk of love or of learning, I had rather for this time be deemed an unthrift in rejecting profit than a Stoic in renouncing pleasure.

'It hath been a question often disputed, but never determined, whether the qualities of the mind or the composition of the man cause women most to like, or whether beauty or wit move men most to love. Certes by how much the more the mind is to be preferred before the body, by so much the more the graces of the one are to be preferred before the gifts of the other; which if it be so, that the contemplation of the inward quality ought to be respected more than the view of the outward beauty, then doubtless women either do or should love those best whose virtue is best, not measuring the deformed man with the reformed mind.

'The foul toad hath a fair stone in his head, the fine gold is found in the filthy earth, the sweet kernel lieth in the hard shell, virtue is harboured in the heart of him that most men esteem misshapen. Contrarywise, if we respect more the outward shape than the inward habit, good God, into how many mischiefs do we fall! Into what blindness are we led! Do we not commonly see that in painted pots is hidden the deadliest poison, that in the greenest grass is the greatest serpent, in the clearest water the ugliest toad? Doth not experience teach us that in the most curious sepulchre are enclosed rotten bones, that the cypress tree beareth a fair leaf but no fruit, that the estridge carrieth fair feathers but rank flesh? How frantic are those lovers which are carried away with the gay glistering of the fine face, the beauty whereof is parched with the summer's blaze and chipped with the winter's blast; which is of so short continuance that it fadeth before one perceive it flourish; of so small profit that it poisoneth those that possess it; of so little value with the wise that they accompt it a delicate bait with a deadly hook, a sweet panther with a devouring paunch, a sour poison in a silver pot.

'Here I could enter into discourse of such fine dames as, being in love with their own looks, make such coarse accompt of their passionate lovers, for commonly if they be adorned with beauty they be straight-laced and made so high in the instep that they disdain them most that most desire them. It is a world to see the doting of their lovers and their dealing with them, the revealing of whose subtle trains would cause me to shed tears and you gentlewomen to shut your modest ears. Pardon me, gentlewomen, if I unfold every wile and show every wrinkle of women's disposition. Two things do they cause their servants to vow unto them: secrecy and sovereignty; the one to conceal their enticing sleights, by the other to assure themselves of their only service. Again—but ho there! If I should have waded any further and sounded the depth of their deceit I should either have procured your displeasure or incurred the suspicion of fraud; either armed you to practise the like subtlety or accused myself of perjury. But I mean not to offend your chaste minds with the rehearsal of their unchaste manners, whose ears I perceive to glow and hearts to be grieved at that which I have already uttered. Not that amongst you there be any such, but that in your sex there should be any such.

'Let not gentlewomen therefore make too much of their painted sheath; let them not be so curious in their own conceit or so currish to their loyal lovers. When the black crow's foot shall appear in their eye, or the black ox tread on their foot,* when their beauty shall be like the blasted rose, their wealth wasted, their bodies worn, their faces wrinkled, their fingers crooked, who will like of them in their age who loved none in their youth? If you will be cherished when you be old, be courteous while you be young; if you look for comfort in your hoary hairs, be not coy when you have your golden locks; if you would be embraced in the waning of your bravery, be not squeamish in the waxing of your beauty; if you desire to be kept like the roses when they have lost their colour, smell sweet as the rose doth in the bud; if you would be tasted for old wine, be in the mouth a pleasant grape. So shall you be cherished for your courtesy, comforted for your honesty, embraced for your amity, so shall you be preserved with the sweet rose and drunk with the pleasant wine.

'Thus far I am bold, gentlewomen, to counsel those that be coy, that they weave not the web of their own woe, nor spin the thread of their own thralldom by their own overthwartness. And seeing we are even in the bowels of love, it shall not be amiss to examine whether man or woman be soonest allured, whether be most constant the male or the female. And in this point I mean not to be mine own carver, lest I should seem either to pick a thank with men or a quarrel with women. If therefore it might stand with your pleasure, Mistress Lucilla, to give your censure, I would take the contrary, for sure I am, though your judgement be sound, yet affection will shadow it.'

Lucilla, seeing his pretence, thought to take advantage of his large proffer, unto whom she said 'Gentleman, in mine opinion women are to be won with every wind, in whose sex there is neither force to withstand the assaults of love neither constancy to remain faithful. And because your discourse hath hitherto bred delight, I am loath to hinder you in the sequel of your devices.'

Euphues, perceiving himself to be taken napping, answered as followeth. 'Mistress Lucilla, if you speak as you think these gentlewomen present have little cause to thank you; if you cause me to commend women my tale will be accompted a mere trifle and your words the plain truth. Yet knowing promise to be debt I will pay it with performance. And I would the gentlemen here present were as ready to credit my proof as the gentlewomen are willing to hear their own praises, or I as able to overcome as Mistress Lucilla would be content to be overthrown. Howsoever the matter shall fall out, I am of the surer side, for if my reasons be weak then is our sex strong; if forcible then your judgement feeble; if I find truth on my side I hope I shall for my wages win the good will of women; if I want proof then gentlewomen of necessity you must yield to men. But to the matter.

'Touching the yielding to love, albeit their hearts seem tender, yet they harden them like the stone of Sicilia, the which the more it is beaten the harder it is; for being framed as it were of the perfection of men they be free from all such cogitations as may any way provoke them to uncleanness, insomuch as they abhor the light love of youth, which is grounded upon lust, and dissolved upon every light occasion. When they see the folly of men turn to fury, their delight to doting, their affection to frenzy; when they see them as it were pine in pleasure and to wax pale through their own peevishness; their suits, their service, their letters, their labours, their loves, their lives, seem to them so odious that they harden their hearts against such concupiscence, to the end they might convert them from rashness to reason, from such lewd disposition to honest discretion. Hereof it cometh that men accuse women of cruelty because they themselves want civility. They accompt them full of wiles in not yielding to their wickedness, faithless for resisting their filthiness.

'But I had almost forgot myself! You shall pardon me, Mistress Lucilla, for this time if this abruptly I finish my discourse. It is neither for want of good will or lack of proof, but that I feel in myself such alteration that I can scarcely utter one word. Ah, Euphues, Euphues . . .' The gentlewomen were struck into such a quandary with this sudden change that they all changed colour. But Euphues, taking Philautus by the hand, and giving the gentlewomen thanks for their patience and his repast, bade them all farewell and went immediately to his chamber. But Lucilla, who now began to fry in the flames of love, all the company being departed to their lodgings, entered into these terms and contrarieties.

'Ah, wretched wench Lucilla, how art thou perplexed? What a doubtful fight dost thou feel betwixt faith and fancy, hope and fear, conscience and concupiscence? O my Euphues, little dost thou know the sudden sorrow that I sustain for thy sweet sake, whose wit hath bewitched me, whose rare qualities have deprived me of mine old quality, whose* courteous behaviour without curiosity, whose comely feature without fault, whose filed speech without fraud, hath wrapped me in this misfortune. And canst thou, Lucilla, be so light of love in forsaking Philautus to fly to Euphues? Canst thou prefer a stranger before thy countryman; a starter before thy companion? Why, Euphues doth perhaps desire my love, but Philautus hath deserved it. Why, Euphues' feature is worthy as good as I, but Philautus his faith is worthy a better. Aye, but the latter love is most fervent; aye, but the first ought to be most faithful. Aye, but Euphues hath greater perfection; aye, but Philautus hath deeper affection.

'Ah, fond wench, dost thou think Euphues will deem thee constant to him when thou hast been unconstant to his friend? Weenest thou that he will have no mistrust of thy faithfulness when he hath had trial of thy fickleness? Will he have no doubt of thine honour when thou thyself callest thine honesty in question? Yes, yes, Lucilla, well doth he know that the glass once crazed will with the least clap be cracked, that the cloth which staineth with milk will soon lose his colour with vinegar, that the eagle's wing will waste the feather as well of the Phoenix as of the pheasant, that she that hath been faithless to one will never be faithful to any.

'But can Euphues convince me of fleeting, seeing for his sake I break my fidelity? Can he condemn me of disloyalty when he is the only cause of my disliking? May he justly condemn me of treachery who hath this testimony as trial of my good will? Doth not he remember that the broken bone once set together is stronger than ever it was; that the greatest blot is taken off with the pumice; that though the spider poison the fly she cannot infect the bee; that although I have been light to Philautus I may be lovely to Euphues? It is not my desire but his deserts that moveth my mind to this choice, neither the want of the like good will in Philautus but the lack of the like good qualities that removeth my fancy from the one to the other.

'For as the bee that gathereth honey out of the weed when she espieth the fair flower flieth to the sweetest; or as the kind spaniel though he hunt after birds yet forsakes them to retrieve the partridge; or as we commonly feed on beef hungerly at the first, yet seeing the quail more dainty change our diet; so I, although I loved Philautus for his good properties, yet seeing Euphues to excel him I ought by nature to like him better. By so much the more therefore my change is to be excused, by how much the more my choice is excellent; and by so much the less I am to be condemned by how much the more Euphues is to be commended. Is not the diamond of more value than the ruby because he is of more virtue? Is not the emerald preferred before the sapphire for his wonderful property? Is not Euphues more praiseworthy than Philautus, being more witty?

'But fie Lucilla, why dost thou flatter thyself in thine own folly? Canst thou fain Euphues thy friend whom by thine own words thou hast made thy foe? Didst not thou accuse women of inconstancy? Didst not thou accompt them easy to be won? Didst not thou condemn them of weakness? What sounder argument can he have against thee than thine own answer? What better proof than thine own speech; what greater trial than thine own talk? If thou hast belied women he will judge thee unkind; if thou have revealed the truth he must needs think thee unconstant; if he perceive thee to be won with a nut he will imagine that thou wilt be lost with an apple;* if he find thee wanton before thou be wooed he will guess thou wilt be wavering when thou art wedded.

'But suppose that Euphues love thee, that Philautus leave thee, will thy father, thinkest thou, give thee liberty to live after thine own lust? Will he esteem him worthy to inherit his possessions whom he accompteth unworthy to enjoy thy person? Is it like that he will match thee in marriage with a stranger, with a Grecian, with a mean man? Aye, but what knoweth my father whether he be wealthy, whether his revenues be able to countervail my father's lands, whether his birth be noble, yea or no? Can anyone make doubt of his

gentle blood that seeth his gentle conditions? Can his honour
be called into question whose honesty is so great? Is he to be
thought thriftless who in all qualities of the mind is peerless?
No, no, the tree is known by his fruit, the gold by his touch,
the son by the sire. And as the soft wax receiveth whatsoever
print be in the seal and showeth no other impression, so the
tender babe, being sealed with his father's gifts, representeth
his image most lively.

'But were I once certain of Euphues' good will I would not
so superstitiously accompt of my father's ill will. Time hath
weaned me from my mother's teat and age rid me from my
father's correction. When children are in their swath-clouts
then are they subject to the whip, and ought to be careful of
the rigour of their parents. As for me, seeing I am not fed with
their pap, I am not to be led by their persuasions. Let my
father use what speeches he list, I will follow mine own lust.
Lust! Lucilla, what sayest thou? No, no, mine own *love*, I
should have said, for I am as far from lust as I am from reason,
and as near to love as I am to folly. Then stick to thy
determination and show thyself what love can do, what love
dares do, what love hath done. Albeit I can no way quench the
coals of desire with forgetfulness, yet will I rake them up in
the ashes of modesty. Seeing I dare not discover my love for
maidenly shamefastness, I will dissemble it till time I have
opportunity. And I hope so to behave myself as Euphues shall
think me his own and Philautus persuade himself I am none
but his. But I would to God Euphues would repair hither that
the sight of him might mitigate some part of my martyrdom.'

She, having thus discoursed with herself her own miseries,
cast herself on the bed. And there let her lie, and return we
to Euphues, who was so caught in the gin of folly that he
neither could comfort himself nor durst ask counsel of his
friend, suspecting that which indeed was true, that Philautus
was corrival with him and cookmate with Lucilla. Amidst,
therefore, these his extremities, between hope and fear, he
uttered these or the like speeches.

'What is he, Euphues, that knowing thy wit, and seeing thy
folly, but will rather punish thy lewdness than pity thy
heaviness? Was there ever any so fickle so soon to be allured?

Any ever so faithless to deceive his friend; ever any so foolish to bathe himself in his own misfortune? Too true it is that, as the sea-crab swimmeth always against the stream, so wit always striveth against wisdom; and as the bee is oftentimes hurt with her own honey, so is wit not seldom plagued with his own conceit.

'O ye Gods, have ye ordained for every malady a medicine, for every sore a salve, for every pain a plaster, leaving only love remediless? Did ye deem no man so mad to be entangled with desire, or thought ye them worthy to be tormented that were so misled? Have ye dealt more favourably with brute beasts than with reasonable creatures?

'The filthy sow, when she is sick, eateth the sea-crab and is immediately recured; the tortoise having tasted the viper sucketh *origanum* and is quickly revived; the bear ready to pine licketh up the ants and is recovered; the dog, having surfeited, to procure his vomit eateth grass and findeth remedy; the hart being pierced with the dart runneth out of hand to the herb *dictanum** and is healed. And can men by no herb, by no art, by no way, procure a remedy for the impatient disease of love? Ah well I perceive that love is not unlike the fig tree whose fruit is sweet, whose root is more bitter than the claw of a bitter; or like the apple in Persia whose blossom savoureth like honey, whose bud is more sour than gall.

'But O impiety! O broad blasphemy against the heavens! Wilt thou be so impudent, Euphues, to accuse the Gods of iniquity? No, fond fool, no! Neither is it forbidden us by the Gods to love, by whose divine providence we are permitted to live; neither do we want remedies to recure our maladies, but reason to use the means. But why go I about to hinder the course of love with the discourse of law? Hast thou not read, Euphues, that he that loppeth the vine causeth it to spread fairer; that he that stoppeth the stream forceth it to swell higher; that he that casteth water on the fire in the smith's forge maketh it to flame fiercer? Even so he that seeketh by counsel to moderate his overlashing affections increaseth his own misfortune.

'Ah my Lucilla, would thou were either less fair or I more fortunate; either I wiser or thou milder; either I would I were out of this mad mood either I would we were both of one mind. But how should she be persuaded of my loyalty that yet had never one simple proof of my love? Will she not rather imagine me to be entangled with her beauty than with her virtue; that my fancy being so lewdly changed at the first will be as lightly changed at the last; that nothing violent can be permanent? Yes, yes she must needs conjecture so, although it be nothing so, for by how much the more my affection cometh on the sudden by so much the less will she think it certain. The rattling thunderbolt hath but his clap, the lightning but his flash, and as they both come in a moment, so do they both end in a minute.

'Aye, but Euphues, hath she not heard also that the dry touchwood is kindled with lime; that the greatest mushromp groweth in one night; that the fire quickly burneth the flax; that love easily entereth into the sharp wit without resistance and is harboured there without repentance. If therefore the Gods have endowed her with as much bounty as beauty, if she have no less wit than she hath comeliness, certes she will neither conceive sinisterly of my sudden suit neither be coy to receive me into her service, neither suspect me of lightness in yielding so lightly neither reject me disdainfully for loving so hastily. Shall I not then hazard my life to obtain my love, and deceive Philautus to receive Lucilla? Yes Euphues, where love beareth sway friendship can have no show. As Philautus brought me for his shadow the last supper, so will I use him for my shadow* till I have gained his saint. And canst thou, wretch, be false to him that is faithful to thee? Shall his courtesy be cause of thy cruelty? Wilt thou violate the league of faith to inherit the land of folly? Shall affection be of more force than friendship, love than law, lust than loyalty? Knowest thou not that he that loseth his honesty hath nothing else to lose?

'Tush, the case is light where reason taketh place; to love and to live well is not granted to Jupiter. Whoso is blinded with the caul of beauty discerneth no colour of honesty. Did not Gyges cut Candaules* a coat by his own measure? Did not Paris, though he were a welcome guest to Menelaus, serve his host a slippery prank? If Philautus had loved Lucilla he would never have suffered Euphues to have seen her. Is it not the prey that enticeth the thief to rifle? Is it not the pleasant bait that causeth the fleetest fish to bite? Is it not a byword amongst us that gold maketh an honest man an ill man? Did Philautus accompt Euphues too simple to decipher beauty, or superstitious not to desire it? Did he deem him a saint in rejecting fancy, or a sot in not discerning; thought he him a Stoic that he would not be moved or a stock that he could not?

'Well, well, seeing the wound that bleedeth inwardly is most dangerous, that the fire kept close burneth most furious, that the oven dammed up baketh soonest, that sores having no vent fester secretly, it is high time to unfold my secret love to my secret friend. Let Philautus behave himself never so craftily, he shall know that it must be a wily mouse that shall breed in the cat's ear, and because I resemble him in wit I mean a little to dissemble with him in wiles. But O my Lucilla, if thy heart be made of that stone which may be mollified only with blood, would I had sipped of that river in Caria which turneth those that drink of it to stones. If thine ears be anointed with the oil of Syria that bereaveth hearing, would mine eyes had been rubbed with the syrup of the cedar tree which taketh away sight.

'If Lucilla be so proud to disdain poor Euphues, would Euphues were so happy to deny Lucilla, or if Lucilla be so mortified to live without love, would Euphues were so fortunate to live in hate. Aye but my cold welcome foretelleth my cold suit. Aye but her privy glances signify some good fortune. Fie, fond fool Euphues, why goest thou about to allege those things to cut off thy hope which she perhaps would never have found, or to comfort myself with those reasons which she never meaneth to propose. Tush, it were no love if it were certain, and a small conquest it is to overthrow those that never resisteth.

'In battles there ought to be a doubtful fight and a desperate end; in pleading a difficult entrance and a diffused determination; in love a life without hope and a death without fear. Fire cometh out of the hardest flint with the steel; oil out of the driest jet by the fire; love out of the stoniest heart by faith, by trust, by time. Had Tarquinius used his love with colours of continuance, Lucretia* would either with some pity have answered his desire or with some persuasion have stayed her death. It was the heat of his lust that made her haste to end her life, wherefore love in neither respect is to be condemned, but he of rashness to attempt a lady furiously and she of rigour to punish his folly in her own flesh, a fact (in mine opinion) more worthy the name of cruelty than chastity, and fitter for a monster in the deserts than a matron of Rome. Penelope, no less constant than she yet more wise, would be weary to unweave that in the night she spun in the day if Ulysses had not come home the sooner. There is no woman, Euphues, but she will yield in time, be not therefore dismayed either with high looks or froward words.'

Euphues having thus talked with himself, Philautus entered the chamber and, finding him so worn and wasted with continual mourning, neither joying in his meat nor rejoicing in his friend, with watery eyes uttered this speech. 'Friend and fellow, as I am not ignorant of thy present weakness, so I am not privy of the cause, and although I suspect many things yet can I assure myself of no one thing. Therefore, my good Euphues, for these doubts and dumps of mine, either remove the cause or reveal it. Thou hast hitherto found me a cheerful companion in thy mirth, and now shalt thou find me as careful with thee in thy moan. If altogether thou mayest not be cured, yet mayest thou be comforted. If there be anything that either by my friends may be procured or by my life attained that may either heal thee in part or help thee in all, I protest to thee by the name of a friend that it shall rather be gotten with the loss of my body than lost by getting a kingdom.

'Thou hast tried me, therefore trust me; thou hast trusted me in many things, therefore try me in this one thing. I never yet failed, and now I will not faint. Be bold to speak and blush not; thy sore is not so angry but I can salve it, the wound not so deep but I can search it; thy grief not so great but I can ease it. If it be ripe it shall be lanced, if it be broken it shall be tainted; be it never so desperate it shall be cured. Rise therefore, Euphues, and take heart at grass;* younger thou shalt never be. Pluck up thy stomach, if love itself have stung thee it shall not stifle thee. Though thou be enamoured of some lady thou shalt not be enchanted. They that begin to pine of a consumption without delay preserve themselves with cullises; he that feeleth his stomach enflamed with heat cooleth it eftsoons with conserves. Delays breed dangers, nothing so perilous as procrastination.'

Euphues, hearing this comfort and friendly counsel, dissembled his sorrowing heart with a smiling face, answering him forthwith as followeth. 'True it is, Philautus, that he which toucheth the nettle tenderly is soonest stung, that the fly which playeth with the fire is singed in the flame, that he that dallieth with women is drawn to his woe. And as the adamant draweth the heavy iron, the harp the fleet dolphin, so beauty allureth the chaste mind to love and the wisest wit to lust. The example whereof I would it were no less profitable than the experience to me is like to be perilous.

'The vine watered with wine is soon withered, the blossom in the fattest ground is quickly blasted, the goat the fatter she is the less fertile she is; yea, man the more witty he is the less happy he is. So it is Philautus (for why should I conceal it from thee of whom I am to take counsel) that since my last and first being with thee at the house of Ferardo, I have felt such a furious battle in mine own body as if it be not speedily repressed by policy it will carry my mind (the grand captain in this fight) into endless captivity. Ah Livia, Livia, thy courtly grace without coyness, thy blazing beauty without blemish, thy courteous demeanour without curiosity, thy sweet speech savoured with wit, thy comely mirth tempered with modesty, thy chaste looks yet lovely, thy sharp taunts yet pleasant, have given me such a check that sure I am at the next view of thy virtues I shall take thee mate.* And taking it not of a pawn but of a prince, the loss is to be accompted the less. And though they be commonly in a great choler that receive the mate, yet would I willingly take every minute ten mates to enjoy Livia for my loving mate.

'Doubtless if ever she herself have been scorched with the flames of desire she will be ready to quench the coals with courtesy in another; if ever she have been attached of love she will rescue him that is drenched in desire; if ever she have been taken with the fever of fancy she will help his ague who by a quotidian fit is converted into frenzy. Neither can there be under so delicate a hue lodged deceit, neither in so beautiful a mould a malicious mind. True it is that the disposition of the mind followeth the composition of the body; how then can she be in mind any way imperfect who in body is perfect every way? I know my success will be good, but I know not how to have access to my goddess. Neither do I want courage to discover my love to my friend, but some colour to cloak my coming to the house of Ferardo; for if they be in Naples as jealous as they be in the other parts of Italy, then it behoveth me to walk circumspectly and to forge some cause for mine often coming.

'If therefore, Philautus, thou canst set but this feather to mine arrow, thou shalt see me shoot so near that thou wilt accompt me for a cunning archer. And verily if I had not loved thee well I would have swallowed mine own sorrow in silence, knowing that in love nothing is so dangerous as to participate the means thereof to another, and that two may keep counsel if one be away. I am therefore enforced perforce to challenge that courtesy at thy hand which erst thou didst promise with thy heart, the performance whereof shall bind me to Philautus and prove thee faithful to Euphues. Now if thy cunning be answerable to thy good will, practise some pleasant conceit upon thy poor patient: one dram of Ovid's art, some of Tibullus' drugs, one of Propertius' pills,* which may cause me either to purge my new disease or recover my hoped desire. But I fear me where so strange a sickness is to be recured of so unskilful a physician that either thou wilt be too bold to practise or my body too weak to purge. But seeing a desperate disease is to be committed to a desperate doctor, I will follow thy counsel and become thy cure, desiring thee to be as wise in ministering thy physic as I have been willing to put my life into thy hands.'

Philautus, thinking all to be gold that glistered and all to be gospel that Euphues uttered, answered his forged gloze with this friendly close. 'In that thou hast made me privy to thy purpose, I will not conceal my practice; in that thou cravest my aid, assure thyself I will be the finger next thy thumb, insomuch as thou shalt never repent thee of the one or the other, for persuade thyself that thou shalt find Philautus during life ready to comfort thee in thy misfortunes and succour thee in thy necessity. Concerning Livia, though she be fair, yet is she not so amiable as my Lucilla, whose servant I have been the term of three years. But lest comparisons should seem odious, chiefly where both the parties be without comparison, I will omit that, and seeing that we had both rather be talking with them than tattling of them we will immediately go to them.

'And truly Euphues, I am not a little glad that I shall have thee not only a comfort in my life but also a companion in my love. As thou hast been wise in thy choice so I hope thou shalt be fortunate in thy chance. Livia is a wench of more wit than beauty, Lucilla of more beauty than wit; both of more honesty than honour, and yet both of such honour as in all Naples there is not one in birth to be compared with any of them both. How much therefore have we to rejoice in our choice. Touching our access be thou secure. I will flap Ferardo in the mouth with some conceit, and fill his old head so full of new fables that thou shalt rather be earnestly entreated to repair to his house than evil entreated to leave it. As old men are very suspicious to mistrust everything, so are they very credulous to believe anything: the blind man doth eat many a fly.'

'Yea but', said Euphues, 'take heed my Philautus that thou thyself swallow not a gudgeon'—which word Philautus did not mark until he had almost digested it. 'But', said Philautus, 'let us go devoutly to the shrine of our saints, there to offer our devotion, for my books teach me that such a wound must be healed where it was first hurt, and for this disease we will use a common remedy but yet comfortable. The eye that blinded thee shall make thee see, the scorpion that stung thee shall heal thee, a sharp sore hath a short cure—let us go.' To the which Euphues consented willingly, smiling to himself to see how he had brought Philautus into a fool's paradise.

Here you may see, gentlemen, the falsehood in fellowship, the fraud in friendship, the painted sheath with the leaden dagger, the fair words that make fools fain. But I will not trouble you with superfluous addition, unto whom I fear me

I have been tedious with the bare discourse of this rude history.

Philautus and Euphues repaired to the house of Ferardo, where they found Mistress Lucilla and Livia accompanied with other gentlewomen neither being idle nor well-employed, but playing at cards. But when Lucilla beheld Euphues she could scarcely contain herself from embracing him, had not womanly shamefastness and Philautus his presence stayed her wisdom. Euphues, on the other side, was fallen into such a trance that he had not the power either to succour himself or salute the gentlewomen. At the last Lucilla began as one that best might be bold on this manner.

'Gentlemen, although your long absence gave me occasion to think that you disliked your late entertainment, yet your coming at the last hath cut off my former suspicion, and by so much the more you are welcome, by how much the more you were wished for. But you gentleman', taking Euphues by the hand, 'were the rather wished for, for that your discourse being left unperfect caused us all to long (as women are wont for things that like them) to have an end thereof.' Unto whom Philautus replied as followeth.

'Mistress Lucilla, though your courtesy made us nothing to doubt of our welcome yet modesty caused us to pinch courtesy* who should first come. As for my friend, I think he was never wished for here so earnestly of any as of himself, whether it might be to renew his talk or to recant his sayings I cannot tell.' Euphues, taking the tale out of Philautus' mouth, answered 'Mistress Lucilla, to recant verities were heresy, and renew the praises of women flattery. The only cause I wished myself here was to give thanks for so good entertainment the which I could no ways deserve, and to breed a greater acquaintance if it might be to make amends.'

Lucilla, inflamed with his presence, said 'Nay Euphues, you shall not escape so, for if my courtesy, as you say, were the cause of your coming, let it also be the occasion of the ending your former discourse, otherwise I shall think your proof naked, and you shall find my reward nothing.' Euphues now as willing to obey as she to command addressed himself to a farther conclusion, who seeing all the gentlewomen ready to give him the hearing, proceeded as followeth.

'I have not yet forgotten that my last talk with these gentlewomen tended to their praises, and therefore the end must tie up the just proof, otherwise I should set down Venus' shadow without the lively substance. As there is no one thing which can be reckoned either concerning love or loyalty wherein women do not excel men, yet in fervency above all others they so far exceed that men are liker to marvel at them than to imitate them, and readier to laugh at their virtues than emulate them. For as they be hard to be won without trial of great faith, so are they hard to be lost without great cause of fickleness. It is long before the cold water seethe, yet being once hot it is long before it be cooled; it is long before salt come to his saltness but being once seasoned it never loseth his savour.

'I for mine own part am brought into a paradise by the only imagination of women's virtues, and were I persuaded that all the devils in hell were women I would never live devoutly to inherit heaven, or that they were all saints in heaven, I would live more strictly for fear of hell. What could Adam have done in his paradise before his fall without a woman, or how would he have rise* again after his fall without* a woman? Artificers are wont in their last works to excel themselves; yea, God, when he had made all things, at the last made man as most perfect, thinking nothing could be framed more excellent, yet after him he created a woman, the express image of eternity, the lively picture of nature, the only steel glass for man to behold his infirmities by comparing them with women's perfections. Are they not more gentle, more witty, more beautiful than men? Are not men so bewitched with their qualities that they become mad for love and women so wise that they detest lust?

'I am entered into so large a field that I shall sooner want time than proof, and so cloy you with variety of praises that I fear me I am like to infect women with pride, which yet they have not, and men with spite, which yet I would not. For as the horse if he knew his own strength were no ways to be bridled, or the unicorn his own virtue were never to be caught, so women, if they knew what excellency were in them, I fear me men should never win them to their wills or wean them from their mind.'

Lucilla began to smile, saying 'In faith Euphues, I would have you stay there, for as the sun when he is at the highest beginneth to go down, so when the praises of women are at the best, if you leave not they will begin to fail.' But Euphues, being rapt with the sight of his saint, answered 'No, no Lucilla,' but whilst he was yet speaking, Ferardo entered, whom they all dutifully welcomed home. Who, rounding Philautus in the ear, desired him to accompany him immediately without farther pausing, protesting it should be as well for his preferment as for his own profit. Philautus consenting, Ferardo said unto his daughter 'Lucilla, the urgent affairs I have in hand will scarce suffer me to tarry with you one hour, yet my return, I hope, will be so short that my absence shall not breed thy sorrow. In the mean season I commit all things into thy custody, wishing thee to use thy accustomable courtesy. And seeing I must take Philautus with me, I will be so bold to crave you, gentleman (his friend) to supply his room, desiring you to take this hasty warning for a hearty welcome, and so to spend this time of mine absence in honest mirth. And thus I leave you.'

Philautus knew well the cause of this sudden departure, which was to redeem certain lands that were mortgaged in his father's time to the use of Ferardo, who on that condition had before time promised him his daughter in marriage. But return we to Euphues.

Euphues was surprised with such incredible joy at this strange event that he had almost sounded, for seeing his corrival to be departed and Ferardo to give him so friendly entertainment, doubted not in time to get the good will of Lucilla. Whom finding in place convenient without company, with a bold courage and comely gesture he began to assay her in this sort.

'Gentlewoman, my acquaintance being so little I am afraid my credit will be less, for that they commonly are soonest believed that are best beloved, and they liked best whom we have known longest. Nevertheless, the noble mind suspecteth no guile without cause, neither condemneth any wight without proof. Having therefore notice of your heroical heart I am the better persuaded of my good hap. So it is, Lucilla, that coming to Naples but to fetch fire, as the byword is, not to make my place of abode, I have found such flames that I can neither quench them with the water of free will neither cool them with wisdom. For as the hop, the pole being never so high, groweth to the end, or as the dry beech, kindled at the root, never leaveth until it come to the top, or as one drop of poison disperseth itself into every vein, so affection having caught hold of my heart, and the sparkles of love kindled my liver, will suddenly though secretly flame up into my head and spread itself into every sinew.

'It is your beauty (pardon my abrupt boldness) lady that hath taken every part of me prisoner, and brought me unto this deep distress, but seeing women when one praiseth them for their deserts deem that he flattereth them to obtain his desire, I am here present to yield myself to such trial as your courtesy in this behalf shall require. Yet will you commonly object this to such as serve you and starve* to win your good will: that hot love is soon cold, that the bavin though it burn bright is but a blaze, that scalding water if it stand awhile turneth almost to ice, that pepper though it be hot in the mouth is cold in the maw, that the faith of men though it fry in their words it freezeth in their works. Which things, Lucilla, albeit they be sufficient to reprove the lightness of someone, yet can they not convince everyone of lewdness; neither ought the constancy of all to be brought in question through the subtlety of a few. For although the worm entereth almost into every wood, yet he eateth not the cedar tree. Though the stone Cylindrus at every thunder clap roll from the hill, yet the pure sleek-stone* mounteth at the noise; though the rust fret the hardest steel, yet doth it not eat into the emerald; though Polypus change his hue, yet the salamander keepeth his colour; though Proteus transform himself into every shape, yet Pygmalion retaineth his old form; though Aeneas were too fickle to Dido, yet Troilus was too faithful to Cressid; though others seem counterfeit in their deeds, yet, Lucilla, persuade yourself that Euphues will be always current in his dealings.

'But as the true gold is tried by the touch, the pure flint by the stroke of the iron, so the loyal heart of the faithful lover is known by the trial of his lady. Of the which trial, Lucilla, if you shall accompt Euphues worthy, assure yourself he will be as ready to offer himself a sacrifice for your sweet sake as yourself shall be willing to employ him in your service. Neither doth he desire to be trusted any way until he shall be tried every way; neither doth he crave credit at the first but a good countenance till time his desire* shall be made manifest by his deserts. Thus not blinded by light affection but dazzled with your rare perfection and boldened by your exceeding courtesy I have unfolded mine entire love, desiring you, having so good leisure, to give so friendly an answer as I may receive comfort and you commendation.'

Lucilla, although she were contented to hear this desired discourse, yet did she seem to be somewhat displeased. And truly I know not whether it be peculiar to that sex to dissemble with those whom they most desire, or whether by craft they have learned outwardly to loath that which inwardly they most love. Yet wisely did she cast this in her head: that if she should yield at the first assault he should think her a light huswife, if she should reject him scornfully a very haggard. Minding therefore that he should neither take hold of her promise, neither unkindness of her preciseness, she fed him indifferently with hope and despair, reason and affection, life and death. Yet in the end, arguing wittily upon certain questions, they fell to such agreement as poor Philautus would not have agreed unto if he had been present, yet always keeping the body undefiled. And thus she replied.

'Gentleman, as you may suspect me of idleness in giving ear to your talk, so may you convince me of lightness in answering such toys. Certes as you have made mine ears glow at the rehearsal of your love, so have you galled my heart with the remembrance of your folly. Though you came to Naples as a stranger, yet were you welcome to my father's house as a friend. And can you then so much transgress the bonds of honour (I will not say of honesty) as to solicit a suit more sharp to me than death? I have hitherto, God be thanked, lived without suspicion of lewdness, and shall I now incur the danger of sensual liberty? What hope can you have to obtain my love, seeing yet I could never afford you a good look? Do you therefore think me easily enticed to the bent of your bow because I was easily entreated to listen to your late discourse? Or seeing me (as finely you gloze) to excel all other in beauty, did you deem that I would exceed all other in beastliness?

'But yet I am not angry, Euphues, but in agony. For who is she that will fret or fume with one that loveth her, if this love to delude me be not dissembled? It is that which causeth me most to fear, not that my beauty is unknown to myself, but that commonly we poor wenches are deluded through light belief, and ye men are naturally inclined craftily to lead your life. When the fox preacheth the geese perish; the crocodile shrowdeth greatest treason under most pitiful tears; in a kissing mouth there lieth a galling mind.

'You have made so large proffer of your service, and so fair promises of fidelity that, were I not over chary of mine honesty, you would inveigle me to shake hands with* chastity. But certes I will either lead a virgin's life on earth (though I lead apes in hell), or else follow thee rather than thy gifts. Yet am I neither so precise to refuse thy proffer neither so peevish to disdain thy good will; so excellent always are the gifts which are made acceptable by the virtue of the giver. I did at the first entrance discern thy love but yet dissemble it. Thy wanton glances, thy scalding sighs, thy loving signs caused me to blush for shame and to look wan for fear lest they should be perceived of any.

'These subtle shifts, these painted practices (if I were to be won) would soon wean me from the teat of Vesta to the toys of Venus. Besides this, thy comely grace, thy rare qualities, thy exquisite perfection, were able to move a mind half mortified to transgress the bonds of maidenly modesty. But God shield, Lucilla, that thou shouldest be so careless of thine honour as to commit the state thereof to a stranger. Learn thou by me, Euphues, to despise things that be amiable, to forgo delightful practices—believe me, it is piety to abstain from pleasure.

'Thou art not the first that hath solicited this suit, but the first that goeth about to seduce me; neither discernest thou more than other, but darest more than any; neither hast thou more art to discover thy meaning, but more heart to open thy mind. But thou preferest me before thy lands, thy livings, thy life; thou offerest thyself a sacrifice for my security; thou profferest me the whole and only sovereignty of thy service. Truly I were very cruel and hard hearted if I should not love thee. Hard hearted albeit I am not, but truly love thee I cannot, whom I doubt to be my lover.

'Moreover I have not been used to the court of Cupid, wherein there be more sleights than there be hares in Athos, than bees in Hybla, than stars in heaven. Besides this, the common people here in Naples are not only both very suspicious of other men's matters and manners, but also very jealous over other men's children and maidens. Either therefore dissemble thy fancy or desist from thy folly.

'But why shouldest thou desist from the one, seeing thou canst cunningly dissemble the other. My father is now gone to Venice, and as I am uncertain of his return, so am I not privy to the cause of his travel. But yet is he so from hence that he seeth me in his absence. Knowest thou not, Euphues, that kings have long arms and rulers large reaches? Neither let this comfort thee, that at his departure he deputed thee in Philautus' place. Although my face cause him to mistrust my loyalty, yet my faith enforceth him to give me this liberty; though he be suspicious of my fair hue, yet is he secure of my firm honesty. But alas, Euphues, what truth can there be found in a traveller? What stay in a stranger, whose words and body both watch but for a wind, whose feet are ever fleeting, whose faith plighted on the shore is turned to perjury when they hoist sail?

'Who more traitorous to Phyllis than Demophon,* yet he a traveller? Who more perjured to Dido than Aeneas, and he a stranger? Both these queens, both they caitiffs. Who more false to Ariadne than Theseus, yet he a sailor? Who more fickle to Medea than Jason, yet he a starter? Both these daughters to great princes, both they unfaithful of their promises. Is it then likely that Euphues will be faithful to Lucilla, being in Naples but a sojourner? I have not yet forgotten the invective (I can no otherwise term it) which thou madest against beauty, saying it was a deceitful bait with a deadly hook and a sweet poison in a painted pot. Canst thou then be so unwise to swallow the bait which will breed thy bane? To swill the drink that will expire thy date? To desire the wight that will work thy death? But it may be that with the scorpion thou canst feed on the earth, or with the quail and roebuck be fat with poison, or with beauty live in all bravery.

'I fear me thou hast the stone continens about thee, which is named of the contrary, that though thou pretend faith in thy words thou devisest fraud in thy heart; that though thou seem to prefer love thou art inflamed with lust. And what for that? Though thou have eaten the seeds of rocket which breed incontinency, yet have I chewed the leaf cress which maintaineth modesty. Though thou bear in thy bosom the herb Araxa most noisome to virginity, yet have I the stone that groweth in the mount Tmolus the upholder of chastity.

'You may, gentleman, accompt me for a cold prophet thus hastily to divine of your disposition. Pardon me, Euphues, if in love I cast beyond the moon, which bringeth us women to endless moan. Although I myself were never burnt whereby I should dread the fire, yet the scorching of others in the flames of fancy warneth me to beware. Though I as yet never tried any faithless whereby I should be fearful, yet have I read of many that have been perjured, which causeth me to be careful. Though I am able to convince none by proof, yet am I enforced to suspect one upon probabilities.

'Alas, we silly souls which have neither wit to decipher the wiles of men nor wisdom to dissemble our affection, neither craft to train in young lovers neither courage to withstand their encounters, neither discretion to discern their doubling neither hard hearts to reject their complaints—we, I say, are soon enticed, being by nature simple, and easily entangled, being apt to receive the impression of love. But, alas, it is both common and lamentable to behold simplicity entrapped by subtlety, and those that have most might to be infected with most malice. The spider weaveth a fine web to hang the fly, the wolf weareth a fair face to devour the lamb, the merlin striketh at the partridge, the eagle often snappeth at the fly, men are always laying baits for women which are the weaker vessels, but as yet I could never hear man by such snares to entrap man. For true it is that men themselves have by use observed that it must be a hard winter when one wolf eateth another.

'I have read that the bull being tied to the fig tree loseth his strength, that the whole herd of deer stand at the gaze if they smell a sweet apple, that the dolphin by the sound of music is brought to the shore. And then no marvel it is that if the fierce bull be tamed with the fig tree, if that women being as weak as sheep be overcome with a fig; if the wild deer be caught with an apple that the tame damsel is won with a blossom; if the fleet dolphin is allured with harmony that women be entangled with the melody of men's speech, fair promises and solemn protestations. But folly it were for me to mark their mischiefs, sith I am neither able neither they willing to amend their manners. It becometh me rather to show what our sex should do than to open what yours doth.

'And seeing I cannot by reason restrain your importunate suit, I will by rigour done on myself cause you to refrain the means. I would to God Ferardo were in this point like to Lysander which would not suffer his daughters to wear gorgeous apparel, saying it would rather make them common than comely. I would it were in Naples a law which was a custom in Egypt, that women should always go barefoot, to the intent they might keep themselves always at home; that they should be ever like to the snail, which hath ever his house on his head. I mean so to mortify myself that instead of silks I will wear sackcloth, for ouches and bracelets, lear and caddis, for the lute use the distaff, for the pen the needle, for lovers' sonnets David's psalms. But yet I am not so senseless altogether to reject your service; which if I were certainly assured to proceed of a simple mind it should not receive so simple a reward. And what greater trial can I have of thy simplicity and truth than thine own request, which desireth a trial?

'Aye, but in the coldest flint there is hot fire, the bee that hath honey in her mouth hath a sting in her tail, the tree that beareth the sweetest fruit hath a sour sap, yea the words of men though they seem smooth as oil yet their hearts are as crooked as the stalk of ivy. I would not, Euphues, that thou shouldest condemn me of rigour in that I seek to assuage thy folly by reason, but take this by the way: that although as yet I am disposed to like of none, yet whensoever I shall love any I will not forget them. In the mean season accompt me thy friend, for thy foe I will never be.'

Euphues was brought into a great quandary, and as it were a cold shivering, to hear this new kind of kindness. Such sweet meat such sour sauce, such fair words such faint promises, such hot love such cold desire, such certain hope such sudden change—and stood like one that had looked on Medusa's head and so had been turned into a stone. Lucilla, seeing him in this pitiful plight, and fearing he would take stand if the lure were not cast out, took him by the hand and wringing him softly with a smiling countenance began thus to comfort him.

'Methinks, Euphues, changing so your colour upon the sudden you will soon change your copy.* Is your mind on your meat? A penny for your thought.'

'Mistress,' quoth he, 'if you would buy all my thoughts at that price I should never be weary of thinking, but seeing it is too dear, read it and take it for nothing.'

'It seems to me', said she, 'that you are in some brown study what colours you might best wear for your lady.'

'Indeed Lucilla, you level shrewdly at my thought by the aim of your own imagination, for you have given unto me a true-love's knot wrought of changeable silk, and you deem that I am devising how I might have my colours changeable also that they might agree. But let this with such toys and devices pass, if it please you to command me any service I am here ready to attend your leisure.'

'No service, Euphues, but that you keep silence until I have uttered my mind, and secrecy when I have unfolded my meaning.'

'If I should offend in the one I were too bold, if in the other too beastly.'

'Well then Euphues,' said she, 'so it is that for the hope that I conceive of thy loyalty, and the happy success that is like to ensue of this our love, I am content to yield thee the place in my heart which thou desirest and deservest above all other, which consent in me, if it may any ways breed thy contentation, sure I am that it will every way work my comfort. But as either thou tenderest mine honour or thine own safety, use such secrecy in this matter that my father have no inkling hereof before I have framed his mind fit for our purpose. And though women have small force to overcome men by reason, yet have they good fortune to undermine them by policy. The soft drops of rain pierce the hard marble, many strokes overthrow the tallest oak, a silly woman in time may make such a breach into a man's heart as her tears may enter without resistance; then doubt not but I will so undermine mine old father as quickly I will enjoy my new friend.

'Tush! Philautus was liked for fashion sake but never loved for fancy sake; and this I vow by the faith of a virgin and by the love I bear thee (for greater bands to confirm my vow I have not) that my father shall sooner martyr me in the fire than marry me to Philautus. No, no, Euphues, thou only hast won me by love and shalt only wear me by law. I force not* Philautus his fury so I may have Euphues his friendship, neither will I prefer his possessions before thy person, neither esteem better of his lands than of thy love. Ferardo shall sooner disherit me of my patrimony than dishonour me in breaking my promise. It is not his great manors but thy good manners that shall make my marriage. In token of which my fierce affection, I give thee my hand in pawn, and my heart forever to be thy Lucilla.' Unto whom Euphues answered in this manner.

'If my tongue were able to utter the joys that my heart hath conceived I fear me, though I be well beloved, yet I should hardly be believed. Ah my Lucilla, how much am I bound to thee, which preferest mine unworthiness before thy father's wrath, my happiness before thine own misfortune, my love before thine own life? How might I excel thee in courtesy, whom no mortal creature can exceed in constancy? I find it now for a settled truth which erst I accompted for a vain talk: that the purple dye will never stain, that the pure civet will never lose his savour, that the green laurel will never change his colour, that beauty can never be blotted with discourtesy. As touching secrecy in this behalf, assure thyself that I will not so much as tell it to myself. Command Euphues to run, to ride, to undertake any exploit be it never so dangerous, to hazard himself in any enterprise be it never so desperate. . . .'

As they were thus pleasantly conferring the one with the other, Livia (whom Euphues made his stale) entered into the parlour, unto whom Lucilla spake in these terms. 'Dost thou not laugh, Livia, to see my ghostly father keep me here so long at shrift?' 'Truly', answered Livia, 'methinks that you smile at some pleasant shift; either he is slow in enquiring of your faults or you slack in answering of his questions.'

And thus, being suppertime, they all sat down, Lucilla well pleased, no man better content than Euphues, who after his repast, having no opportunity to confer with his lover, had small lust to continue with the gentlewomen any longer. Seeing therefore he could frame no means to work his delight, he coined an excuse to hasten his departure, promising the next morning to trouble them again as a guest more bold than welcome, although indeed he thought himself to be the better welcome, in saying that he would come.

But as Ferardo went in post so he returned in haste, having concluded with Philautus that the marriage should immediately be consummated, which wrought such a content in Philautus that he was almost in an ecstasy through the extremity of his passions; such is the fullness and force of pleasure that there is nothing so dangerous as the fruition. Yet knowing that delays bring dangers, although he nothing doubted of Lucilla whom he loved, yet feared he the fickleness of old men, which is always to be mistrusted. He urged therefore Ferardo to break with his daughter, who being willing to have the match made was content incontinently to procure the means. Finding therefore his daughter at leisure, and having knowledge of her former love, spake to her as followeth.

'Dear daughter, as thou hast long time lived a maiden, so now thou must learn to be a mother, and as I have been careful to bring thee up a virgin so am I now desirous to make thee a wife. Neither ought I in this matter to use any persuasions, for that maidens commonly nowadays are no sooner born but they begin to bride it, neither to offer any great portions, for that thou knowest thou shalt inherit all my possessions. Mine only care hath been hitherto to match thee with such an one as should be of good wealth, able to maintain thee; of great worship, able to compare with thee in birth; of honest conditions, to deserve thy love; and an Italian born, to enjoy my lands. At the last I have found one answerable to my desire: a gentleman of great revenues, of a noble progeny, of honest behaviour, of comely personage, born and brought up in Naples—Philautus, thy friend as I guess, thy husband, Lucilla, if thou like it; neither canst thou dislike him who wanteth nothing that should cause thy liking, neither hath anything that should breed thy loathing.

'And surely I rejoice the more that thou shalt be linked to him in marriage whom thou hast loved, as I hear, being a maiden, neither can there any jars kindle between them where the minds be so united, neither any jealousy arise where love hath so long been settled. Therefore, Lucilla, to the end the desire of either of you may now be accomplished to the delight of you both, I am here come to finish the contract by giving hands, which you have already begun between yourselves by joining of hearts, that as God doth witness the one in your consciences so the world may testify the other by your conversations. And therefore, Lucilla, make such answer to my request as may like me and satisfy thy friend.'

Lucilla, abashed with this sudden speech of her father, yet boldened by the love of her friend, with a comely bashfulness answered him in this manner. 'Reverend sir, the sweetness that I have found in the undefiled estate of virginity causeth me to loathe the sour sauce which is mixed with matrimony, and the quiet life which I have tried being a maiden maketh me to shun the cares that are always incident to a mother. Neither am I so wedded to the world that I should be moved with great possessions, neither so bewitched with wantonness that I should be enticed with any man's proportion, neither if I were so disposed would I be so proud to desire one of noble progeny, or so precise to choose one only in mine own country for that commonly these things happen always to the contrary. Do we not see the noble to match with the base, the rich with the poor, the Italian oftentimes with the Portingale?

As love knoweth no laws so it regardeth no conditions; as the lover maketh no pause where he liketh so he maketh no conscience of these idle ceremonies.

'In that Philautus is the man that threateneth such kindness at my hands and such courtesy at yours that he should accompt me his wife before he woo me, certainly he is like for me to make his reckoning twice because he reckoneth without his hostess. And in this Philautus would either show himself of great wisdom to persuade, or me of great lightness to be allured. Although the loadstone draw iron yet it cannot move gold, though the jet gather up the light straw yet can it not take up the pure steel. Although Philautus think himself of virtue sufficient to win his lover yet shall he not obtain Lucilla. I cannot but smile to hear that a marriage should be solemnized where never was any mention of assuring, and that the wooing should be a day after the wedding.

'Certes if when I looked merrily on Philautus he deemed it in the way of marriage, or if seeing me disposed to jest he took me in good earnest, then sure he might gather some presumption of my love, but no promise. But methinks it is good reason that I should be at mine own bridal, and not given in the church before I know the bridegroom.

'Therefore, dear father, in mine opinion as there can be no bargain where both be not agreed, neither any indenture sealed where the one will not consent, so can there be no contract where both be not content; no bans asked lawfully where one of the parties forbiddeth them; no marriage made where no match was meant. But I will hereafter frame myself to be coy seeing I am claimed for a wife because I have been courteous, and give myself to melancholy seeing I am accompted won in that I have been merry. And if every gentleman be made of the metal that Philautus is, then I fear I shall be challenged of as many as I have used to company with, and be a common wife to all those that have commonly resorted hither.

'My duty therefore ever reserved, I here on my knees forswear Philautus for my husband although I accept him for my friend, and seeing I shall hardly be induced ever to match with any, I beseech you, if by your fatherly love I shall be compelled, that I may match with such a one as both I may love and you may like.'

Ferardo, being a grave and wise gentleman, although he were throughly angry, yet he dissembled his fury to the end he might by craft discover her fancy, and whispering Philautus in the ear (who stood as though he had a flea in his ear) desired him to keep silence until he had undermined her by subtlety, which Philautus having granted, Ferardo began to sift his daughter with this device. 'Lucilla, thy colour showeth thee to be in a great choler, and thy hot words bewray thy heavy wrath, but be patient, seeing all my talk was only to try thee. I am neither so unnatural to wrest thee against thine own will, neither so malicious to wed thee to any against thine own liking, for well I know what jars, what jealousy, what strife, what storms ensue where the match is made rather by the compulsion of the parents than by the consent of the parties. Neither do I like thee the less in that thou likest Philautus so little, neither can Philautus love thee the worse in that thou lovest thyself so well, wishing rather to stand to thy chance than to the choice of any other.

'But this grieveth me most, that thou art almost vowed to the vain order of the vestal virgins, despising or at the least not desiring the sacred bands of Juno her bed.* If thy mother had been of that mind when she was a maiden thou hadst not now been born to be of this mind to be a virgin. Weigh with thyself what slender profit they bring to the commonwealth, what slight pleasure to themselves, what great grief to their parents, which joy most in their offspring and desire most to enjoy the noble and blessed name of a grandfather. Thou knowest that the tallest ash is cut down for fuel because it beareth no good fruit, that the cow that gives no milk is brought to the slaughter, that the drone that gathereth no honey is contemned, that the woman that maketh herself barren by not marrying is accompted among the Grecian ladies worse than a carrion, as Homer reporteth.

'Therefore Lucilla, if thou have any care to be a comfort to my hoary hairs or a commodity to thy commonweal, frame thyself to that honourable estate of matrimony, which was sanctified in paradise, allowed of the patriarchs, hallowed of the old prophets, and commended of all persons. If thou like any, be not ashamed to tell it me which only am to exhort thee, yea and as much as in me lieth to command thee, to love one. If he be base thy blood will make him noble, if beggarly thy goods shall make him wealthy, if a stranger thy freedom may enfranchise him, if he be young he is the more fitter to be thy fere, if he be old the liker to thine aged father. For I had rather thou shouldest lead a life to thine own liking in earth than to thy great torments lead apes in hell. Be bold therefore to make me partaker of thy desire which will be partaker of thy disease; yea, and a furtherer of thy delights as far as either my friends or my lands or my life will stretch.'

Lucilla, perceiving the drift of the old fox her father, weighed with herself what was the best to be done. At the last, not weighing her father's ill will, but encouraged by love, shaped him an answer which pleased Ferardo but a little, and pinched Philautus on the parson's side,* on this manner.

'Dear father Ferardo, although I see the bait you lay to catch me, yet I am content to swallow the hook, neither are you more desirous to take me napping than I willing to confess my meaning. So it is that love hath as well inveigled me as others which make it as strange as I. Neither do I love him so meanly that I should be ashamed of his name, neither is his personage so mean that I should love him shamefully. It is Euphues that lately arrived here at Naples that hath battered the bulwark of my breast and shall shortly enter as conqueror into my bosom. What his wealth is I neither know it nor weigh it; what his wit is all Naples doth know it and wonder at it; neither have I been curious to enquire of his progenitors, for that I know so noble a mind could take no original but from a noble man, for as no bird can look against the sun but those that be bred of the eagle, neither any hawk soar so high as the brood of the hobby, so no wight can have such excellent qualities except he descend of a noble race, neither be of so high capacity unless he issue of a high progeny. And I hope Philautus will not be my foe seeing I have chosen his dear friend, neither you, father, be displeased in that Philautus is displaced. You need not muse that I should so suddenly be entangled; love gives no reason of choice, neither will it suffer any repulse.

Myrrha* was enamoured of her natural father, Biblis* of her brother, Phaedra* of her son-in-law. If nature can no way resist the fury of affection, how should it be stayed by wisdom?'

Ferardo interrupting her in the middle of her discourse, although he were moved with inward grudge, yet he wisely repressed his anger, knowing that sharp words would but sharpen her froward will, and thus answered her briefly.

'Lucilla, as I am not presently to grant my good will, so mean I not to reprehend thy choice, yet wisdom willeth me to pause until I have called what may happen to my remembrance, and warneth thee to be circumspect lest thy rash conceit bring a sharp repentance. As for you Philautus, I would not have you despair, seeing a woman doth oftentimes change her desire.' Unto whom Philautus in few words made answer.

'Certainly Ferardo I take the less grief in that I see her so greedy after Euphues, and by so much the more I am content to leave my suit by how much the more she seemeth to disdain my service. But as for hope, because I would not by any means taste one dram thereof, I will abjure all places of her abode and loathe her company whose countenance I have so much loved. As for Euphues—' And there staying his speech, he flung out of the doors and, repairing to his lodging, uttered these words.

'Ah, most dissembling wretch Euphues! O counterfeit companion! Couldst thou under the show of a steadfast friend cloak the malice of a mortal foe? Under the colour of simplicity shroud the image of deceit? Is thy Livia turned to my Lucilla; thy love to my lover; thy devotion to my saint? Is this the courtesy of Athens, the cavilling of scholars, the craft of Grecians? Couldst thou not remember, Philautus, that Greece is never without some wily Ulysses, never void of some Sinon,* never to seek of some deceitful shifter? Is it not commonly said of Grecians that craft cometh to them by kind, that they learn to deceive in their cradle? Why then did his pretended courtesy bewitch thee with such credulity? Shall my good will be the cause of his ill will? Because I was content to be his friend, thought he me meet to be made his fool? I see now that as the fish Scolopidus in the flood Araris at the waxing of the moon is as white as the driven snow, and at the waning as black as the burnt coal, so Euphues, which at the first increasing of our familiarity was very zealous, is now at the last cast become most faithless.

'But why rather exclaim I not against Lucilla, whose wanton looks caused Euphues to violate his plighted faith? Ah, wretched wench, canst thou be so light of love as to change with every wind; so unconstant as to prefer a new lover before thine old friend? Ah well I wot that a new broom sweepeth clean, and a new garment maketh thee leave off the old though it be fitter, and new wine causeth thee to forsake the old though it be better; much like to the men in the island Scyrum which pull up the old tree when they see the young begin to spring, and not unlike unto the widow of Lesbos which changed all her old gold for new glass. Have I served thee three years faithfully and am I served so unkindly? Shall the fruit of my desire be turned to disdain?

'But unless Euphues had inveigled thee thou hadst yet been constant. Yea, but if Euphues had not seen thee willing to be won he would never have wooed thee. But had not Euphues enticed thee with fair words thou wouldst never have loved him. But hadst thou not given him fair looks he would never have liked thee. Aye, but Euphues gave the onset; aye, but Lucilla gave the occasion. Aye, but Euphues first brake his mind; aye, but Lucilla first bewrayed her meaning. Tush, why go I about to excuse any of them, seeing I have just cause to accuse them both? Neither ought I to dispute which of them hath proffered me the greatest villainy, sith that either of them hath committed perjury. Yet although they have found me dull in perceiving their falsehood they shall not find me slack in revenging their folly. As for Lucilla, seeing I mean altogether to forget her, I mean also to forgive her, lest in seeking means to be revenged mine old desire be renewed.'

Philautus having thus discoursed with himself began to write to Euphues as followeth.

'Although hitherto, Euphues, I have shrined thee in my heart for a trusty friend, I will shun thee hereafter as a trothless foe, and although I cannot see in thee less wit than I was wont, yet do I find less honesty. I perceive at the last (although being deceived it be too late) that musk, though it be sweet in the smell, is sour in the smack; that the leaf of the cedar tree, though it be fair to be seen, yet the syrup depriveth sight; that friendship, though it be plighted by shaking the hand, yet it is shaken off by fraud of the heart. But thou hast not much to boast of, for as thou hast won a fickle lady so hast thou lost a faithful friend. How canst thou be secure of her constancy when thou hast had such trial of her lightness? How canst thou assure thyself that she will be faithful to thee which hath been faithless to me?

'Ah Euphues, let not my credulity be an occasion hereafter for thee to practise the like cruelty. Remember this, that yet there hath never been any faithless to his friend that hath not also been fruitless to his God. But I weigh the treachery the less in that it cometh from a Grecian, in whom is no truth. Though I be too weak to wrestle for a revenge, yet God, who permitteth no guile to be guiltless, will shortly requite this injury. Though Philautus have no policies to undermine thee, yet thine own practices will be sufficient to overthrow thee.

'Couldst thou, Euphues, for the love of a fruitless pleasure violate the league of faithful friendship? Didst thou weigh more the enticing looks of a lewd wench than the entire love of a loyal friend? If thou didst determine with thyself at the first to be false, why didst thou swear to be true? If to be true, why art thou false? If thou wast minded both falsely and forgedly to deceive me, why didst thou flatter and dissemble with me at the first? If to love me, why dost thou flinch at the last? If the sacred bands of amity did delight thee, why didst thou break them? If dislike thee, why didst thou praise them? Dost thou not know that a perfect friend should be like the glazeworm which shineth most bright in the dark, or like the pure frankincense which smelleth most sweet when it is in the fire, or at the least not unlike to the damask rose which is sweeter in the still than on the stalk?

'But thou, Euphues, dost rather resemble the swallow which in the summer creepeth under the eaves of every house and in the winter leaveth nothing but dirt behind her, or the humble bee which having sucked honey out of the fair flower doth leave it and loathe it, or the spider which in the finest web doth hang the fairest fly. Dost thou think, Euphues, that thy craft in betraying me shall any whit cool my courage in revenging thy villainy, or that a gentleman of Naples will put up such an injury at the hands of a scholar? And if I do, it is not for want of strength to maintain my just quarrel, but of will which thinketh scorn to get so vain a conquest.

'I know that Menelaus for his ten years' war endured ten years' woe, that after all his strife he won but a strumpet, that for all his travail* he reduced (I cannot say reclaimed) but a straggler, which was as much in my judgement as to strive for a broken glass which is good for nothing. I wish thee rather Menelaus' care than myself his conquest, that thou, being deluded by Lucilla, mayest rather know what it is to be deceived than I, having conquered thee, should prove what it were to bring back a dissembler. Seeing therefore there can no greater revenge light upon thee than that as thou hast reaped where another hath sown, so another may thresh that which thou hast reaped. I will pray that thou mayest be measured unto with the like measure that thou hast meten unto others; that as thou hast thought it no conscience to betray me, so others may deem it no dishonesty to deceive thee; that as Lucilla made it a light matter to forswear her old friend Philautus, so she may make it a mock to forsake her new fere Euphues. Which if it come to pass, as it is like by my compass, then shalt thou see the troubles and feel the torments which thou hast already thrown into the hearts and eyes of others.

'Thus hoping shortly to see thee as hopeless as myself is hapless, I wish my wish were as effectually ended as it is heartily looked for. And so I leave thee.

Thine once
Philautus'

Philautus, dispatching a messenger with this letter speedily to Euphues, went into the fields to walk there, either to digest his choler or chew upon his melancholy. But Euphues, having read the contents, was well content, setting his talk at naught and answering his taunts in these gibing terms.

'I remember, Philautus, how valiantly Ajax boasted in the feats of arms, yet Ulysses bare away the armour, and it may be that though thou crake of thine own courage thou mayest easily lose the conquest. Dost thou think Euphues such a dastard that he is not able to withstand thy courage, or such a dullard that he cannot descry thy craft? Alas good soul! It fareth with thee as with the hen which, when the puttock hath caught her chicken, beginneth to cackle, and thou having lost thy lover beginnest to prattle. Tush Philautus, I am in this point of Euripides his mind, who thinks it lawful for the desire of a kingdom to transgress the bonds of honesty, and for the love of a lady to violate and break the bonds of amity.

'The friendship between man and man as it is common so is it of course, between man and woman as it is seldom so is it sincere; the one proceedeth of the similitude of manners, the other of the sincerity of the heart. If thou hadst learned the first point of hawking thou wouldst have learned to have held fast, or the first note of descant thou wouldst have kept thy *sol fa* to thyself.

'But thou canst blame me no more of folly in leaving thee to love Lucilla than thou mayest reprove him of foolishness that having a sparrow in his hand letteth her go to catch the pheasant; or him of unskilfulness that seeing the heron leaveth to level his shot at the stockdove; or that woman of coyness that having a dead rose in her bosom throweth it away to gather the fresh violet. Love knoweth no laws. Did not Jupiter transform himself into the shape of Amphitrio to embrace Alcmene; into the form of a swan to enjoy Leda; into a bull to beguile Io;* into a shower of gold to win Danaë? Did not Neptune change himself into a heifer, a ram, a flood, a dolphin, only for the love of those he lusted after? Did not Apollo convert himself into a shepherd, into a bird, into a lion, for the desire he had to heal his disease? If the Gods thought no scorn to become beasts to obtain their best beloved, shall Euphues be so nice in changing his copy to gain his lady?

'No, no, he that cannot dissemble in love is not worthy to live. I am of this mind, that both might and malice, deceit and treachery, all perjury, any impiety may lawfully be committed in love, which is lawless. In that thou arguest Lucilla of lightness, thy will hangs in the light of thy wit. Dost thou not know that the weak stomach, if it be cloyed with one diet, doth soon surfeit? That the clown's garlic cannot ease the courtier's

disease so well as the pure treacle?* That far fet and dear
bought is good for ladies? That Euphues, being a more dainty
morsel than Philautus, ought better to be accepted? Tush
Philautus, set thy heart at rest, for thy hap willeth thee to give
over all hope both of my friendship and her love. As for
revenge, thou art not so able to lend a blow as I to ward it;
neither more venturous to challenge the combat than I valiant
to answer the quarrel. As Lucilla was caught by fraud so that
she be kept by force, and as thou wast too simple to espy my
craft, so I think thou wilt be too weak to withstand my
courage. But if thy revenge stand only upon thy wish, thou
shalt never live to see my woe or have thy will, and so farewell.

Euphues'

This letter being dispatched, Euphues sent it, and
Philautus read it, who disdaining those proud terms disdained
also to answer them, being ready to ride with Ferardo.
Euphues, having for a space absented himself from the house
of Ferardo because he was at home, longed sore to see Lucilla,
which now opportunity offered unto him, Ferardo being gone
again to Venice with Philautus. But in this his absence one
Curio, a gentleman of Naples of little wealth and less wit,
haunted Lucilla her company, and so enchanted her that
Euphues was also cast off with Philautus. Which thing being
unknown to Euphues caused him the sooner to make his
repair to the presence of his lady, whom he finding in her
muses began pleasantly to salute in this manner.

'Mistress Lucilla, although my long absence might breed
your just anger (for that lovers desire nothing so much as often
meeting), yet I hope my presence will dissolve your choler (for
that lovers are soon pleased when of their wishes they be fully
possessed). My absence is the rather to be excused in that your
father hath been always at home, whose frowns seemed to
threaten my ill fortune, and my presence at this present the
better to be accepted in that I have made such speedy repair
to your presence.' Unto whom Lucilla answered with this
gleke.

'Truly Euphues, you have missed the cushion,* for I was
neither angry with your long absence, neither am I well

pleased at your presence. The one gave me rather a good hope hereafter never to see you, the other giveth me a greater occasion to abhor you.' Euphues, being nipped on the head, with a pale countenance as though his soul had forsaken his body, replied as followeth.

'If this sudden change, Lucilla, proceed of any desert of mine I am here not only to answer the fact but also to make amends for my fault; if of any new motion or mind to forsake your new friend, I am rather to lament your inconstancy than revenge it. But I hope that such hot love cannot be so soon cold, neither such sure faith be rewarded with so sudden forgetfulness.' Lucilla, not ashamed to confess her folly, answered him with this frump.

'Sir, whether your deserts or my desire have wrought this change it will boot you little to know, neither do I crave amends, neither fear revenge. As for fervent love, you know there is no fire so hot but it is quenched with water, neither affection so strong but is weakened with reason. Let this suffice thee: that thou know I care not for thee.'

'Indeed,' said Euphues, 'to know the cause of your alteration would boot me little, seeing the effect taketh such force. I have heard that women either love entirely or hate deadly, and seeing you have put me out of doubt of the one I must needs persuade myself of the other. This change will cause Philautus to laugh me to scorn, and double thy lightness in turning so often. Such was the hope that I conceived of thy constancy that I spared not in all places to blaze thy loyalty, but now my rash conceit will prove me a liar and thee a light huswife.'

'Nay,' said Lucilla, 'now shalt thou not laugh Philautus to scorn, seeing you have both drunk of one cup. In misery, Euphues, it is great comfort to have a companion. I doubt not but that you will both conspire against me to work some mischief, although I nothing fear your malice. Whosoever accompteth you a liar for praising me may also deem you a lecher for being enamoured of me, and whosoever judgeth me light in forsaking of you may think thee as lewd in loving of me; for thou that thoughtest it lawful to deceive thy friend must take no scorn to be deceived of thy foe.'

'Then I perceive Lucilla', said he, 'that I was made thy stale and Philautus thy laughing-stock, whose friendship (I must confess indeed) I have refused to obtain thy favour. And sithens another hath won that we both have lost, I am content for my part, neither ought I to be grieved, seeing thou art fickle.'

'Certes Euphues,' said Lucilla, 'you spend your wind in waste, for your welcome is but small and your cheer is like to be less. Fancy giveth no reason of his change, neither will be controlled for any choice. This is therefore to warn you that, from henceforth, you neither solicit this suit neither offer any way your service. I have chosen one (I must needs confess) neither to be compared to Philautus in wealth nor to thee in wit, neither in birth to the worst of you both. I think God gave it me for a just plague for renouncing Philautus and choosing thee, and sithens I am an ensample to all women of lightness I am like also to be a mirror to them all of unhappiness, which ill-luck I must take by so much the more patiently by how much the more I acknowledge myself to have deserved it worthily.'

'Well Lucilla,' answered Euphues, 'this case breedeth my sorrow the more in that it is so sudden, and by so much the more I lament it by how much the less I looked for it. In that my welcome is so cold and my cheer so simple it nothing toucheth me, seeing your fury is so hot and my misfortune so great that I am neither willing to receive it nor you to bestow it. If tract of time or want of trial had caused this metamorphosis my grief had been more tolerable and your fleeting more excusable, but coming in a moment undeserved, unlooked for, unthought of, it increaseth my sorrow and thy shame.'

'Euphues,' quoth she, 'you make a long harvest for a little corn, and angle for the fish that is already caught. Curio, yea Curio, is he that hath my love at his pleasure and shall also have my life at his commandment, and although you deem him unworthy to enjoy that which erst you accompted no wight worthy to embrace, yet seeing I esteem him more worth than any, he is to be reputed as chief. The wolf chooseth him for her make that hath or doth endure most travail for her sake. Venus was content to take the blacksmith with his polt-foot; Cornelia here in Naples disdained not to love a rude miller. As for changing, did not Helen, the pearl of Greece thy countrywoman, first take Menelaus, then Theseus, and last of all Paris? If brute beasts give us ensamples that those are most to be liked of whom we are best beloved, or if the princess of beauty Venus and her heirs Helen and Cornelia show that our affection standeth on our free will, then am I rather to be excused than accused. Therefore, good Euphues, be as merry as you may be, for time may so turn that once again you may be.'

'Nay Lucilla,' said he, 'my harvest shall cease seeing others have reaped my corn, as for angling for the fish that is already caught, that were but mere folly. But in my mind if you be a fish you are either an eel, which as soon as one hath hold on her tail will slip out of his hand, or else a minnow which will be nibbling at every bait but never biting. But what fish soever you be, you have made both me and Philautus to swallow a gudgeon.

'If Curio be the person, I would neither wish thee a greater plague nor him a deadlier poison. I for my part think him worthy of thee, and thou unworthy of him, for although he be in body deformed, in mind foolish, an innocent born, a beggar by misfortune, yet doth he deserve a better than thyself, whose corrupt manners have stained thy heavenly hue, whose light behaviour hath dimmed the lights of thy beauty, whose unconstant mind hath betrayed the innocency of so many a gentleman.

'And in that you bring in the example of a beast to confirm your folly, you show therein your beastly disposition which is ready to follow such beastliness. But Venus played false! And what for that? Seeing her lightness served for an example I would wish thou mightest try her punishment for a reward, that being openly taken in an iron net* all the world might judge whether thou be fish or flesh—and certes in my mind no angle will hold thee, it must be a net. Cornelia loved a miller and thou a miser; can her folly excuse thy fault? Helen of Greece, my countrywoman born, but thine by profession, changed and rechanged at her pleasure I grant. Shall the lewdness of others animate thee in thy lightness? Why then dost thou not haunt the stews because Laïs frequented them? Why dost thou not love a bull, seeing Pasiphaë* loved one? Why art thou not enamoured of thy father, knowing that Myrrha was so incensed? These are set down that we, viewing their incontinency, should fly the like impudency, not follow the like excess, neither can they excuse thee of any inconstancy. Merry I will be as I may, but if I may hereafter as thou meanest I will not. And therefore farewell Lucilla, the most inconstant that ever was nursed in Naples, farewell Naples the most cursed town in all Italy, and women all farewell!'

Euphues having thus given her his last farewell, yet being solitary, began afresh to recount his sorrow on this manner. 'Ah Euphues, into what misfortune art thou brought! In what sudden misery art thou wrapped! It is like to fare with thee as with the eagle, which dieth neither for age nor with sickness but with famine, for although thy stomach hunger, yet thy heart will not suffer thee to eat. And why shouldst thou torment thyself for one in whom is neither faith nor fervency? Oh the counterfeit love of women! Oh inconstant sex! I have lost Philautus, I have lost Lucilla. I have lost that which I shall hardly find again: a faithful friend. Ah, foolish Euphues! Why didst thou leave Athens, the nurse of wisdom, to inhabit Naples, the nourisher of wantonness? Had it not been better for thee to have eaten salt with the philosophers in Greece than sugar with the courtiers of Italy? But behold the course of youth, which always inclineth to pleasure. I forsook mine old companions to search for new friends, I rejected the grave and fatherly counsel of Eubulus to follow the brainsick humour of mine own will. I addicted myself wholly to the service of women to spend my life in the laps of ladies, my lands in maintenance of bravery, my wit in the vanities of idle sonnets.

'I had thought that women had been as we men, that is true, faithful, zealous, constant; but I perceive they be rather woe unto men by their falsehood, jealousy, inconstancy. I was half persuaded that they were made of the perfection of men, and would be comforters, but now I see they have tasted of the infection of the serpent, and will be corrosives. The physician saith it is dangerous to minister physic unto the patient that hath a cold stomach and a hot liver, lest in giving warmth to the one he inflame the other; so verily it is hard to deal with a woman, whose words seem fervent, whose heart is congealed into hard ice, lest trusting their outward talk he be betrayed with their inward treachery. I will to Athens, there to toss my books, no more in Naples to live with fair looks.

'I will so frame myself as all youth hereafter shall rather rejoice to see mine amendment than be animated to follow my former life. Philosophy, physic, divinity, shall be my study. Oh the hidden secrets of nature, the express image of moral virtues, the equal balance of justice, the medicines to heal all diseases, how they begin to delight me! The axioms of Aristotle, the maxims of Justinian, the aphorisms of Galen,* have suddenly made such a breach into my mind that I seem only to desire them which did only erst detest them. If wit be employed in the honest study of learning, what thing so precious as wit; if in the idle trade of love, what thing more pestilent than wit? The proof of late hath been verified in me, whom nature hath endued with a little wit which I have abused with an obstinate will. Most true it is that the thing the better it is the greater is the abuse, and that there is nothing but through the malice of man may be abused.

'Doth not the fire (an element so necessary that without it man cannot live) as well burn the house as burn in the house if it be abused? Doth not treacle as well poison as help if it be taken out of time? Doth not wine if it be immoderately taken kill the stomach, inflame the liver, mischief the drunken? Doth not physic destroy if it be not well-tempered? Doth not law accuse if it be not rightly interpreted? Doth not divinity condemn if it be not faithfully construed? Is not poison taken out of the honeysuckle by the spider, venom out of the rose by the canker, dung out of the maple tree by the scorpion? Even so the greatest wickedness is drawn out of the greatest wit, if it be abused by will, or entangled with the world, or inveigled with women.

'But seeing I see my own impiety, I will endeavour myself to amend all that is past and to be a mirror of Godliness hereafter. The rose, though a little it be eaten with the canker, yet being distilled yieldeth sweet water. The iron, though fretted with the rust, yet being burnt in the fire shineth brighter. And wit, although it hath been eaten with the canker of his own conceit, and fretted with the rust of vain love, yet being purified in the still of wisdom and tried in the fire of zeal, will shine bright and smell sweet in the nostrils of all young novices.

'As therefore I gave a farewell to Lucilla, a farewell to Naples, a farewell to women, so now do I give a farewell to the world, meaning rather to macerate myself with melancholy than pine in folly, rather choosing to die in my study amidst my books than to court it in Italy in the company of ladies.' Euphues, having thus debated with himself, went to his bed, there either with sleep to deceive his fancy or with musing to renew his ill-fortune or recant his old follies.

But it happened immediately Ferardo to return home who, hearing this strange event, was not a little amazed, and was now more ready to exhort Lucilla from the love of Curio than before to the liking of Philautus. Therefore in all haste, with watery eyes and a woeful heart, began on this manner to reason with his daughter. 'Lucilla (daughter I am ashamed to call thee, seeing thou hast neither care of thy father's tender affection nor of thine own credit), what sprite hath enchanted thy spirit that every minute thou alterest thy mind? I had thought that my hoary hairs should have found comfort by thy golden locks, and my rotten age great ease by thy ripe years. But alas I see in thee neither wit to order thy doings, neither will to frame thyself to discretion; neither the nature of a child, neither the nurture of a maiden; neither (I cannot without tears speak it) any regard of thine honour, neither any care of thine honesty.

'I am now enforced to remember thy mother's death, who I think was a prophetess in her life, for oftentimes she would say that thou hadst more beauty than was convenient for one that should be honest, and more cockering than was meet for one that should be a matron.

'Would I had never lived to be so old or thou to be so obstinate, either would I had died in my youth in the court or thou in thy cradle. I would to God that either I had never been born or thou never bred. Is this the comfort that the parent reapeth for all his care? Is obstinacy paid for obedience, stubbornness rendered for duty, malicious desperateness for filial fear? I perceive now that the wise painter saw more than the foolish parent can, who painted love going downward, saying it might well descend but ascend it could never. Danaus,* whom they report to be the father of fifty children, had among them all but one that disobeyed him in a thing most dishonest, but I that am father to one more than I would be, although one be all, have that one most disobedient to me in a request lawful and reasonable. If Danaus, seeing but one of his daughters without awe, became himself without mercy, what shall Ferardo do in this case, who hath one and all most unnatural to him in a most just cause? Shall Curio enjoy the fruit of my travails, possess the benefit of my labours, inherit the patrimony of mine ancestors, who hath neither wisdom to increase them nor wit to keep them?

'Wilt thou, Lucilla, bestow thyself on such an one as hath neither comeliness in his body nor knowledge in his mind nor credit in his country? Oh I would thou hadst either been ever faithful to Philautus or never faithless to Euphues, or would thou wouldst be most fickle to Curio. As thy beauty hath made thee the blaze of Italy, so will thy lightness make thee the byword of the world. Oh Lucilla, Lucilla, would thou wert less fair or more fortunate, either of less honour or greater honesty, either better minded or soon buried! Shall thine old father live to see thee match with a young fool? Shall my kind heart be rewarded with such unkind hate? Ah Lucilla, thou knowest not the care of a father nor the duty of a child, and as far art thou from piety as I from cruelty.

'Nature will not permit me to disherit my daughter, and yet it will suffer thee to dishonour thy father. Affection causeth me to wish thy life, and shall it entice thee to procure my death? It is mine only comfort to see thee flourish in thy youth, and is it thine to see me fade in mine age? To conclude, I desire to live to see thee prosper, and thou to see me perish. But why cast I the effect of this unnaturalness in thy teeth, seeing I myself was the cause? I made thee a wanton and thou hast made me a fool. I brought thee up like a cockney, and thou hast handled me like a cockscomb (I speak it to mine own shame), I made more of thee than became a father and thou less of me than beseemed a child. And shall my loving care be cause of thy wicked cruelty? Yea, yea, I am not the first that hath been too careful, nor the last that shall be handled so unkindly. It is common to see fathers too fond and children too froward.

'Well Lucilla, the tears which thou seest trickle down my cheeks, and my drops of blood (which thou canst not see) that fall from my heart, enforce me to make an end of my talk, and if thou have any duty of a child or care of a friend or courtesy of a stranger or feeling of a Christian or humanity of a reasonable creature, then release thy father of grief and acquit thyself of ungratefulness. Otherwise thou shalt but hasten my death and increase thine own defame; which if thou do, the gain is mine and the loss thine, and both infinite.'

Lucilla, either so bewitched that she could not relent or so wicked that she would not yield to her father's request, answered him on this manner. 'Dear father, as you would have me to show the duty of a child, so ought you to show the care of a parent, for as the one standeth in obedience so the other is grounded upon reason. You would have me as I owe duty to you to leave Curio, and I desire you as you owe me any love that you suffer me to enjoy him. If you accuse me of unnaturalness in that I yield not to your request, I am also to condemn you of unkindness in that you grant not my petition. You object I know not what to Curio, but it is the eye of the master that fatteth the horse, and the love of the woman that maketh the man. To give reason for fancy were to weigh the fire and measure the wind. If therefore my delight be the cause of your death, I think my sorrow would be an occasion of your solace. And if you be angry because I am pleased, certes I deem you would be content if I were deceased; which if it be so that my pleasure breed your pain and mine annoy your joy, I may well say that you are an unkind father and I an unfortunate child. But good father, either content yourself with my choice or let me stand to the main chance, otherwise the grief will be mine and the fault yours, and both untolerable.'

Ferardo, seeing his daughter to have neither regard of her own honour nor his request, conceived such an inward grief that in short space he died, leaving Lucilla the only heir of his lands, and Curio to possess them. But what end came of her,* seeing it is nothing incident to the history of Euphues, it were superfluous to insert it, and so incredible that all women would rather wonder at it than believe it; which event being so strange I had rather leave them in a muse what it should be than in a maze in telling what it was.

Philautus, having intelligence of Euphues his success and the falsehood of Lucilla, although he began to rejoice at the misery of his fellow, yet seeing her fickleness could not but lament her folly and pity his friend's misfortune, thinking that the lightness of Lucilla enticed Euphues to so great liking.

Euphues and Philautus having conference between themselves, casting discourtesy in the teeth each of the other, but chiefly noting disloyalty in the demeanour of Lucilla, after much talk renewed their old friendship, both abandoning Lucilla as most abominable. Philautus was earnest to have Euphues tarry in Naples, and Euphues desirous to have Philautus to Athens, but the one was so addicted to the court, the other so wedded to the university, that each refused the offer of the other. Yet this they agreed between themselves, that though their bodies were by distance of place severed, yet the conjunction of their minds should neither be separated by the length of time nor alienated by change of soil. 'I for my part', said Euphues, 'to confirm this league give thee my hand and my heart.' And so likewise did Philautus, and so shaking hands, they bid each other farewell.*

ROBERT GREENE

Pandosto. The Triumph of Time
(1588)

Pandosto. The Triumph of Time. Wherein is discovered by a pleasant history that although by the means of sinister fortune truth may be concealed, yet by time in spite of fortune it is most manifestly revealed. Pleasant for age to avoid drowsy thoughts, profitable for youth to eschew other wanton pastimes, and bringing to both a desired content. *Temporis filia veritas.** By Robert Greene, Master of Arts in Cambridge. *Omne tulit punctum qui miscuit utile dulci.**

To the Gentlemen Readers, Health.

THE paltering poet Aphranius,* being blamed for troubling the Emperor Trajan with so many doting poems, adventured notwithstanding still to present him with rude and homely verses, excusing himself with the courtesy of the emperor, which did as friendly accept as he fondly offered. So gentlemen, if any condemn my rashness for troubling your ears with so many unlearned pamphlets, I will straight shroud myself under the shadow of your courtesies, and with Aphranius lay the blame on you as well for your friendly reading them as on myself for fondly penning them. Hoping, though fond, curious, or rather currish, backbiters breathe out slanderous speeches, yet the courteous readers (whom I fear to offend) will requite my travail at the least with silence; and in this hope I rest, wishing you health and happiness.

Robert Greene

To the Right Honourable George Clifford,* Earl of Cumberland, Robert Greene wisheth increase of honour and virtue.

THE Rascians, right honourable, when by long gazing against the sun they become half-blind, recover their sights by looking on the black loadstone. Unicorns, being glutted with browsing on roots of liquorice, sharpen their stomachs with crushing bitter grass.

Alexander vouchsafed as well to smile at the crooked picture of Vulcan as to wonder at the curious counterfeit of Venus.

The mind is sometimes delighted as much with small trifles as with sumptuous triumphs, and as well pleased with hearing of Pan's homely fancies as of Hercules' renowned labours.

Silly Baucis could not serve Jupiter in a silver plate but in a wooden dish. All that honour Aesculapius deck not his shrine with jewels. Apollo gives oracles as well to the poor man for his mite as to the rich man for his treasure. The stone echites is not so much liked for the colour as for virtue, and gifts are not to be measured by the worth but by the will. Myson, that unskilful painter of Greece, adventured to give unto Darius the shield of Pallas so roughly shadowed as he smiled more at the folly of the man than at the imperfection of his art. So I present unto your honour the triumph of time, so rudely finished as I fear your honour will rather frown at my impudency than laugh at my ignorancy. But I hope my willing mind shall excuse my slender skill, and your honour's courtesy shadow my rashness.

They which fear the biting of vipers do carry in their hands the plumes of a Phoenix. Phidias drew Vulcan sitting in a chair of ivory. Caesar's crow durst never cry '*Ave*' but when she was perched on the capitol. And I seek to shroud this imperfect pamphlet under your honour's patronage, doubting the dint of such envenomed vipers as seek with their slanderous reproaches to carp at all, being oftentimes most unlearned of all, and assure myself that your honour's renowned valour and virtuous disposition shall be a sufficient defence to protect me from the poisoned tongues of such scorning sycophants; hoping that as Jupiter vouchsafed to lodge in Philemon's thatched cottage, and Philip of Macedon to take a bunch of grapes of a country peasant, so I hope your honour, measuring my work by my will, and weighing more the mind than the matter, will when you have cast a glance at this toy, with Minerva, under your golden target cover a deformed owl. And in this hope I rest, wishing unto you and the virtuous countess your wife such happy success as your honours can desire or I imagine.

Your Lordship's most dutifully to command,
Robert Greene

THE HISTORY OF DORASTUS
AND FAWNIA

AMONG all the passions wherewith human minds are perplexed there is none that so galleth with restless despite as that infectious sore of jealousy, for all other griefs are either to be appeased with sensible persuasions, to be cured with wholesome counsel, to be relieved in want, or by tract of time to be worn out—jealousy only excepted, which is so sauced with suspicious doubts and pinching mistrust that whoso seeks by friendly counsel to raze out this hellish passion, it forthwith suspecteth that he giveth this advice to cover his own guiltiness. Yea, whoso is pained with this restless torment doubteth all, distrusteth himself, is always frozen with fear and fired with suspicion, having that wherein consisteth all his joy to be the breeder of his misery. Yea, it is such a heavy enemy to that holy estate of matrimony, sowing between the married couples such deadly seeds of secret hatred as, love being once razed out by spiteful distrust, there oft ensueth bloody revenge, as this ensuing history manifestly proveth. Wherein Pandosto, furiously incensed by causeless jealousy, procured the death of his most loving and loyal wife and his own endless sorrow and misery.

In the country of Bohemia there reigned a king called Pandosto, whose fortunate success in wars against his foes, and bountiful courtesy towards his friends in peace, made him to be greatly feared and loved of all men. This Pandosto had to wife a lady called Bellaria, by birth royal, learned by education, fair by nature, by virtues famous, so that it was hard to judge whether her beauty, fortune or virtue won the greatest commendations. These two, linked together in perfect love, led their lives with such fortunate content that their subjects greatly rejoiced to see their quiet disposition. They had not been married long but fortune (willing to increase their happiness) lent them a son, so adorned with the gifts of nature as the perfection of the child greatly augmented the love of the parents and the joy of their commons, insomuch that the Bohemians, to show their inward joys by outward actions, made bonfires and triumphs throughout all the kingdom, appointing jousts and tourneys for the honour of their young prince. Whither resorted not only his nobles but also diverse kings and princes which were his neighbours, willing to show their friendship they ought to Pandosto and to win fame and glory by their prowess and valour.

Pandosto, whose mind was fraught with princely liberality, entertained the kings, princes, and noble men with such submiss courtesy and magnifical bounty that they all saw how willing he was to gratify their good wills, making a general feast for his subjects which continued by the space of twenty days; all which time the jousts and tourneys were kept to the great content both of the lords and ladies there present. This solemn triumph being once ended, the assembly taking their leave of Pandosto and Bellaria, the young son (who was called Garinter) was nursed up in the house to the great joy and content of the parents.

Fortune, envious of such happy success, willing to show some sign of her inconstancy, turned her wheel and darkened their bright sun of prosperity with the misty clouds of mishap and misery. For it so happened that Egistus, King of Sicilia,* who in his youth had been brought up with Pandosto, desirous to show that neither tract of time nor distance of place could diminish their former friendship, provided a navy of ships and sailed into Bohemia to visit his old friend and companion who, hearing of his arrival, went himself in person and his wife Bellaria, accompanied with a great train of lords and ladies, to meet Egistus; and espying him, alighted from his horse, embraced him very lovingly, protesting that nothing in the world could have happened more acceptable to him than his coming, wishing his wife to welcome his old friend and acquaintance. Who (to show how she liked him whom her husband loved) entertained him with such familiar courtesy as Egistus perceived himself to be very well welcome.

After they had thus saluted and embraced each other, they mounted again on horseback and rode toward the city, devising and recounting how, being children, they had passed their youth in friendly pastimes, where by the means of the citizens Egistus was received with triumphs and shows in such sort that he marvelled how on so small a warning they could make such preparation. Passing the streets thus with such rare sights they rode on to the palace, where Pandosto entertained Egistus and his Sicilians with such banqueting and sumptuous cheer so royally as they all had cause to commend his princely liberality. Yea, the very basest slave that was known to come from Sicilia was used with such courtesy that Egistus might easily perceive how both he and his were honoured for his friend's sake.

Bellaria, who in her time was the flower of courtesy, willing to show how unfeignedly she loved her husband by his friend's entertainment, used him likewise so familiarly that her countenance bewrayed how her mind was affected towards him, oftentimes coming herself into his bedchamber to see that nothing should be amiss to mislike him. This honest familiarity increased daily more and more betwixt them, for Bellaria, noting in Egistus a princely and bountiful mind adorned with sundry and excellent qualities, and Egistus, finding in her a virtuous and courteous disposition, there grew such a secret uniting of their affections that the one could not well be without the company of the other; insomuch that when Pandosto was busied with such urgent affairs that he could not be present with his friend Egistus, Bellaria would walk with him into the garden, where they two in private and pleasant devices would pass away the time to both their contents.

This custom still continuing betwixt them, a certain melancholy passion, entering the mind of Pandosto, drave him into sundry and doubtful thoughts. First he called to mind the beauty of his wife Bellaria, the comeliness and bravery of his friend Egistus, thinking that love was above all laws, and therefore to be stayed with no law; that it was hard to put fire and flax together without burning; that their open pleasures might breed his secret displeasures. He considered with himself that Egistus was a man and must needs love; that his wife was a woman and therefore subject unto love; and that where fancy forced, friendship was of no force.

These and such like doubtful thoughts a long time

smothering in his stomach began at last to kindle in his mind a secret mistrust which, increased by suspicion, grew at last to a flaming jealousy that so tormented him as he could take no rest. He then began to measure all their actions and to misconstrue of their too private familiarity, judging that it was not for honest affection but for disordinate fancy, so that he began to watch them more narrowly to see if he could get any true or certain proof to confirm his doubtful suspicion.

While thus he noted their looks and gestures and suspected their thoughts and meanings, they two silly souls, who doubted nothing of this his treacherous intent, frequented daily each other's company, which drave him into such a frantic passion that he began to bear a secret hate to Egistus and a louring countenance to Bellaria who, marvelling at such unaccustomed frowns, began to cast beyond the moon and to enter into a thousand sundry thoughts which way she should offend her husband; but finding in herself a clear conscience, ceased to muse until such time as she might find fit opportunity to demand the cause of his dumps.

In the meantime Pandosto's mind was so far charged with jealousy that he did no longer doubt, but was assured (as he thought) that his friend Egistus had entered a wrong point in his tables* and so had played him false play. Whereupon, desirous to revenge so great an injury, he thought best to dissemble the grudge with a fair and friendly countenance, and so under the shape of a friend to show him the trick of a foe. Devising with himself a long time how he might best put away Egistus without suspicion of treacherous murder, he concluded at last to poison him; which opinion pleasing his humour, he became resolute in his determination, and the better to bring the matter to pass, he called unto him his cupbearer, with whom in secret he brake the matter, promising to him for the performance thereof to give him a thousand crowns of yearly revenues.

His cupbearer, either being of a good conscience or willing for fashion sake to deny such a bloody request, began with great reasons to persuade Pandosto from his determinate mischief, showing him what an offence murder was to the gods, how such unnatural actions did more displease the

heavens than men,* and that causeless cruelty did seldom or
never escape without revenge. He laid before his face that
Egistus was his friend, a king, and one that was come into his
kingdom to confirm a league of perpetual amity betwixt them;
that he had and did show him a most friendly countenance;
how Egistus was not only honoured of his own people by
obedience but also loved of the Bohemians for his courtesy.
And that if now he should without any just or manifest cause
poison him, it would not only be a great dishonour to his
majesty and a means to sow perpetual enmity between the
Sicilians and the Bohemians, but also his own subjects would
repine at such treacherous cruelty.

These and such like persuasions of Franion (for so was his
cupbearer called) could no whit prevail to dissuade him from
his devilish enterprise, but remaining resolute in his
determination, his fury so fired with rage as it could not be
appeased with reason. He began with bitter taunts to take up
his man and to lay before him two baits: preferment and
death, saying that if he would poison Egistus he should
advance him to high dignities, if he refused to do it of an
obstinate mind no torture should be too great to requite his
disobedience.

Franion, seeing that to persuade Pandosto any more was but
to strive against the stream, consented as soon as opportunity
would give him leave to dispatch Egistus, wherewith Pandosto
remained somewhat satisfied, hoping now he should be fully
revenged of such mistrusted injuries, intending also as soon as
Egistus was dead to give his wife a sop of the same sauce and
to be rid of those which were the cause of his restless sorrow.
While thus he lived in this hope, Franion, being secret in his
chamber, began to meditate with himself in these terms.

'Ah Franion, treason is loved of many, but the traitor hated
of all. Unjust offences may for a time escape without danger,
but never without revenge. Thou art servant to a king, and
must obey at command; yet Franion, against law and
conscience it is not good to resist a tyrant with arms, nor to
please an unjust king with obedience. What shalt thou do?
Folly refused gold, and frenzy preferment. Wisdom seeketh
after dignity and counsel looketh for gain. Egistus is a stranger

to thee and Pandosto thy sovereign; thou hast little cause to respect the one and oughtest to have great care to obey the other. Think this Franion: that a pound of gold is worth a ton of lead, great gifts are little gods, and preferment to a mean man is a whetstone to courage. There is nothing sweeter than promotion nor lighter than report; care not then though most count thee a traitor so all call thee rich. Dignity, Franion, advanceth thy posterity and evil report can hurt but thyself. Know this: where eagles build, falcons may prey; where lions haunt, foxes may steal. Kings are known to command, servants are blameless to consent. Fear not thou then to lift at Egistus, Pandosto shall bear the burden. Yea, but Franion, conscience is a worm that ever biteth but never ceaseth, that which is rubbed with the stone galactites will never be hot, flesh dipped in the sea Aegeum will never be sweet, the herb tragion being once bit with an aspis never groweth, and conscience once stained with innocent blood is always tied to a guilty remorse. Prefer thy content before riches, and a clear mind before dignity; so being poor thou shalt have rich peace or else rich thou shalt enjoy disquiet.'

Franion having muttered out these or such like words, seeing either he must die with a clear mind or live with a spotted conscience, he was so cumbered with diverse cogitations that he could take no rest until at last he determined to break the matter to Egistus. But fearing that the King should either suspect or hear of such matters, he concealed the device till opportunity would permit him to reveal it. Lingering thus in doubtful fear, in an evening he went to Egistus' lodging and, desirous to break with him of certain affairs that touched the King, after all were commanded out of the chamber, Franion made manifest the whole conspiracy which Pandosto had devised against him, desiring Egistus not to accompt him a traitor for bewraying his master's counsel but to think that he did it for conscience, hoping that although his master, inflamed with rage or incensed by some sinister reports or slanderous speeches, had imagined such causeless mischief, yet when time should pacify his anger and try those talebearers but flattering parasites, then he would count him as a faithful servant that with such care had kept his master's credit.

Egistus had not fully heard Franion tell forth his tale but a quaking fear possessed all his limbs, thinking that there was some treason wrought, and that Franion did but shadow his craft with these false colours. Wherefore he began to wax in choler, and said that he doubted not Pandosto, sith he was his friend, and there had never as yet been any breach of amity. He had not sought to invade his lands, to conspire with his enemies, to dissuade his subjects from their allegiance, but in word and thought he rested his at all times. He knew not, therefore, any cause that should move Pandosto to seek his death, but suspected it to be a compacted knavery of the Bohemians to bring the King and him at odds.

Franion, staying him in the midst of his talk, told him that to dally with princes was with the swans to sing against their death, and that if the Bohemians had intended any such secret mischief it might have been better brought to pass than by revealing the conspiracy. Therefore his Majesty did ill to misconstrue of his good meaning, sith his intent was to hinder treason, not to become a traitor; and to confirm his premises, if it please his Majesty to flee into Sicilia for the safeguard of his life, he would go with him. And if then he found not such a practice to be pretended, let his imagined treachery be repaid with most monstrous torments.

Egistus, hearing the solemn protestation of Franion, began to consider that in love and kingdoms neither faith nor law is to be respected, doubting that Pandosto thought by his death to destroy his men and with speedy war to invade Sicilia. These and such doubts throughly weighed, he gave great thanks to Franion, promising if he might with life return to Syracusa that he would create him a duke in Sicilia, craving his counsel how he might escape out of the country.

Franion, who, having some small skill in navigation, was well acquainted with the ports and havens and knew every danger in the sea, joining in counsel with the master of Egistus' navy, rigged all their ships and setting them afloat, let them lie at anchor to be in the more readiness when time and wind should serve. Fortune, although blind, yet by chance favouring this just cause, sent them within six days a good gale of wind, which Franion seeing fit for their purpose, to put Pandosto out of suspicion, the night before they should sail he went to him and promised that the next day he would put the device in practice, for he had got such a forcible poison as the very smell thereof should procure sudden death.

Pandosto was joyful to hear this good news, and thought every hour a day till he might be glutted with bloody revenge. But his suit had but ill success, for Egistus, fearing that delay might breed danger, and willing that the grass should not be cut from under his feet, taking bag and baggage with the help of Franion, conveyed himself and his men out of a postern gate of the city, so secretly and speedily that without any suspicion they got to the sea shore where, with many a bitter curse, taking their leave of Bohemia, they went aboard. Weighing their anchors and hoisting sail they passed as fast as wind and sea would permit towards Sicilia, Egistus being a joyful man that he had safely passed such treacherous perils.

But as they were quietly floating on the sea, so Pandosto and his citizens were in an uproar, for seeing that the Sicilians without taking their leave were fled away by night, the Bohemians feared some treason, and the King thought that without question his suspicion was true, seeing his cupbearer had bewrayed the sum of his secret pretence. Whereupon he began to imagine that Franion and his wife Bellaria had conspired with Egistus, and that the fervent affection she bare him was the only means of his secret departure, insomuch that, incensed with rage, he commanded that his wife should be carried to straight prison* until they heard further of his pleasure.

The guard, unwilling to lay their hands on such a virtuous princess, and yet fearing the King's fury, went very sorrowfully to fulfil their charge. Coming to the Queen's lodging they found her playing with her young son Garinter, unto whom with tears doing the message, Bellaria astonished at such a hard censure, and finding her clear conscience a sure advocate to plead in her case, went to the prison most willingly; where with sighs and tears she passed away the time until she might come to her trial.

But Pandosto, whose reason was suppressed with rage, and whose unbridled folly was incensed with fury, seeing Franion had bewrayed his secrets and that Egistus might well be railed on but not revenged, determined to wreak all his wrath on poor Bellaria. He therefore caused a general proclamation to be made through all his realm that the Queen and Egistus had by the help of Franion not only committed most incestuous adultery but also had conspired the King's death, whereupon the traitor Franion was fled away with Egistus, and Bellaria was most justly imprisoned. This proclamation being once blazed through the country, although the virtuous disposition of the Queen did half discredit the contents, yet the sudden and speedy passsage of Egistus, and the secret departure of Franion, induced them (the circumstances throughly considered) to think that both the proclamation was true and the King greatly injured. Yet they pitied her case, as sorrowful that so good a lady should be crossed with such adverse fortune.

But the King, whose restless rage would admit no pity, thought that although he might sufficiently requite his wife's falsehood with the bitter plague of pinching penury, yet his mind should never be glutted with revenge till he might have fit time and opportunity to repay the treachery [of] Egistus with a fatal injury. But a curst cow hath ofttimes short horns,* and a willing mind but a weak arm, for Pandosto, although he felt that revenge was a spur to war, and that envy always proffereth steel, yet he saw that Egistus was not only of great puissance and prowess to withstand him but had also many kings of his alliance to aid him if need should serve, for he married to the Emperor's daughter of Russia. These and such like considerations something daunted Pandosto his courage, so that he was content rather to put up a manifest injury with peace than hunt after revenge with dishonour and loss, determining, since Egistus had escaped scot free, that Bellaria should pay for all at an unreasonable price.

Remaining thus resolute in his determination, Bellaria continuing still in prison and hearing the contents of the proclamation, knowing that her mind was never touched with such affection, nor that Egistus had ever offered her such discourtesy, would gladly have come to her answer, that both she might have known her unjust accusers and cleared herself of that guiltless crime.

But Pandosto was so inflamed with rage and infected with jealousy, as he would not vouchsafe to hear her nor admit any just excuse, so that she was fain to make a virtue of her need, and with patience to bear these heavy injuries. As thus she lay crossed with calamities (a great cause to increase her grief) she found herself quick with child. Which, as soon as she felt stir in her body, she burst forth into bitter tears, exclaiming against fortune in these terms.

'Alas Bellaria, how infortunate art thou because fortunate! Better hadst thou been born a beggar than a prince, so shouldest thou have bridled fortune with want, where now she sporteth herself with thy plenty. Ah happy life, where poor thoughts and mean desires live in secure content, not fearing fortune because too low for fortune. Thou seest now, Bellaria, that care is a companion to honour not to poverty, that high cedars are frushed with tempests when low shrubs are not touched with the wind; precious diamonds are cut with the file when despised pebbles lie safe in the sand; Delphos is sought to by princes not beggars, and fortune's altars smoke with kings' presents not with poor men's gifts. Happy are such, Bellaria, that curse fortune for contempt, not fear, and may wish they were, not sorrow they have been. Thou art a princess, Bellaria, and yet a prisoner, born to the one by descent, assigned to the other by despite, accused without cause and therefore oughtest to die without care, for patience is a shield against fortune, and a guiltless mind yieldeth not to sorrow.

'Ah, but infamy galleth unto death, and liveth after death! Report is plumed with time's feathers and envy oftentimes soundeth fame's trumpet. Thy suspected adultery shall fly in the air, and thy known virtues shall lie hid in the earth. One mole staineth a whole face, and what is once spotted with infamy can hardly be worn out with time. Die then Bellaria; Bellaria die! For if the gods should say thou art guiltless, yet envy would hear the gods but never believe the gods. Ah, hapless wretch, cease these terms. Desperate thoughts are fit for them that fear shame, not for such as hope for credit. Pandosto hath darkened thy fame but shall never discredit thy virtues. Suspicion may enter a false action but proof shall never put in his plea. Care not then for envy, sith report hath a blister on her tongue, and let sorrow bite them which offend, not touch thee that are faultless. But alas, poor soul, how canst thou but sorrow? Thou art with child, and by him that instead of kind pity pincheth thee in cold prison.' And with that such gasping sighs so stopped her breath that she could not utter any mo words, but wringing her hands, and gushing forth streams of tears, she passed away the time with bitter complaints.

The jailor, pitying these her heavy passions, thinking that if the King knew she were with child he would somewhat appease his fury and release her from prison, went in all haste and certified Pandosto what the effect of Bellaria's complaint was. Who no sooner heard the jailor say she was with child but, as one possessed with a frenzy, he rose up in a rage, swearing that she and the bastard brat she was withal should die if the gods themselves said no—thinking assuredly by computation of time that Egistus, and not he, was father to the child. This suspicious thought galled afresh this half-healed sore, insomuch as he could take no rest until he might mitigate his choler with a just revenge, which happened presently after. For Bellaria was brought to bed of a fair and beautiful daughter, which no sooner Pandosto heard but he determined that both Bellaria and the young infant should be burnt with fire.

His nobles, hearing of the King's cruel sentence, sought by persuasions to divert him from this bloody determination, laying before his face the innocency of the child and the virtuous disposition of his wife, how she had continually loved and honoured him so tenderly that without due proof he could not, nor ought not to appeach her of that crime. And if she had faulted, yet it were more honourable to pardon with mercy than to punish with extremity, and more kingly to be commended of pity than accused of rigour. And as for the child, if he should punish it for the mother's offence, it were to strive against nature and justice, and that unnatural actions do more offend the gods than men; how causeless cruelty nor innocent blood never scapes without revenge.

These and such like reasons could not appease his rage, but

he rested resolute in this: that Bellaria, being an adulteress, the child was a bastard, and he would not suffer that such an infamous brat should call him father. Yet at last, seeing his noblemen were importunate upon him, he was content to spare the child's life, and yet to put it to a worser death. For he found out this device: that seeing (as he thought) it came by fortune, so he would commit it to the charge of fortune, and therefore he caused a little cock-boat to be provided, wherein he meant to put the babe and then send it to the mercy of the seas and the destinies. From this his peers in no wise could persuade him, but that he sent presently two of his guard to fetch the child who, being come to the prison, and with weeping tears recounting their master's message, Bellaria no sooner heard the rigorous resolution of her merciless husband but she fell down in a sound, so that all thought she had been dead. Yet at last, being come to herself, she cried and screeched out in this wise.

'Alas, sweet infortunate babe, scarce born before envied by fortune! Would the day of thy birth had been the term of thy life, then shouldest thou have made an end to care and prevented thy father's rigour. Thy faults cannot yet deserve such hateful revenge, thy days are too short for so sharp a doom, but thy untimely death must pay thy mother's debts, and her guiltless crime must be thy ghastly curse. And shalt thou, sweet babe, be committed to fortune when thou art already spited by fortune? Shall the seas be thy harbour and the hard boat thy cradle? Shall thy tender mouth instead of sweet kisses be nipped with bitter storms? Shalt thou have the whistling winds for thy lullaby and the salt sea foam instead of sweet milk? Alas, what destinies would assign such hard hap? What father would be so cruel? Or what gods will not revenge such rigour? Let me kiss thy lips, sweet infant, and wet thy tender cheeks with my tears, and put this chain about thy little neck, that if fortune save thee it may help to succour thee. Thus, since thou must go to surge in the ghastful seas, with a sorrowful kiss I bid thee farewell, and I pray the gods thou mayest fare well.'

Such and so great was her grief that, her vital spirits being suppressed with sorrow, she fell again down in a trance, having her senses so sotted with care that after she was revived, yet she lost her memory, and lay for a great time without moving, as one in a trance. The guard left her in this perplexity, and carried the child to the King who, quite* devoid of pity, commanded that without delay it should be put in the boat, having neither sail nor other* to guide it, and so to be carried into the midst of the sea and there left to the wind and wave as the destinies please to appoint.

The very shipmen, seeing the sweet countenance of the young babe, began to accuse the King of rigour, and to pity the child's hard fortune. But fear constrained them to that which their nature did abhor, so that they placed it in one of the ends of the boat, and with a few green boughs made a homely cabin to shroud it as they could from wind and weather. Having thus trimmed the boat, they tied it to a ship and so haled it into the main sea, and then cut in sunder the cord, which they had no sooner done but there arose a mighty tempest which tossed the little boat so vehemently in the waves that the shipmen thought it could not continue long without sinking. Yea, the storm grew so great that with much labour and peril they got to the shore.

But leaving the child to her fortunes, again to Pandosto, who, not yet glutted with sufficient revenge, devised which way he should best increase his wife's calamity. But first assembling his nobles and counsellors, he called her for the more reproach into open court, where it was objected against her that she had committed adultery with Egistus and conspired with Franion to poison Pandosto her husband, but their pretence being partly spied, she counselled them to fly away by night for their better safety.

Bellaria, who, standing like a prisoner at the bar, feeling in herself a clear conscience to withstand her false accusers, seeing that no less than death could pacify her husband's wrath, waxed bold, and desired that she might have law and justice, for mercy she neither craved nor hoped for, and that those perjured wretches which had falsely accused her to the King might be brought before her face to give in evidence. But Pandosto, whose rage and jealousy was such as no reason nor equity could appease, told her that for her accusers, they were of such credit as their words were sufficient witness, and that the sudden and secret flight of Egistus and Franion confirmed that which they had confessed. And as for her, it was her part to deny such a monstrous crime and to be impudent in forswearing the fact, since she had passed all shame in committing the fault. But her stale countenance should stand for no coin, for as the bastard which she bare was served, so she should with some cruel death be requited.

Bellaria, no whit dismayed with this rough reply, told her husband Pandosto that he spake upon choler and not conscience, for her virtuous life had been ever such as no spot of suspicion could ever stain. And if she had borne a friendly countenance to Egistus it was in respect he was his friend, and not for any lusting affection. Therefore, if she were condemned without any further proof, it was rigour and not law.

The noblemen which sat in judgement said that Bellaria spake reason, and entreated the King that the accusers might be openly examined and sworn, and if then the evidence were such as the jury might find her guilty (for seeing she was a prince she ought to be tried by her peers) then let her have such punishment as the extremity of the law will assign to such malefactors. The King presently made answer that in this case he might and would dispense with the law, and that the jury being once panelled they should take his word for sufficient evidence, otherwise he would make the proudest of them repent it.

The noblemen, seeing the King in choler, were all whist. But Bellaria, whose life then hung in the balance, fearing more perpetual infamy than momentary death, told the King if his fury might stand for a law, that it were vain to have the jury yield their verdict; and therefore she fell down upon her knees and desired the King that for the love he bare to his young son Garinter, whom she brought into the world, that he would grant her a request, which was this: that it would please his Majesty to send six of his noblemen whom he best trusted to the Isle of Delphos, there to enquire of the Oracle of Apollo whether she had committed adultery with Egistus or conspired to poison him with Franion; and if the God

Apollo, who by his divine essence knew all secrets, gave answer that she was guilty, she were content to suffer any torment, were it never so terrible.

The request was so reasonable that Pandosto could not for shame deny it unless he would be counted of all his subjects more wilful than wise. He therefore agreed that with as much speed as might be, there should be certain ambassadors dispatched to the Isle of Delphos, and in the mean season he commanded that his wife should be kept in close prison.

Bellaria, having obtained this grant, was now more careful for her little babe that floated on the seas than sorrowful for her own mishap. For of that she doubted; of herself she was assured, knowing if Apollo should give oracle according to the thoughts of the heart yet the sentence should go on her side, such was the clearness of her mind in this case. But Pandosto, whose suspicious head still remained in one song, chose out six of his nobility whom he knew were scarce indifferent men in the Queen's behalf, and providing all things fit for their journey, sent them to Delphos.

They, willing to fulfil the King's command, and desirous to see the situation and custom of the island, dispatched their affairs with as much speed as might be, and embarked themselves on this voyage, which (the wind and weather serving fit for their purpose) was soon ended. For within three weeks they arrived at Delphos, where they were no sooner set on land but with great devotion they went to the temple of Apollo, and there offering sacrifice to the God and gifts to the priest, as the custom was, they humbly craved an answer of their demand. They had not long kneeled at the altar but Apollo with a loud voice said 'Bohemians, what you find behind the altar take, and depart.' They forthwith, obeying the oracle, found a scroll of parchment wherein was written these words in letters of gold.

THE ORACLE

Suspicion is no proof. Jealousy is an unequal judge. Bellaria is chaste, Egistus blameless, Franion a true subject, Pandosto treacherous, his babe an innocent, and the King shall live without an heir if that which is lost be not found.

As soon as they had taken out this scroll, the priest of the God commanded them that they should not presume to read it before they came in the presence of Pandosto unless they would incur the displeasure of Apollo. The Bohemian lords carefully obeying his command, taking their leave of the priest, with great reverence departed out of the temple and went to their ships, and as soon as wind would permit them, sailed toward Bohemia. Whither, in short time, they safely arrived, and with great triumph issuing out of their ships, went to the King's palace, whom they found in his chamber accompanied with other noblemen.

Pandosto no sooner saw them but with a merry countenance he welcomed them home, asking what news. They told his Majesty that they had received an answer of the God written in a scroll, but with this charge: that they should not read the contents before they came in the presence of the King; and with that they delivered him the parchment. But his noblemen entreated him that sith therein was contained either the safety of his wife's life and honesty, or her death and perpetual infamy, that he would have his nobles and commons assembled in the judgement hall, where the Queen, brought in as prisoner, should hear the contents. If she were found guilty by the oracle of the God, then all should have cause to think his rigour proceeded of due desert; if her grace were found faultless, then she should be cleared before all, sith she had been accused openly.

This pleased the King, so that he appointed the day, and assembled all his lords and commons, and caused the Queen to be brought in before the judgement seat, commanding that the indictment should be read, wherein she was accused of adultery with Egistus and of conspiracy with Franion. Bellaria, hearing the contents, was no whit astonished, but made this cheerful answer.

'If the divine powers be privy to human actions, as no doubt they are, I hope my patience shall make fortune blush and my unspotted life shall stain spiteful* discredit. For although lying report hath sought to appeach mine honour, and suspicion hath intended to soil my credit with infamy, yet where virtue keepeth the fort, report and suspicion may assail but never sack. How I have led my life before Egistus' coming I appeal, Pandosto, to the gods and to thy conscience. What hath passed betwixt him and me the gods only know, and I hope will presently reveal. That I loved Egistus I cannot deny, that I honoured him I shame not to confess; to the one I was forced by his virtues, to the other for his dignities. But as touching lascivious lust, I say Egistus is honest, and hope myself to be found without spot. For Franion, I can neither accuse him nor excuse him, for I was not privy to his departure. And that this is true which I have here rehearsed I refer myself to the divine oracle.'

Bellaria had no sooner said but the King commanded that one of his dukes should read the contents of the scroll; which after the commons had heard, they gave a great shout, rejoicing and clapping their hands that the Queen was clear of that false accusation. But the King, whose conscience was a witness against him of his witless fury and false suspected jealousy, was so ashamed of his rash folly that he entreated his nobles to persuade Bellaria to forgive and forget these injuries, promising not only to show himself a loyal and loving husband but also to reconcile himself to Egistus and Franion, revealing then before them all the cause of their secret flight and how treacherously he thought to have practised his death if the good mind of his cupbearer had not prevented his purpose.

As thus he was relating the whole matter, there was word brought him that his young son Garinter was suddenly dead, which news, so soon as Bellaria heard, surcharged before with extreme joy and now suppressed with heavy sorrow, her vital spirits were so stopped that she fell down presently dead, and could be never revived. This sudden sight so appalled the King's senses that he sank from his seat in a sound so as he was fain to be carried by his nobles to his palace, where he lay by the space of three days without speech.

His commons were as men in despair, so diversely distressed. There was nothing but mourning and lamentation to be heard throughout Bohemia—their young prince dead, their virtuous Queen bereaved of her life, and their King and sovereign in great hazard. This tragical discourse of fortune so daunted them as they went like shadows, not men. Yet somewhat to comfort their heavy hearts, they heard that Pandosto was come to himself and had recovered his speech, who as in a fury brayed out these bitter speeches.

'O miserable Pandosto, what surer witness than conscience? What thoughts more sour than suspicion? What plague more bad than jealousy? Unnatural actions offend the gods more than men, and causeless cruelty never scapes without revenge. I have committed such a bloody fact as repent I may but recall I cannot. Ah jealousy—a hell to the mind and a horror to the conscience, suppressing reason and inciting rage, a worse passion than frenzy, a greater plague than madness. Are the gods just? Then let them revenge such brutish cruelty. My innocent babe I have drowned in the seas; my loving wife I have slain with slanderous suspicion; my trusty friend I have sought to betray—and yet the gods are slack to plague such offences. Ah, unjust Apollo, Pandosto is the man that hath committed the fault! Why should Garinter, seely child, abide the pain? Well, sith the gods mean to prolong my days to increase my dolour, I will offer my guilty blood a sacrifice to those sackless souls whose lives are lost by my rigorous folly.'

And with that he reached at a rapier, to have murdered himself, but his peers being present stayed him from such a bloody act, persuading him to think that the commonwealth consisted on his safety, and that those sheep could not but perish that wanted a shepherd; wishing that if he would not live for himself yet he should have care of his subjects, and to put such fancies out of his mind sith in sores past help salves do not heal but hurt, and in things past cure care is a corrasive.

With these and such like persuasions the King was overcome, and began somewhat to quiet his mind, so that as soon as he could go abroad he caused his wife to be embalmed and wrapped in lead with her young son Garinter, erecting a rich and famous sepulchre wherein he entombed them both, making such solemn obsequies at her funeral as all Bohemia might perceive he did greatly repent him of his forepassed folly, causing this epitaph to be engraven on her tomb in letters of gold.

THE EPITAPH

Here lies entombed Bellaria fair,
  Falsely accused to be unchaste;
Cleared by Apollo's sacred doom
  Yet slain by jealousy at last.

What ere thou be that passest by
Curse him that caused this Queen to die.

This epitaph being engraven, Pandosto would once a day repair to the tomb, and there with watery plaints bewail his misfortune, coveting no other companion but sorrow, nor no other harmony but repentance.

But leaving him to his dolorous passions, at last let us come to show the tragical discourse of the young infant; who, being tossed with wind and wave, floated two whole days without succour, ready at every puff to be drowned in the sea. Till at last the tempest ceased and the little boat was driven with the tide into the coast of Sicilia where, sticking upon the sands, it rested. Fortune, minding to be wanton, willing to show that as she hath wrinkles on her brows so she hath dimples in her cheeks, thought after so many sour looks to lend a feigned smile, and after a puffing storm to bring a pretty calm; she began thus to dally.

It fortuned a poor mercenary shepherd that dwelled in Sicilia, who got his living by other men's flocks, missed one of his sheep, and thinking it had strayed into the covert that was hard by, sought very diligently to find that which he could not see, fearing either that the wolves or eagles had undone him (for he was so poor as a sheep was half his substance), wandered down toward the sea cliffs to see if perchance the sheep was browsing on the sea ivy, whereon they greatly do feed. But not finding her there, as he was ready to return to his flock he heard a child cry. But knowing there was no house near, he thought he had mistaken the sound, and that it was the bleating of his sheep. Wherefore, looking more narrowly, as he cast his eye to the sea he spied a little boat from whence as he attentively listened he might hear the cry to come. Standing a good while in a maze, at last he went to the shore and, wading to the boat, as he looked in he saw the little babe lying all alone, ready to die for hunger and cold, wrapped in a mantle of scarlet richly embroidered with gold and having a chain about the neck.

The shepherd, who before had never seen so fair a babe nor so rich jewels, thought assuredly that it was some little god, and began with great devotion to knock on his breast. The babe, who writhed with the head to seek for the pap, began again to cry afresh, whereby the poor man knew that it was a child which by some sinister means was driven thither in distress of weather, marvelling how such a seely infant, which by the mantle and the chain could not be but born of noble parentage, should be so hardly crossed with deadly mishap.

The poor shepherd, perplexed thus with diverse thoughts, took pity of the child and determined with himself to carry it to the King, that there it might be brought up according to the worthiness of birth; for his ability could not afford to foster it, though his good mind was willing to further it. Taking therefore the child in his arms, as he folded the mantle together the better to defend it from cold, there fell down at his foot a very fair and rich purse, wherein he found a great sum of gold, which sight so revived the shepherd's spirits as he was greatly ravished with joy and daunted with fear—joyful to see such a sum in his power and fearful, if it should be known, that it might breed his further danger. Necessity wished him at the least to retain the gold, though he would not keep the child; the simplicity of his conscience feared him from such deceitful bribery.

Thus was the poor man perplexed with a doubtful dilemma, until at last the covetousness of the coin overcame him, for what will not the greedy desire of gold cause a man to do? So that he was resolved in himself to foster the child, and with the sum to relieve his want. Resting thus resolute in this point, he left seeking of his sheep and as covertly and secretly as he could went by a byway to his house, lest any of his neighbours should perceive his carriage.

As soon as he was got home, entering in at the door, the child began to cry, which his wife hearing, and seeing her husband with a young babe in his arms, began to be somewhat jealous, yet marvelling that her husband should be so wanton abroad sith he was so quiet at home. But as women are naturally given to believe the worst, so his wife, thinking it was some bastard, began to crow against her goodman, and taking up a cudgel (for the most, master went breechless)* sware solemnly that she would make clubs trumps if he brought any bastard brat within her doors.

The goodman, seeing his wife in her majesty with her mace in her hand, thought it was time to bow for fear of blows, and desired her to be quiet for there was none such matter, but if she could hold her peace they were made for ever. And with that he told her the whole matter: how he had found the child in a little boat, without any succour, wrapped in that costly mantle, and having that rich chain about the neck. But at last, when he showed her the purse full of gold, she began to simper something sweetly, and taking her husband about the neck kissed him after her homely fashion, saying that she hoped God had seen their want and now meant to relieve their poverty, and seeing they could get no children had sent them this little babe to be their heir.

'Take heed in any case', quoth the shepherd, 'that you be secret, and blab it not out when you meet with your gossips, for if you do we are like not only to lose the gold and jewels but our other goods and lives.' 'Tush,' quoth his wife, 'profit is a good hatch before the door. Fear not, I have other things to talk of than of this. But I pray you, let us lay up the money surely, and the jewels, lest by any mishap it be spied.'

After that they had set all things in order, the shepherd went to his sheep with a merry note, and the goodwife learned to sing lullaby at home with her young babe, wrapping it in a homely blanket instead of a rich mantle, nourishing it so cleanly and carefully as it began to be a jolly girl, insomuch that they began, both of them, to be very fond of it, seeing as it waxed in age so it increased in beauty. The shepherd every night at his coming home would sing and dance it on his knee and prattle, that in a short time it began to speak and call him 'Dad' and her 'Mam'.

At last, when it grew to ripe years that it was about seven years old, the shepherd left keeping of other men's sheep, and with the money he found in the purse, he bought him the lease of a pretty farm and got a small flock of sheep, which when Fawnia (for so they named the child) came to the age of ten years, he set her to keep, and she with such diligence performed her charge as the sheep prospered marvellously under her hand.

Fawnia thought Porrus had been her father and Mopsa her mother (for so was the shepherd and his wife called), honoured and obeyed them with such reverence that all the neighbours praised the dutiful obedience of the child. Porrus grew in short time to be a man of some wealth and credit, for fortune so favoured him in having no charge but Fawnia that he began to purchase land, intending after his death to give it to his daughter, so that diverse rich farmers' sons came as wooers to his house, for Fawnia was something cleanly attired, being of such singular beauty and excellent wit that whoso saw her would have thought she had been some heavenly nymph and not a mortal creature. Insomuch that, when she came to the age of sixteen years, she so increased with exquisite perfection, both of body and mind, as her natural disposition did bewray that she was born of some high parentage. But the people, thinking she was daughter to the shepherd Porrus, rested only amazed at her beauty and wit. Yea, she won such favour and commendations in every man's eye as her beauty was not only praised in the country but also spoken of in the court. Yet such was her submiss modesty that, although her praise daily increased, her mind was no whit puffed up with pride, but humbled herself as became a country maid and the daughter of a poor shepherd.

Every day she went forth with her sheep to the field, keeping them with such care and diligence as all men thought she was very painful, defending her face from the heat of the sun with no other veil but with a garland made of bows* and flowers, which attire became her so gallantly as she seemed to be the goddess Flora herself for beauty.

Fortune, who all this while had showed a friendly face, began now to turn her back and to show a louring countenance, intending as she had given Fawnia a slender check, so she would give her a harder mate, to bring which to pass she laid her train on this wise. Egistus had but one only son, called Dorastus, about the age of twenty years; a prince so decked and adorned with the gifts of nature, so fraught with beauty and virtuous qualities, as not only his father joyed to have so good a son, but* all his commons rejoiced that God had lent them such a noble prince to succeed in the kingdom.

Egistus, placing all his joy in the perfection of his son, seeing that he was now marriageable, sent ambassadors to the King of Denmark, to entreat a marriage between him and his daughter, who, willingly consenting, made answer that the next spring, if it please Egistus with his son to come into Denmark, he doubted not but they should agree upon reasonable conditions. Egistus, resting satisfied with this friendly answer, thought convenient in the meantime to break with* his son. Finding therefore on a day fit opportunity, he spake to him in these fatherly terms.

'Dorastus, thy youth warneth me to prevent the worst, and mine age to provide the best. Opportunities neglected are signs of folly. Actions measured by time are seldom bitten with repentance. Thou art young and I old; age hath taught me that which thy youth cannot yet conceive.

'I therefore will counsel thee as a father, hoping thou wilt obey as a child. Thou seest my white hairs are blossoms for the grave, and thy fresh colour fruit for time and fortune, so that it behoveth me to think how to die, and for thee to care how to live. My crown I must leave by death, and thou enjoy my kingdom by succession, wherein I hope thy virtue and prowess shall be such as, though my subjects want my person, yet they shall see in thee my perfection. That nothing either may fail to satisfy thy mind or increase thy dignities, the only care I have is to see thee well married before I die, and thou become old.'

Dorastus, who from his infancy delighted rather to die with Mars in the field than to dally with Venus in the chamber, fearing to displease his father, and yet not willing to be wed, made him this reverent answer.

'Sir, there is no greater bond than duty, nor no straiter law than nature. Disobedience in youth is often galled with despite in age. The command of the father ought to be a constraint to the child; so parents' wills are laws, so they pass not all laws. May it please your grace, therefore, to appoint whom I shall love, rather than by denial I should be appeached of disobedience. I rest content to love, though it be the only thing I hate.'

Egistus, hearing his son to fly far from the mark, began to be somewhat choleric, and therefore made him this hasty answer.

'What Dorastus, canst thou not love? Cometh this cynical passion of prone desires or peevish frowardness? What, dost thou think thyself too good for all, or none good enough for thee? I tell thee, Dorastus, there is nothing sweeter than youth, nor swifter decreasing while it is increasing. Time passed with folly may be repented, but not recalled. If thou marry in age, thy wife's fresh colours will breed in thee dead thoughts and suspicion, and thy white hairs her loathsomeness and sorrow. For Venus' affections are not fed with kingdoms or treasures, but with youthful conceits and sweet amours. Vulcan was allotted to shake the tree, but Mars allowed to reap the fruit. Yield, Dorastus, to thy father's persuasions, which may prevent thy perils. I have chosen thee a wife fair by nature, royal by birth, by virtues famous, learned by education, and rich by possessions, so that it is hard to judge whether her bounty or fortune, her beauty or virtue, be of greater force. I mean, Dorastus, Euphania, daughter and heir to the king of Denmark.'

Egistus, pausing here a while, looking when his son should make him answer, and seeing that he stood still as one in a trance, he shook him up thus sharply.

'Well Dorastus, take heed. The tree alpya wasteth not with fire but withereth with the dew. That which love nourisheth not, perisheth with hate. If thou like Euphania thou breedest my content, and in loving her thou shalt have my love, otherwise—' And with that he flung from his son in a rage, leaving him a sorrowful man, in that he had by denial displeased his father, and half-angry with himself that he could not yield to that passion whereto both reason and his father persuaded him. But see how fortune is plumed with time's feathers, and how she can minister strange causes to breed strange effects.

It happened not long after this that there was a meeting of all the farmers' daughters in Sicilia, whither Fawnia was also bidden as the mistress of the feast, who having attired herself in her best garments, went among the rest of her companions to the merry meeting, there spending the day in such homely pastimes as shepherds use. As the evening grew on and their sports ceased, each taking their leave at* other, Fawnia, desiring one of her companions to bear her company, went home by the flock to see if they were well folded, and as they returned it fortuned that Dorastus (who all that day had been hawking and killed store of game) encountered by the way these two maids, and casting his eye suddenly on Fawnia he was half afraid, fearing that with Actaeon* he had seen Diana, for he thought such exquisite perfection could not be found in any mortal creature. As thus he stood in a maze, one of his pages told him that the maid with the garland on her head was Fawnia, the fair shepherd, whose beauty was so much talked of in the court.

Dorastus, desirous to see if nature had adorned her mind with any inward qualities as she had decked her body with outward shape, began to question with her whose daughter she was, of what age, and how she had been trained up, who answered him with such modest reverence and sharpness of wit that Dorastus thought her outward beauty was but a counterfeit to darken her inward qualities, wondering how so courtly behaviour could be found in so simple a cottage, and cursing fortune that had shadowed wit and beauty with such hard fortune.

As thus he held her a long while with chat, Beauty seeing him at discovert, thought not to lose the vantage, but struck him so deeply with an envenomed shaft as he wholly lost his liberty and became a slave to love, which before contemned love, glad now to gaze on a poor shepherd who before refused the offer of a rich princess. For the perfection of Fawnia had so fixed his fancy as he felt his mind greatly changed and his affections altered, cursing love that had wrought such a change, and blaming the baseness of his mind that would make such a choice. But thinking these were but passionate toys that might be thrust out at pleasure, to avoid the siren that enchanted him he put spurs to his horse and bade this fair shepherd farewell.

Fawnia, who all this while had marked the princely gesture of Dorastus, seeing his face so well featured and each limb so perfectly framed, began greatly to praise his perfection, commending him so long till she found herself faulty, and perceived that if she waded but a little further she might slip over her shoes. She therefore, seeking to quench that fire which never was put out, went home and, feigning herself not well at ease, got her to bed, where, casting a thousand thoughts in her head, she could take no rest. For, if she waked, she began to call to mind his beauty and, thinking to beguile such thoughts with sleep, she then dreamed of his perfection. Pestered thus with these unacquainted passions, she passed the night as she could in short slumbers.

Dorastus, who all this while rode with a flea in his ear,* could not by any means forget the sweet favour of Fawnia, but rested so bewitched with her wit and beauty as he could take no rest. He felt fancy to give the assault, and his wounded mind ready to yield as vanquished. Yet he began with diverse considerations to suppress this frantic affection, calling to mind that Fawnia was a shepherd, one not worthy to be looked at of a prince, much less to be loved of such a potentate, thinking what a discredit it were to himself, and what a grief it would be to his father, blaming fortune and accusing his own folly that should be so fond as but once to cast a glance at such a country slut.

As thus he was raging against himself, love, fearing if she dallied long to lose her champion, stepped more nigh and gave him such a fresh wound as it pierced him at the heart, that he was fain to yield maugre his face,* and to forsake the company and get him to his chamber. Where, being solemnly set, he burst into these passionate terms.

'Ah Dorastus, art thou alone? No, not alone while thou art tired with these unacquainted passions. Yield to fancy thou canst not by thy father's counsel, but in a frenzy thou art by just destinies. Thy father were content if thou couldst love, and thou therefore discontent because thou dost love. O divine love, feared of men because honoured of the gods, not to be suppressed by wisdom because not to be comprehended by reason. Without law, and therefore above all law.

'How now Dorastus, why dost thou blaze that with praises which thou hast cause to blaspheme with curses? Yet why should they curse love that are in love? Blush, Dorastus, at thy fortune, thy choice, thy love. Thy thoughts cannot be uttered without shame, nor thy affections without discredit. Ah Fawnia, sweet Fawnia, thy beauty, Fawnia! Shamest not thou, Dorastus, to name one unfit for thy birth, thy dignities, thy kingdoms? Die Dorastus, Dorastus die! Better hadst thou perish with high desires than live in base thoughts. Yea, but beauty must be obeyed, because it is beauty, yet framed of the gods to feed the eye, not to fetter the heart.

'Ah, but he that striveth against love shooteth with them of Scyrum against the wind, and with the cockatrice pecketh against the steel. I will therefore obey, because I must obey. Fawnia, yea Fawnia shall be my fortune in spite of fortune. The gods above disdain not to love women beneath. Phoebus liked Sibylla,* Jupiter Io, and why not I then Fawnia, one something inferior to these in birth but far superior to them in beauty, born to be a shepherd but worthy to be a goddess?

'Ah Dorastus, wilt thou so forget thyself as to suffer affection to suppress wisdom, and love to violate thine honour? How sour will thy choice be to thy father, sorrowful to thy subjects, to thy friends a grief, most gladsome to thy foes! Subdue, then, thy affections, and cease to love her whom thou couldst not love unless blinded with too much love. Tush, I talk to the wind, and in seeking to prevent the causes I further the effects. I will yet praise Fawnia, honour, yea and love Fawnia, and at this day follow content, not counsel. Do Dorastus, thou canst but repent—'

And with that, his page came into the chamber, whereupon he ceased from his complaints, hoping that time would wear out that which fortune had wrought. As thus he was pained, so poor Fawnia was diversely perplexed. For the next morning, getting up very early, she went to her sheep, thinking with hard labours to pass away her new conceived amours. Beginning very busily to drive them to the field, and then to shift the folds, at last, wearied with toil, she sate her down where (poor soul) she was more tried with fond affections. For love began to assault her, insomuch that, as she sate upon the side of a hill, she began to accuse her own folly in these terms.

'Infortunate Fawnia, and therefore infortunate because Fawnia, thy shepherd's hook showeth thy poor state, thy proud desires an aspiring mind; the one declareth thy want, the other thy pride. No bastard hawk must soar so high as the hobby, no fowl gaze against the sun but the eagle, actions wrought against nature reap despite and thoughts above fortune, disdain.

'Fawnia, thou art a shepherd, daughter to poor Porrus. If thou rest content with this, thou art like to stand, if thou climb thou art sure to fall. The herb anita, growing higher than six inches, becometh a weed. Nilus, flowing more than twelve cubits, procureth a dearth. Daring affections that pass measure are cut short by time or fortune. Suppress then, Fawnia, those thoughts which thou mayest shame to express. But ah Fawnia, love is a lord who will command by power and constrain by force!

'Dorastus, ah Dorastus is the man I love, the worse is thy hap, and the less cause hast thou to hope. Will eagles catch at flies, will cedars stoop to brambles, or mighty princes look at such homely trulls? No, no, think this: Dorastus' disdain is greater than thy desire. He is a prince respecting his honour, thou a beggar's brat forgetting thy calling. Cease then not only to say but to think to love Dorastus, and dissemble thy love, Fawnia, for better it were to die with grief than to live with shame. Yet in despite of love I will sigh to see if I can sigh out love.'

Fawnia, somewhat appeasing her griefs with these pithy persuasions, began after her wonted manner to walk about her sheep, and to keep them from straying into the corn, suppressing her affection with the due consideration of her base estate, and with the impossibilities of her love, thinking it were frenzy, not fancy, to covet that which the very destinies did deny her to obtain.

But Dorastus was more impatient in his passions, for love so fiercely assailed him that neither company nor music could mitigate his martyrdom, but did rather far the more increase his malady. Shame would not let him crave counsel in this case, nor fear of his father's displeasure reveal it to any secret friend; but he was fain to make a secretary of himself and to participate his thoughts with his own troubled mind. Lingering thus awhile in doubtful suspense, at last stealing secretly from the court without either men or page, he went to see if he could espy Fawnia walking abroad in the field. But as one having a great deal more skill to retrieve the partridge with his spaniels than to hunt after such a strange prey, he sought but was little the better; which cross luck drave him into a great choler, that he began both to accuse love and fortune. But as he was ready to retire, he saw Fawnia sitting all alone under the side of a hill, making a garland of such homely flowers as the fields did afford.

This sight so revived his spirits that he drew nigh with more judgement to take a view of her singular perfection, which he found to be such as in that country attire she stained all the courtly dames of Sicilia. While thus he stood gazing with piercing looks on her surpassing beauty, Fawnia cast her eye aside and spied Dorastus, which* sudden sight made the poor girl to blush and to dye her crystal cheeks with a vermilion red, which gave her such a grace as she seemed far more beautiful. And with that she rose up, saluting the prince with such modest courtesies as he wondered how a country maid could afford such courtly behaviour. Dorastus, repaying her courtesy with a smiling countenance, began to parley with her on this manner.

'Fair maid,' quoth he, 'either your want is great, or a shepherd's life very sweet, that your delight is in such country labours. I cannot conceive what pleasure you should take, unless you mean to imitate the nymphs, being yourself so like a nymph. To put me out of this doubt, show me what is to be commended in a shepherd's life, and what pleasures you have to countervail these drudging labours.'

Fawnia, with blushing face, made him this ready answer. 'Sir, what richer state than content, or what sweeter life than quiet? We shepherds are not born to honour, nor beholding unto beauty, the less care we have to fear fame or fortune. We count our attire brave enough if warm enough, and our food dainty if to suffice nature. Our greatest enemy is the wolf; our only care in safekeeping our flock. Instead of courtly ditties we spend the days with country songs. Our amorous conceits are homely thoughts; delighting as much to talk of Pan and his country pranks as ladies to tell of Venus and her wanton toys. Our toil is in shifting the folds and looking to the lambs: easy labours; oft singing and telling tales: homely pleasures. Our greatest wealth not to covet, our honour not to climb, our quiet not to care. Envy looketh not so low as shepherds; shepherds gaze not so high as ambition; we are rich in that we are poor with content, and proud only in this: that we have no cause to be proud.'

This witty answer of Fawnia so inflamed Dorastus' fancy as he commended himself for making so good a choice, thinking if her birth were answerable to her wit and beauty that she were a fit mate for the most famous prince in the world. He therefore began to sift her more narrowly on this manner.

'Fawnia, I see thou art content with country labours because thou knowest not courtly pleasures. I commend thy wit and pity thy want. But wilt thou leave thy father's cottage and serve a courtly mistress?' 'Sir,' quoth she, 'beggars ought not to strive against fortune, nor to gaze after honour, lest either their fall be greater or they become blind. I am born to toil for the court, not in the court, my nature unfit for their nurture. Better live, then, in mean degree than in high disdain.'

'Well said Fawnia,' quoth Dorastus, 'I guess at thy thoughts. Thou art in love with some country shepherd.' 'No sir,' quoth she, 'shepherds cannot love, that are so simple, and maids may not love that are so young.' 'Nay therefore', quoth Dorastus, 'maids must love because they are young, for Cupid is a child, and Venus, though old, is painted with fresh colours.' 'I grant,' quoth she, 'age may be painted with new shadows, and youth may have imperfect affections, but what art concealeth in one, ignorance revealeth in the other.'

Dorastus, seeing Fawnia held him so hard, thought it was vain so long to beat about the bush. Therefore he thought to have given her a fresh charge, but he was so prevented by certain of his men who, missing their master, came posting to seek him, seeing that he was gone forth all alone. Yet before they drew so nigh that they might hear their talk, he used these speeches.

'Why Fawnia, perhaps I love thee, and then thou must needs yield, for thou knowest I can command and constrain.' 'Truth sir,' quoth she, 'but not to love, for constrained love is force, not love; and know this sir, mine honesty is such as I had rather die than be a concubine, even to a king, and my birth is so base as I am unfit to be a wife to a poor farmer.' 'Why then,' quoth he, 'thou canst not love Dorastus?' 'Yes,' said Fawnia, 'when Dorastus becomes a shepherd,' and with that the presence of his men broke off their parley, so that he went with them to the palace and left Fawnia sitting still on the hillside who, seeing that the night drew on, shifted her folds and busied herself about other work to drive away such fond fancies as began to trouble her brain.

But all this could not prevail, for the beauty of Dorastus had made such a deep impression in her heart as it could not be worn out without cracking, so that she was forced to blame her own folly in this wise.

'Ah Fawnia, why dost thou gaze against the sun, or catch at the wind. Stars are to be looked at with the eye not reached at with the hand. Thoughts are to be measured by fortunes, not by desires. Falls come not by sitting low but by climbing too high; what then, shall all fear to fall because some hap to fall? No—luck cometh by lot, and fortune windeth those threads which the destinies spin. Thou art favoured, Fawnia, of a prince, and yet thou art so fond to reject desired favours. Thou hast denial at thy tongue's end, and desire at thy heart's bottom. A woman's fault, to spurn at that with her foot which she greedily catcheth at with her hand. Thou lovest Dorastus, Fawnia, and yet seemest to lour. Take heed, if he retire thou wilt repent, for unless he love thou canst but die. Die then Fawnia, for Dorastus doth but jest. The lion never preyeth on the mouse, nor falcons stoop not to dead stales. Sit down then in sorrow, cease to love, and content thyself that Dorastus will vouchsafe to flatter Fawnia though not to fancy Fawnia. Heigh ho! Ah fool, it were seemlier for thee to whistle as a shepherd than to sigh as a lover,' and with that she ceased from these perplexed passions, folding her sheep and hieing home to her poor cottage.

But such was the incessant sorrow of Dorastus to think on

the wit and beauty of Fawnia, and to see how fond he was, being a prince, and how froward she was, being a beggar, that* he began to lose his wonted appetite, to look pale and wan, instead of mirth to feed on melancholy, for courtly dances to use cold dumps, insomuch that not only his own men but his father and all the court began to marvel at his sudden change, thinking that some lingering sickness had wrought him into this state. Wherefore he caused physicians to come, but Dorastus neither would let them minister nor so much as suffer them to see his urine, but remained still so oppressed with these passions as he feared in himself a farther inconvenience.

His honour wished him to cease from such folly, but love forced him to follow fancy; yea, and in despite of honour, love won the conquest, so that his hot desires caused him to find new devices, for he presently made himself a shepherd's coat, that he might go unknown, and with the less suspicion to prattle with Fawnia, and conveyed it secretly into a thick grove hard joining to the palace. Whither, finding fit time and opportunity, he went all alone and, putting off his princely apparel, got on those shepherd's robes and, taking a great hook in his hand (which he had also gotten), he went very anciently to find out the mistress of his affection. But as he went by the way, seeing himself clad in such unseemly rags, he began to smile at his own folly, and to reprove his fondness in these terms.

'Well,' said Dorastus, 'thou keepest a right decorum: base desires and homely attires. Thy thoughts are fit for none but a shepherd, and thy apparel such as only become a shepherd. A strange change from a prince to a peasant! What is it? Thy wretched fortune or thy wilful folly? Is it thy cursed destinies or thy crooked desires that appointeth thee this penance? Ah Dorastus, thou canst but love, and unless thou love, thou art like to perish for love. Yet, fond fool, choose flowers, not weeds; diamonds, not pebbles; ladies which may honour thee, not shepherds which may disgrace thee. Venus is painted in silks not in rags, and Cupid treadeth on disdain when he reacheth at dignity. And yet Dorastus, shame not at thy shepherd's weed. The heavenly gods have sometime earthly thoughts. Neptune became a ram, Jupiter a bull, Apollo a shepherd. They gods, and yet in love, and thou a man appointed to love.'

Devising thus with himself, he drew nigh to the place where Fawnia was keeping her sheep who, casting her eye aside, and seeing such a mannerly shepherd, perfectly limbed and coming with so good a pace, she began half to forget Dorastus and to favour this pretty shepherd, whom she thought she might both love and obtain. But as she was in these thoughts, she perceived then it was the young prince Dorastus, wherefore she rose up and reverently saluted him. Dorastus, taking her by the hand, repaid her courtesy with a sweet kiss and, praying her to sit down by him, he began thus to lay the battery.

'If thou marvel, Fawnia, at my strange attire, thou wouldst more muse at my unaccustomed thoughts. The one disgraceth but my outward shape, the other disturbeth my inward senses. I love Fawnia, and therefore what love liketh I cannot mislike. Fawnia, thou hast promised to love, and I hope thou wilt perform no less. I have fulfilled thy request, and now thou canst but grant my desire. Thou wert content to love Dorastus when he ceased to be a prince and to become* a shepherd; and see—I have made the change, and therefore not* to miss of my choice.'

'Truth,' quoth Fawnia, 'but all that wear cools are not monks. Painted eagles are pictures, not eagles; Zeuxis' grapes were like grapes, yet shadows; rich clothing make not princes, nor homely attire beggars. Shepherds are not called shepherds because they wear hooks and bags but that they are born poor and live to keep sheep. So this attire hath not made Dorastus a shepherd, but to seem like a shepherd.'

'Well Fawnia,' answered Dorastus, 'were I a shepherd I could not but like thee, and being a prince I am forced to love thee. Take heed Fawnia, be not proud of beauty's painting, for it is a flower that fadeth in the blossom. Those which disdain in youth are despised in age. Beauty's shadows are tricked up with time's colours which, being set to dry in the sun, are stained with the sun, scarce pleasing the sight ere they begin not to be worth the sight, not much unlike the herb ephemeron, which flourisheth in the morning and is withered before the sun setting. If my desire were against law thou mightest justly deny me by reason, but I love thee Fawnia, not to misuse thee as a concubine, but to use thee as my wife. I can promise no more, and mean to perform no less.'

Fawnia, hearing this solemn protestation of Dorastus, could no longer withstand the assault, but yielded up the fort in these friendly terms.

'Ah Dorastus, I shame to express that thou forcest me with thy sugared speech to confess; my base birth causeth the one and thy high dignities the other. Beggars' thoughts ought not to reach so far as kings, and yet my desires reach as high as princes. I dare not say, Dorastus, I love thee, because I am a shepherd. But the gods know I have honoured Dorastus (pardon if I say amiss), yea, and loved Dorastus with such dutiful affection as Fawnia can perform or Dorastus desire. I yield, not overcome with prayers but with love, resting Dorastus' handmaid, ready to obey his will, if no prejudice at all to his honour nor to my credit.'

Dorastus, hearing this friendly conclusion of Fawnia, embraced her in his arms, swearing that neither distance, time, nor adverse fortune should diminish his affection, but that in despite of the destinies he would remain loyal unto death. Having thus plight their troth each to other, seeing they could not have the full fruition of their love in Sicilia, for that Egistus' consent would never be granted to so mean a match, Dorastus determined, as soon as time and opportunity would give them leave, to provide a great mass of money and many rich and costly jewels for the easier carriage and then to transport themselves and their treasure into Italy, where they should lead a contented life until such time as either he could be reconciled to his father, or else by succession come to the kingdom.

This device was greatly praised of Fawnia, for she feared if the King his father should but hear of the contract that his fury would be such as no less than death would stand for payment. She therefore told him that delay bred danger, that many mishaps did fall out between the cup and the lip, and that to avoid danger it were best with as much speed as might be to pass out of Sicilia, lest fortune might prevent their pretence with some new despite.

Dorastus, whom love pricked forward with desire, promised to dispatch his affairs with as great haste as either time or opportunity would give him leave, and so, resting upon this point, after many embracings and sweet kisses, they departed. Dorastus, having taken his leave of his best-loved Fawnia, went to the grove where he had his rich apparel and there, uncasing himself as secretly as might be, hiding up his shepherd's attire till occasion should serve again to use it, he went to the palace, showing by his merry countenance that either the state of his body was amended or the case of his mind greatly redressed.

Fawnia, poor soul, was no less joyful that, being a shepherd, fortune had favoured her so as to reward her with the love of a prince, hoping in time to be advanced from the daughter of a poor farmer to be the wife of a rich king; so that she thought every hour a year till by their departure they might prevent danger, not ceasing still to go every day to her sheep, not so much for the care of her flock as for the desire she had to see her love and lord Dorastus. Who oftentimes, when opportunity would serve, repaired thither to feed his fancy with the sweet content of Fawnia's presence. And although he never went to visit her but in his shepherd's rags, yet his oft repair made him not only suspected but known to diverse of their neighbours, who for the good will they bare to old Porrus told him secretly of the matter, wishing him to keep his daughter at home lest she went so oft to the field that she brought him home a young son. For they feared that Fawnia being so beautiful, the young prince would allure her to folly. Porrus was stricken into a dump at these news,* so that, thanking his neighbours for their good will, he hied him home to his wife and, calling her aside, wringing his hands and shedding forth tears, he brake the matter to her in these terms.

'I am afraid, wife, that my daughter Fawnia hath made herself so fine that she will buy repentance too dear. I hear news which, if they be true, some will wish they had not proved true. It is told me by my neighbours that Dorastus, the King's son, begins to look at our daughter Fawnia. Which, if it be so, I will not give her a halfpenny for her honesty at the year's end. I tell thee wife, nowadays beauty is a great stale to trap young men, and fair words and sweet promises are two great enemies to a maiden's honesty. And thou knowest where poor men entreat and cannot obtain, there princes may command and will obtain. Though kings' sons dance in nets, they may not be seen, but poor men's faults are spied at a little hole. Well, it is a hard case where kings' lusts are laws, and that they should bind poor men to that which they themselves wilfully break.'

'Peace husband,' quoth his wife, 'take heed what you say. Speak no more than you should, lest you hear what you would not. Great streams are to be stopped by sleight, not by force, and princes to be persuaded by submission, not by rigour. Do what you can, but no more than you may, lest in saving Fawnia's maidenhead you lose your own head. Take heed, I say, it is ill jesting with edged tools,* and bad sporting with kings. The wolf had his skin pulled over his ears for but looking into the lion's den.'

'Tush wife,' quoth he, 'thou speakest like a fool. If the King should know that Dorastus had begotten our daughter with child (as I fear it will fall out little better) the King's fury would be such as no doubt we should both lose our goods and lives. Necessity therefore hath no law, and I will prevent this mischief with a new device that is come in my head, which shall neither offend the King nor displease Dorastus. I mean to take the chain and the jewels that I found with Fawnia, and carry them to the King, letting him then to understand how she is none of my daughter, but that I found her beaten up with the water alone in a little boat wrapped in a rich mantle wherein was enclosed this treasure. By this means I hope the King will take Fawnia into his service and we, whatsoever chanceth, shall be blameless.'

This device pleased the goodwife very well, so that they determined as soon as they might know the King at leisure to make him privy to this case. In the meantime Dorastus was not slack in his affairs, but applied his matters with such diligence that he provided all things fit for their journey. Treasure and jewels he had gotten great store, thinking there was no better friend than money in a strange country. Rich attire he had provided for Fawnia, and because he could not bring the matter to pass without the help and advice of someone, he made an old servant of his called Capnio, who had served him from his childhood, privy to his affairs; who, seeing no persuasions could prevail to divert him from his settled determination, gave his consent and dealt so secretly in the cause that within short space he had gotten a ship ready for their passage.

The mariners, seeing a fit gale of wind for their purpose, wished Capnio to make no delays, lest if they pretermitted this good weather they might stay long ere they had such a fair wind. Capnio, fearing that his negligence should hinder the journey, in the night time conveyed the trunks full of treasure into the ship, and by secret means let Fawnia understand that the next morning they meant to depart. She, upon this news, slept very little that night, but got up very early and went to her sheep, looking every minute when she should see Dorastus, who tarried not long for fear delay might breed danger, but came as fast as he could gallop and, without any great circumstance, took Fawnia up behind him and rode to the haven where the ship lay, which was not three quarters of a mile distant from that place.

He no sooner came there but the mariners were ready with their cockboat to set them aboard where, being couched together in a cabin, they passed away the time in recounting their old loves till their man Capnio should come. Porrus, who had heard that this morning the King would go abroad to take the air, called in haste to his wife to bring him his holiday hose and his best jacket, that he might go like an honest, substantial man to tell his tale. His wife, a good cleanly wench, brought him all things fit, and sponged him up very handsomely, giving him the chain and the jewels in a little box, which Porrus for the more safety put in his bosom.

Having thus all his trinkets in a readiness, taking his staff in his hand, he bade his wife kiss him for good luck, and so he went towards the palace. But as he was going, fortune (who meant to show him a little false play) prevented his purpose in this wise. He met by chance in his way Capnio who, trudging as fast as he could with a little coffer under his arm to the ship, and spying Porrus, whom he knew to be Fawnia's father, going towards the palace, being a wily fellow began to doubt the worst and therefore crossed him the way and asked him whither he was going so early this morning.

Porrus, who knew by his face that he was one of the court, meaning simply,* told him that the King's son Dorastus dealt hardly with him, for he had but one daughter who was a little beautiful, and that his neighbours told him the young prince had allured her to folly. He went, therefore, now to complain to the King how greatly he was abused.

Capnio, who straightway smelt the whole matter, began to soothe him in his talk, and said that Dorastus dealt not like a prince to spoil any poor man's daughter in that sort. He therefore would do the best for him he could because he knew he was an honest man. 'But', quoth Capnio, 'you lose your labour in going to the palace, for the King means this day to take the air of the sea and to go abroad of a ship that lies in the haven. I am going before, you see, to provide all things in a readiness, and if you will follow my counsel, turn back with me to the haven, where I will set you in such a fit place as you may speak to the King at your pleasure.'

Porrus, giving credit to Capnio's smooth tale, gave him a thousand thanks for his friendly advice and went with him to the haven, making all the way his complaints of Dorastus, yet concealing secretly the chain and the jewels. As soon as they were come to the seaside, the mariners, seeing Capnio, came aland with their cockboat, who, still dissembling the matter, demanded of Porrus if he would go see the ship; who, unwilling and fearing the worst because he was not well acquainted with Capnio, made his excuse that he could not brook the sea, therefore would not trouble him.

Capnio, seeing that by fair means he could not get him aboard, commanded the mariners that by violence they should carry him into the ship, who like sturdy knaves hoisted the poor shepherd on their backs and, bearing him to the boat, launched from the land. Porrus, seeing himself so cunningly betrayed, durst not cry out, for he saw it would not prevail, but began to entreat Capnio and the mariners to be good to him and to pity his estate; he was but a poor man that lived by his labour. They, laughing to see the shepherd so afraid, made as much haste as they could and set him aboard.

Porrus was no sooner in the ship but he saw Dorastus walking with Fawnia, yet he scarce knew her, for she had attired herself in rich apparel which so increased her beauty that she resembled rather an angel than a mortal creature. Dorastus and Fawnia were half astonished to see the old shepherd, marvelling greatly what wind had brought him thither till Capnio told them all the whole discourse: how Porrus was going to make his complaint to the King if by policy he had not prevented him, and therefore now sith he was aboard, for the avoiding of further danger, it were best to carry him into Italy. Dorastus praised greatly his man's device and allowed of his counsel, but Fawnia (who still feared Porrus as her father) began to blush for shame that by her means he should either incur danger or displeasure.

The old shepherd, hearing this hard sentence that he should on such a sudden be carried from his wife, his country and kinsfolk into a foreign land amongst strangers, began with bitter tears to make his complaint, and on his knees to entreat Dorastus that, pardoning his unadvised folly, he would give him leave to go home, swearing that he would keep all things as secret as they could wish. But these protestations could not prevail, although Fawnia entreated Dorastus very earnestly. But the mariners hoisting their main sails weighed anchors and haled into the deep, where we leave them to the favour of the wind and seas and return to Egistus.

Who, having appointed this day to hunt in one of his forests, called for his son Dorastus to go sport himself, because he saw that of late he began to lour. But his men made answer that he was gone abroad none knew whither, except he were gone to the grove to walk all alone as his custom was to do every day. The King, willing to waken him out of his dumps, sent one of his men to go seek him, but in vain, for at last he returned but find him he could not, so that the King went himself to go see the sport; where, passing away the day, returning at night from hunting he asked for his son, but he could not be heard of, which drave the King into a great choler.

Whereupon most of his noblemen and other courtiers posted abroad to seek him, but they could not hear of him through all Sicilia; only they missed Capnio his man, which again made the King suspect that he was not gone far.

Two or three days being passed and no news heard of Dorastus, Egistus began to fear that he was devoured with some wild beasts, and upon that made out a great troup of men to go seek him, who coasted through all the country and searched in every dangerous and secret place until at last they met with a fisherman that was sitting in a little covert hard by the seaside mending his nets when Dorastus and Fawnia took shipping; who, being examined if he either knew or heard where the King's son was, without any secrecy at all revealed the whole matter, how he was sailed two days past and had in his company his man Capnio, Porrus, and his fair daughter Fawnia.

This heavy news was presently carried to the King who, half dead for sorrow, commanded Porrus' wife to be sent for. She being come to the palace, after due examination confessed that her neighbours had oft told her that the King's son was too familiar with Fawnia her daughter, whereupon her husband, fearing the worst, about two days past (hearing the King should go an hunting) rose early in the morning and went to make his complaint, but since she neither heard of him nor saw him.

Egistus, perceiving the woman's unfeigned simplicity, let her depart without incurring further displeasure, concealing such secret grief for his son's reckless folly that he had so forgotten his honour and parentage by so base a choice to dishonour his father and discredit himself, that with very care and thought he fell into a quartan fever, which was so unfit for his aged years and complexion that he became so weak as the physicians would grant him no life.

But his son Dorastus little regarded either father, country or kingdom in respect of his lady Fawnia, for fortune, smiling on this young novice, lent him so lucky a gale of wind for the space of a day and a night that the mariners lay and slept upon the hatches. But on the next morning, about the break of the day, the air began to overcast, the winds to rise, the seas to swell—yea presently there arose such a fearful tempest as the ship was in danger to be swallowed up with every sea. The main mast with the violence of the wind was thrown overboard, the sails were torn, the tackling went in sunder, the storm raging still so furiously that poor Fawnia was almost dead for fear but that she was greatly comforted with the presence of Dorastus. The tempest continued three days, all which time the mariners every minute looked for death, and the air was so darkened with clouds that the master could not tell by his compass in what coast they were. But upon the fourth day, about ten of the clock, the wind began to cease, the sea to wax calm, and the sky to be clear, and the mariners descried the coast of Bohemia, shooting off their ordnance for joy that they had escaped such a fearful tempest.

Dorastus, hearing that they were arrived at some harbour, sweetly kissed Fawnia and bade her be of good cheer. When they told him that the port belonged unto the chief city of Bohemia, where Pandosto kept his court, Dorastus began to be sad, knowing that his father hated no man so much as Pandosto, and that the King himself had sought secretly to betray Egistus. This considered, he was half afraid to go on land, but that Capnio counselled him to change his name and his country until such time as they could get some other bark to transport them into Italy. Dorastus, liking this device, made his case privy to the mariners, rewarding them bountifully for their pains, and charging them to say that he was a gentleman of Trapalonia* called Meleagrus.

The shipmen, willing to show what friendship they could to Dorastus, promised to be as secret as they could or he might wish, and upon this they landed in a little village a mile distant from the city where, after they had rested a day, thinking to make provision for their marriage, the fame of Fawnia's beauty was spread throughout all the city so that it came to the ears of Pandosto, who then being about the age of fifty had, notwithstanding, young and fresh affections so that he desired greatly to see Fawnia. And to bring this matter the better to pass, hearing they had but one man, and how they rested at a very homely house, he caused them to be apprehended as spies, and sent a dozen of his guard to take them who, being

come to their lodging, told them the King's message.
Dorastus, no whit dismayed, accompanied with Fawnia and
Capnio went to the court (for they left Porrus to keep the
stuff)* who, being admitted to the King's presence, Dorastus
and Fawnia with humble obeisance saluted his Majesty.

Pandosto, amazed at the singular perfection of Fawnia,
stood half astonished viewing her beauty, so that he had
almost forgot himself what he had to do. At last, with stern
countenance, he demanded their names and of what country
they were and what caused them to land in Bohemia. 'Sir,'
quoth Dorastus, 'know that my name Meleagrus is, a knight
born and brought up in Trapalonia, and this gentlewoman,
whom I mean to take to my wife, is an Italian born in Padua,
from whence I have now brought her. The cause I have so
small a train with me is for that, her friends unwilling to
consent, I intended secretly to convey her into Trapalonia,
whither as I was sailing by distress of weather I was driven
into these coasts. Thus have you heard my name, my country,
and the cause of my voyage.'

Pandosto, starting from his seat as one in choler, made this
rough reply. 'Meleagrus, I fear this smooth tale hath but small
truth, and that thou coverest a foul skin with fair paintings.
No doubt this lady by her grace and beauty is of her degree
more meet for a mighty prince than for a simple knight, and
thou, like a perjured traitor, hast bereft her of her parents to
their present grief and her ensuing sorrow. Till, therefore, I
hear more of her parentage and of thy calling I will stay you
both here in Bohemia.'

Dorastus, in whom rested nothing but kingly valour, was
not able to suffer the reproaches of Pandosto but that he made
him this answer. 'It is not meet for a king without due proof
to appeach any man of ill behaviour, nor upon suspicion to
infer belief. Strangers ought to be entertained with courtesy,
not to be entreated with cruelty, lest being forced by want to
put up injuries the gods revenge their cause with rigour.'

Pandosto, hearing Dorastus utter these words, commanded
that he should straight be committed to prison until such time
as they heard further of his pleasure. But as for Fawnia, he
charged that she should be entertained in the court with such

courtesy as belonged to a stranger and her calling. The rest of the shipmen he put into the dungeon.

Having thus hardly handled the supposed Trapalonians, Pandosto, contrary to his aged years, began to be somewhat tickled with the beauty of Fawnia, insomuch that he could take no rest, but cast in his old head a thousand new devices. At last he fell into these thoughts. 'How art thou pestered, Pandosto, with fresh affections and unfit fancies, wishing to possess with an unwilling mind and a hot desire troubled with a cold disdain! Shall thy mind yield in age to that thou hast resisted in youth? Peace Pandosto, blab not out that which thou mayest be ashamed to reveal to thyself. Ah, Fawnia is beautiful, and it is not for thine honour (fond fool) to name her that is thy captive and another man's concubine. Alas, I reach at that with my hand which my heart would fain refuse, playing like the bird Ibis in Egypt, which hateth serpents yet feedeth on their eggs.

'Tush, hot desires turn oftentimes to cold disdain. Love is brittle where appetite, not reason, bears the sway. Kings' thoughts ought not to climb so high as the heavens, but to look no lower than honour. Better it is to peck at the stars with the young eagles than to prey on dead carcasses with the vulture. 'Tis more honourable for Pandosto to die by concealing love than to enjoy such unfit love. Doth Pandosto then love? Yea. Whom? A maid unknown, yea and perhaps immodest, straggled out of her own country. Beautiful but not therefore chaste; comely in body but perhaps crooked in mind. Cease then, Pandosto, to look at Fawnia, much less to love her. Be not overtaken with a woman's beauty, whose eyes are framed by art to enamour, whose heart is framed by nature to enchant, whose false tears know their true times, and whose sweet words pierce deeper than sharp swords.'

Here Pandosto ceased from his talk but not from his love; for although he sought by reason and wisdom to suppress this frantic affection yet he could take no rest, the beauty of Fawnia had made such a deep impression in his heart. But on a day, walking abroad into a park which was hard adjoining to his house, he sent by one of his servants for Fawnia, unto whom he uttered these words.

'Fawnia, I commend thy beauty and wit and now pity thy distress and want. But if thou wilt forsake Sir Meleagrus, whose poverty, though a knight, is not able to maintain an estate answerable to thy beauty, and yield thy consent to Pandosto, I will both increase thee with dignities and riches.' 'No sir,' answered Fawnia, 'Meleagrus is a knight that hath won me by love, and none but he shall wear me. His sinister mischance shall not diminish my affection, but rather increase my good will. Think not, though your grace hath imprisoned him without cause, that fear shall make me yield my consent. I had rather be Meleagrus' wife and a beggar than live in plenty and be Pandosto's concubine.'

Pandosto, hearing the assured answer of Fawnia, would, notwithstanding, prosecute his suit to the uttermost, seeking with fair words and great promises to scale the fort of her chastity, swearing that if she would grant to his desire, Meleagrus should not only be set at liberty but honoured in his court amongst his nobles. But these alluring baits could not entice her mind from the love of her new-betrothed mate Meleagrus; which Pandosto seeing, he left her alone for that time to consider more of the demand. Fawnia, being alone by herself, began to enter into these solitary meditations.

'Ah, infortunate Fawnia, thou seest to desire above fortune is to strive against the gods and fortune. Who gazeth at the sun weakeneth his sight; they which stare at the sky fall oft into deep pits. Hadst thou rested content to have been a shepherd, thou needest not to have feared mischance. Better had it been for thee, by sitting low, to have had quiet, than by climbing high to have fallen into misery. But alas, I fear not mine own danger, but Dorastus' displeasure. Ah sweet Dorastus, thou art a prince, but now a prisoner, by too much love, procuring thine own loss. Hadst thou not loved Fawnia thou hadst been fortunate. Shall I then be false to him that hath forsaken kingdoms for my cause? No! Would my death might deliver him, so mine honour might be preserved.'

With that, fetching a deep sigh, she ceased from her complaints, and went again to the palace, enjoying a liberty without content, and proffered pleasure with small joy. But poor Dorastus lay all this while in close prison, being pinched with a hard restraint, and pained with the burden of cold and heavy irons, sorrowing sometimes that his fond affection had procured him this mishap, that by the disobedience of his parents he had wrought his own despite; another while cursing the gods and fortune that they should cross him with such sinister chance, uttering at last his passions in these words.

'Ah, unfortunate wretch born to mishap, now thy folly hath his desert. Art thou not worthy for thy base mind to have bad fortune? Could the destinies favour thee, which hast forgot thine honour and dignities? Will not the gods plague him with despite that paineth his father with disobedience? Oh gods, if any favour or justice be left, plague me, but favour poor Fawnia, and shroud her from the tyrannies of wretched Pandosto. But let my death free her from mishap, and then welcome death!'

Dorastus, pained with these heavy passions, sorrowed and sighed, but in vain, for which he used the more patience. But again to Pandosto who, broiling at the heat of unlawful lust, could take no rest but still felt his mind disquieted with his new love, so that his nobles and subjects marvelled greatly at this sudden alteration, not being able to conjecture the cause of this his continued care. Pandosto, thinking every hour a year till he had talked once again with Fawnia, sent for her secretly into his chamber whither, though Fawnia unwillingly coming, Pandosto entertained her very courteously, using these familiar speeches, which Fawnia answered as shortly in this wise.

PANDOSTO

Fawnia, are you become less wilful and more wise, to prefer the love of a king before the liking of a poor knight? I think ere this you think it is better to be favoured of a king than of a subject.

FAWNIA

Pandosto, the body is subject to victories, but the mind not to be subdued by conquest. Honesty is to be preferred before honour, and a dram of faith weigheth down a ton of gold. I have promised Meleagrus to love, and will perform no less.

PANDOSTO

Fawnia, I know thou art not so unwise in thy choice as to refuse the offer of a king, nor so ingrateful as to despise a good turn. Thou art now in that place where I may command, and yet thou seest I entreat. My power is such as I may compel by force, and yet I sue by prayers. Yield, Fawnia, thy love to him which burneth in thy love. Meleagrus shall be set free, thy countrymen discharged and thou both loved and honoured.

FAWNIA

I see, Pandosto, where lust ruleth it is a miserable thing to be a virgin. But know this, that I will always prefer fame before life, and rather choose death than dishonour.

Pandosto, seeing that there was in Fawnia a determinate courage to love Meleagrus, and a resolution without fear to hate him, flung away from her in a rage, swearing if in short time she would not be won with reason he would forget all courtesy and compel her to grant by rigour. But these threatening words no whit dismayed Fawnia, but that she still both despited and despised Pandosto.

While thus these two lovers strove, the one to win love, the other to live in hate, Egistus heard certain news by merchants of Bohemia that his son Dorastus was imprisoned by Pandosto, which made him fear greatly that his son should be but hardly entreated. Yet considering that Bellaria and he was cleared by the oracle of Apollo from that crime wherewith Pandosto had unjustly charged them, he thought best to send with all speed to Pandosto that he should set free his son Dorastus, and put to death Fawnia and her father Porrus.

Finding this by the advice of counsel the speediest remedy to release his son, he caused presently two of his ships to be rigged and thoroughly furnished with provision of men and victuals, and sent diverse of his nobles ambassadors into

Bohemia; who, willing to obey their King and receive their young prince, made no delays for fear of danger, but with as much speed as might be, sailed towards Bohemia. The wind and seas favoured them greatly, which made them hope of some good hap, for within three days they were landed. Which Pandosto no sooner heard of their arrival but he in person went to meet them, entreating them with such sumptuous and familiar courtesy that they might well perceive how sorry he was for the former injuries he had offered to their King, and how willing (if it might be) to make amends.

As Pandosto made report to them how one Meleagrus, a knight of Trapalonia, was lately arrived with a lady called Fawnia in his land, coming very suspiciously accompanied only with one servant and an old shepherd, the ambassadors perceived by the half what the whole tale meant, and began to conjecture that it was Dorastus, who for fear to be known had changed his name. But dissembling the matter, they shortly arrived at the court where, after they had been very solemnly and sumptuously feasted, the noblemen of Sicilia being gathered together, they made report of their embassage, where they certified Pandosto that Meleagrus was son and heir to the King Egistus, and that his name was Dorastus; how, contrary to the King's mind, he had privily conveyed away that Fawnia, intending to marry her, being but daughter to that poor shepherd Porrus. Whereupon the King's request was that Capnio, Fawnia, and Porrus might be murthered and put to death, and that his son Dorastus might be sent home in safety.

Pandosto, having attentively and with great marvel heard their embassage, willing to reconcile himself to Egistus and to show him how greatly he esteemed his labour, although love and fancy forbade him to hurt Fawnia, yet in despite of love he determined to execute Egistus' will without mercy, and therefore he presently sent for Dorastus out of prison who, marvelling at this unlooked for courtesy, found at his coming to the King's presence that which he least doubted of: his father's ambassadors. Who no sooner saw him but with great reverence they honoured him; and Pandosto, embracing Dorastus, set him by him very lovingly in a chair of estate.

Dorastus, ashamed that his folly was bewrayed, sat a long time as one in a muse, till Pandosto told him the sum of his father's embassage, which he had no sooner heard but he was touched at the quick for the cruel sentence that was pronounced against Fawnia. But neither could his sorrow nor persuasions prevail, for Pandosto commanded that Fawnia, Porrus, and Capnio should be brought to his presence; who were no sooner come but Pandosto, having his former love turned to a disdainful hate, began to rage against Fawnia in these terms.

'Thou disdainful vassal, thou currish kite, assigned by the destinies to base fortune and yet with an aspiring mind gazing after honour! How durst thou presume, being a beggar, to match with a prince? By thy alluring looks to enchant the son of a king to leave his own country to fulfil thy disordinate lusts? O despiteful mind, a proud heart in a beggar is not unlike to a great fire in a small cottage, which warmeth not the house but burneth it. Assure thyself thou shalt die, and thou, old doting fool, whose folly hath been such as to suffer thy daughter to reach above thy fortune, look for no other meed but the like punishment. But Capnio, thou which hast betrayed the King, and hast consented to the unlawful lust of thy lord and master, I know not how justly I may plague thee. Death is too easy a punishment for thy falsehood, and to live (if not in extreme misery) were not to show thee equity. I therefore award that thou shall have thine eyes put out, and continually while thou diest grind in a mill like a brute beast.'

The fear of death brought a terrible silence upon Fawnia and Capnio, but Porrus, seeing no hope of life, burst forth into these speeches. 'Pandosto, and ye noble ambassadors of Sicily, seeing without cause I am condemned to die, I am yet glad I have opportunity to disburden my conscience before my death. I will tell you as much as I know, and yet no more than is true. Whereas I am accused that I have been a supporter of Fawnia's pride, and she disdained as a vilde beggar, so it is that I am neither father unto her, nor she daughter unto me.

'For so it happened that I, being a poor shepherd in Sicilia, living by keeping other men's flocks, one of my sheep straying down to the seaside, as I went to seek her I saw a little boat driven upon the shore, wherein I found a babe of six days old, wrapped in a mantle of scarlet, having about the neck this chain. I, pitying the child, and desirous of the treasure, carried it home to my wife, who with great care nursed it up and set it to keep sheep. Here is the chain and the jewels, and this Fawnia is the child whom I found in the boat. What she is, or of what parentage, I know not, but this I am assured, that she is none of mine.'

Pandosto would scarce suffer him to tell out his tale but that he enquired the time of the year, the manner of the boat, and other circumstances, which when he found agreeing to his count, he suddenly leaped from his seat and kissed Fawnia, wetting her tender cheeks with his tears, and crying 'My daughter Fawnia, ah sweet Fawnia, I am thy father, Fawnia.' This sudden passion of the King drave them all into a maze, especially Fawnia and Dorastus. But when the King had breathed himself awhile in this new joy, he rehearsed before the ambassadors the whole matter: how he had entreated his wife Bellaria for jealousy, and that this was the child whom he sent to float in the seas.

Fawnia was not more joyful that she had found such a father than Dorastus was glad he should get such a wife. The ambassadors rejoiced that their young prince had made such a choice, that those kingdoms which through enmity had long time been dissevered should now through perpetual amity be united and reconciled. The citizens and subjects of Bohemia, hearing that the King had found again his daughter, which was supposed dead, joyful that there was an heir apparent to his kingdom, made bonfires and shows throughout the city. The courtiers and knights appointed jousts and tourneys to signify their willing minds in gratifying the King's hap.

Eighteen days being passed in these princely sports, Pandosto, willing to recompense old Porrus, of a shepherd made him a knight; which done, providing a sufficient navy to receive him and his retinue, accompanied with Dorastus, Fawnia, and the Sicilian ambassadors, he sailed towards Sicilia, where he was most princely entertained by Egistus who, hearing this comical event, rejoiced greatly at his son's good hap, and without delay (to the perpetual joy of the two young lovers) celebrated the marriage. Which was no sooner ended but Pandosto, calling to mind how first he betrayed his friend Egistus, how his jealousy was the cause of Bellaria's death, that contrary to the law of nature he had lusted after his own daughter, moved with these desperate thoughts, he fell in a melancholy fit, and to close up the comedy with a tragical stratagem, he slew himself; whose death being many days bewailed of Fawnia, Dorastus, and his dear friend Egistus, Dorastus, taking leave of his father, went with his wife and the dead corpse into Bohemia where, after they were sumptuously entombed, Dorastus ended his days in contented quiet.

THOMAS NASHE

The Unfortunate Traveller
(1594)

The Unfortunate Traveller; or, The Life of Jack Wilton. *Qui audiunt audita dicunt.** Tho. Nashe.

To the Right Honourable Lord Henry Wriothesley, Earl of Southampton and Baron of Tichfield.*

INGENUOUS, honourable lord, I know not what blind custom methodical antiquity hath thrust upon us, to dedicate such books as we publish to one great man or other; in which respect, lest any man should challenge these my papers as goods uncustomed and so extend upon them as forfeit to contempt, to the seal of your excellent censure lo here I present them to be seen and allowed. Prize them as high or as low as you list; if you set any price on them, I hold my labour well satisfied. Long have I desired to approve my wit unto you. My reverent, dutiful thoughts, even from their infancy, have been retainers to your glory. Now at last I have enforced an opportunity to plead my devoted mind. All that in this fantastical treatise I can promise is some reasonable conveyance of history and variety of mirth. By diverse of my good friends have I been dealt with to employ my dull pen in this kind, it being a clean different vein from other my former courses of writing. How well or ill I have done in it I am ignorant; the eye that sees round about itself sees not into itself. Only your Honour's applauding encouragement hath power to make me arrogant. Incomprehensible is the height of your spirit, both in heroical resolution and matters of conceit. Unreprievably perisheth that book whatsoever to waste paper which on the diamond rock of your judgement disasterly chanceth to be shipwrecked. A dear lover and cherisher you are, as well of the lovers of poets, as of poets themselves. Amongst their sacred number I dare not ascribe myself, though now and then I speak English. That small brain I have, to no further use I convert save to be kind to my friends and fatal to my enemies. A new brain, a new wit, a new style, a new soul will I get me, to canonize your name to posterity, if in this my first attempt I be not taxed of presumption. Of your gracious favour I despair not, for I am not altogether fame's outcast. This handful of leaves I offer to your view to the leaves on trees I compare which, as they cannot grow of themselves except they have some branches or boughs to cleave to, and with whose juice and sap they be evermore recreated and nourished, so except these unpolished leaves of mine have some branch of nobility whereon to depend and cleave, and with the vigorous nutriment of whose authorized commendation they may be continually fostered and refreshed, never will they grow to the world's good liking, but forthwith fade and die on the first hour of their birth. Your lordship is the large spreading branch of renown from whence these my idle leaves seek to derive their whole nourishing. It resteth you either scornfully shake them off as worm-eaten and worthless, or in pity preserve them and cherish them for some little summer fruit you hope to find amongst them.

> Your Honour's in all humble service,
> Tho. Nashe

THE INDUCTION TO THE DAPPER MONSIEUR PAGES OF THE COURT

Gallant squires, have amongst you. At mumchance I mean not, for so I might chance come to short commons, but at *novus, nova, novum,** which is, in English, news of the maker. A proper fellow page of yours, called Jack Wilton, by me commends him unto you, and hath bequeathed for waste paper here amongst you certain pages of his misfortunes. In any case, keep them preciously as a privy token of his good will towards you. If there be some better than other, he craves you would honour them in their death so much as to dry and kindle tobacco with them. For a need, he permits you to wrap velvet pantofles in them also, so they be not woebegone at the heels, or weather-beaten like a black head with grey hairs, or mangy at the toes like an ape about the mouth. But as you love good fellowship and ambs-ace rather turn them to stop mustard pots than the grocers should have one patch of them to wrap mace in—a strong, hot, costly spice it is, which above all things he hates. To any use about meat or drink put them to and spare not, for they cannot do their country better service. Printers are mad whoresons; allow them some of them for napkins.

Just a little nearer to the matter and the purpose. *Memorandum*: every one of you after the perusing of this pamphlet is to provide him a case of poniards that, if you come in company with any man which shall dispraise it or speak against it, you may straight cry '*Sic respondeo*',* and give him the stoccado. It stands not with your honours (I assure ye) to have a gentleman and a page abused in his absence. Secondly, whereas you were wont to swear men on a pantofle to be true to your puissant order, you shall swear them on nothing but this chronicle of the King of pages henceforward. Thirdly, it shall be lawful for any whatsoever to play with false dice in a corner on the cover of this foresaid *Acts and Monuments*.* None of the fraternity of the minorites shall refuse it for a pawn in the times of famine and necessity. Every stationer's stall they pass by, whether by day or by night, they shall put off their hats to and make a low leg, in regard their grand printed Capitano is there entombed. It shall be flat treason for any of this fore-mentioned catalogue of the point-trussers* once to name him within forty foot of an alehouse. Marry, the tavern is honourable.

Many special, grave articles more had I to give you in charge, which your wisdoms, waiting together at the bottom of the great chamber stairs or sitting in a porch (your parliament house) may better consider of than I can deliver. Only let this suffice for a taste to the text, and a bit to pull on a good wit with, as a rasher on the coals is to pull on a cup of wine.

Hey pass, come aloft. Every man of you take your places and hear Jack Wilton tell his own tale.

THE UNFORTUNATE TRAVELLER

ABOUT that time that the terror of the world and fever quartan of the French, Henry the Eight (the only true subject of chronicles) advanced his standard against the two hundred and fifty towers of Turney and Turwin,* and had the emperor and all the nobility of Flanders, Holland and Brabant as mercenary attendants on his full-sailed fortune, I, Jack Wilton, a gentleman at least, was a certain kind of an appendix or page belonging or appertaining in or unto the confines of the English court, where what my credit was a number of my creditors that I cozened can testify. *Coelum petimus stultitia;* * which of us all is not a sinner? Be it known to as many as will pay money enough to peruse my story that I followed the camp or the court, or the court and the camp, when Turwin lost her maidenhead and opened her gates to more than Jane Tross* did. There did I (soft, let me drink before I go any further) reign sole king of the cans and blackjacks, prince of the pigmies, county palatine of clean straw and provant and, to conclude, lord high regent of rashers of the coals and red herring cobs. *Paulo maiora canamus.* *

Well, to the purpose. What stratagemical acts and monuments do you think an ingenious infant of my age might enact? You will say it were sufficient if he slur a die,* pawn his master to the utmost penny, and minister the oath on the pantofle artificially. These are signs of good education, I must confess, and arguments of 'in grace and virtue to proceed'.* Oh, but *aliquid latet quod non patet,** there's a farther path I must trace. Examples confirm—list, lordings, to my proceedings.

Whosoever is acquainted with the state of a camp understands that in it be many quarters, and yet not so many as on London Bridge. In those quarters are many companies. Much company, much knavery; as true as that old adage 'much courtesy much subtlety'. Those companies, like a great deal of corn, do yield some chaff. The corn are cormorants, the chaff are good fellows which are quickly blown to nothing with bearing a light heart in a light purse. Amongst this chaff was I winnowing my wits to live merrily, and by my troth so I did. The prince could but command men spend their blood in his service, I could make them spend all the money they had for my pleasure. But poverty in the end parts friends. Though I was prince of their purses, and exacted of my unthrift subjects as much liquid allegiance as any kaiser in the world could do, yet where it is not to be had the king must lose his right.* Want cannot be withstood, men can do no more than they can do. What remained then, but the fox's case must help when the lion's skin is out at the elbows.

There was a lord in the camp, let him be a lord of misrule if you will, for he kept a plain alehouse without welt or guard of any ivy bush, and sold cider and cheese by pint and by pound to all that came (at that very name of cider I can but sigh, there is so much of it in rhenish wine nowadays). Well, *tendit ad sidera virtus*,* there's great virtue belongs (I can tell you) to a cup of cider, and very good men have sold it, and at sea it is *aqua celestis**—but that's neither here nor there, if it had no other patrons but this peer of quart pots to authorize it, it were sufficient. This great lord, this worthy lord, this noble lord, thought no scorn (Lord have mercy upon us) to have his great velvet breeches larded with the droppings of this dainty liquor, and yet he was an old servitor, a cavalier of an ancient house, as it might appear by the arms of his ancestry, drawn very amiably in chalk on the inside of his tent door.

He, and no other, was the man I chose out to damn with a lewd moneyless device; for, coming to him on a day as he was counting his barrels and setting the price in chalk on the head of every one of them, I did my duty very devoutly and told his aley honour I had matters of some secrecy to impart unto him, if it pleased him to grant me private audience. 'With me, young Wilton,' quoth he, 'marry and shalt. Bring us a pint of cider of a fresh tap into the Three Cups here. Wash the pot!'

So into a back room he led me where, after he had spit on his finger and picked off two or three motes of his old, moth-eaten velvet cap, and sponged and wrung all the rheumatic drivel from his ill-favoured goat's beard, he bade me declare my mind, and thereupon he drank to me on the same. I up with a long circumstance—alias a cunning shift of the seventeens—and discoursed unto him what entire affection I had borne him time out of mind, partly for the high descent and lineage from whence he sprung, and partly for the tender care and provident respect he had of poor soldiers, that whereas the vastity of that place (which afforded them no indifferent supply of drink or of victuals) might humble them to some extremity, and so weaken their hands, he vouchsafed in his own person to be a victualer to the camp (a rare example of magnificence and honourable courtesy) and diligently provided that, without far travel, every man might for his money have cider and cheese his bellyful.

Nor did he sell his cheese by the way only, or his cider by the great, but abased himself with his own hands to take a shoemaker's knife (a homely instrument for such a high personage to touch) and cut it out equally like a true justiciary in little pennyworths, that it would do a man good for to look upon. So likewise of his cider, the poor man might have his moderate draught of it (as there is a moderation in all things) as well for his doit or his dandiprat, as the rich man for his half-souse or his denier.*

'Not so much,' quoth I, 'but this tapster's linen apron, which you wear before you to protect your apparel from the imperfections of the spigot, most amply bewrays your lowly mind. I speak it with tears. Too few such humble-spirited noblemen have we, that will draw drink in linen aprons. Why, you are every child's fellow; any man that comes under the name of a soldier and a good fellow you will sit and bear company to the last pot. Yea, and you take in as good part the homely phrase of "Mine host, here's to you" as if one saluted you by all the titles of your barony. These considerations, I say, which the world suffers to slip by in the channel of carelessness, have moved me in ardent zeal of your welfare to forewarn you of some dangers that have beset you and your barrels.'

At the name of dangers he start* up and bounced with his fist on the board so hard that his tapster, overhearing him, cried 'Anon, anon sir, by and by', and came and made a low leg and asked him what he lacked. He was ready to have stricken his tapster for interrupting him in attention of this his so much desired relation, but for fear of displeasing me he moderated his fury and, only sending him for the other fresh pint, willed him look to the bar and come when he is called with a devil's name.

Well, at his earnest importunity, after I had moistened my

lips to make my lie run glib to his journey's end, forward I went as followeth. 'It chanced me the other night, amongst other pages, to attend where the King with his lords and many chief leaders sat in counsel. There, amongst sundry serious matters that were debated, and intelligences from the enemy given up, it was privily informed (no villains to these privy informers) that you, even you that I now speak to, had (O would I had no tongue to tell the rest)—by this drink it grieves me so I am not able to repeat it.'

Now was my drunken lord ready to hang himself for the end of the full point, and over my neck he throws himself very lubberly, and entreated me, as I was a proper young gentleman, and ever looked for pleasure at his hands, soon to rid him out of this hell of suspense and resolve him of the rest. Then fell he on his knees, wrung his hands, and I think, on my conscience, wept out all the cider that he had drunk in a week before, to move me to have pity on him. He rose and put his rusty ring on my finger, gave me his greasy purse with that single money that was in it, promised to make me his heir, and a thousand more favours if I would expire the misery of his unspeakable tormenting uncertainty. I, being by nature inclined to mercy (for indeed I knew two or three good wenches of that name) bade him harden his ears and not make his eyes abortive before their time, and he should have the inside of my breast turned outward, hear such a tale as would tempt the utmost strength of life to attend it and not die in the midst of it.

'Why,' quoth I, 'myself that am but a poor, childish wellwiller of yours, with the very thought that a man of your desert and state by a number of peasants and varlets should be so injuriously abused in hugger mugger, have wept all my urine upward. The wheel under our city bridge carries not so much water over the city as my brain hath welled forth gushing streams of sorrow. I have wept so immoderately and lavishly that I thought verily my palate had been turned to Pissing Conduit in London. My eyes have been drunk, outrageously drunk, with giving but ordinary intercourse through their sea-circled islands to my distilling dreariment. What shall I say? That which malice hath said is the mere overthrow and murder of your days. Change not your colour. None can slander a clear conscience to itself; receive all your fraught of misfortune in at once. It is buzzed in the King's head that you are a secret friend to the enemy and, under pretence of getting a licence to furnish the camp with cider and such like provant, you have furnished the enemy, and in empty barrels sent letters of discovery and corn innumerable.'

I might well have left here, for by this time his white liver had mixed itself with the white of his eye, and both were turned upwards, as if they had offered themselves a fair white for death to shoot at. The troth was, I was very loath mine host and I should part to heaven with dry lips, wherefore the best means that I could imagine to wake him out of his trance was to cry loud in his ear 'Hough host! What's to pay? Will no man look to the reckoning here?'; and in plain verity it took expected effect, for with the noise he started and bustled like a man that had been scared with fire out of his sleep, and ran hastily to his tapster and all to-belaboured him about the ears for letting gentlemen call so long and not look in to them. Presently he remembered himself, and had like to have fallen into his memento again, but that I met him halfways and asked his lordship what he meant to slip his neck out of the collar so suddenly and, being revived, strike his tapster so rashly.

'Oh,' quoth he, 'I am bought and sold for doing my country such good service as I have done. They are afraid of me because my good deeds have brought me into such estimation with the commonalty. I see, I see it is not for the lamb to live with the wolf.'

The world is well amended, thought I, with your Cidership. Such another forty years' nap together as Epimenides* had would make you a perfect wise man. 'Answer me,' quoth he, 'my wise young Wilton, is it true that I am thus underhand dead and buried by these bad tongues?'

'Nay,' quoth I, 'you shall pardon me, for I have spoken too much already. No definitive sentence of death shall march out of my well meaning lips; they have but lately sucked milk, and shall they so suddenly change their food and seek after blood?'

'Oh but', quoth he, 'a man's friend is his friend. (Fill the other pint, tapster.) What said the King? Did he believe it when he heard it? I pray thee say! I swear to thee by my nobility, none in the world shall ever be made privy that I received any light of this matter from thee.'

'That firm affiance', quoth I, 'had I in you before, or else I would never have gone so far over the shoes to pluck you out of the mire. Not to make many words, since you will needs know, the King says flatly you are a miser and a snudge, and he never hoped better of you.' 'Nay then,' quoth he, 'questionless some planet that loves not cider hath conspired against me.'

'Moreover, which is worse, the King hath vowed to give Turwin one hot breakfast only with the bungs that he will pluck out of your barrels. I cannot stay at this time to report each circumstance that passed, but the only counsel that my long-cherished kind inclination can possibly contrive is now in your old days to be liberal, such victuals or provision as you have, presently distribute it frankly amongst poor soldiers. I would let them burst their bellies with cider and bathe in it, before I would run into my prince's ill opinion for a whole sea of it. The hunter pursuing the beaver* for his stones, he bites them off and leaves them behind for him to gather up, whereby he lives quiet. If greedy hunters and hungry tell-tales pursue you, it is for a little pelf which you have. Cast it behind you, neglect it, let them have it, lest it breed a further inconvenience. Credit my advice, you shall find it prophetical, and thus I have discharged the part of a poor friend.' With some few like phrases of ceremony, 'your honour's suppliant' and so forth, and 'Farewell my good youth, I thank thee and will remember thee', we parted.

But the next day I think we had a dole of cider. Cider in bowls, in scuppets, in helmets, and to conclude, if a man would have filled his boots full there he might have had it. Provant thrust itself into poor soldiers' pockets whether they would or no. We made five peals of shot into the town together of nothing but spiggots and faucets of discarded empty barrels. Every under-footsoldier had a dis-tenanted tun, as Diogenes had his tub, to sleep in. I myself got as many confiscated tapsters' aprons as made me a tent as big as any ordinary commander's in the field. But in conclusion, my wellbeloved baron of double beer got him humbly on his mary-bones to the King, and complained he was old and stricken in years, and had ne'er an heir to cast at a dog, wherefore if it might please his Majesty to take his lands into his hands and allow him some reasonable pension to live on, he should be marvellous well pleased. As for the wars, he was weary of them, and yet as long as his Highness should venture his own person he would not flinch a foot, but make his withered body a buckler to bear off any blow that should be advanced against him.

The King, marvelling at this strange alteration of his great merchant of cider (for so he would often pleasantly term him), with a little further talk bolted out the whole complotment. Then was I pitifully whipped for my holiday lie, although they made themselves merry with it many a fair winter's evening after. Yet notwithstanding, his good ass-headed honour mine host persevered in his former simple request to the King to accept of the surrender of his lands and allow him a beadsmanry or out-brothership of brachet,* which at length, through his vehement instancy, took effect, and the King jestingly said since he would needs have it so, he would distrain on part of his land for impost of cider—which he was behindhand with him, and never paid.

This was one of my famous achievements, insomuch as I never light upon the like famous fool—but I have done a thousand better jests if they had been booked in order as they were begotten. It is pity posterity should be deprived of such precious records, and yet there is no remedy—and yet there is too, for when all fails welfare* a good memory. Gentle readers (look you be gentle now, since I have called you so), as freely as my knavery was mine own, it shall be yours to use in the way of honesty.

Even in this expedition of Turwin (for the King stood not long thrumming of buttons* there) it happened me fall out* (I would it had fallen out otherwise for his sake) with an ugly, mechanical captain. You must think in an army, where truncheons are in their state house, it is a flat stab once to name a captain without cap in hand. Well, suppose he was a captain, and had ne'er a good cap of his own, but I was fain to lend him one of my lord's cast velvet caps and a weather-beaten feather, wherewith he threatened his soldiers afar off, as Jupiter is said with the shaking of his hair to make heaven and earth to quake. Suppose out of the parings of a pair of false dice I apparelled both him and myself many a time and oft; and surely, not to slander the devil, if any man ever deserved the golden dice the King of the Parthians sent to Demetrius it was I. I had the right vein of sucking up a die twixt the dints of my fingers; not a crevice in my hand but could swallow a quarter trey* for a need. In the line of life many a dead lift* did there lurk, but it was nothing towards the maintenance of a family.

This monsieur capitano eat up the cream of my earnings, and *crede mihi res est ingeniosa dare,** any man is a fine fellow as long as he hath any money in his purse. That money is like the marigold, which opens and shuts with the sun. If fortune smileth, or one be in favour, it floweth; if the evening of age comes on, or he falleth into disgrace, it fadeth and is not to be found. I was my craft's master though I was but young, and could as soon decline *nominativo hic asinus** as a greater clerk, wherefore I thought it not convenient my soldado should have my purse any longer for his drum to play upon, but I would give him Jack Drum's entertainment* and send him packing.

This was my plot. I knew a piece of service of intelligence which was presently to be done that required a man with all his five senses to affect it, and would overthrow any fool that should undertake it. To this service did I animate and egg my foresaid costs and charges, alias senior velvet cap, whose head was not encumbered with too much forecast, and coming to him in his cabin about dinner time, where I found him very devoutly paring of his nails for want of other repast, I entertained him with this solemn oration.

'Captain, you perceive how near both of us are driven. The dice of late are grown as melancholy as a dog; high men and low men both prosper alike; langrets, fulhams* and all the whole fellowship of them will not afford a man his dinner. Some other means must be invented to prevent imminent extremity. My state, you are not ignorant, depends on trencher service; your advancement must be derived from the valour of your arm. In the delays of siege, desert hardly gets a day of hearing; 'tis gowns must direct and guns enact all the wars that is to be made against walls. Resteth no way for you to climb suddenly but by doing some strange stratagem that the like hath not been heard of heretofore, and fitly at this instant occasion is ministered.

'There is a feat the King is desirous to have wrought on some great man of the enemy's side. Marry, it requireth not so much resolution as discretion to bring it to pass, and yet resolution enough shall be shown in it too, being so full of hazardous jeopardy as it is. Hark in your ear. Thus it is. Without more drumbling or pausing, if you will undertake it and work it through stitch* (as you may ere the King hath determined which way to go about it) I warrant you are made while you live. You need not care which way your staff falls.* If it prove not so, then cut off my head.'

Oh my auditors, had you seen him how he stretched out his limbs, scratched his scabbed elbows at this speech! How he set his cap over his eyebrows like a politician, and then folded his arms one in another and nodded with the head, as who should say 'Let the French beware, for they shall find me a devil.' If, I say, you had seen but half the actions that he used of shrucking up his shoulders, smiling scornfully, playing with his fingers on his buttons, and biting the lip, you would have laughed your face and your knees together.

The iron being hot, I thought to lay on load, for in any case I would not have his humour cool. As before I laid open unto him the brief sum of the service, so now I began to urge the honourableness of it, and what a rare thing it was to be a right politician; how much esteemed of kings and princes and how diverse of mean parentage have come to be monarchs by it. Then I discoursed of the qualities and properties of him in every respect; how, like the wolf, he must draw the breath from a man before he be seen; how, like a hare, he must sleep with his eyes open; how, as the eagle in flying casts dust in the eyes of crows and other fowls for to blind them, so he must cast dust in the eyes of his enemies, delude their sight by one means or other that they dive not into his subtleties. How he must be familiar with all and trust none; drink, carouse, and lecher with him out of whom he hopes to wring any matter; swear and forswear rather than be suspected; and, in a word, have the art of dissembling at his fingers' ends as perfect as any courtier.

'Perhaps', quoth I, 'you may have some few greasy cavaliers that will seek to dissuade you from it, and they will not stick to stand on their three-halfpenny honour, swearing and staring that a man were better be an hangman than an intelligencer, and call him a sneaking eavesdropper, a scraping hedgecreeper, and a piperly pickthank. But you must not be discouraged by their talk, for the most part of these beggarly contemners of wit are huge, burlyboned butchers like Ajax, good for nothing but to strike right-down blows on a wedge with a cleaving beetle, or stand hammering all day upon bars of iron. The whelps of a bear never grow but sleeping, and these bear-wards, having big limbs, shall be preferred though they do nothing.

'You have read stories' (I'll be sworn he never looked in book in his life) 'how many of the Roman worthies were there that have gone as spies into their enemy's camp? Ulysses, Nestor, Diomede, went as spies together in the night into the tents of Rhoesus and intercepted Dolon, the spy of the Trojans. Never any discredited the trade of intelligencers but Judas, and he hanged himself. Danger will put wit into any man. Architas made a wooden dove to fly, by which proportion I see no reason that the veriest block in the world should despair of anything. Though nature be contrary inclined, it may be altered; yet usually those whom she denies her ordinary gifts in one thing she doubles them in another. That which the ass wants in wit he hath in honesty. Who ever saw him kick or winch or use any jade's tricks? Though he live an hundred years, you shall never hear that he breaks pasture.

'Amongst men, he that hath not a good wit lightly hath a good iron memory, and he that hath neither of both hath some bones to carry burthens. Blind men have better noses than other men; the bull's horns serve him as well as hands to fight withal; the lion's paws are as good to him as a poleaxe to knock down any that resists him; so the boar's tushes serve him in

better stead than a sword and buckler; what need the snail care
for eyes when he feels the way with his two horns as well as
if he were as sharp-sighted as a decipherer? There is a fish
that, having no wings, supports herself in the air with her fins.
Admit that you had neither wit nor capacity, as sure in my
judgement there is none equal unto you in idiotism, yet if you
have simplicity and secrecy, serpents themselves will think
you a serpent, for what serpent is there but hideth his sting?
And yet whatsoever be wanting, a good, plausible, alluring
tongue in such a man of employment can hardly be spared;
which, as the forenamed serpent with his winding tail fetcheth
in those that come near him, so with a ravishing tale it gathers
all men's hearts unto him—which if he have not, let him never
look to engender by the mouth, as ravens and doves do; that
is, mount or be great by undermining.

'Sir, I am ascertained that all these imperfections I speak of
in you have their natural resiance. I see in your face that you
were born with the swallow, to feed flying, to get much
treasure and honour by travel. None so fit as you for so
important an enterprise. Our vulgar reputed politicians are
but flies swimming on the stream of subtlety superficially in
comparison of your singularity. Their blind, narrow eyes
cannot pierce into the profundity of hypocrisy. You alone
with Palamed can pry into Ulysses' mad counterfeiting. You
can discern Achilles from a chamber maid, though he be
decked with his spindle and distaff. As Jove, dining with
Lycaon, could not be beguiled with human flesh dressed like
meat, so no human brain may go beyond you, none beguile
you—you gull all, all fear you, love you, stoop to you.
Therefore, good sir, be ruled by me. Stoop your fortune so
low as to bequeath yourself wholly to this business.'

This silver sounding tale made such sugared harmony in
his ears that, with the sweet meditation what a more than
miraculous politician he should be, and what kingly promotion should come tumbling on him thereby, he could have
found in his heart to have packed up his pipes and to have
gone to heaven without a bait.* Yea, he was more inflamed
and ravished with it than a young man called Taurimontanus
was with the Phrygian melody, who was so incensed and fired

therewith that he would needs run presently upon it and set a courtesan's house on fire that had angered him.

No remedy there was but I must help to furnish him with money. I did so, as who will not make his enemy a bridge of gold to fly by. Very earnestly he conjured me to make no man living privy to his departure in regard of his place and charge, and on his honour assured me his return should be very short and successful. Ay, ay, shorter by the neck, thought I, in the mean time let this be thy posy: 'I live in hope to scape the rope.'

Gone he is. God send him good shipping to Wapping,* and by this time, if you will, let him be a pitiful poor fellow and undone for ever. For mine own part, if he had been mine own brother I could have done no more for him than I did, for straight after his back was turned I went in all love and kindness to the marshal general of the field and certified him that such a man was lately fled to the enemy, and got his place begged for another immediately. What became of him after, you shall hear. To the enemy he went and offered his service, railing egregiously on the King of England. He swore, as he was a gentleman and a soldier, he would be revenged on him, and let but the King of France follow his counsel, he would drive him from Turwin walls yet ere three* days to an end. All these were good humours, but the tragedy followeth.

The French King, hearing of such a prating fellow that was come, was desirous to see him, but yet he feared treason, wherefore he willed one of his minions to take upon him his person, and he would stand by as a private man whilst he was examined. Why should I use any idle delays? In was captain Gog's Wounds* brought after he was throughly searched; not a louse in his doublet was let pass but was asked 'Quevela?'* and charged to stand in the King's name. The moulds of his buttons they turned out to see if they were not bullets covered over with thread. The codpiece in his devil's breeches (for they were then in fashion) they said plainly was a case for a pistol. If he had had ever a hobnail in his shoes it had hanged him, and he should never have known who had harmed him. But as luck was, he had not a mite of any metal about him; he took part with none of the four ages, neither the golden age, the silver age, the brazen, nor the iron age. Only his purse was aged in emptiness, and I think verily a Puritan, for it kept itself from any pollution of crosses.*

Standing before the supposed King, he was asked what he was and wherefore he came. To the which, in a glorious bragging humour, he answered that he was a gentleman, a captain commander, a chief leader that came away from the King of England upon discontentment. Questioned particular of the cause of his discontentment, he had not a word to bless himself with, yet fain he would have patched out a polt-foot tale, but (God he knows) it had not one true leg to stand on. Then began he to smell on the villain so rammishly that none there but was ready to rent him in pieces, yet the minion King kept in his choler and propounded unto him farther what of the King of England's secrets so advantageable he was privy to as might remove him from the siege of Turwin in three days. He said diverse, diverse matters which asked longer conference, but in good honesty they were lies which he had not yet stamped. Hereat the true King stepped forth and commanded to lay hands on the losel, and that he should be tortured to confess the truth, for he was a spy and nothing else.

He no sooner saw the wheel and the torments set before him but he cried out like a rascal, and said he was a poor captain in the English camp suborned by one Jack Wilton, a nobleman's page, and no other, to come and kill the French King in a bravery and return, and that he had no other intention in the world. This confession could not choose but move them all to laughter, in that he made it as light a matter to kill their King and come back as to go to Islington and eat a mess of cream and come home again. Nay, and besides he protested that he had no other intention, as if that were not enough to hang him.

Adam never fell till God made fools. All this could not keep his joints from ransacking on the wheel, for they vowed either to make him a confessor or a martyr in a trice. When still he sung all one song, they told the King he was a fool, and some shrewd head had knavishly wrought on him, wherefore it should stand with his honour to whip him out of the camp and send him home. That persuasion took place, and soundly was he lashed out of their liberties and sent home by a herald with this message: that so the King his master hoped to whip home all the English fools very shortly. Answer was returned that that shortly was a long lie, and they were shrewd fools that should drive the Frenchman out of his kingdom and make him glad, with Corinthian Dionysius, to play the school-master.

The herald being dismissed, our afflicted intelligencer was called *coram nobis*.* How he sped, judge you, but something he was adjudged too. The sparrow for his lechery liveth but a year, he for his treachery was turned on the toe.* *Plura dolor prohibet*.*

Here let me triumph a while and ruminate a line or two on the excellence of my wit. But I will not breathe neither till I have disfraughted all my knavery. Another Switzer captain that was far gone for want of the wench I led astray most notoriously, for he being a monstrous unthrift of battle axes (as one that cared not in his anger to bid 'fly out scuttles'* to five score of them) and a notable emboweller of quart pots, I came disguised unto him in the form of a half-a-crown wench, my gown and attire according to the custom then in request. Iwis I had my courtesies in cue*—or in quart pot rather, for they dived into the very entrails of the dust, and I simpered with my countenance like a porridge pot on the fire when it first begins to seethe. The sobriety of the circumstance is that, after he had courted me and all, and given me the earnest penny of impiety, some six crowns at least for an antepast to iniquity, I fained an impregnable excuse to be gone and never came at him after.

Yet left I not here, but committed a little more scutchery. A company of coistrel clerks, who were in band with Satan and not of any soldier's colour, pinched a number of good minds to Godward of their provant. They would not let a dram of dead pay* overslip them. They would not lend a groat of the week to come to him that had spent his money before this week was done. They out-faced the greatest and most magnanimous servitors in their sincere and finigraphical clean shirts and cuffs. A louse that was any gentleman's companion they thought scorn of. Their near bitten beards must in a devil's name be dewed every day with rosewater; hogs could have ne'er a hair on their backs for making them rubbing brushes to rouse their crab lice. They would in no wise permit that the motes in the sunbeams should be full-mouthed beholders of their clean finified apparel. Their shoes shined as bright as a slick-stone; their hands troubled and soiled more water with washing than the camel doth, that ne'er drinks till the whole stream be troubled. Summarily, never any were so fantastical the one half as they.

My masters, you may conceive of me what you list, but I think confidently I was ordained God's scourge from above for their dainty finicality. The hour of their punishment could no longer be prorogued but vengeance must have at them at all aventures. So it was that the most of these above named goosequill braggadocios were mere cowards and cravens, and durst not so much as throw a pen-full of ink into the enemy's face if proof were made; wherefore, on the experience of their pusillanimity, I thought to raise the foundation of my roguery.

What did I now but one day made a false alarm in the quarter where they lay to try how they would stand to their tackling, and with a pitiful outcry warned them to fly, for there was treason afoot, they were environed and beset. Upon the first watchword of treason that was given, I think they betook them to their heels very stoutly, left their pen and ink-horns and papers behind them for spoil, resigned their desks with the money that was in them to the mercy of the vanquisher, and in fine, left me and my fellows (their fool-catchers) lords of the field. How we dealt with them their disburdened desks can best tell, but this I am assured, we fared the better for it a fortnight of fasting days after.

I must not place a volume in the precincts of a pamphlet. Sleep an hour or two, and dream that Turney and Turwin is won, that the King is shipped again into England, and that I am close at hard meat* at Windsor or at Hampton Court. What, will you in your indifferent opinions allow me for my travel no more seigniory over the pages than I had before? Yes, whether you will part with so much probable friendly suppose or no, I'll have it in spite of your hearts. For your instruction and godly consolation, be informed that at that time I was no common squire, no undertrodden torchbearer. I had my feather in my cap as big as a flag in the fore-top, my French doublet gelt in the belly as though, like a pig ready to be spitted, all my guts had been plucked out, a pair of side-paned hose that hung down like two scales filled with Holland cheeses, my long stock that sat close to my dock and smothered not a scab or a lecherous, hairy sinew on the calf of my leg, my rapier pendant like a round stick fastened in the tacklings for skippers the better to climb by, my cape cloak of black cloth overspreading my back like a thornback or an elephant's ear that hangs on his shoulders like a country huswife's banskin which she thirleth her spindle on, and in consummation of my curiosity, my hands without gloves, all a-more French, and a black budge* edging of a beard on the upper lip, and the like sable auglet of excrements in the first rising of the angle of my chin.

I was the first that brought in the order of passing into the court, which I derived from the common word '*Qui passa?*', and the herald's phrase of arms *passant*, thinking in sincerity he was not a gentleman, nor his arms current, who was not first passed by the pages. If any prentice or other came into the court that was not a gentleman, I thought it was an indignity to the preeminence of the court to include such a one, and could not be salved except we gave him arms passant to make him a gentleman. Besides, in Spain none can pass* any far way but he must be examined what he is, and give threepence for his pass. In which regard it was considered of by the common table of the cupbearers what a perilsome thing it was to let any stranger or out-dweller approach so near the precincts of the prince as the great chamber without examining what he was and giving him his pass. Whereupon we established the like order, but took no money of them as they did, only for a sign that he had not passed our hands unexamined we set a red mark on either of his ears, and so let him walk as authentical.

I must not discover what ungodly dealing we had with the black jacks, or how oft I was crowned king of the drunkards with a court cup. Let me quietly descend to the waning of my youthful days, and tell a little of the sweating sickness* that made me in a cold sweat take my heels and run out of England.

This sweating sickness was a disease that a man then might catch and never go to a hot-house. Many masters desire to have such servants as would work till they sweat again, but in those days he that sweat never wrought again. That scripture then was not thought so necessary which says 'Earn thy living with the sweat of thy brows', for then they earned their dying with the sweat of their brows. It was enough if a fat man did but truss his points to turn him over the perch. Mother Cornelius' tub,* why it was like hell, he that came into it never came out of it. Cooks that stand continually basting their faces before the fire were now all cashiered with this sweat into kitchen-stuff; their hall fell into the King's hands for want of one of the trade to uphold it. Felt-makers and furriers, what the one with the hot steam of their wool new taken out of the pan, and the other with the contagious heat of their slaughter budge and coney-skins, died more thick than of the pestilence. I have seen an old woman at that season, having three chins, wipe them all away one after another as they melted to water and left herself nothing of a mouth but an upper chap. Look how in May or the heat of the summer we lay butter in water for fear it should melt away, so then were men fain to wet their clothes in water as dyers do, and hide themselves in wells from the heat of the sun.

Then happy was he that was an ass, for nothing will kill an ass but cold, and none died but with extreme heat. The fishes called sea-stars, that burn one another by excessive heat, were not so contagious as one man that had the sweat was to another. Masons payed nothing for hair to mix their lime, nor glovers to stuff their balls* with, for then they had it for nothing, it dropped off men's heads and beards faster than any barber could shave it. O, if hair breeches had then been in fashion, what a fine world had it been for tailors. And so it was a fine world for tailors nevertheless, for he that could make a garment slightest and thinnest carried it away. Cutters, I can tell you, then stood upon it to have their trade one of the twelve companies,* for who was it then that would not have his doublet cut to the skin and his shirt cut into it too, to make it more cold. It was as much as a man's life was worth once to name a frieze jerkin. It was treason for a fat, gross man to come within five miles of the court. I heard where they died up* all in one family and not a mother's child escaped, insomuch as they had but an Irish rug locked up in a press, and not laid upon any bed neither. If those that were sick of this malady slept on it they never waked more.

Physicians with their simples in this case were simple fellows, and knew not which way to bestir them. Galen might go shoe the gander for any good he could do; his secretaries had so long called him divine that now he had lost all his virtue upon earth. Hippocrates might well help almanac makers, but here he had not a word to say, a man might sooner catch the sweat with plodding over him to no end than cure the sweat with any of his impotent principles. Paracelsus, with his spirit of the buttery and his spirits of minerals, could not so much as say 'God amend him' to the matter. *Plus erat in artifice quam arte*;* there was more infection in the physician himself than his art could cure.

This mortality first began amongst old men, for they, taking a pride to have their breasts loose basted with tedious beards, kept their houses so hot with these hairy excrements that not so much but their very walls sweat out saltpetre with the smothering perplexity. Nay, a number of them had marvellous hot breaths which, sticking in the briars of their bushy beards, could not choose but (as close air long imprisoned) engender corruption. Wiser was our brother Banks* of these latter days, who made his juggling horse a cut, for fear if at any time he should foist, the stink sticking in his thick, bushy tail might be noisome to his auditors.

Should I tell you how many pursuivants with red noses and sergeants with precious faces shrunk away in this sweat you would not believe me. Even as the salamander with his very sight blasteth apples on the trees, so a pursuivant or a sergeant at this present, with the very reflex of his fiery facias,* was able to spoil a man afar off. In some places of the world there is no shadow of the sun; *diebus illis** if it had been so in England, the generation of Brute had died all and some. To

knit up this description in a pursenet, so fervent and scorching
was the burning air which enclosed them that the most blessed
man then alive would have thought that God had done fairly
by him if he had turned him to a goat, for goats take breath
not at the mouth or nose only but at the ears also.

Take breath how they would, I vowed to tarry no longer
amongst them. As at Turwin I was a demi-soldier in jest, so
now I became a martialist in earnest. Over sea with my
implements I got me, where, hearing the King of France and
the Switzers* were together by the ears, I made towards them
as fast as I could, thinking to thrust myself into that faction
that was strongest. It was my good luck or my ill, I know not
which, to come just to the fighting of the battle, where I saw
a wonderful spectacle of bloodshed on both sides. Here the
unwieldy Switzers wallowing in their gore like an ox in his
dung, there the sprightly French sprawling and turning on the
stained grass like a roach new taken out of the stream. All the
ground was strewed as thick with battleaxes as the carpenter's
yard with chips.

The plain appeared like a quagmire, overspread as it was
with trampled dead bodies. In one place might you behold a
heap of dead murthered men overwhelmed with a falling steed
instead of a tombstone, in another place a bundle of bodies
fettered together in their own bowels, and as the tyrant
Roman emperors used to tie condemned living caitiffs face to
face to dead corses, so were the half-living here mixed with
squeezed carcasses long putrified. Any man might give arms
that was an actor in that battle, for there were more arms and
legs scattered in the field that day than will be gathered up till
doomsday. The French King himself in this conflict was
much distressed, the brains of his own men sprinkled in his
face. Thrice was his courser slain under him, and thrice was
he struck on the breast with a spear. But in the end, by the
help of the Venetians, the Helvetians or Switzers were
subdued, and he crowned victor, a peace concluded, and the
city of Milan surrendered unto him as a pledge of
reconciliation.

That war thus blown over and the several bands dissolved,
like a crow that still follows aloof where there is carrion, I flew

me over to Munster* in Germany, which an Anabaptistical brother named John Leyden kept at that instant against the Emperor and the Duke of Saxony. Here I was in good hope to set up my staff for some reasonable time, deeming that no city would drive it to a siege except they were able to hold out, and prettily well had these Munsterians held out, for they kept the Emperor and the Duke of Saxony sound play for the space of a year, and longer would have done but that Dame Famine came amongst them, whereupon they were forced by messengers to agree upon a day of fight when, according to their Anabaptistical error, they might be all new-christened in their own blood.

That day come, flourishing entered John Leyden the botcher into the field, with a scarf made of lists like a bowcase; a cross on his breast like a thread-bottom; a round twilted tailor's cushion buckled like a tankard-bearer's device to his shoulders for a target, the pike whereof was a pack needle; a tough prentice's club for his spear; a great brewer's cow on his back for a corslet; and on his head for a helmet a huge high shoe with the bottom turned upward, embossed as full of hobnails as ever it might stick. His men were all base handicrafts, as cobblers and curriers and tinkers, whereof some had bars of iron, some hatchets, some cool staves, some dung forks, some spades, some mattocks, some wood knives, some addises for their weapons. He that was best provided had but a piece of rusty brown bill bravely fringed with cobwebs to fight for him. Perchance here and there you might see a fellow that had a canker-eaten skull on his head, which served him and his ancestors for a chamber pot two hundred years, and another that had bent a couple of iron dripping-pans armour-wise to fence his back and his belly; another that had thrust a pair of dry old boots as a breast-plate before his belly of his doublet because he would not be dangerously hurt; another that had twilted all his truss full of counters, thinking if the enemy should take him he would mistake them for gold and so save his life for his money.

Very devout asses they were, for all they were so dunstically set forth, and such as thought they knew as much of God's mind as richer men. Why, inspiration was their ordinary familiar, and buzzed in their ears like a bee in a box every hour what news from heaven, hell, and the land of whipperginnie. Displease them who durst, he should have his mittimus* to damnation *ex tempore*. They would vaunt there was not a pease difference twixt them and the apostles; they were as poor as they, of as base trades as they, and no more inspired than they, and with God there is no respect of persons. Only herein may seem some little diversity to lurk, that Peter wore a sword, and they count it flat hellfire for any man to wear a dagger. Nay, so grounded and gravelled were they in this opinion that now when they should come to battle there's ne'er a one of them would bring a blade (no, not an onion blade) about him to die for it. It was not lawful, said they, for any man to draw the sword but the magistrate, and in fidelity, which I had wellnigh forgot, Jack Leyden their magistrate had the image or likeness of a piece of a rusty sword like a lusty lad by his side. Now I remember me, it was but a foil neither, and he wore it to show that he should have the foil of his enemies, which might have been an oracle for his two-hand interpretation.

*Quid plura?** His battle is pitched. By pitched I do not mean set in order, for that was far from their order. Only as sailors do pitch their apparel to make it storm proof, so had most of them pitched their patched clothes to make them impierceable. A nearer way than to be at the charges of armour by half, and in another sort he might be said to have pitched the field, for he had pitched or set up his rest whither to fly if they were discomfited.

Peace, peace there in the belfry, service begins! Upon their knees before they join, falls John Leyden and his fraternity very devoutly. They pray, they howl, they expostulate with God to grant them victory, and use such unspeakable vehemence a man would think them the only well-bent men under heaven. Wherein let me dilate a little more gravely than the nature of this history requires, or will be expected of so young a practitioner in divinity, that not those that intermissively cry 'Lord open unto us, Lord open unto us' enter first into the kingdom of heaven; that not the greatest professors have the greatest portion in grace; that all is not gold that glisters. When Christ said the kingdom of heaven must suffer violence, he meant not the violence of long babbling prayers to no purpose, nor the violence of tedious invective sermons without wit, but the violence of faith, the violence of good works, the violence of patient suffering. The ignorant arise and snatch the kingdom of heaven to themselves with greediness, when we with all our learning sink down into hell.

Where did Peter and John in the third of the Acts find the lame cripple but in the gate of the temple called Beautiful? In the beautifullest gates of our temple, in the forefront of professors, are many lame cripples—lame in life, lame in good works, lame in everything, yet will they always sit at the gates of the temple. None be more forward than they to enter into matters of reformation, yet none more behindhand to enter into the true temple of the Lord by the gates of good life.

You may object that those which I speak against are more diligent in reading the scriptures, more careful to resort unto sermons, more sober in their looks and modest in their attire than any else. But I pray you, let me answer you. Doth not Christ say that before the latter day the sun shall be turned into darkness and the moon into blood, whereof what may the meaning be but that the glorious sun of the gospel shall be eclipsed with the dim cloud of dissimulation; that that which is the brightest planet of salvation shall be a means of error and darkness. And 'the moon shall be turned into blood'— those that shine fairest make the simplest show, seem most to favour religion, shall rent out the bowels of the church, be turned into blood, and all this shall come to pass before the notable day of the Lord, whereof this age is the eve.

Let me use a more familiar example since the heat of a great number hath outraged so excessively. Did not the devil lead Christ to the pinnacle or highest part of the temple to tempt him? If he led Christ, he will lead a whole army of hypocrites to the top or highest part of the temple, the highest step of religion and holiness, to seduce them and subvert them. I say unto you that which this our tempted saviour, with many other words, besought his disciples: 'Save yourselves from this froward generation; verily, verily, the servant is not greater than his master; verily, verily, sinful men are not holier than holy Jesus their maker.' That holy Jesus again repeats this holy sentence: 'Remember the words I said unto you, the servant is not holier or greater than his master', as if he should say 'Remember them, imprint in your memory, your pride and singularity will make you forget them, the effects of them many years hence will come to pass.' 'Whosoever will seek to save his soul shall lose it'—whosoever seeks by headlong means to enter into heaven and disannul God's ordinance shall, with the giants that thought to scale heaven in contempt of Jupiter, be overwhelmed with Mount Ossa and Pelion and dwell with the devil in eternal dissolution.

Though the High Priest's office was expired when Paul said unto one of them 'God rebuke thee, thou painted sepulchre', yet when a stander-by reproved him, saying 'Revilest thou the High Priest?', he repented and asked forgiveness. That which I suppose I do not grant; the lawfulness of the authority they oppose themselves against is sufficiently proved. Far be it my under-age arguments should intrude themselves as a green, weak prop to support so high a building. Let it suffice if you know Christ you know his Father also. But a great number of you with Philip have been long with Christ and have not known him, have long professed yourselves Christians and not known his true ministers. You follow the French and Scottish fashion and faction, and in all points are like the Switzers, *qui quaerunt cum qua gente cadunt*: that seek with what nation they may first miscarry.

In the days of Nero there was an odd fellow that had found out an exquisite way to make glass as hammer-proof as gold. Shall I say that the like experiment he made upon glass we have practised on the Gospel? Aye, confidently will I. We have found out a sleight to hammer it to any heresy whatsoever. But those furnaces of falsehood and hammer-heads of heresy must be dissolved and broken as his was, or else I fear me the false, glittering glass of innovation will be better esteemed of than the ancient gold of the gospel. The fault of faults is this: that your dead-born faith is begotten by too, too infant fathers. Cato, one of the wisest men Roman histories canonized, was not born till his father was fourscore years old. None can be a perfect father of faith and beget men aright unto God but those that are aged in experience, have many years imprinted in their mild conversation, and have with Zacchaeus sold all their possessions of vanities to enjoy the sweet fellowship not of the human but spiritual messiahs.

Ministers and pastors sell away your sects and schisms to the decrepit churches in contention beyond sea. They have been so long inured to war, both about matters of religion and regiment, that now they have no peace of mind but in troubling all other men's peace. Because the poverty of their provinces will allow them no proportionable maintenance for higher callings of ecclesiastical magistrates, they would reduce us to the precedent of their rebellious persecuted beggary, much like the sect of philosophers called cynics who, when they saw they were born to no lands or possessions nor had any possible means to support their desperate estates but they must live despised and in misery do what they could, they plotted and consulted with themselves how to make their poverty better esteemed of than rich dominion and sovereignty.

The upshot of their plotting and consultation was this: that they would live to themselves, scorning the very breath or company of all men. They professed, according to the rate of their lands, voluntary poverty, thin fare, and lying hard, contemning and inveighing against all those as brute beasts whatsoever whom the world had given any reputation for riches or prosperity. Diogenes was one of the first and foremost of the ring-leaders of this rusty morosity, and he, for all his nice dogged disposition and blunt deriding of worldly dross and the gross felicity of fools, was taken notwithstanding a little after very fairly coining money in his cell.

So fares it up and down with our cynical, reformed foreign churches, they will digest no grapes of great bishoprics, forsooth, because they cannot tell how to come by them. They must shape their coats, good men, according to their cloth, and do as they may, not as they would, yet they must give us leave here in England that are their honest neighbours, if we have more cloth than they, to make our garment somewhat larger.

What was the foundation or groundwork of this dismal declining of Munster but the banishing of their bishop, their confiscating and casting lots for church livings, as the soldiers cast lots for Christ's garments, and, in short terms, their making the house of God a den of thieves. The house of God a number of hungry church-robbers in these days have made a den of thieves. Thieves spend loosely what they have got lightly. Sacrilege is no sure inheritance; Dionysius was ne'er the richer for robbing Jupiter of his golden coat—he was driven in the end to play the schoolmaster at Corinth. The name of religion, be it good or bad, that is ruinated, God never suffers unrevenged. I'll say it as Ovid* said of eunuchs:

> *Qui primus pueris genitalia membra recidit,*
> *Vulnera quae fecit debuit ipse pati.*
>
> Who first deprived young boys of their best part,
> With self-same wounds he gave he ought to smart.

So would he that first gelt religion or church-livings had been first gelt himself or never lived. Cardinal Wolsey is the man I aim at, *qui in suas poenas ingeniosus erat,** first gave others a light to his own overthrow. How it prospered with him and his instruments that after wrought for themselves, chronicles largely report though not apply, and some parcel of their punishment yet unpaid I do not doubt but will be required of their posterity.

To go forward with my story of the overthrow of that usurper John Leyden, he and all his army (as I said before) falling prostrate on their faces, and fervently given over to prayer, determined never to cease or leave soliciting of God till he had showed them from heaven some manifest miracle of success. Note that it was a general received tradition both with J. Leyden and all the crew of Cnipperdolings and Muncers,* if God at any time at their vehement outcries and clamours did not condescend to their requests, to rail on Him and curse Him to his face, to dispute with Him and argue Him of injustice for not being so good as His word with them, and to urge His many promises in the scripture against Him. So that they did not serve God simply, but that He should serve their turns, and after that tenure are many content to serve as bondmen to save the danger of hanging.

But he that serves God aright, whose upright conscience hath for his mot *Amor est mihi causa sequendi*, I serve because I love, he says *Ego te potius domine quam tua dona sequar*, I'll rather follow thee, O Lord, for thine own sake than for any covetous respect of that thou canst do for me. Christ would have no followers but such as forsook all and follow him, such as forsake all their own desires, such as abandon all expectations of reward in this world, such as neglected and contemned their lives, their wives and children in comparison of him, and were content to take up their cross and follow him.

These Anabaptists had not yet forsook all and followed Christ. They had not forsook their own desires of revenge and innovation, they had not abandoned their expectation of the spoil of their enemies, they regarded their lives, they looked after their wives and children, they took not up their cross of humility and followed him, but would cross him, upbraid him, and set him at naught if he assured not by some sign their prayers and supplications. *Deteriora sequunter,** they followed God as daring him. God heard their prayers; *quod petitur poena est,** it was their speedy punishment that they prayed for. Lo, according to the sum of their impudent supplications, a sign in the heavens appeared: the glorious sign of the rainbow, which agreed just with the sign of their ensign that was a rainbow likewise. Whereupon, assuring themselves of victory (*miseri quod volunt facile credunt*, that which wretches would have they easily believe) with shouts and clamours they presently ran headlong on their well-deserved confusion.

Pitiful and lamentable was their unpitied and well-performed slaughter. To see even a bear, which is the most cruellest of all beasts, too too bloodily overmatched and deformedly rent in pieces by an unconscionable number of curs, it would move compassion against kind, and make those that beholding him at the stake yet uncoped with wished him a suitable death to his ugly shape, now to recall their hard-hearted wishes and moan him suffering as a mild beast in comparison of the foul-mouthed mastiffs his butchers. Even such compassion did those overmatched, ungracious Munsterians obtain of many indifferent eyes, who now thought them, suffering, to be as sheep brought innocent to the shambles, whenas before they deemed them as a number of wolves up in arms against the shepherds.

The imperials themselves, that were their executioners, like a father that weeps when he beats his child, yet still weeps and still beats, not without much ruth and sorrow prosecuted that lamentable massacre. Yet drums and trumpets, sounding nothing but stern revenge in their ears, made them so eager that their hands had no leisure to ask counsel of their effeminate eyes. Their swords, their pikes, their bills, their bows, their calivers slew, empierced, knocked down, shot through, and overthrew as many men every minute of the battle as there falls ears of corn before the scythe at one blow. Yet all their weapons so slaying, empiercing, knocking down, shooting through, overthrowing, dis-soul-joined not half so many as the hailing thunder of their great ordinance. So ordinary at every footstep was the imbruement of iron in blood that one could hardly discern heads from bullets, or clotted hair from mangled flesh hung with gore.

This tale must at one time or other give up the ghost, and as good now as stay longer. I would gladly rid my hands of it cleanly if I could tell you how, for what with talking of cobblers and tinkers and ropemakers and botchers and dirt-daubers, the mark is clean gone out of my muse's mouth, and I am, as it were, more than duncified twixt divinity and poetry. What is there more as touching this tragedy that you would be resolved of? Say quickly, for now my pen is got upon his feet again! How J. Leyden died, is that it? He died like a dog; he was hanged and the halter paid for. For his companions, do they trouble you? I can tell you they troubled some men before, for they were all killed, and none escaped— no, not so much as one to tell the tale of the rainbow. Hear what it is to be Anabaptists, to be puritans, to be villains. You may be counted illuminate botchers for a while, but your end will be 'Good people, pray for me.'

With the tragical catastrophe of this Munsterian conflict did I cashier the new vocation of my cavaliership. There was no more honourable wars in christendom then towards wherefore, after I had learned to be half an hour in bidding a man *bonjour* in German sunonimas, I travelled along the country towards England as fast as I could. What with wagons and bare ten-toes having attained to Middleborough (good Lord see the changing chances of us knight-arrant infants) I met with the right honourable Lord Henry Howard,* Earl of Surrey, my late master. Jesu, I was persuaded I should not be more glad to see heaven than I was to see him. Oh it was a right noble lord, liberality itself—if in this iron age there were any such creature as liberality left on the earth. A prince in content because a poet without peer. Destiny never defames herself but when she lets an excellent poet die. If there be any spark of Adam's paradised perfection yet embered up in the breasts of mortal men, certainly God hath bestowed that his perfectest image on poets. None come so near to God in wit, none more contemn the world. *Vatis avarus non temere est animus*, saith Horace, *versus amat, hoc studet unum*: seldom have you seen any poet possessed with avarice; only verses he loves, nothing else he delights in. And as they contemn the world, so contrarily of the mechanical world are none more contemned. Despised they are of the world because they are not of the world; their thoughts are exalted above the world of ignorance and all earthly conceits.

As sweet, angelical queristers they are continually conversant in the heaven of arts. Heaven itself is but the highest height of knowledge; he that knows himself and all things else knows the means to be happy. Happy, thrice happy, are they whom God hath doubled his spirit upon, and given a double soul unto to be poets. My heroical master exceeded in this supernatural kind of wit. He entertained no gross, earthly spirit of avarice, nor weak womanly spirit of pusillanimity and fear that are feigned to be of the water, but admirable airy and fiery spirits, full of freedom, magnanimity, and bountihood. Let me not speak any more of his accomplishments for fear I spend all my spirits in praising him and leave myself no vigour of wit or effects of a soul to go forward with my history.

Having thus met him I so much adored, no interpleading

was there of opposite occasions, but back I must return and bear half stakes with him in the lottery of travel. I was not altogether unwilling to walk along with such a good purse-bearer, yet musing what changeable humour had so suddenly seduced him from his native soil to seek out needless perils in these parts beyond sea, one night very boldly I demanded of him the reason that moved him thereto.

'Ah,' quoth he, 'my little page, full little canst thou perceive how far metamorphosed I am from myself since I last saw thee. There is a little god called Love that will not be worshipped of any leaden brains, one that proclaims himself sole king and emperor of piercing eyes and chief sovereign of soft hearts. He it is that, exercising his empire in my eyes, hath exorcized and clean conjured me from my content. Thou knowest stately Geraldine*—too stately, I fear, for me to do homage to her statue or shrine. She it is that is come out of Italy to bewitch all the wise men of England. Upon Queen Katherine Dowager she waits, that hath a dowry of beauty sufficient to make her wooed of the greatest kings in Christendom. Her high exalted sunbeams have set the phoenix nest of my breast on fire, and I myself have brought Arabian spiceries of sweet passions and praises to furnish out the funeral flame of my folly.

'Those who were condemned to be smothered to death by sinking down into the soft bottom of an high-built bed of roses never died so sweet a death as I should die if her rose-coloured disdain were my deathsman. Oh thrice imperial Hampton Court, Cupid's enchanted castle, the place where I first saw the perfect omnipotence of the Almighty expressed in mortality, 'tis thou alone that, tithing all other men solace in thy pleasant situation, affordest me nothing but an excellent begotten sorrow out of the chief treasury of all thy recreations.

'Dear Wilton, understand that there it was where I first set eye on my more than celestial Geraldine. Seeing her I admired her; all the whole receptacle of my sight was unhabited with her rare worth. Long suit and uncessant protestations got me the grace to be entertained. Did never unloving servant so prenticelike obey his never-pleased mistress as I did her. My life, my wealth, my friends, had all their destiny depending on her command.

'Upon a time I was determined to travel. The fame of Italy, and an especial affection I had unto poetry, my second mistress, for which Italy was so famous, had wholly ravished me unto it. There was no dehortment from it, but needs thither I would, wherefore coming to my mistress as she was then walking with other ladies of estate in Paradise* at Hampton Court, I most humbly besought her of favour that she would give me so much gracious leave to absent myself from her service as to travel a year or two into Italy. She very discreetly answered me that, if my love were so hot as I had often avouched, I did very well to apply the plaster of absence unto it, for absence, as they say, causeth forgetfulness.

' "Yet nevertheless, since it is Italy, my native country, you are so desirous to see, I am the more willing to make my will yours. Aye, *pete Italiam*, go and seek Italy with Aeneas, but be more true than Aeneas. I hope that kind, wit-cherishing climate will work no change in so witty a breast. No country of mine shall it be more if it conspire with thee in any new love against me. One charge I will give thee, and let it be rather a request than a charge. When thou comest to Florence, the fair city from whence I fetched the pride of my birth, by an open challenge defend my beauty against all comers.

' "Thou hast that honourable carriage in arms that it shall be no discredit for me to bequeath all the glory of my beauty to thy well-governed arm. Fain would I be known where I was born; fain would I have thee known where fame sits in her chiefest theatre. Farewell; forget me not. Continued deserts will eternize me unto thee. Thy full wishes shall be expired when thy travel shall be once ended."

'Here did tears step out before words, and intercepted the course of my kind conceived speech even as wind is allayed with rain. With heart-scalding sighs I confirmed her parting request, and vowed myself hers while living heat allowed me to be mine own. *Hinc illae lacrimae*:* here hence proceedeth the whole cause of my peregrination.'

Not a little was I delighted with this unexpected love story, especially from a mouth out of which was naught wont to march but stern precepts of gravity and modesty. I swear unto you, I thought his company the better by a thousand crowns because he had discarded those nice terms of chastity and continency. Now I beseech God love me so well as I love a plain dealing man. Earth is earth, flesh is flesh; earth will to earth and flesh unto flesh; frail earth, frail flesh, who can keep you from the work of your creation.

Dismissing this fruitless annotation *pro et contra*, towards Venice we progressed, and took Rotterdam in our way, that was clean out of our way. There we met with aged learning's chief ornament, that abundant and superingenious clerk Erasmus,* as also with merry Sir Thomas More our countryman, who was come purposely over a little before us to visit the said grave father Erasmus. What talk, what conference we had then it were here superfluous to rehearse, but this I can assure you: Erasmus in all his speeches seemed so much to mislike the indiscretion of princes in preferring of parasites and fools that he decreed with himself to swim with the stream and write a book forthwith in commendation of folly.

Quick-witted Sir Thomas More travelled in a clean contrary province, for he, seeing most commonwealths corrupted by ill custom, and that principalities were nothing but great piracies which, gotten by violence and murther, were maintained by private undermining and bloodshed; that in the chiefest flourishing kingdoms there was no equal or well-divided weal one with another, but a manifest conspiracy of rich men against poor men, procuring their own unlawful commodities under the name and interest of the commonwealth—he concluded with himself to lay down a perfect plot of a commonwealth or government which he would entitle his *Utopia*. So left we them to prosecute their discontented studies, and made our next journey to Wittenberg.

At the very point of our entrance into Wittenberg* we were spectators of a very solemn, scholastical entertainment of the Duke of Saxony thither; whom, because he was the chief patron of their university, and had took Luther's part in banishing the mass and all like papal jurisdiction out of their town, they crouched unto extremely. The chief ceremonies of their entertainment were these: first, the heads of their university (they were great heads of certainty) met him in their hooded hypocrisy and doctorly accoutrements, *secundum formam statuti*,* where by the orator of the university, whose pickerdevant was very plentifully besprinkled with rosewater, a very learned—or rather ruthful—oration was delivered (for it rained all the while) signifying thus much: that it was all by patch and by piecemeal stolen out of Tully, and he must pardon them, though in emptying their phrase books the air emptied his* entrails, for they did it not in any ostentation of wit (which they had not) but to show the extraordinary good will they bare the Duke—to have him stand in the rain till he was thorough wet. A thousand *quemadmodums* and *quaopropters*,* he came over him with. Every sentence he concluded with *esse posse videatur*.* Through all the nine worthies he ran with praising and comparing him. Nestor's years he assured him of under the broad seal of their supplications, and with that crow-trodden verse in Virgil, *dum iuga montis aper*,* he packed up his pipes and cried *dixi*.*

That pageant overpassed, there rushed upon him a miserable rabblement of junior graduates that all cried out upon him mightily in their gibrige like a company of beggars 'God save your grace, God save your grace, Jesus preserve your highness, though it be but for an hour.' Some three halfpennyworth of Latin here also had he thrown at his face, but it was choice stuff I can tell you, as there is a choice even amongst rags gathered up from the dunghill. At the town's end met him the burghers and dunstical incorporationers of Wittenberg in their distinguished liveries—their distinguished, livery faces I mean, for they were most of them hot-livered drunkards, and had all the coat colours of sanguine, purple, crimson, copper, carnation, that were to be had in their countenances. Filthy knaves, no cost had they bestowed on the town for his welcome saving new painted their houghs and boozing houses, which commonly are built fairer than their churches, and over their gates set the town arms,* which sounded gulping after this sort: '*Vanhotten slotten, irk bloshen glotten gelderlike*.' Whatever the words were, the sense was this: good drink is a medicine for all diseases.

A bursten-belly inkhorn orator called Vanderhulk they picked out to present him with an oration; one that had a sulphurous big swollen large face like a Saracen, eyes like two Kentish oysters, a mouth that opened as wide every time he spake as one of those old knit* trap doors, a beard as though it had been made of a bird's nest plucked in pieces, which consisteth of straw, hair, and dirt mixed together. He was apparelled in black leather new liquored and a short gown without any gathering in the back, faced before and behind with a boisterous bear skin, and a red nightcap on his head. To this purport and effect was this broccing double-beer oration.

'Right noble Duke, *ideo nobilis quasi no bilis*, for you have no bile or choler in you, know that our present incorporation of Wittenberg by me, the tongueman of their thankfulness, a townsman by birth, a free German by nature, an orator by art, and a scrivener by education, in all obedience and chastity most bountifully bid you welcome to Wittenberg. Welcome said I? O orificial rhetoric, wipe thy everlasting mouth and afford me a more Indian metaphor than that for the brave princely blood of a Saxon. Oratory, uncask the barred hutch of thy compliments, and with the triumphantest troup in thy treasury do trewage unto him. What impotent speech with his eight parts may not specify, this unestimable gift holding his peace shall as it were (with tears I speak it) do whereby as it may seem or appear to manifest or declare, and yet it is, and yet it is not, and yet it may be a diminutive oblation meritorious to your high pusillanimity and indignity. Why should I go gadding and fizgigging after firking flantado amphibologies?* Wit is wit, and good will is good will. With all the wit I have I here, according to the premises, offer up unto you the city's general good will, which is a gilded can, in manner and form following for you and the heirs of your body lawfully begotten to drink healths in. The scholastical squitter-books clout you up canopies and footcloths of verses. We that are good fellows, and live as merry as cup and can, will not verse upon you as they do, but must do as we can, and entertain you if it be but with a plain empty can. He hath learning enough that hath learned to drink to his first man.

'Gentle Duke, without paradox be it spoken, thy horses at our own proper costs and charges shall knead up to the knees all the while thou art here in spruce beer and lubeck liquor. Not a dog thou bringest with thee but shall be banqueted with rhenish wine and sturgeon. On our shoulders we wear no lambskin or miniver like these academics, yet we can drink to the confusion of all thy enemies. Good lambswool have we for their lambskins, and for their miniver large minerals in our coffers. Mechanical men they call us, and not amiss, for most of us being *Maechi*,* that is, cuckolds and whoremasters, fetch our antiquity from the temple of *Maecha*, where Mahomet is hung up. Three parts of the world, America, Africk, and Asia, are of this our mechanic religion. Nero, when he cried *O quantus artifex pereo*,* professed himself of our freedom, insomuch as *artifex* is a citizen or craftsman as well as *carnifex*, a scholar or hangman. Pass on by leave into the precincts of our abomination. Bonny Duke, frolic in our bower and persuade thyself that even as garlic hath three properties, to make a man wink, drink, and stink, so we will wink on thy imperfections, drink to thy favourites, and all thy foes shall stink before us. So be it. Farewell.'

The Duke laughed not a little at this ridiculous oration, but that very night as great an ironical occasion was ministered, for he was bidden to one of the chief schools to a comedy handled by scholars. *Acolastus the Prodigal Child** was the name of it, which was so filthily acted, so leathernly set forth, as would have moved laughter in Heraclitus. One, as if he had been planing a clay floor, stampingly trod the stage so hard with his feet that I thought verily he had resolved to do the carpenter that set it up some utter shame. Another flung his arms like cudgels at a pear tree, insomuch as it was mightily dreaded that he would strike the candles that hung above their heads out of their sockets and leave them all dark. Another did nothing but wink and make faces. There was a parasite, and he with clapping his hands and thripping his fingers seemed to dance an antic to and fro. The only thing they did well was the prodigal child's hunger, most of their scholars being hungerly kept, and surely you would have said they had been brought up in hog's academy to learn to eat acorns if you had seen how sedulously they fell to them. Not a jest had they to keep their auditors from sleep but of swill and draff. Yes, now and then the servant put his hand into the dish before his master and almost choked himself, eating slovenly and ravenously to cause sport.

The next day they had solemn disputations, where Luther and Carolostadius* scolded level coil. A mass of words I wot well they heaped up against the mass and the Pope, but farther particulars of their disputations I remember not. I thought verily they would have worried one another with words, they were so earnest and vehement. Luther had the louder voice, Carolostadius went beyond him in beating and bouncing with his fists. *Quae supra nos nihil ad nos.** They uttered nothing to make a man laugh, therefore I will leave them.

Marry, their outward gestures now and then would afford a man a morsel of mirth. Of those two I mean not so much as of all the other train of opponents and respondents. One pecked like a crane with his forefinger at every half syllable he brought forth, and nodded with his nose like an old singing man teaching a young querister to keep time. Another would be sure to wipe his mouth with his handkercher at the end of every full point, and ever when he thought he had cast a figure so curiously as he dived over head and ears into his auditors' admiration, he would take occasion to stroke up his hair and twine up his mustachios twice or thrice over while they might have leisure to applaud him. A third wavered and waggled his head like a proud horse playing with his bridle, or as I have seen some fantastical swimmer at every stroke train his chin sidelong over his left shoulder. A fourth sweat and foamed at the mouth for very anger his adversary had denied that part of his syllogism which he was not prepared to answer. A fifth spread his arms like an usher that goes before to make room, and thripped with his finger and his thumb when he thought he had tickled it with a conclusion. A sixth hung down his countenance like a sheep, and stuttered and slavered very pitifully when his invention was stepped aside out of the way. A seventh gasped and gaped for wind and groaned in his pronunciation as if he were hard bound with some bad argument.

Gross plodders they were all, that had some learning and reading but no wit to make use of it. They imagined the Duke took the greatest pleasure and contentment under heaven to hear them speak Latin, and as long as they talked nothing but Tully he was bound to attend them. A most vain thing it is in many universities at this day, that they count him excellent eloquent who stealeth not whole phrases but whole pages out of Tully. If of a number of shreds of his sentences he can shape an oration, from all the world he carries it away, although in truth it be no more than a fool's coat of many colours. No invention or matter have they of their own, but tack up a style of his stale gallimaufries. The leaden-headed Germans first began this, and we Englishmen have surfeited of their absurd imitation. I pity Nizolius,* that had nothing to do but pick threads' ends out of an old, overworn garment.

This is but by the way; we must look back to our disputants. One amongst the rest, thinking to be more conceited than his fellows, seeing the Duke have a dog he loved well which sat by him on the terrace, converted all his oration to him, and not a hair of his tail but he combed out with comparisons. So to have courted him if he were a bitch had been very suspicious. Another commented and descanted on the Duke's staff, new tipping it with many quaint epithets. Some cast his nativity and promised him he should not die till the day of judgement.

Omitting further superfluities of this stamp, in this general assembly we found intermixed that abundant scholar Cornelius Agrippa.* At that time he bare the fame to be the greatest conjurer in Christendom. Scoto, that did the juggling tricks here before the Queen, never came near him one quarter in magic reputation. The doctors of Wittenberg, doting on the rumour that went of him, desired him before the Duke and them to do something extraordinary memorable.

One requested to see pleasant Plautus, and that he would show them in what habit he went, and with what countenance he looked when he ground corn in the mill. Another had half a month's mind to Ovid and his hook nose. Erasmus, who was not wanting to that honourable meeting, requested to see Tully in that same grace and majesty he pleaded his oration *pro Roscio Amerino*, affirming that till in person he beheld his importunity of pleading he would not be persuaded any man could carry away a manifest case with rhetoric so strangely. To Erasmus' petition he easily condescended, and willing the doctors at such an hour to hold their convocation, and every one to keep him in his place without moving, at the time prefixed in entered Tully, ascended his pleading place, and declaimed verbatim the forenamed oration, but with such astonishing amazement, with such fervent exaltation of spirit, with such soul-stirring gestures, that all his auditors were ready to install his guilty client for a god.

Great was the concourse of glory Agrippa drew to him with this one feat. And indeed he was so cloyed with men which came to behold him that he was fain sooner than he would to return to the Emperor's court from whence he came, and leave Wittenberg before he would. With him we travelled along, having purchased his acquaintance a little before. By the way as we went my master and I agreed to change names. It was concluded betwixt us that I should be the Earl of Surrey and he my man, only because in his own person, which he would not have reproached, he meant to take more liberty of behaviour. As for my carriage, he knew he was to tune it at a key either high or low or as he list.

To the Emperor's court we came, where our entertainment was every way plentiful. Carouses we had in whole gallons instead of quart pots. Not a health was given us but contained well near a hogshead. The customs of the country we were eager to be instructed in, but nothing we could learn but this: that ever at the Emperor's coronation there is an ox roasted with a stag in the belly, and that stag in his belly hath a kid, and that kid is stuffed full of birds. Some courtiers, to weary out time, would tell us further tales of Cornelius Agrippa, and how when Sir Thomas More our countryman was there he showed him the whole destruction of Troy in a dream. How the Lord Cromwell* being the King's ambassador there, in like case in a perspective glass he set before his eyes King Henry the Eight with all his lords hunting in his forest at Windsor; and when he came into his study and was very urgent to be partaker of some rare experiment that he might report when he came into England, he willed him amongst two thousand great books to take down which he list and begin to read one line in any place, and without book he would rehearse twenty leaves following. Cromwell did so, and in many books tried him, when in everything he exceeded his promise and conquered his expectation. To Charles the Fifth, then Emperor, they reported how he showed the nine worthies, David, Solomon, Gideon, and the rest, in that similitude and likeness that they lived upon earth.

My master and I, having by the highway side gotten some reasonable familiarity with him, upon this access of miracles imputed to him resolved to request him something in our own behalfs. I, because I was his suborned lord and master, desired him to see the lively image of Geraldine his love in the glass, and what at that instant she did, and with whom she was talking. He showed her us without more ado, sick, weeping on her bed, and resolved all into devout religion for the absence of her lord. At the sight thereof he could in no wise refrain, though he had took upon him the condition of a servant, but he must forthwith frame this extemporal ditty.

> All soul, no earthly flesh, why dost thou fade?
> All gold, no worthless dross, why look'st thou pale?
> Sickness, how dar'st thou one so fair invade,
> Too base infirmity to work her bale?
>   Heaven be distempered since she grieved pines,
>   Never be dry, these my sad plaintive lines.

> Perch thou, my spirit, on her silver breasts,
> And with their pain-redoubled music beatings
> Let them toss thee to world where all toil rests,
> Where bliss is subject to no fear's defeatings.
>   Her praise I tune, whose tongue doth tune the spheres,
>   And gets new muses in her hearers' ears.

> Stars fall to fetch fresh light from her rich eyes,
> Her bright brow drives the sun to clouds beneath,
> Her hairs reflex with red strakes paints the skies,
> Sweet morn and evening dew flows from her breath.
>   Phoebe rules tides, she my tears' tides forth draws,
>   In her sickbed love sits and maketh laws.

Her dainty limbs tinsel her silk soft sheets,
Her rose-crowned cheeks eclipse my dazzled sight,
O glass, with too much joy my thoughts thou greets,
And yet thou showest me day but by twilight.
    I'll kiss thee for the kindness I have felt,
    Her lips one kiss would unto nectar melt.

Though the Emperor's court and the extraordinary edifying company of Cornelius Agrippa might have been arguments of weight to have arrested us a little longer there, yet Italy still stuck as a great mote in my master's eye. He thought he had travelled no farther than Wales till he had took survey of that country which was such a curious moulder of wits.

To cut off blind ambages by the highway side, we made a long stride and got to Venice in short time where, having scarce looked about us, a precious supernatural pander, apparelled in all points like a gentleman and having half a dozen several languages in his purse, entertained us in our own tongue very paraphrastically and eloquently, and maugre all other pretended acquaintance would have us in a violent kind of courtesy to be the guests of his appointment. His name was Petro de Campo Frego, a notable practitioner in the policy of bawdry. The place whither he brought us was a pernicious courtesan's house named Tabitha the Temptress's, a wench that could set as civil a face on it as chastity's first martyr Lucretia.

What will you conceit to be in any saint's house that was there to seek? Books, pictures, beads, crucifixes—why there was a haberdasher's shop of them in every chamber. I warrant you should not see one set of her neckercher perverted or turned awry, not a piece of hair displaced. On her beds there was not a wrinkle of any wallowing to be found; her pillows bare out as smooth as a groaning wife's belly, and yet she was a Turk and an infidel, and had more doings than all her neighbours besides. Us for our money they used like emperors. I was master, as you heard before, and my master the Earl was but as my chief man, whom I made my companion. So it happened (as iniquity will out at one time or other) that she, perceiving my expense had no more vents than it should have, fell in with my supposed servant, my man, and gave him half a promise of marriage if he would help to make me away, that she and he might enjoy the jewels and wealth that I had.

The indifficulty of the condition thus she explained unto him: her house stood upon vaults which in two hundred years together were never searched; who came into her house none took notice of; his fellow servants that knew of his master's abode there should all be dispatched by him as from his master into sundry parts of the city about business, and when they returned answer should be made that he lay not there any more but had removed to Padua since their departure, and thither they must follow him. 'Now', quoth she, 'if you be disposed to make him away in their absence, you shall have my house at command. Stab, poison, or shoot him through with a pistol—all is one, into the vault he shall be thrown when the deed is done.'

On my bare honesty, it was a crafty quean, for she had enacted with herself if he had been my legitimate servant, as he was one that served and supplied my necessities, when he had murthered me to have accused him of the murther, and made all that I had hers, as I carried all my master's wealth—money, jewels, rings, or bills of exchange—continually about me. He very subtly consented to her stratagem at the first motion. Kill me he would, that heavens could not withstand, and a pistol was the predestinate engine which must deliver the parting blow. God wot I was a raw young squire, and my master dealt Judasly with me, for he told me but* everything that she and he agreed of, wherefore I could not possibly prevent it, but as a man would say avoid it.

The execution day aspired to his utmost devolution, into my chamber came my honourable attendant with his pistol charged by his side, very suspiciously and sullenly. Lady Tabitha and Petro de Campo Frego, her pander, followed him at the hard heels. At their entrance I saluted them all very familiarly and merrily, and began to impart unto them what disquiet dreams had disturbed me the last night. 'I dreamed', quoth I, 'that my man Brunquell here (for no better name got he of me) came into my chamber with a pistol charged under his arm to kill me, and that he was suborned by you, Mistress Tabitha, and my very good friend here Petro de Campo Frego. God send it turn to good, for it hath affrighted me above measure.'

As they were ready to enter into a colourable commonplace of the deceitful frivolousness of dreams, my trusty servant Brunquell stood quivering and quaking every joint of him, and (as it was before compacted between us) let his pistol drop from him on the sudden, wherewith I started out of my bed and drew my rapier and cried 'Murther, murther!', which made goodwife Tabitha ready to bepiss her.

My servant, or my master, which you will, I took roughly by the collar, and threatened to run him through incontinent, if he confessed not the truth. He, as it were stricken with remorse of conscience (God be with him, for he could counterfeit most daintily), down on his knees, asked me forgiveness, and impeached Tabitha and Petro de Campo Frego as guilty of subornation. I very mildly and gravely gave him audience; rail on them I did not after his tale was ended, but said I would try what the law could do. Conspiracy by the custom of their country was a capital offence, and what custom or justice might afford they should be all sure to feel.

'I could', quoth I, 'acquit myself otherwise, but it is not for a stranger to be his own carver in revenge.' Not a word more with Tabitha, but die she would before God or the devil would have her. She sounded and revived and then sounded again, and after she revived again sighed heavily, spoke faintly and pitifully, yea and so pitifully as if a man had not known the pranks of harlots before, he would have melted in commiseration. Tears, sighs, and doleful tuned words could not make any forcible claim to my stony ears, it was the glistering crowns that I hungered and thirsted after, and with them, for all her mock holy day gestures, she was fain to come off before I would condescend to any bargain of silence.

So it fortuned (fie upon that unfortunate word of Fortune) that this whore, this quean, this courtesan, this common of ten thousand, so bribing me not to bewray her, had given me a great deal of counterfeit gold which she had received of a coiner to make away a little before, amongst the gross sum of my bribery. I, silly milksop, mistrusting no deceit, under an angel of light took what she gave me, ne'er turned it over, for which (O falsehood in fair show) my master and I had like to have been turned over. He that is a knight errant exercised in the affairs of ladies and gentlewomen hath more places to send money to than the devil hath to send his spirits to.

There was a delicate wench called Flavia Amelia, lodging in St Mark's Street at a goldsmith's, which I would fain have had to the grand test to try whether she were current in alchemy or no. Ay me! She was but a counterfeit slip, for she not only gave me the slip but had well nigh made me a slipstring. To her I sent my gold to beg an hour of grace. Ah, graceless fornicatress! My hostess and she were confederate, who, having gotten but one piece of my ill gold into their hands, devised the means to make me immortal. I could drink for anger till my head ached to think how I was abused.

Shall I shame the devil and speak the truth? To prison was I sent as principal and my master as accessory; nor was it to a prison neither, but to the master of the Mint's house, who though partly our judge, and a most severe upright justice in his own nature, extremely seemed to condole our ignorant estate, and without all peradventure a present redress he had ministered if certain of our countrymen, hearing an English earl was apprehended for coining, had not come to visit us. An ill planet brought them thither, for at the first glance they knew the servant of my secrecies to be the Earl of Surrey, and I (not worthy to be named I) an outcast of his cup or his pantofles.

Thence, thence sprung the full period of our infelicity. The master of the Mint, our whilom refresher and consolation, now took part against us. He thought we had a mint in our head of mischievous conspiracies against their state. Heavens bear witness with us it was not so (heavens will not always come to witness when they are called). To a straiter ward were we committed; that which we have imputatively transgressed must be answered. O the heathen hey pass, and the intrinsical legerdemain of our special approved good pander Petro de Campo Frego. He, although he dipped in the same dish with us every day, seeming to labour our cause very importunately, and had interpreted for us to the state from the beginning, yet was one of those treacherous Brother Trulies,* and abused us most clerkly. He interpreted to us with a pestilence, for whereas we stood obstinately upon it we were wrongfully detained, and that it was naught but a malicious practice of sinful Tabitha our late hostess, he by a fine coney-catching corrupt translation made us plainly to confess and cry *Miserere* ere we had need of our neck-verse.*

Detestable, detestable, that the flesh and the devil should deal by their factors! I'll stand to it, there is not a pander but hath vowed paganism. The devil himself is not such a devil as he, so be he perform his function aright. He must have the back of an ass, the snout of an elephant, the wit of a fox, and the teeth of a wolf; he must fawn like a spaniel, crouch like a Jew, leer like a sheepbiter. If he be half a puritan and have scripture continually in his mouth he speeds the better. I can tell you it is a trade of great promotion, and let none ever think to mount by service in foreign courts, or creep near to some magnifique lords, if they be not seen in this science. O, it is the art of arts, and ten thousand times goes beyond the intelligencer. None but a staid, grave civil man is capable of it; he must have exquisite courtship in him or else he is not old who; he wants the best point in his tables.*

God be merciful to our pander (and that were for God to work a miracle), he was seen in all the seven liberal deadly sciences; not a sin but he was as absolute in as Satan himself. Satan could never have supplanted us so as he did. I may say to you he planted in us the first Italianate wit that we had.

During the time we lay close and took physic in this castle of contemplation, there was a magnifico's wife of good calling sent in to bear us company. Her husband's name was Castaldo, she hight Diamante. The cause of her committing was an ungrounded jealous suspicion which her doting husband had conceived of her chastity. One Isaac Medicus, a Bergomast, was the man he chose to make him a monster, who—being a courtier and repairing to his house very often, neither for love of him nor his wife, but only with a drift to borrow money of a pawn of wax and parchment—when he saw his expectation deluded, and that Castaldo was too chary for him to close with, he privily with purpose of revenge gave out amongst his copesmates that he resorted to Castaldo's house for no other end but to cuckold him, and doubtfully he talked that he had and he had not obtained his suit. Rings which he borrowed of a light courtesan that he used to, he would feign to be taken from her fingers; and in sum so handled the matter that Castaldo exclaimed 'Out whore, strumpet, six-penny hackster! Away with her to prison!'

As glad were we almost as if they had given us liberty that fortune lent us such a sweet pew-fellow. A pretty, round-faced wench was it, with black eyebrows, a high forehead, a little mouth and a sharp nose, as fat and plum every part of her as a plover, a skin as sleek and soft as the back of a swan. It doth me good when I remember her. Like a bird she tripped on the ground, and bare out her belly as majestical as an ostrich. With a licorous, rolling eye fixed piercing on the earth, and sometimes scornfully darted on the t'one side, she figured forth a high, discontented disdain, much like a prince puffing and storming at the treason of some mighty subject fled lately out of his power. Her very countenance repiningly wrathful, and yet clear and unwrinkled, would have confirmed the clearness of her conscience to the austerest judge in the world.

If in anything she were culpable, it was in being too melancholy chaste, and showing herself as covetous of her beauty as her husband was of his bags. Many are honest because they know not how to be dishonest; she thought there was no pleasure in stolen bread because there was no pleasure in an old man's bed. It is almost impossible that any woman should be excellently witty and not make the utmost penny of her beauty. This age and this country of ours admits of some miraculous exceptions, but former times are my constant informers. Those that have quick motions of wit have quick motions in everything. Iron only needs many strokes; only iron wits are not won without a long siege of entreaty. Gold easily bends; the most ingenious minds are easiest moved. *Ingenium nobis molle Thalia dedit,** saith Sappho to Phao. Who hath no merciful mild mistress, I will maintain, hath no witty but a clownish, dull phlegmatic puppy to his mistress.

This magnifico's wife was a good, loving soul, that had mettle enough in her to make a good wit of, but being never removed from under her mother's and her husband's wing, it was not moulded and fashioned as it ought. Causeless distrust is able to drive deceit into a simple woman's head. I durst pawn the credit of a page, which is worth ambs-ace at all times, that she was immaculate honest till she met with us in prison. Marry, what temptations she had then, when fire and wax were put together, conceit with yourselves, but hold my master excusable.

Alack, he was too virtuous to make her vicious; he stood upon religion and conscience, what a heinous thing it was to subvert God's ordinance. This was all the injury he would offer her: sometimes he would imagine her in a melancholy humour to be his Geraldine, and court her in terms correspondent. Nay, he would swear she was his Geraldine, and take her white hand and wipe his eyes with it as though the very touch of her might stanch his anguish. Now would he kneel and kiss the ground as holy ground which she vouchsafed to bless from barrenness by her steps. Who would have learned to write an excellent passion might have been a perfect tragic poet had he but attended half the extremity of his lament. Passion upon passion would throng one on another's neck. He would praise her beyond the moon and stars, and that so sweetly and ravishingly as I persuade myself he was more in love with his own curious forming fancy than her face; and truth it is, many become passionate lovers only to win praise to their wits.

He praised, he prayed, he desired and besought her to pity him that perished for her. From this his entranced mistaking ecstasy could no man remove him. Who loveth resolutely will include everything under the name of his love. From prose he would leap into verse, and with these or such like rhymes assault her.

> If I must die, O let me choose my death,
> Suck out my soul with kisses, cruel maid,
> In thy breasts' crystal balls embalm my breath,
> Dole it all out in sighs when I am laid.
> Thy lips on mine like cupping glasses clasp,
> Let our tongues meet and strive as they would sting,
> Crush out my wind with one straight girting grasp,
> Stabs on my heart keep time whilst thou dost sing.
> Thy eyes like searing irons burn out mine,
> In thy fair tresses stifle me outright,

Like Circes change me to a loathsome swine
So I may live forever in thy sight.
    Into heaven's joys can none profoundly see,
    Except that first they meditate on thee.

Sadly and verily, if my master said true, I should if I were a wench make many men quickly immortal. What is't, what is't for a maid fair and fresh to spend a little lip salve on a hungry lover? My master beat the bush and kept a coil and a prattling, but I caught the bird; simplicity and plainness shall carry it away in another world. God wot he was Petro Desperato when I, stepping to her with a dunstable tale, made up my market. A holy requiem to their souls that think to woo women with riddles. I had some cunning plot, you must suppose, to bring this about. Her husband had abused her, and it was very necessary she should be revenged. Seldom do they prove patient martyrs who are punished unjustly. One way or other they will cry quittance, whatsoever it cost them. No other apt means had this poor she-captived Ciccly to work her hoddy-peak husband a proportionable plague to his jealousy but to give his head his full loading of infamy. She thought she would make him complain for something, that now was so hard bound with an heretical opinion. How I dealt with her, guess gentle reader! *Subaudi*.* that I was in prison and she was my jailor.

Means there was made after a month's or two durance by Mr John Russell,* a gentleman of King Henry the Eighth's chamber, who then lay lieger at Venice for England, that our cause should be favourably heard. At that time was Monsieur Petro Aretino* searcher and chief inquisitor for the college of courtesans. Diverse and sundry ways was this Aretino beholding to the King of England, especially for by this foresaid Mr Russell a little before he had sent him a pension of four hundred crowns yearly during his life. Very forcibly was he dealt withal to strain the utmost of his credit for our delivery. Nothing at his hands we sought but that the courtesan might be more narrowly sifted and examined. Such and so extraordinary was his care and industry herein that within few days after, Mistress Tabitha and her pander cried '*Peccavi, confiteor*!'* and we were presently discharged, they

for example sake executed. Most honourably, after our enlargement, of the state were we used, and had sufficient
recompense for all our troubles and wrongs.

Before I go any further, let me speak a word or two of this
Aretine. It was one of the wittiest knaves that ever God made.
If out of so base a thing as ink there may be extracted a spirit,
he writ with nought but the spirit of ink, and his style was the
spirituality of arts and nothing else, whereas all others of his
age were but the lay temporality of inkhorn terms. For indeed
they were mere temporizers and no better. His pen was sharp
pointed like a poniard. No leaf he wrote on but was like a
burning glass to set on fire all his readers. With more than
musket-shot did he charge his quill, where he meant to
inveigh. No one hour but he sent a whole legion of devils into
some herd of swine or other. If Martial had ten muses (as he
saith of himself) when he but tasted a cup of wine, he had ten
score when he determined to tyrannize. Ne'er a line of his but
was able to make a man drunken with admiration. His sight
pierced like lightning into the entrails of all abuses. This I
must needs say, that most of his learning he got by hearing the
lectures at Florence. It is sufficient that learning he had, and
a conceit exceeding all learning to quintessence everything
which he heard.

He was no timorous, servile flatterer of the commonwealth
wherein he lived. His tongue and his invention were forborne;
what they thought, they would confidently utter. Princes he
spared not that in the least point transgressed. His life he
contemned in comparison of the liberty of speech. Whereas
some dull-brain maligners of his accuse him of that treatise
De Tribus Impostoribus Mundi,* which was never contrived
without a general council of devils, I am verily persuaded it
was none of his, and of my mind are a number of the most
judicial Italians. One reason is this: because it was published
forty years after his death, and he never in all his life wrote
anything in Latin. Certainly I have heard that one of
Machiavel's followers and disciples was the author of that
book, who, to avoid discredit, filched it forth under Aretino's
name a great while after he had sealed up his eloquent spirit
in the grave. Too much gall did that wormwood of Ghibelline

wits put in his ink who engraved that rhubarb epitaph on this excellent poet's tombstone. Quite forsaken of all good angels was he, and utterly given over to an artless envy. Four universities honoured Aretino with these rich titles: *Il flagello de principi*, *Il veritiero*, *Il divino*, and *L'unico Aretino*.*

The French King, Francis the First, he kept in such awe that, to chain his tongue, he sent him a huge chain of gold in the form of tongues fashioned. Singularly hath he commented of the humanity of Christ. Besides, as Moses set forth his Genesis, so hath he set forth his Genesis also, including the contents of the whole Bible. A notable treatise hath he compiled, called *I sette psalmi poenetentiarii*. All the Thomasos have cause to love him because he hath dilated so magnificently of the life of Saint Thomas. There is a good thing that he hath set forth, *La Vita della Virgine Maria*, though it somewhat smell of superstition, with a number more which here for tediousness, I suppress. If lascivious he were, he may answer with Ovid *Vita verecunda est, musa jocosa mea est*: my life is chaste though wanton be my verse. Tell me, who is most travelled in histories, what good poet is or ever was there who hath not had a little spice of wantonness in his days? Even Beza* himself, by your leave. Aretino, as long as the world lives shalt thou live. Tully, Virgil, Ovid, Seneca, were never such ornaments to Italy as thou hast been. I never thought of Italy more religiously than England till I heard of thee. Peace to thy ghost, and yet methinks so indefinite a spirit should have no peace or intermission of pains, but be penning ditties to the archangels in another world. Puritans, spew forth the venom of your dull inventions! A toad swells with thick, troubled poison; you swell with poisonous perturbations; your malice hath not a clear dram of any inspired disposition.

My principal subject plucks me by the elbow. Diamante, Castaldo the magnifico's wife, after my enlargement, proved to be with child, at which instant there grew an unsatiable famine in Venice wherein, whether it were for mere niggardise, or that Castaldo still ate out his heart with jealousy, Saint Anne be our record, he turned up the heels very devoutly. To Master Aretino after this once more very dutifully I appealed, requested him of favour, acknowledged former gratuities. He made no more humming or halting, but in despite of her husband's kinsfolks gave her *nunc dimittis*,* and so established her free of my company.

Being out, and fully possessed of her husband's goods, she invested me in the state of a monarch. Because the time of childbirth drew nigh, and she could not remain in Venice but discredited, she decreed to travel whither soever I would conduct her. To see Italy throughout was my proposed scope, and that way if she would travel, have with her, I had wherewithal to relieve her.

From my master by her full-hand provokement I parted without leave; the state of an Earl he had thrust upon me before, and now I would not bate him an inch of it. Through all the cities passed I by no other name but the young Earl of Surrey; my pomp, my apparel, train, and expense was nothing inferior to his; my looks were as lofty, my words as magnifical. Memorandum: that Florence being the principal scope of my master's course, missing me, he journeyed thither without interruption. By the way as he went he heard of another Earl of Surrey besides himself, which caused him make more haste to fetch me in, whom he little dreamed of had such art in my budget to separate the shadow from the body. Overtake me at Florence he did where, sitting in my pontificalibus with my courtesan at supper, like Antony and Cleopatra when they quaffed standing bowls of wine spiced with pearl together, he stole in ere we sent for him, and bade much good it us, and asked us whether we wanted any guests. If he had asked me whether I would have hanged myself, his question had been more acceptable. He that had then ungartered me might have plucked out my heart at my hams.

My soul, which was made to soar upward, now sought for passage downward; my blood, as the blushing Sabine maids surprised on the sudden by the soldiers of Romulus ran to the noblest of blood amongst them for succour that were in no less (if not greater) danger, so did it run for refuge to the noblest of his blood about my heart assembled, that stood in more need itself of comfort and refuge. A trembling earthquake or shaking fever assailed either of us, and I think unfeignedly if he, seeing our faint-heart agony, had not soon cheered and refreshed us, the dogs had gone together by the ears under the table for our fear-dropped limbs.

Instead of menacing or affrighting me with his sword or his frowns for my superlative presumption, he burst out into a laughter above e-la,* to think how bravely napping he had took us, and how notably we were damped and struck dead in the nest with the unexpected view of his presence.

'Ah,' quoth he, 'my noble lord' (after his tongue had borrowed a little leave of his laughter), 'is it my luck to visit you thus unlooked for? I am sure you will bid me welcome if it be but for the name's sake. It is a wonder to see two English earls of one house at one time together in Italy.'

I, hearing him so pleasant, began to gather up my spirits, and replied as boldly as I durst. 'Sir, you are welcome; your name, which I have borrowed, I have not abused. Some large sums of money this my sweet mistress Diamante hath made me master of, which I knew not how better to employ for the honour of my country than by spending it munificently under your name. No Englishman would I have renowned for bounty, magnificence, and courtesy but you; under your colours all my meritorious works I was desirous to shroud. Deem it no insolence to add increase to your fame. Had I basely and beggarly, wanting ability to support any part of your royalty, undertook the estimation of this high calling, your allegement of injury had been the greater, and my defence less authorized. It will be thought but a policy of yours thus to send one before you who, being a follower of yours, shall keep and uphold the estate and port of an earl. I have known many earls myself that in their own persons would go very plain, but delighted to have one that belonged to them, being loaden with jewels, apparelled in cloth of gold and all the rich embroidery that might be, to stand bareheaded unto him, arguing thus much: that if the greatest men went not more sumptuous, how more great than the greatest was he that could command one going so sumptuous. A nobleman's glory appeareth in nothing so much as in the pomp of his attendants. What is the glory of the sun but that the moon and so many millions of stars borrow their light from him? If you can reprehend me of any one illiberal, licentious action I have disparaged your name with, heap shame on me prodigally; I beg no pardon or pity.'

Non veniunt in idem pudor et amor;* he was loath to detract from one that he loved so. Beholding with his eyes that I clipped not the wings of his honour, but rather increased them with additions of expense, he entreated me as if I had been an ambassador; he gave me his hand and swore he had no more hearts but one, and I should have half of it, in that I so enhanced his obscured reputation. 'One thing,' quoth he, 'my sweet Jack, I will entreat thee (it shall be but one): that though I am well pleased thou shouldest be the ape of my birthright (as what nobleman hath not his ape and his fool), yet that thou be an ape without a clog, not carry thy courtesan with thee.'

I told him that a king could do nothing without his treasury; this courtesan was my purse-bearer, my countenance, and supporter. My earldom I would sooner resign than part with such a special benefactress. 'Resign it I will, however, since I am thus challenged of stolen goods by the true owner. Lo, into my former state I return again; poor Jack Wilton and your servant am I, as I was at the beginning, and so will I persevere to my life's ending.'

That theme was quickly cut off, and other talk entered in place; of what I have forgot, but talk it was, and talk let it be, and talk it shall be, for I do not mean here to remember it. We supped, we got to bed, we rose in the morning; on my master I waited, and the first thing he did after he was up, he went and visited the house where his Geraldine was born, at sight whereof he was so impassioned that in the open street, but for me, he would have made an oration in praise of it. Into it we were conducted, and showed each several room thereto appertaining. O, but when he came to the chamber where his Geraldine's clear sunbeams first thrust themselves into this cloud of flesh and acquainted mortality with the purity of angels, then did his mouth overflow with magnificats, his tongue thrust the stars out of heaven and eclipsed the sun and moon with comparisons. Geraldine was the soul of heaven, sole daughter and heir to *primus motor*.* The alchemy of his eloquence, out of the incomprehensible drossy matter of clouds and air, distilled no more quintessence than would make his Geraldine complete fair.

In praise of the chamber that was so illuminatively honoured with her radiant conception, he penned this sonnet.

> Fair room, the presence of sweet beauty's pride,
> The place the sun upon the earth did hold
> When Phaeton his chariot did misguide,
> The tower where Jove rained down himself in gold.
> Prostrate as holy ground I'll worship thee,
> Our Lady's chapel henceforth be thou named,
> Here first love's queen put on mortality,
> And with her beauty all the world inflamed.
> Heaven's chambers harbouring fiery cherubins
> Are not with thee in glory to compare,
> Lightning it is, not light, which in thee shines,
> None enter thee but straight entranced are.
> O if Elysium be above the ground,
> Then here it is, where naught but joy is found.

Many other poems and epigrams in that chamber's patient alabaster enclosure, which her melting eyes long sithens had softened, were curiously engraved. Diamonds thought themselves *dii mundi** if they might but carve her name on the naked glass. With them on it did he anatomize these body-wanting mots: *Dulce puella malum est; Quod fugit ipse sequor; Amor est mihi causa sequendi; O infelix ego; Cur vidi, cur perii; Non patienter amo, tantum patiatur amari.**

After the view of these venereal monuments, he published a proud challenge in the Duke of Florence's court against all comers (whether Christians, Turks, Cannibals, Jews, or Saracens) in defence of his Geraldine's beauty. More mildly was it accepted in that she whom he defended was a town-born child of that city, or else the pride of the Italian would have prevented him ere he should have come to perform it. The Duke of Florence nevertheless sent for him, and demanded him of his estate and the reason that drew him thereto, which when he was advertised of to the full he granted all countries whatsoever, as well enemies and outlaws as friends and confederates, free access and regress into his dominions unmolested until that insolent trial were ended.

The right honourable and ever renowned Lord Henry Howard, Earl of Surrey, my singular good lord and master, entered the lists after this order. His armour was all intermixed with lilies and roses, and the bases thereof bordered with nettles and weeds, signifying stings, crosses, and overgrowing encumbrances in his love; his helmet round proportioned like a gardener's water-pot from which seemed to issue forth small threads of water, like cithern strings, that not only did moisten the lilies and roses but did fructify as well the nettles and weeds and made them overgrow their liege lords. Whereby he did import thus much, that the tears that issued from his brain, as those artificial distillations issued from the well-counterfeit water-pot on his head, watered and gave life as well to his mistress's disdain (resembled to nettles and weeds) as increase of glory to her care-causing beauty (comprehended under the lilies and roses). The symbol thereto annexed was this: *ex lachrimis lachrimae.* *

The trappings of his horse were pounced and bolstered out with rough-plumed silver plush in full proportion and shape of an ostrich. On the breast of the horse were the foreparts of this greedy bird advanced whence, as his manner is, he reached out his long neck to the reins of the bridle, thinking they had been iron, and still seemed to gape after the golden bit and ever, as the courser did raise or curvet, to have swallowed it half in. His wings, which he never useth but running, being spreaded full sail, made his lusty steed as proud under him as he had been some other Pegasus, and so quiveringly and tenderly were these his broad wings bound to either side of him that, as he paced up and down the tilt-yard in his majesty ere the knights were entered, they seemed wantonly to fan in his face and make a flickering sound such as eagles do, swiftly pursuing their prey in the air. On either of his wings, as the ostrich hath a sharp goad or prick wherewith he spurreth himself forward in his sail-assisted race, so this artificial ostrich on the inbent knuckle of the pinion of either wing had embossed crystal eyes affixed, wherein wheelwise were circularly engrafted sharp pointed diamonds, as rays from those eyes derived, that like the rowels of a spur ran deep into his horse's sides and made him more eager in his course.

Such a fine, dim shine did these crystal eyes and these round enranked diamonds make through their bollen swelling bowers of feathers, as if it had been a candle in a paper lantern, or a glow-worm in a bush by night glistering through the leaves and briars. The tail of the ostrich being short and thick served very fitly as a plume to trick up his horse's tail with, so that every part of him was as naturally co-apted as might be. The word to this device was *Aculeo alatus*:* I spread my wings only spurred with her eyes. The moral of the whole is this: that as the ostrich (the most burning-sighted bird of all others, insomuch as the female of them hatcheth not her eggs by covering them but by the effectual rays of her eyes), as he, I say, outstrippeth the nimblest trippers of his feathered condition in footmanship, only spurred on with the needle-quickening goad under his side, so he, no less burning-sighted than the ostrich, spurred on to the race of honour by the sweet rays of his mistress's eyes, persuaded himself he should outstrip all other in running to the goal of glory only animated and incited by her excellence. And as the ostrich will eat iron, swallow any hard metal whatsoever, so would he refuse no iron adventure, no hard task whatsoever, to sit in the grace of so fair a commander.

The order of his shield was this: it was framed like a burning-glass, beset round with flame-coloured feathers, on the outside whereof was his mistress's picture adorned as beautiful as art could portraiture; on the inside a naked sword tied in a true love knot, the mot *Militat omnis amans*,* signifying that in a true love knot his sword was tied to defend and maintain the high features of his mistress.

Next him entered the black knight, whose beaver was pointed all torn and bloody, as though he had new come from combat-ting with a bear. His headpiece seemed to be a little oven fraught full with smothering flames, for nothing but sulphur and smoke voided out at the clefts of his beaver. His bases were all embroidered with snakes and adders engendered of the abundance of innocent blood that was shed. His horse's trappings were throughout bespangled with honey spots, which are no blemishes but ornaments. On his shield he bare the sun full-shining on a dial at his going down, the word *Sufficit tandem*.*

After him followed the knight of the owl, whose armour was a stubbed tree overgrown with ivy, his helmet fashioned like an owl sitting on the top of this ivy. On his bases were wrought all kind of birds as on the ground wandering about him, the word *Ideo mirum quia monstrum.** His horse's furniture was framed like a cart, scattering whole sheaves of corn amongst hogs, the word *Liberalitas liberalitate perit.** On his shield a bee entangled in sheep's wool, the mot *Frontis nulla fides.**

The fourth that succeeded was a well-proportioned knight in an armour imitating rust, whose headpiece was prefigured like flowers growing in a narrow pot where they had not any space to spread their roots or disperse their flourishing. His bases embellished with open-armed hands scattering gold amongst truncheons, the word *Cura futuri est.** His horse was harnessed with leaden chains, having the outside gilt, or at least saffroned instead of gilt, to decipher a holy or golden pretence of a covetous purpose, the sentence *Cani capilli mei compedes.** On his target he had a number of crawling worms kept under by a block, the faburden *Speramus lucent.**

The fifth was the forsaken knight, whose helmet was crowned with nothing but cypress and willow garlands. Over his armour he had on Hymen's nuptial robe dyed in a dusky yellow, and all to be defaced and discoloured with spots and stains. The enigma *Nos quoque florimus*,* as who should say 'We have been in fashion'. His steed was adorned with orange tawny eyes, such as those have that have the yellow jaundice that make all things yellow they look upon, with this brief: *Qui invident egent*, those that envy are hungry.

The sixth was the knight of the storms, whose helmet was round moulded like the moon, and all his armour like waves whereon the shine of the moon, sleightly silvered, perfectly represented moonshine in the water; his bases were the banks or shores that bounded in the streams. The spoke was this: *Frustra pius*, as much to say as fruitless service. On his shield he set forth a lion driven from his prey by a dunghill cock, the word *Non vi sed voce*, not by violence but by his voice.

The seventh had, like the giants that sought to scale heaven in despite of Jupiter, a mount overwhelming his head and whole body. His bases outlaid with arms and legs which the skirts of that mountain left uncovered. Under this did he characterize a man desirous to climb to the heaven of honour, kept under with the mountain of his prince's command, and yet had he arms and legs exempted from the suppression of that mountain. The word *Tu mihi criminis author* (alluding to his prince's command): thou art the occasion of my imputed cowardice. His horse was trapped in the earthy strings of tree roots which, though their increase was stubbed down to the ground, yet were they not utterly deaded, but hoped for an after resurrection. The word *Spe alor*,* I hope for a spring. Upon his shield he bare a ball stricken down with a man's hand that it might mount. The word *Ferior ut efferar*, I suffer myself to be contemned because I will climb.

The eighth had all his armour throughout engrailed like a crabbed briary hawthorn bush, out of which notwithstanding sprung (as a good child of an ill father) fragrant blossoms of delightful May flowers that made (according to the nature of May) a most odoriferous smell. In midst of this his snowy curled top, round wrapped together, on the ascending of his crest sat a solitary nightingale close encaged with a thorn at her breast, having this mot in her mouth: *Luctus monumenta manebunt*.* At the foot of this bush represented on his bases lay a number of black swollen toads gasping for wind, and summer-lived grasshoppers gaping after dew, both which were choked with excessive drouth and for want of shade. The word *Non sine vulnere viresco*, I spring not without impediments—alluding to the toads and suchlike, that erst lay sucking at his roots but now were turned out and near choked with drought. His horse was suited in black sandy earth (as adjacent to this bush) which was here and there patched with short burnt grass, and as thick ink, dropped with toiling ants and emmets as ever it might crawl, who in the full of the summer moon (ruddy garnished on his horse's forehead) hoarded up their provision of grain against winter. The word *Victrix fortunae sapientia*, providence prevents misfortune. On his shield he set forth the picture of death doing alms-deeds to a number of poor desolate children. The word *Nemo alius explicat*, no other man takes pity upon us. What his meaning was herein I cannot imagine, except death had done him and his brethren some great good turn in ridding them of some untoward parent or kinsman that would have been their confusion, for else I cannot see how death should have been said to do alms-deeds, except he had deprived them suddenly of their lives to deliver them out of some further misery; which could not in any wise be, because they were yet living.

The ninth was the infant knight, who on his armour had enamelled a poor young infant put into a ship without tackling, masts, furniture, or anything. This weather-beaten and ill-apparelled ship was shadowed on his bases, and the slender compass of his body set forth the right picture of an infant. The waves wherein the ship was tossed were fretted on his steed's trappings so movingly that ever as he offered to bound or stir they seemed to bounce and toss and sparkle brine out of their hoary silver billows. Their mot *Inopem me copia fecit*,* as much to say as the rich prey makes the thief. On his shield he expressed an old goat that made a young tree to wither only with biting it; the word thereto *Primo extinguor in aevo*, I am frost-bitten ere I come out of the blade.

It were here too tedious to manifest all the discontented or amorous devices that were used in that tournament. The shields only of some few I will touch to make short work. One bare for his impresa the eyes of young swallows coming again after they were plucked out with this mot: *Et addit et addimit*, your beauty both bereaves and restores my sight. Another, a siren smiling when the sea rageth and ships are overwhelmed, including a cruel woman that laughs, sings, and scorns at her lover's tears and the tempests of his despair, the word *Cuncta pereunt*, all my labour is ill employed. A third, being troubled with a cursed, a treacherous and wanton, wanton wife, used this similitude. On his shield he caused to be limned Pompey's ordinance for parricides, as namely a man put into a sack with a cock, a serpent, and an ape, interpreting that his wife was a cock for her crowing, a serpent for her stinging, and an ape for her unconstant wantonness, with which ill qualities he was so beset that thereby he was thrown into a sea of grief. The word *Extremum malorum mulier*, the utmost of evils is a woman. A fourth who, being a person of suspected religion, was continually haunted with intelligencers and spies that thought to prey upon him for that he had, he could not devise which way to shake them off but by making away that he had. To obscure this he used no other fancy but a number of blind flies whose eyes the cold had closed, the word *Aurum reddit acutissimum*, Gold is the only physic for the eyesight. A fifth, whose mistress was fallen into a consumption and yet would condescend to no treaty of love, emblazoned for his complaint grapes that withered for want of pressing. The ditty to the mot *Quid regna sine usu?**

I will rehearse no more, but I have an hundred other; let this be the upshot of those shows: they were the admirablest that ever Florence yielded. To particularize their manner of encounter were to describe the whole art of tilting. Some had like to have fallen over their horse's neck and so break their necks in breaking their staves. Others ran at a buckle instead of a button, and peradventure whetted their spears' points idly gliding on their enemy's sides but did no other harm. Others ran across at their adversary's left elbow, yea and by your leave sometimes let not the lists scape scot-free, they were so eager. Others, because they would be sure not to be unsaddled with the shock, when they came to the spear's utmost proof they threw it over the right shoulder and so tilted backward, for forward they durst not. Another had a monstrous spite at the pommel of his rival's saddle, and thought to have thrust his spear twixt his legs without raising any skin, and carried him clean away on it as a coolstaff. Another held his spear to his nose, or his nose to his spear, as though he had been discharging a caliver, and ran at the right foot of his fellow's steed. Only the Earl of Surrey, my master, observed the true measures of honour, and made all his encounterers new scour their armour in the dust. So great was his glory that day as Geraldine was thereby eternally glorified. Never such a bountiful master came amongst the heralds; not that he did enrich them with any plentiful purse largess, but that by his stern assaults he tithed them more rich offals of bases, of helmets, of armour, than the rent of their offices came to in ten years before.

What would you have more? The trumpets proclaimed him master of the field, the trumpets proclaimed Geraldine the exceptionless fairest of women. Everyone strived to magnify him more than other. The Duke of Florence, whose name (as my memory serveth me) was Paschal de Medices,* offered him such large proffers to stay with him as it were uncredible to report. He would not; his desire was as he had done in Florence so to proceed throughout all the chief cities in Italy. If you ask why he began not this at Venice first, it was because he would let Florence, his mistress's native city, have the maidenhead of his chivalry. As he came back again, he thought to have enacted something there worthy the annals of posterity, but he was debarred both of that and all his other determinations; for, continuing in feasting and banqueting with the Duke of Florence and the princes of Italy there assembled, post haste letters came to him from the King his master to return as speedily as he could possible into England, whereby his fame was quite cut off by the shins, and there was no reprieve but *bazelus manos*, he must into England, and I with my courtesan travelled forward in Italy.

What adventures happened him after we parted I am ignorant, but Florence we both forsook; and I, having a wonderful ardent inclination to see Rome, the queen of the world and metropolitan mistress of all other cities, made thither with my bag and baggage as fast as I could.

Attained thither, I was lodged at the house of one Johannes de Imola, a Roman cavaliero who, being acquainted with my courtesan's deceased doting husband, for his sake used us with all the familiarity that might be. He showed us all the monuments that were to be seen, which are as many as there have been emperors, consuls, orators, conquerors, famous painters, or players in Rome. Till this day not a Roman (if he be a right Roman indeed) will kill a rat but he will have some registered remembrance of it.

There was a poor fellow during my remainder there that, for a new trick he had invented of killing cimeces and scorpions, had his mountebank banner hung up on a high pillar with an inscription about it longer than the King of Spain's style. I thought these cimices, like the Cymbrians, had been some strange nation he had brought under, and they were no more but things like sheep lice which alive have the most venomous* sting that may be, and being dead do stink out of measure. Saint Austin compareth heretics unto them. The chiefest thing that my eyes delighted in was the church of the seven sibyls, which is a most miraculous thing, all their prophecies and oracles being there enrolled, as also the beginning and ending of their whole catalogue of the heathen gods, with their manner of worship. There are a number of other shrines and statues also dedicated to their emperors and withal some statues of idolatry reserved for detestation. I was at Pontius Pilate's house, and pissed against it.* There is the prison yet packed up together (an old rotten thing) where the man that was condemned to death and could have nobody come to him and succour him but was searched, was kept alive a long space by sucking his daughter's breasts.

These are but the shop dust of the sights that I saw, and in truth I did not behold with any care hereafter to report, but contented my eye for the present, and so let them pass. Should I memorize half the miracles which they there told me had been done about martyrs' tombs, or the operations of the earth of the sepulchre and other relics brought from Jerusalem I should be counted the [most] monstrous* liar that ever came in print.

The ruins of Pompey's theatre, reputed one of the nine wonders of the world, Gregory the Sixth's tomb, Priscilla's grate, or the thousands of pillars arreared amongst the razed foundations of old Rome it were here frivolous to specify, since he that hath but once drunk with a traveller talks of them. Let me be a historiographer of my own misfortunes, and not meddle with the continued trophies of so old a triumphing city.

At my first coming to Rome, I, being a youth of the English cut, ware my hair long, went apparelled in light colours, and imitated four or five sundry nations in my attire at once; which no sooner was noted but I had all the boys of the city in a swarm wondering about me. I had not gone a little farther but certain officers crossed the way of me and demanded to see my rapier which when they found (as also my dagger) with his point unblunted, they would have haled me headlong to the strappado but that with money I appeased them. And my fault was more pardonable in that I was a stranger altogether ignorant of their customs.

Note, by the way, that it is the use in Rome for all men whatsoever to wear their hair short, which they do not so much for conscience sake or any religion they place in it, but because the extremity of the heat is such there that, if they should not do so, they should not have a hair left on their heads to stand upright when they were scared with sprites. And he is counted no gentleman amongst them that goes not in black; they dress their jesters and fools only in fresh colours, and say variable garments do argue unstaidness and unconstancy of affections.

The reason of their strait ordinance for carrying weapons without points is this: the bandettos, which are certain outlaws that lie betwixt Rome and Naples, and besiege the passage that none can travel that way without robbing. Now and then, hired for some few crowns, they will steal to Rome and do a murther and betake them to their heels again. Disguised as they go, they are not known from strangers; sometimes they will shroud themselves under the habit of grave citizens. In this consideration, neither citizen nor stranger, gentleman, knight, marquis, or any may wear any weapon endamageable upon pain of the strappado. I bought it out, let others buy experience of me better cheap.

To tell you of the rare pleasures of their gardens, their baths, their vineyards, their galleries, were to write a second part of *The Gorgeous Gallery of Gallant Devices*.* Why, you should not come into any man's house of account but he had fish-ponds and little orchards on the top of his leads. If by rain or any other means those ponds were so full they need to be sluiced or let out, even of their superfluities they made melodious use, for they had great wind instruments instead of leaden spouts, that went duly in consort only with this water's rumbling descent.

I saw a summer banqueting house belonging to a merchant that was the marvel of the world, and could not be matched except God should make another paradise. It was built round of green marble, like a theatre without; within there was a heaven and earth comprehended both under one roof. The heaven was a clear overhanging vault of crystal, wherein the sun and moon and each visible star had his true similitude, shine, situation, and motion, and by what enwrapped art I cannot conceive these spheres in their proper orbs observed their circular wheelings and turnings, making a certain kind of soft angelical murmuring music in their often windings and going about, which music the philosophers say in the true heaven, by reason of the grossness of our senses, we are not capable of.

For the earth, it was counterfeited in that likeness that Adam lorded over it* before his fall. A wide, vast, spacious room it was, such as we would conceit Prince Arthur's hall to be, where he feasted all his knights of the round table together every Pentecost. The floor was painted with the beautifullest flowers that ever man's eye admired, which so lineally* were delineated that he that viewed them afar off and had not directly stood poringly over them would have sworn they had lived indeed. The walls round about were hedged with olives and palm trees and all other odoriferous fruit-bearing plants, which at any solemn entertainment dropped myrrh and frankincense. Other trees that bare no fruit were set in just order one against another, and divided the room into a number of shady lanes, leaving but one overspreading pine tree arbour where we sat and banqueted.

On the well-clothed boughs of this conspiracy of pine trees, against the resembled sunbeams, were perched as many sorts of shrill-breasted birds as the summer hath allowed for singing men in her silvan chapels. Who, though there* were bodies without souls, and sweet resembled substances without sense, yet by the mathematical experiments of long silver pipes secretly inrinded in the entrails of the boughs whereon they sat, and undiscernible conveyed under their bellies into their small throats sloping, they whistled and freely carolled their natural field note. Neither went those silver pipes straight, but by many-edged unsundered writhings and crankled wanderings aside strayed from bough to bough into an hundred throats. But into this silver pipe so writhed and wandering aside, if any demand how the wind was breathed, forsooth, the tail of the silver pipe stretched itself into the mouth of a great pair of bellows where it was close soldered and baled about with iron: it could not stir or have any vent betwixt. Those bellows, with the rising and falling of leaden plummets wound up on a wheel, did beat up and down uncessantly, and so gathered in wind, serving with one blast all the snarled pipes to and fro of one tree at once. But so closely were all those organizing implements obscured in the corpulent trunks of the trees, that every man there present renounced conjectures of art and said it was done by enchantment.

One tree for his fruit bare nothing but enchained chirping birds, whose throats, being conduit-piped with squared narrow shells and charged syringe-wise with searching sweet water driven in by a little wheel for the nonce that fed it afar off, made a spurting sound, such as chirping is, in bubbling upwards through the rough crannies of their closed bills.

Under tuition of the shade of every tree that I have signified to be in this round hedge, on delightful leafy cloisters, lay a wild tyrannous beast asleep, all prostrate. Under some, two together, as the dog nuzzling his nose under the neck of the deer, the wolf glad to let the lamb lie upon him to keep him warm, the lion suffering the ass to cast his leg over him; preferring one honest unmannerly friend before a number of crouching pickthanks. No poisonous beast there reposed (poison was not before our parent Adam transgressed). There were no sweet-breathing panthers that would hide their terrifying heads to betray; no men-imitating hyenas that changed their sex to seek after blood. Wolves as now when they are hungry eat earth, so then did they feed on earth only, and abstained from innocent flesh. The unicorn did not put his horn into the stream to chase away venom before he drunk, for there was no such thing as venom extant in the water or on the earth. Serpents were as harmless to mankind as they are still one to another; the rose had no canker, the leaves no caterpillars, the sea no sirens, the earth no usurers. Goats then bare wool, as it is recorded in Sicily they do yet. The torrid zone was habitable. Only jays loved to steal gold and silver to build their nests withal, and none cared for covetous clientry or running to the Indies. As the elephant understands his country speech, so every beast understood what men spoke. The ant did not hoard up against winter, for there was no winter but a perpetual spring, as Ovid saith. No frosts to make the green almond tree counted rash and improvident in budding soonest of all other, or the mulberry tree a strange politician in blooming late and ripening early. The peach tree at the first planting was fruitful and wholesome, whereas now till it be transplanted it is poisonous and hateful. Young plants for their sap had balm, for their yellow gum glistering amber. The evening dewed not water on flowers but honey. Such a golden age, such a good age, such an honest age was set forth in this banqueting house!

O Rome, if thou hast in thee such soul-exalting objects, what a thing is heaven in comparison of thee, of which Mercator's globe* is a perfecter model than thou art? Yet this I must say to the shame of us Protestants: if good works may merit heaven, they do them, we talk of them. Whether superstition or no makes them unprofitable servants, that let pulpits decide; but there you shall have the bravest ladies, in gowns of beaten gold, washing pilgrims and poor soldiers' feet and doing nothing, they and their waiting maids, all the year long but making shirts and bands for them against they come by in distress. Their hospitals are more like noblemen's houses than otherwise; so richly furnished, clean kept, and hot perfumed that a soldier would think it a sufficient recompense for his travail and his wounds to have such a heavenly retiring place. For the Pope and his pontificalibus I will not deal with, only I will dilate unto you what happened whilst* I was in Rome.

So it fell out that, it being a vehement hot summer when I was a sojourner there, there entered such a hotspurred plague as hath not been heard of. Why it was but a word and a blow, 'Lord have mercy upon us' and he was gone. Within three quarters of a year in that one city there died of it a hundred thousand. Look in Lanquet's chronicle* and you shall find it. To smell of a nosegay that was poisoned, and turn your nose to a house that had the plague, it was all one. The clouds, like a number of cormorants that keep their corn till it stink and is musty, kept in their stinking exhalations till they had almost stifled all Rome's inhabitants. Physicians' greediness of gold made them greedy of their destiny. They would come to visit those with whose infirmities their art had no affinity, and even as a man with a fee should be hired to hang himself, so would they quietly go home and die presently after they had been with their patients. All day and all night long car-men did nothing but go up and down the streets with their carts and cry 'Have you any dead to bury? Have you any dead to bury?', and had many times out of one house their whole loading. One grave was the sepulchre of seven score, one bed was the altar whereon whole families were offered.

The walls were hoared and furred with the moist scorching steam of their desolation. Even as, before a gun is shot off, a stinking smoke funnels out and prepares the way for him, so before any gave up the ghost, death, arrayed in a stinking smoke, stopped his nostrils and crammed itself full into his mouth that closed up his fellow's eyes, to give him warning to prepare for his funeral. Some died sitting at their meat, others as they were asking counsel of the physician for their friends. I saw at the house where I was hosted, a maid bring her master warm broth for to comfort him, and she sink down dead herself ere he had half eat it up.

During this time of visitation, there was a Spaniard, one Esdras of Granado, a notable bandetto, authorized by the Pope because he assisted him in some murthers. This villain, colleagued with one Bartol, a desperate Italian, practised to break into those rich men's houses in the night where the plague had most reigned and, if there were none but the mistress and maid left alive, to ravish them both and bring away all the wealth they could fasten on. In a hundred chief citizens' houses where the hand of God had been, they put this outrage in ure. Though the women so ravished cried out, none durst come near them for fear of catching their deaths by them, and some thought they cried out only with the tyranny of the malady. Amongst the rest, the house where I lay he invaded, where all being snatched up by the sickness but the good wife of the house, a noble and chaste matron called Heraclide, and her zany* and I and my courtesan, he, knocking at the door late in the night, ran in to the matron and left me and my love to the mercy of his companion who, finding me in bed (as the time required) ran at me full with his rapier, thinking I would resist him, but as good luck was I escaped him and betook me to my pistol in the window uncharged. He, fearing it had been charged, threatened to run her through if I once offered but to aim at him. Forth the chamber he dragged her, holding his rapier at her heart, whilst I still cried out 'Save her, kill me, and I'll ransom her with a thousand ducats!' But lust prevailed, no prayers would be heard.

Into my chamber I was locked, and watchmen charged (as he made semblance when there was none there) to knock me down with their halberds if I stirred but a foot down the stairs. So threw I myself pensive again on my pallet, and dared all the devils in hell now I was alone to come and fight with me one after another in defence of that detestable rape. I beat my head against the walls and called them bawds because they would see such a wrong committed and not fall upon him.

To return to Heraclide below, whom the ugliest of all bloodsuckers, Esdras of Granado, had under shrift. First he assailed her with rough means, and slew her zany at her foot that stepped before her in rescue. Then when all armed resist was put to flight, he assayed her with honey speech, and promised her more jewels and gifts than he was able to pilfer in an hundred years after. He discoursed unto her how he was countenanced and borne out by the Pope, and how many execrable murthers with impunity he had executed upon them that displeased him. 'This is the eight score house', quoth he, 'that hath done homage unto me, and here I will prevail or I will be torn in pieces.' 'Ah,' quoth Heraclide, with a heart-renting sigh, 'art thou ordained to be a worse plague to me than the plague itself? Have I escaped the hands of God to fall into the hands of man? Hear me, Jehovah, and be merciful in ending my misery. Dispatch me incontinent, dissolute homicide, death's usurper. Here lies my husband, stone cold on the dewy floor. If thou beest of more power than God to strike me speedily, strike home, strike deep, send me to heaven with my husband. Ay me, it is the spoil of my honour thou seekest in my soul's troubled departure; thou art some devil sent to tempt me. Avoid from me Satan, my soul is my Saviour's, to him have I bequeathed it, from him can no man take it. Jesu, Jesu, spare me undefiled for thy spouse; Jesu, Jesu, never fail those that put their trust in thee.'

With that she fell in a swoon, and her eyes in their closing seemed to spawn forth in their outward sharp corners new-created seed pearl, which the world before never set eye on. Soon he rigorously revived her, and told her that he had a charter above scripture; she must yield, she should yield, see who durst remove her out of his hands. Twixt life and death thus she faintly replied.

'How thinkest thou, is there a power above thy power? If there be, He is here present in punishment, and on thee will take present punishment if thou persistest in thy enterprise. In the time of security every man sinneth, but when death substitutes one friend his special baily to arrest another by infection, and disperseth his quiver into ten thousand hands at once, who is it but looks about him? A man that hath an unevitable huge stone hanging only by a hair over his head, which he looks every paternoster while to fall and pash him in pieces, will not he be submissively sorrowful for his transgressions, refrain himself from the least thought of folly, and purify his spirit with contrition and penitence? God's hand, like a huge stone, hangs inevitably over thy head. What is the plague but death playing the provost marshal to execute all those that will not be called home by any other means? This my dear knight's body is a quiver of his arrows which already are shot into thee invisible. Even as the age of goats is known by the knots on their horns, so think the anger of God apparently visioned or shown unto thee in the knitting of my brows. A hundred have I buried out of my house, at all whose departures I have been present. A hundred's infection is mixed with my breath; lo, now I breathe upon thee a hundred deaths come upon thee. Repent betimes, imagine there is a hell though not a heaven; that hell thy conscience is thoroughly acquainted with, if thou hast murdered half so many as thou unblushingly braggest. As Maecenas in the latter end of his days was seven years without sleep, so these seven weeks have I took no slumber; my eyes have kept continual watch against the devil my enemy. Death I deemed my friend (friends fly from us in adversity); death, the devil, and all the ministering spirits of temptation are watching about thee to entrap thy soul by my abuse to eternal damnation. It is thy soul only thou mayest save by saving mine honour. Death will have thy body infallibly for breaking into my house that he had selected for his private habitation. If thou ever camest of a woman, or hopest to be saved by the seed of a woman, spare a woman. Deers oppressed with dogs, when they cannot take soil, run to men for succour; to whom should women in their disconsolate and desperate estate run but to men, like the deer, for succour and sanctuary. If thou be a man, thou wilt succour me, but if thou be a dog and a brute beast, thou wilt spoil me, defile me and tear me. Either renounce God's image, or renounce the wicked mind that thou bearest.'

These words might have moved a compound heart of iron and adamant, but in his heart they obtained no impression, for he, sitting in his chair of state against the door all the while that she pleaded, leaning his overhanging gloomy eyebrows on the pommel of his unsheathed sword, he never looked up or gave her a word. But when he perceived she expected his answer of grace or utter perdition, he start up and took her currishly by the neck, and asked her how long he should stay for her ladyship.

'Thou tellest me', quoth he, 'of the plague, and the heavy hand of God, and thy hundred infected breaths in one. I tell thee I have cast the dice an hundred times for the galleys in Spain and yet still missed the ill chance. Our order of casting is this: if there be a general or captain new come home from the wars, and hath some four or five hundred crowns overplus of the King's in his hand, and his soldiers all paid, he makes proclamation that whatsoever two resolute men will go to dice for it, and win the bridle or lose the saddle, to such a place let them repair and it shall be ready for them. Thither go I and find another such needy squire resident. The dice run, I win, he is undone. I, winning, have the crowns; he, losing, is carried to the galleys. This is our custom, which a hundred times and more hath paid me custom of crowns when the poor fellows have gone to Gehenna, had coarse bread and whipping there all their life after. Now thinkest thou that I, who so oft have escaped such a number of hellish dangers, only depending on the turning of a few pricks, can be scarebugged with the plague? What plague canst thou name worse than I have had? Whether diseases, imprisonment, poverty, banishment, I have passed through them all. My own mother gave I a box of the ear to and brake her neck down a pair of stairs, because she would not go in to a gentleman when I bade her. My sister I sold to an old leno to make his best of her. Any kinswoman that I have, knew I she were not a whore, myself would make her one. Thou art a whore, thou shalt be a whore in spite of religion or precise ceremony.'

Therewith he flew upon her, and threatened her with his sword, but it was not that he meant to wound her with. He grasped her by the ivory throat and shook her as a mastiff would shake a young bear, swearing and staring he would tear out her weasand if she refused. Not content with that savage constraint, he slipped his sacrilegious hand from her lily lawn-skinned neck and enscarfed it in her long silver locks, which with struggling were unrolled. Backward he dragged her, even as a man backward would pluck a tree down by the twigs, and then like a traitor that is drawn to execution on a hurdle, he traileth her up and down the chamber by those tender untwisted braids and, setting his barbarous foot on her bare snowy breast, bade her yield or have her wind stamped out.

She cried 'Stamp, stifle me in my hair, hang me up by it on a beam, and so let me die rather than I should go to heaven with a beam in my eye!' 'No,' quoth he, 'nor stamped, nor stifled, nor hanged, nor to heaven shalt thou go till I have had my will of thee. Thy busy arms in these silken fetters I'll enfold.' Dismissing her hair from his fingers, and pinioning her elbows therewithal, she struggled, she wrestled, but all was in vain. So struggling and so resisting, her jewels did sweat, signifying there was poison coming towards her. On the hard boards he threw her, and used his knee as an iron ram to beat ope the two-leaved gate of her chastity. Her husband's dead body he made a pillow to his abomination.

Conjecture the rest; my words stick fast in the mire and are clean tired. Would I had never undertook this tragical tale. Whatsoever is born is born to have an* end. Thus endeth my tale. His boorish lust was glutted, his beastly desire satisfied; what in the house of any worth was carriageable he put up and went his way.

Let not your sorrow die, you that have read the proem and narration of this elegiacal history. Show you have quick wits in sharp conceit of compassion. A woman that hath viewed all her children sacrificed before her eyes, and after the first was slain wiped the sword with her apron to prepare it for the cleanly murther of the second, and so on forward till it* came to the empiercing of the seventeenth of her loins—will you not give her great allowance of anguish? This woman, this matron, this forsaken Heraclide, having buried fourteen children in five days, whose eyes she howlingly closed, and caught many wrinkles with funeral kisses, besides having her husband within a day after laid forth as a comfortless corpse, a carrionly block that could neither eat with her, speak with her, nor weep with her—is she not to be borne withal though her body swells with a tympany of tears, though her speech be as impatient as unhappy Hecuba's, though her head raves and her brain dotes? Devise with yourselves that you see a corpse rising from his hearse after he is carried to church, and such another suppose Heraclide to be, rising from the couch of enforced adultery.

Her eyes were dim, her cheeks bloodless, her breath smelt earthy, her countenance was ghastly. Up she rose after she was deflowered, but loth she arose, as a reprobate soul rising to the day of judgement. Looking on the t'one side as she rose, she spied her husband's body lying under her head. Ah, then she bewailed as Cephalus when he had killed Procris unwittingly, or Oedipus when, ignorant, he had slain his own father and known his mother incestuously. Thus was her subdued reason's discourse:

'Have I lived to make my husband's body the bier to carry me to hell; had filthy pleasure no other pillow to lean upon but his spreaded limbs? On thy flesh my fault shall be imprinted at the day of resurrection. O beauty, the bait ordained to ensnare the irreligious! Rich men are robbed for their wealth, women are dishonested for being too fair. No blessing is beauty, but a curse. Cursed be the time that ever I was begotten; cursed be the time that my mother brought me forth to tempt. The serpent in paradise did no more; the serpent in paradise is damned sempiternally. Why should not I hold myself damned (if predestination's opinions be true) that am predestinate to this horrible abuse. The hog dieth presently if he loseth an eye; with the hog have I wallowed in the mire; I have lost the eye of honesty, it is clean plucked out with a strong hand of unchastity. What remaineth but I die? Die I will, though life be unwilling. No recompense is there for me to redeem my compelled offence but with a rigorous compelled death. Husband, I'll be thy wife in heaven; let not thy pure deceasing spirit despise me when we meet because I am tyrannously polluted. The devil, the belier of our frailty and common accuser of mankind, cannot accuse me, though he would, of unconstrained submitting. If any guilt be mine, this is my fault: that I did not deform my face ere it should so impiously allure.'

Having passioned thus a while, she hastily ran and looked herself in her glass to see if her sin were not written on her forehead. With looking she blushed, though none looked upon her but her own reflected image. Then began she again. '*Heu quam difficile est crimen non prodere vultu*, how hard is it not to bewray a man's fault by his forehead. Myself do but behold myself and yet I blush; then, God beholding me, shall not I be ten times more ashamed? The angels shall hiss at me, the saints and martyrs fly from me, yea, God himself shall add to the devil's damnation because he suffered such a wicked creature to come before him. Agamemnon, thou wert an infidel, yet when thou went'st to the Trojan war, thou left'st a musician at home with thy wife who, by playing the foot spondaeus* till thy return, might keep her in chastity. My husband, going to war with the devil and his enticements, when he surrendered left no musician with me but mourning and melancholy. Had he left any, as Aegisthus killed Agamemnon's musician ere he could be successful, so surely would he have been killed ere this Aegisthus surceased. My distressed heart, as the hart when he loseth his horns is astonied and sorrowfully runneth to hide himself, so be thou afflicted and distressed; hide thyself under the Almighty's wings of mercy; sue, plead, entreat; grace is never denied to them that ask. It may be denied; I may be a vessel ordained to dishonour. The only repeal we have from God's undefinite chastisement is to chastise ourselves in this world; and so I will. Naught but death be my penance; gracious and acceptable may it be. My hand and my knife shall manumit me out of the horror of mind I endure. Farewell life that hast lent me nothing but sorrow; farewell sin-sowed flesh that hast more weeds than flowers, more woes than joys. Point pierce, edge enwiden; I patiently afford thee a sheath. Spur forth my soul to mount post to heaven. Jesu forgive me; Jesu receive me.'

So, throughly stabbed, fell she down and knocked her head against her husband's body; wherewith he, not having been aired his full four and twenty hours, start as out of a dream, whiles I, through a cranny of my upper chamber unsealed, had beheld all this sad spectacle. Awaking, he rubbed his head to and fro and, wiping his eyes with his hand, began to look about him. Feeling something lie heavy on his breast, he turned it off and, getting upon his legs, lighted a candle.

Here beginneth my purgatory. For he, good man, coming into the hall with the candle, and spying his wife with her hair about her ears defiled and massacred and his simple zany, Capestrano, run through, took a halberd in his hand and, running from chamber to chamber to search who in his house was likely to do it, at length found me lying on my bed, the door locked to me on the outside, and my rapier unsheathed on the window. Wherewith he straight conjectured it was I and, calling the neighbours hard by, said I had caused myself to be locked into my chamber after that sort, sent away my courtesan whom I called my wife, and made clean my rapier because I would not be suspected. Upon this was I laid in prison, should have been hanged, was brought to the ladder, had made a ballad for my farewell in a readiness called *Wilton's Wantonness*—and yet for all that scaped dancing in a hempen circle. He that hath gone through many perils and returned safe from them makes but a merriment to dilate them. I had the knot under my ear, there was fair play, the hangman had one halter and another about my neck which was fastened to the gallows; the riding device was almost thrust home and his foot on my shoulder to press me down when I made my saint-like confession as you have heard before: that such and such men at such an hour brake into the house, slew the zany, took my courtesan, locked me into my chamber, ravished Heraclide, and finally how she slew herself.

Present at the execution was there a banished English earl who, hearing that a countryman of his was to suffer for such a notable murder, came to hear his confession and see if he knew him. He had not heard me tell half of that I have recited but he craved audience and desired the execution might be stayed.

'Not two days since it is, gentlemen and noble Romans,' said he, 'since, going to be let blood in a barber's shop against the infection, all on a sudden in a great tumult and uproar was there brought in one Bartol, an Italian, grievously wounded and bloody. I, seeming to commiserate his harms, courteously questioned him with what ill debtors he had met, or how or by what casualty he came to be so arrayed. "Oh," quoth he, "long I have lived sworn brothers in sensuality with one Esdras of Granado; five hundred rapes and murders have we committed betwixt us. When our iniquities were grown to the height, and God had determined to countercheck our amity, we came to the house of Johannes de Imola" (whom this young gentleman hath named); there did he justify all those rapes in manner and form as the prisoner here hath confessed. But lo, an accident after, which neither he nor this audience is privy to. Esdras of Granado, not content to have ravished the matron Heraclide and robbed her, after he had betook him from thence to his heels, light on his companion Bartol with his courtesan, whose pleasing face he had scarce winkingly glanced on but he picked a quarrel with Bartol to have her from him. On this quarrel they fought; Bartol was wounded to the death, Esdras fled, and the fair dame left to go whither she would. This Bartol in the barber's shop freely acknowledged, as both the barber and his man and other here present can amply depose.'

Deposed they were, their oaths went for current; I was quit by proclamation. To the banished earl I came to render thanks, when thus he examined me and schooled me.

'Countryman, tell me what is the occasion of thy straying so far out of England to visit this strange nation. If it be languages, thou mayest learn them at home; naught but lasciviousness is to be learned here. Perhaps to be better accounted of than other of thy condition thou ambitiously undertakest this voyage. These insolent fancies are but Icarus' feathers, whose wanton wax melted against the sun will betray thee into a sea of confusion. The first traveller was Cain, and he was called a vagabond runagate on the face of the earth. Travel, like the travail wherein smiths put wild horses when they shoe them, is good for nothing but to tame and bring men under. God had no greater curse to lay upon the Israelites than by leading them out of their own country to live as slaves in a strange land. That which was their curse, we Englishmen count our chief blessedness; he is nobody that hath not travelled. We had rather live as slaves in another land, crouch and cap and be servile to every jealous Italian's and proud Spaniard's humour, where we may neither speak, look, nor do anything but what pleaseth them—than live as free men and lords in our own country. He that is a traveller must have the back of an ass to bear all, a tongue like the tail of a dog to flatter all, the mouth of a hog to eat what is set before him, the ear of a merchant to hear all and say nothing; and if this be not the highest step of thralldom, there is no liberty or freedom. It is but a mild kind of subjection to be the servant of one master at once, but when thou hast a thousand thousand masters, as the veriest botcher, tinker, or cobbler freeborn will domineer over a foreigner, and think to be his better or master in company, then shalt thou find there's no such hell as to leave thy father's house (thy natural habitation) to live in the land of bondage.

'If thou dost but lend half a look to a Roman's or Italian's wife, thy porridge shall be prepared for thee and cost thee nothing but thy life. Chance some of them break a bitter jest on thee and thou retortest it severely or seemest discontented, go to thy chamber and provide a great banquet, for thou shalt be sure to be visited with guests in a mask the next night when in kindness and courtship thy throat shall be cut and the doers return undiscovered. Nothing so long of memory as a dog; these Italians are old dogs and will carry an injury a whole age in memory. I have heard of a box on the ear that hath been revenged thirty year after. The Neapolitan carrieth the bloodiest wreakful mind, and is the most secret fleering murderer; whereupon it is grown to a common proverb, "I'll give him the Neapolitan shrug", when one means to play the villain and makes no boast of it.

'The only precept that a traveller hath most use of, and shall find most ease in, is that of Epicharcus:* *Vigila et memor sis ne quid credas*, believe nothing, trust no man—yet seem thou as thou swallowedst all, suspectedst none, but wert easy to be gulled by everyone. *Multi fallere docuerunt* (as Seneca saith) *dum timent falli*, many by showing their jealous suspect of deceit have made men seek more subtle means to deceive them. Alas, our Englishmen are the plainest dealing souls that ever God put life in. They are greedy of news, and love to be fed in their humours and hear themselves flattered the best that may be. Even as Philemon, a comic poet, died with extreme laughter at the conceit of seeing an ass eat figs, so have the Italians no such sport as to see poor English asses how soberly they swallow Spanish figs;* devour any hook baited for them. He is not fit to travel that cannot with the Candians live on serpents, make nourishing food even of poison. Rats and mice engender by licking one another; he must lick, he must crouch, he must cog, lie, and prate that either in the court or a foreign country will engender and come to preferment. Be his feature what it will, if he be fair spoken he winneth friends. *Non formosus erat, sed erat facundus Ulysses*; Ulysses, the long traveller, was not amiable but eloquent.

'Some allege they travel to learn wit, but I am of this opinion: that as it is not possible for any man to learn the art of memory, whereof Tully, Quintilian, Seneca, and Hermannus Buschius have written so many books, except he had a natural memory before, so is it* not possible for any man to attain any great wit by travel except he have the grounds of it rooted in him before. That wit which is thereby to be perfected or made staid is nothing but *experientia longa malorum*, the experience of many evils; the experience that such a man lost his life by this folly, another by that. Such a young gallant consumed his substance on such a courtesan, these courses of revenge a merchant of Venice took against a merchant of Ferrara, and this point of justice was showed by the duke upon the murtherer. What is here but we may read in books and a great deal more too without stirring our feet out of a warm study.

> *Vobis alii ventorum praelia narrent* (saith Ovid)
> *Quasque Scilla infestat, quasque Charybdis aquas*
> Let others tell you wonders of the wind,
> How Scilla or Charybdis is inclined,
> *—vos quod quisque loquetur*
> *Credite**
> Believe you what they say, but never try.

So let others tell you strange accidents, treasons, poisonings, close packings in France, Spain, and Italy; it is no harm for you to hear of them, but come not near them.

'What is there in France to be learned more than in England but falsehood in fellowship, perfect slovenry, to love no man but for my pleasure, to swear *Ah par la mort Dieu* when a man's hams are scabbed? For the idle traveller (I mean not for the soldier) I have known some that have continued there by the space of half a dozen year, and when they come home they have hid a little wearish lean face under a broad French hat, kept a terrible coil with the dust in the street in their long cloaks of grey paper, and spoke English strangely. Naught else have they profited by their travel save learnt to distinguish of the true Bordeaux grape, and know a cup of neat Gascon wine from wine of Orleans. Yea and, peradventure, this also: to esteem of the pox as a pimple, to wear a velvet patch on their face, and walk melancholy with their arms folded.

'From Spain what bringeth our traveller? A scull-crowned hat of the fashion of an old deep porringer, a diminutive alderman's ruff with short strings like the droppings of a man's nose, a close-bellied doublet coming down with a peak behind as far as the crupper and cut off before by the breast bone like a partlet or neckercher, a wide pair of gaskins which ungathered would make a couple of women's riding-kirtles, huge hangers that have half a cow hide in them, a rapier that is lineally descended from half a dozen dukes at the least. Let his cloak be as long or as short as you will; if long, it is faced with turkey grogeran ravelled, if short, it hath a cape like a calf's tongue and is not so deep in his whole length, nor hath so much cloth in it I will justify, as only the standing cape of a Dutchman's cloak. I have not yet touched all, for he hath in either shoe as much taffety for his tyings as would serve for an ancient, which serveth him (if you will have the mystery of it) of the own accord for a shoe-rag. A soldier and a braggart he is (that's concluded); he jetteth strutting, dancing on his toes with his hands under his sides. If you talk with him, he makes a dish-cloth of his own country in comparison of Spain, but if you urge him more particularly wherein it exceed, he can give no instance but in Spain they have better bread than any we have—when (poor hungry slaves) they may crumble it into water well enough and make misers* with it, for they have not a good morsel of meat except it be salt pilchers to eat with it all the year long and, which is more, they are poor beggars and lie in foul straw every night.

'Italy, the paradise of the earth and the epicure's heaven, how doth it form our young master? It makes him to kiss his hand like an ape, cringe his neck like a starveling, and play at "hey pass repass come aloft" when he salutes a man. From thence he brings the art of atheism, the art of epicurizing, the art of whoring, the art of poisoning, the art of sodomitry. The only probable good thing they have to keep us from utterly condemning it is that it maketh a man an excellent courtier, a curious carpet knight—which is, by interpretation, a fine close lecher, a glorious hypocrite. It is now a privy note amongst the better sort of men when they would set a singular mark or brand on a notorious villain to say he hath been in Italy.

'With the Dane and the Dutchman I will not encounter, for they are simple honest men that, with Danaus' daughters, do nothing but fill bottomless tubs and will be drunk and snort in the midst of dinner. He hurts himself only that goes thither;

he cannot lightly be damned, for the vintners, the brewers, the maltmen, and alewives pray for him. Pitch and pay, they will pray all day; score and borrow, they will wish him much sorrow. But lightly a man is ne'er the better for their prayers, for they commit all deadly sin, for the most part of them, in mingling their drink, the vintners in the highest degree.

'Why jest I in such a necessary, persuasive discourse? I am a banished exile from my country, though near linked in consanguinity to the best; an earl born by birth, but a beggar now as thou seest. These many years in Italy have I lived an outlaw. A while I had a liberal pension of the Pope, but that lasted not for he continued not; one succeeded in his chair that cared neither for Englishmen nor his own countrymen. Then was I driven to pick up my crumbs amongst the cardinals, to implore the benevolence and charity of all the dukes of Italy, whereby I have since made a poor shift to live, but so live as I wish myself a thousand times dead.

> *Cum patriam amisi, tunc me periisse putato.**
> When I was banished, think I caught my bane.

'The sea is the native soil to fishes; take fishes from the sea, they take no joy nor thrive but perish straight. So likewise the birds removed from the air (the abode whereto they were born), the beasts from the earth, and I from England. Can a lamb take delight to be suckled at the breasts of a she-wolf? I am a lamb nourished with the milk of wolves; one that, with the Ethiopians inhabiting over against Meroe, feed on nothing but scorpions. Use is another nature, yet ten times more contentive were nature restored to her kingdom from whence she is excluded. Believe me, no air, no bread, no fire, no water agree with a man or doth him any good out of his own country. Cold fruits never prosper in a hot soil, nor hot in a cold. Let no man for any transitory pleasure sell away the inheritance of breathing he hath in the place where he was born. Get thee home, my young lad; lay thy bones peaceably in the sepulchre of thy fathers; wax old in overlooking thy grounds; be at hand to close the eyes of thy kindred. The devil and I am desperate; he of being restored to heaven, I of being recalled home.'

Here he held his peace and wept. I, glad of any opportunity of a full point to part from him, told him I took his counsel in worth, what lay in me to requite in love should not be lacking. Some business that concerned me highly called me away very hastily, but another time I hoped we should meet. Very hardly he let me go, but I earnestly overpleading my occasions, at length he dismissed me, told me where his lodging was, and charged me to visit him without excuse very often.

Here's a stir, thought I to myself after I was set at liberty, that is worse than an upbraiding lesson after a britching. Certainly if I had bethought me like a rascal, as I was, he should have had an Ave Mary of me for his cynic exhortation. God plagued me for deriding such a grave fatherly advertiser. List the worst throw of ill lucks. Tracing up and down the city to seek my courtesan till the evening began to grow well in age, it fortuned the element, as if it had drunk too much in the afternoon, poured down so profoundly that I was forced to creep like one afraid of the watch close under the pentices, where the cellar door of a Jew's house called Zadok (over which in my direct way I did pass) being unbarred on the inside, over head and ears I fell into it as a man falls in a ship from the orlop into the hold, or as in an earthquake the ground should open and a blind man, come feeling pad pad over the open gulf with his staff, should stumble on sudden into hell. Having worn out the anguish of my fall a little with wallowing up and down, I cast up mine eyes to see under what continent I was and lo (O destiny) I saw my courtesan kissing very lovingly with a prentice!

My back and my sides I had hurt with my fall, but now my head swelled and ached worse than both. I was even gathering wind to come upon her with a full blast of contumely when the Jew (awaked with the noise of my fall) came bustling down the stairs and, raising his other servants, attached both the courtesan and me for breaking his house and conspiring with his prentice to rob him.

It was then the law in Rome that if any man had a felon fallen into his hands, either by breaking into his house, or robbing him by the highway, he might choose whether he would make him his bondman or hang him. Zadok (as all Jews are covetous) casting with himself he should have no benefit by casting me off the ladder, had another policy in his head. He went to one Doctor Zachary, the Pope's physician, that was a Jew and his countryman likewise, and told him he had the finest bargain for him that might be.

'It is not concealed from me', saith he, 'that the time of your accustomed yearly anatomy is at hand, which it behoves you under forfeiture of the foundation of your college very carefully to provide for. The infection is great, and hardly will you get a sound body to deal upon. You are my countryman, therefore I come to you first. Be it known unto you, I have a young man at home fallen to me for my bondman, of the age of eighteen, of stature tall, straight limbed, of as clear a complexion as any painter's fancy can imagine. Go to, you are an honest man, and one of the scattered children of Abraham; you shall have him for five hundred crowns.' 'Let me see him,' quoth Doctor Zachary, 'and I will give you as much as another.'

Home he sent for me; pinioned and shackled I was transported alongst the streets where, passing under Juliana's, the Marquis of Mantua's wife's window, that was a lusty bona roba, one of the Pope's concubines, as she had her casement half open she looked out and spied me. At the first sight she was enamoured with my age and beardless face that had in it no ill sign of physiognomy fatal to fetters. After me she sent to know what I was, wherein I had offended and whither I was going. My conducts resolved them all. She, having received this answer, with a lustful collachrymation lamenting my Jewish praemunire, that body and goods I should light into the hands of such a cursed generation, invented the means of my release.

But first I'll tell you what betided me after I was brought to Doctor Zachary's. The purblind doctor put on his spectacles and looked upon me, and when he had throughly viewed my face, he caused me to be stripped naked, to feel and grope whether each limb were sound and my skin not infected. Then he pierced my arm to see how my blood ran; which assays and searchings ended, he gave Zadok his full price and sent him away, then locked me up in a dark chamber till the day of anatomy.

O the cold, sweating cares which I conceived after I knew I should be cut like a French summer-doublet. Methought already the blood began to gush out at my nose. If a flea on the arm had but bit me, I deemed the instrument had pricked me. Well, well, I may scoff at a shrowd* turn but there's no such ready way to make a man a true Christian as to persuade himself he is taken up for an anatomy. I'll depose I prayed then more than I did in seven year before. Not a drop of sweat trickled down my breast and my sides but I dreamed it was a smooth-edged razor tenderly slicing down my breast and my sides. If any knocked at door, I supposed it was the beadle of Surgeon's Hall come for me. In the night I dreamed of nothing but phlebotomy, bloody fluxes, incarnatives, running ulcers. I durst not let out a wheal for fear through it I should bleed to death.

For meat in this distance I had plum porridge of purgations ministered me one after another to clarify my blood that it should not lie cloddered in the flesh. Nor did he it so much for clarifying physic as to save charges. Miserable is that mouse that lives in a physician's house; Tantalus lives not so hunger-starved in hell as she doth there. Not the very crumbs that fall from his table but Zachary sweeps together and of them moulds up a manna. Of the ashy parings of his bread he would make conserve of chippings. Out of bones after the meat was eaten off he would alchemize an oil that he sold for a shilling a dram. His snot and spittle a hundred times he hath put over to his apothecary for snow-water. Any spider he would temper to perfect mithridate. His rheumatic eyes when he went in the wind, or rose early in a morning, dropped as cool alum water as you would request. He was Dame Niggardise's sole heir and executor.

A number of old books had he, eaten with the moths and worms. Now all day would not he study a dodkin, but pick those worms and moths out of his library, and of their mixture make a preservative against the plague. The liquor out of his shoes he would wring to make a sacred balsamum against barrenness.

Spare we him a line or two, and look back to Juliana, who, conflicted in her thoughts about me very debatefully, adventured to send a messenger to Doctor Zachary in her name, very boldly to beg me of him, and if she might not beg me, to buy me with what sums of money soever he would ask. Zachary, Jewishly and churlishly, withstood both her suits, and said if there were no more Christians on the earth he would thrust his incision knife in his throat bowl immediately. Which reply she taking at his hands most despitefully, thought to cross him over the shins with as sore an overwhart blow yet ere a month to an end.

The Pope (I know not whether at her entreaty or no) within two days after fell sick. Doctor Zachary was sent for to minister unto him who, seeing a little danger in his water, gave him a gentle confortative for the stomach, and desired those near about him to persuade his Holiness to take some rest and he doubted not but he would be forthwith well. Who should receive this mild physic of him but the concubine Juliana, his utter enemy. She, being not unprovided of strong poison at that instant, in the Pope's outward chamber so mingled it that, when his grand sublimity taster came to relish it, he sunk down stark dead on the pavement.

Herewith the Pope called Juliana and asked her what strong concocted broth she had brought him. She kneeled down on her knees and said it was such as Zachary the Jew had delivered her with his own hands and therefore, if it misliked his Holiness, she craved pardon. The Pope, without further sifting into the matter, would have had Zachary and all Jews in Rome put to death, but she hung about his knees and with crocodile tears desired him the sentence might be lenified, and they be all but banished at most. 'For Doctor Zachary,' quoth she, 'your ten times ungrateful physician, since notwithstanding his treacherous intent he hath much art and many sovereign simples, oils, gargarisms, and syrups in his closet and house that may stand your Mightiness in stead, I beg all his goods only for your Beatitude's preservation and good.'

This request at the first was sealed with a kiss, and the Pope's edict without delay proclaimed throughout Rome; namely that all foreskin-clippers, whether male or female, belonging to the Old Jewry should depart and avoid open pain of hanging within twenty days after the date thereof.

Juliana, two days before the proclamation came out, sent her servants to extend upon Zachary's territories, his goods, his moveables, his chattels, and his servants; who performed their commission to the utmost tittle, and left him not so much as master of an urinal case or a candle-box. It was about six a clock in the evening when those boot-halers entered. Into my chamber they rushed when I sat leaning on my elbow, and my left hand under my side, devising what a kind of death it might be to let blood till a man die. I called to mind the assertion of some philosophers who said the soul was nothing but blood. Then, thought I, what a filthy thing were this if I should let my soul fall and break his neck into a basin? I had but a pimple rose with heat in that part of the vein where they use to prick, and I fearfully misdeemed it was my soul searching for passage. Fie upon it, a man's breath to be let out a back door, what a villainy it is! To die bleeding is all one as if a man should die pissing. Good drink makes good blood, so that piss is nothing but blood under age. Seneca and Lucan were lobcocks to choose that death of all other; a pig or a hog, or any edible brute beast a cook or a butcher deals upon, dies bleeding. To die with a prick, wherewith the faintest-hearted woman under heaven would not be killed—O God, it is infamous!

In this meditation did they seize upon me; in my cloak they muffled me that no man might know me, nor I see which way I was carried. The first ground I touched after I was out of Zachary's house was the Countess Juliana's chamber. Little did I surmise that fortune reserved me to so fair a death. I made no other reckoning all the while they had me on their shoulders but that I was on horseback to heaven, and carried to church on a bier, excluded forever from* drinking any more ale or beer. Juliana scornfully questioned them thus (as if I had fallen into her hands beyond expectation).

'What proper apple-squire is this you bring so suspiciously into my chamber? What hath he done? Or where had you him?' They answered likewise afar off that in one of Zachary's chambers they found him close prisoner, and thought themselves guilty of the breach of her Ladyship's commandment if they should have left him behind.

'O,' quoth she, 'ye love to be double-diligent, or thought peradventure that I, being a lone woman, stood in need of a love. Bring you me a princox beardless boy (I know not whence he is, nor whither he would) to call my name in suspense? I tell you, you have abused me, and I can hardly brook it at your hands. You should have led him to the magistrate; no commission received you of me but for his goods and his servants.'

They besought her to excuse their overweening error; it proceeded from a zealous care of their duty, and no negligent default. 'But why should not I conjecture the worst?' quoth she. 'I tell you troth, I am half in a jealousy he is some fantastical, amorous youngster who to dishonour me hath hired you to this stratagem. It is a likely matter that such a man as Zachary should make a prison of his house and deal in matters of state. By your leave, sir gallant, under lock and key shall you stay with me till I have enquired further of you; you shall be sifted thoroughly ere you and I part. Go maid, show him to the further chamber at the end of the gallery that looks into the garden. You, my trim panders, I pray guard him thither as you took pains to bring him hither. When you have so done, see the doors be made fast and come your way.'

Here was a wily wench had her liripoop without book. She was not to seek in her knacks and shifts. Such are all women; not one of them but hath a cloak for the rain, and can blear her husband's eyes as she list.

Not too much of this Madam Marquess at once. We'll step a little back and dilate what Zadok the Jew did with my courtesan after he had sold me to Zachary. Of an ill tree I hope you are not so ill-sighted in grafting to expect good fruit. He was a Jew, and entreated her like a Jew. Under shadow of enforcing her to tell how much money she had of his prentice so to be trained to his cellar, he stripped her and scourged her from top to toe tantara. Day by day he digested his meat with leading her the measures. A diamond delphinical dry lecher it was. The ballad of the whipper of late days here in England was but a scoff in comparison of him. All the colliers of Romford, who hold their corporation by yarking the blind bear at Paris Garden,* were but bunglers to him. He had the right agility of the lash, there were none of them could make the cord come aloft with a twang half like him.

Mark the ending; mark the ending. The tribe of Judah is adjudged from Rome to be trudging; they may no longer be lodged there. All the Albumazars, Rabisaks, Gideons, Tebeths, Benhadads, Benrodans, Zedekiahs, Halies of them were bankrouts and turned out of house and home. Zachary came running to Zadok's in sackcloth and ashes presently after his goods were confiscated, and told him how he was served, and what decree was coming out against them all. Descriptions stand by! Here is to be expressed the fury of Lucifer when he was turned over heaven bar for a wrangler. There is a toad-fish which, taken out of the water, swells more than one would think his skin could hold, and bursts in his face that toucheth him. So swelled Zadok, and was ready to burst out of his skin and shoot his bowels like chainshot full at Zachary's face for bringing him such baleful tidings. His eyes glared and burnt blue like brimstone and aqua vitae set on fire in an eggshell; his very nose lightened glowworms. His teeth crashed and grated together like the joints of a high building cracking and rocking like a cradle whenas a tempest takes her full butt against his broad side. He swore, he cursed, and said:

'These be they that worship that crucified God of Nazareth. Here's the fruits of their new-found gospel; sulphur and gunpowder carry them all quick to Gehenna! I would spend my soul willingly to have this triple-headed Pope, with all his sin-absolved whores and oil-greased priests, borne with a black sant on the devils' backs in procession to the pit of perdition. Would I might sink presently into the earth so I might blow up this Rome, this whore of Babylon, into the air with my breath. If I must be banished, if those heathen dogs will needs rob me of my goods, I will poison their springs and conduit heads whence they receive all their water round about the city. I'll 'tice all the young children into my house that I can get and, cutting their throats, barrel them up in powdering beef tubs, and so send them to victual all the Pope's galleys. Ere the officers come to extend, I'll bestow a hundred pounds on a dole of bread which I'll cause to be kneaded with scorpions' oil that may kill more than the plague. I'll hire them that make their wafers or sacramentary gods to ming them after the same sort, so in the zeal of their superstitious religion shall they languish and drop like carrion. If there be ever a blasphemous conjurer that can call the winds from their brazen caves and make the clouds travel before their time, I'll give him the other hundred pounds to disturb the heavens a whole week together with thunder and lightning, if it be for nothing but to sour all the wines in Rome and turn them to vinegar. As long as they have either oil or wine, this plague feeds but pinglingly upon them.'

'Zadok, Zadok,' said Doctor Zachary, cutting him off, 'thou threatenest the air whiles we perish here on earth. It is the Countess Juliana, the Marquess of Mantua's wife and no other that hath complotted our confusion. Ask not how, but insist in my words, and assist in revenge.'

'As how, as how,' said Zadok, shrugging and shrubbing. 'More happy than the patriarchs were I if, crushed to death with the greatest torments Rome's tyrants have tried, there might be quintessenced out of me one quart of precious poison. I have a leg with an issue, shall I cut it off and from his fount of corruption extract a venom worse than any serpent's? If thou wilt, I'll go to a house that is infected where, catching the plague, and having got a running sore upon me, I'll come and deliver her a supplication and breathe upon her. I know my breath stinks so already that it is within half a degree of poison. I'll pay her home if I perfect it with any more putrefaction.'

'No, no, brother Zadok,' answered Zachary, 'that is not the way. Canst thou provide me ere a bondmaid endued with singular and divine qualified beauty, whom as a present from our synagogue thou mayest commend unto her, desiring her to be good and gracious unto us?'

'I have; I am for you,' quoth Zadok. 'Diamante, come forth. Here's a wench', said he, 'of as clear a skin as Susanna. She hath not a wem on her flesh from the sole of the foot to the crown of the head. How think you, Master Doctor, will she not serve the turn?'

'She will,' said Zachary, 'and therefore I'll tell you what charge I would have committed to her. But I care not if I disclose it only to her. Maid (if thou beest a maid) come hither to me. Thou must be sent to the Countess of Mantua's about a small piece of service whereby, being now a bondwoman, thou shalt purchase freedom, and gain a large dowry to thy marriage. I know thy master loves thee dearly, though he will not let thee perceive so much. He intends after he is dead to make thee his heir, for he hath no children. Please him in that I shall instruct thee, and thou art made forever. So it is that the Pope is far out of liking with the Countess of Mantua his concubine, and hath put his trust in me his physician to have her quietly and charitably made away. Now I cannot intend it, for I have many cures in hand which call upon me hourly. Thou, if thou beest placed with her as her waiting maid or cup-bearer, mayest temper poison with her broth, her meat, her drink, her oils, her syrups, and never be bewrayed. I will not say whether the Pope hath heard of thee, and thou mayest come to be his leman in her place if thou behave thyself wisely. What, hast thou the heart to go through with it or no?'

Diamante, deliberating with herself in what hellish servitude she lived with the Jew, and that she had no likelihood to be released of it, but fall from evil to worse if she omitted this opportunity, resigned herself over wholly to be disposed and employed as seemed best unto them. Thereupon, without further consultation, her wardrobe was richly rigged, her tongue smooth-filed and new-edged on the whetstone, her drugs delivered her, and presented she was by Zadok her master to the Countess, together with some other slight newfangles, as from the whole congregation, desiring her to stand their merciful mistress and solicit the Pope for them that through one man's ignorant offence were all generally in disgrace with him, and had incurred the cruel sentence of loss of goods and of banishment.

Juliana, liking well the pretty round face of my black-browed Diamante, gave the Jew better countenance than otherwise she would have done, and told him for her own part she was but a private woman, and could promise nothing confidently of his Holiness; for though he had suffered himself to be overruled by her in some humours, yet in this that touched him so nearly she knew not how he would be inclined; but what lay in her either to pacify or persuade him they should be sure of, and so craved his absence.

His back turned, she asked Diamante what country-woman she was, what friends she had, and how she fell into the hands of that Jew. She answered that she was a magnifico's daughter of Venice, stolen when she was young from her friends and sold to this Jew for a bondwoman. 'Who', quoth she, 'hath used me so Jewishly and tyrannously that for ever I must celebrate the memory of this day wherein I am delivered from his jurisdiction. Alas,' quoth she, deep sighing, 'why did I enter into any mention of my own misusage? It will be thought that that which I am now to reveal proceeds of malice not truth. Madam, your life is sought by these Jews that sue to you. Blush not, nor be troubled in your mind, for with warning I shall arm you against all their intentions. Thus and thus', quoth she, 'said Doctor Zachary unto me, this poison he delivered me. Before I was called in to them such and such consultation through the crevice of the door fast locked did I hear betwixt them. Deny it if they can, I will justify it. Only I beseech you to be favourable, lady, unto me, and let me not fall again into the hands of those vipers.'

Juliana said little, but thought unhappily; only she thanked her for detecting it and vowed, though she were her bondwoman, to be a mother unto her. The poison she took of her, and set it up charily on a shelf in her closet, thinking to keep it for some good purposes; as, for example, when I was consumed and worn to the bones through her abuse she would give me but a dram too much and pop me into a privy. So she had served some of her paramours ere that, and if God had not sent Diamante to be my redeemer undoubtedly I had drunk of the same cup.

In a leaf or two before, was I locked up. Here in this page the foresaid goodwife Countess comes to me. She is no longer a judge but a client. How she came, in what manner of attire, with what immodest and uncomely words she courted me, if I should take upon me to enlarge all modest ears would abhor me. Some inconvenience she brought me to by her harlot-like behaviour, of which enough I can never repent me.

Let that be forgiven and forgotten; fleshly delights could not make her slothful or slumbering in revenge against Zadok. She set men about him to incense and egg him on in courses of discontentment, and other supervising espials to ply, follow, and spur forward those suborning incensers, both which played their parts so that Zadok, of his own nature violent, swore by the ark of Jehovah to set the whole city on fire ere he went out of it. Zachary, after he had furnished the wench with the poison and given her instructions to go to the devil, durst not stay one hour for fear of disclosing, but fled to the Duke of Bourbon that after sacked Rome, and there practised with his Bastardship all the mischief against the Pope and Rome that envy could put into his mind.

Zadok was left behind for the hangman. According to his oath, he provided balls of wildfire in a readiness, and laid trains of gunpowder in a hundred several places of the city to blow it up, which he had set fire to, as also bandied his balls abroad, if his attendant spies had not taken him with the manner. To the straitest prison in Rome he was dragged, where from top to toe he was clogged with fetters and manacles. Juliana informed the Pope of Zachary's and his practice; Zachary was sought for but *non est inventus*,* he was packing long before. Commandment was given that Zadok, whom they had under hand and seal of lock and key, should be executed with all the fiery torments that could be found out.

I'll make short work, for I am sure I have wearied all my readers. To the execution place was he brought, where first and foremost he was stripped, then on a sharp iron stake fastened in the ground had he his fundament pitched, which stake ran up along into his body like a spit. Under his armholes two of like sort. A great bonfire they made round about him, wherewith his flesh roasted, not burned; and ever as with the heat his skin blistered, the fire was drawn aside and they basted him with a mixture of aqua fortis, alum water, and mercury sublimatum, which smarted to the very soul of him and searched him to the marrow. Then did they scourge his back parts so blistered and basted with burning whips of red hot wire. His head they 'nointed over with pitch and tar, and so inflamed it. To his privy members they tied streaming fireworks; the skin from the crest of his shoulder, as also from his elbows, his huckle bones, his knees, his ankles, they plucked and gnawed off with sparkling pincers. His breast and his belly with seal-skins they grated over, which as fast as they grated and rawed one stood over and laved with smith's cindery water and aqua vitae. His nails they half raised up, and then underpropped them with sharp pricks like a tailor's shop window half open on a holiday. Every one of his fingers they rent up to the wrist. His toes they brake off by the roots and let them still hang by a little skin. In conclusion, they had a small oil fire such as men blow light bubbles of glass with, and beginning at his feet, they let him lingeringly burn up limb by limb, till his heart was consumed, and then he died. Triumph women! This was the end of the whipping Jew, contrived by a woman in revenge of two women, herself and her maid.

I have told you, or should tell you, in what credit Diamante grew with her mistress. Juliana never dreamed but she was an authentical maid. She made her the chief of her bedchamber, she appointed none but her to look in to me and serve me of such necessaries as I lacked. You must suppose when we met there was no small rejoicing on either part, much like the three brothers that went three several ways to seek their fortunes and at the year's end at those three crossways met again and told one another how they sped. So after we had been long asunder seeking our fortune, we commented one to another most kindly what cross haps had encountered us. Ne'er a six hours but the Countess cloyed me with her company. It grew to this pass, that either I must find out some miraculous means of escape or drop away in a consumption as one pined for lack of meat. I was clean spent and done, there was no hope of me.

The year held on his course to doomsday, when St Peter's Day dawned. That day is a day of supreme solemnity in Rome, when the ambassador of Spain comes and presents a milk white jennet to the Pope that kneels down upon his own accord in token of obeisance and humility before him, and lets him stride on his back as easy as one strides over a block. With this jennet is offered a rich purse of a yard length full of Peter pence. No music that hath the gift of utterance but sounds all the while. Copes and costly vestments deck the hoarsest and beggarliest singing man. Not a clerk or sexton is absent, no nor a mule nor a foot-cloth belonging to any cardinal but attends on the tail of the triumph. The Pope himself is borne in his pontificalibus through the Burgo (which is the chief street in Rome) to the ambassador's house to dinner, and thither resorts all the assembly; where, if a poet should spend all his lifetime in describing a banquet, he could not feast his auditors half so well with words as he doth his guests with junkets.

To this feast Juliana addressed herself like an angel. In a litter of green needlework wrought like an arbour, and open on every side, was she borne by four men hidden under cloth rough-plushed and woven like eglantine and woodbine. At the four corners it was topped with four round crystal cages of nightingales. For footmen on either side of her went four virgins clad in lawn with lutes in their hands playing. Next before her, two and two in order, a hundred pages in suits of white cypress and long horsemen's coats of cloth of silver who, being all in white, advanced every one of them her picture enclosed in a white round screen of feathers, such as is carried over great princesses' heads when they ride in summer to keep them from the heat of the sun. Before them went a fourscore beadwomen she maintained, in green gowns, scattering strewing-herbs and flowers. After her followed the blind, the halt, and the lame, sumptuously apparelled like lords. And thus passed she on to St Peter's.

Interea quid agitur domi, how is't at home all this while? My courtesan is left my keeper, the keys are committed unto her, she is mistress factotum. Against our Countess we conspire, pack up all her jewels, plate, money that was extant, and to the waterside send them; to conclude, courageously rob her and run away. *Quid non auri sacra fames*, what defame will not gold salve? He mistook himself that invented the proverb *Dimicandum est pro aris et focis*, for it should have been *pro auro et fama*: not for altars and fires we must contend, but for gold and fame.

Oars nor wind could not stir nor blow faster than we toiled out of Tiber; a number of good fellows would give size ace and the dice* that with as little toil they could leave Tyburn* behind them. Out of ken we were ere the Countess came from the feast. When she returned and found her house not so much pestered as it was wont, her chests, her closets, and her cupboards broke open to take air, and that both I and my keeper was missing—O then she fared like a frantic bacchanal. She stamped, she stared, she beat her head against the walls, scratched her face, bit her fingers, and strewed all the chamber with her hair. None of her servants durst stay in her sight, but she beat them out in heaps, and bade them go seek, search, they knew not where, and hang themselves and never look her in the face more if they did not hunt us out.

After her fury had reasonably spent itself, her breast began to swell with the mother* caused by her former fretting and chafing, and she grew very ill at ease. Whereupon she knocked for one of her maids and bade her run into her closet and fetch her a little glass that stood on the upper shelf wherein there was *spiritus vini*.* The maid went and, mistaking, took the glass of poison which Diamante had given her and she kept in store for me. Coming with it as fast as her legs could carry her, her mistress at her return was in a swound, and lay for dead on the floor, whereat she shrieked out and fell a rubbing and chafing her very busily. When that would not serve, she took a key and opened her mouth and, having heard that *spiritus vini* was a thing of mighty operation, able to call a man from death to life, she took the poison and, verily thinking it to be *spiritus vini* (such as she was sent for), poured a large quantity of it into her throat, and jogged on her back to digest it. It revived her with a merry vengeance, for it killed her outright; only she awakened and lift up her hands, but spake ne'er a word. Then was the maid in her grandame's beans,* and knew not what should become of her. I heard the Pope took pity on her and, because her trespass was not voluntary but chance-medley, he assigned her no other punishment but this: to drink out the rest of the poison in the glass that was left, and so go scot free.

We, careless of these mischances, held on our flight, and

saw no man come after us but we thought had pursued us. A thief, they say, mistakes every bush for a true man; the wind rattled not in any bush by the way as I rode but I straight drew my rapier. To Bologna with a merry gale we posted, where we lodged ourselves in a blind street out of the way, and kept secret many days. But when we perceived we sailed in the haven, that the wind was laid and no alarum made after us, we boldly came abroad, and one day hearing of a more desperate murderer than Cain that was to be executed, we followed the multitude, and grudged not to lend him our eyes at his last parting.

Who should it be but one Cutwolf, a wearish, dwarfish, writhen-faced cobbler, brother to Bartol the Italian that was confederate with Esdras of Granado, and at that time stole away my courtesan when he ravished Heraclide. It is not so natural for me to epitomize his impiety as to hear him in his own person speak upon the wheel where he was to suffer.

Prepare your ears and your tears, for never, till this, thrust I any tragical matter upon you. Strange and wonderful are God's judgements; here shine they in their glory. Chaste Heraclide, thy blood is laid up in heaven's treasury, not one drop of it was lost, but lent out to usury. Water poured forth sinks down quietly into the earth, but blood spilt on the ground sprinkles up to the firmament. Murder is wide-mouthed, and will not let God rest till he grant revenge. Not only the blood of the slaughtered innocent but the soul ascendeth to his throne, and there cries out and exclaims for justice and recompense. Guiltless souls that live every hour subject to violence, and with your despairing fears do much impair God's providence, fasten your eyes on this spectacle that will add to your faith. Refer all your oppressions, afflictions, and injuries to the even-balanced eye of the Almighty. He it is that, when your patience sleepeth, will be most exceeding mindful of you. This is but a gloss upon the text; thus Cutwolf begins his insulting oration:

'Men and people that have made holiday to behold my pained flesh toil on the wheel, expect not of me a whining penitent slave that shall do nothing but cry and say his prayers and so be crushed in pieces. My body is little but my mind is as great as a giant's. The soul which is in me is the very soul of Julius Caesar by reversion. My name is Cutwolf, neither better nor worse by occupation than a poor cobbler of Verona—cobblers are men, and kings are no more. The occasion of my coming hither at this present is to have a few of my bones broken (as we are all born to die) for being the death of the emperor of homicides Esdras of Granado. About two years since in the streets of Rome he slew the only and eldest brother I had, named Bartol, in quarrelling about a courtesan. The news brought to me as I was sitting in my shop under a stall, knocking in of tacks I think, I raised up my bristles, sold pritch-awl, sponge, blacking tub, and punching iron, bought me rapier and pistol and to go I went.

'Twenty months together I pursued him, from Rome to Naples, from Naples to Caiete passing over the river, from Caiete to Siena, from Siena to Florence, from Florence to Parma, from Parma to Pavia, from Pavia to Sion, from Sion to Geneva, from Geneva back again towards Rome, where in the way it was my chance to meet him in the nick here at Bologna, as I will tell you how. I saw a great fray in the streets as I passed along and many swords walking, whereupon drawing nearer, and enquiring who they were, answer was returned me it was that notable bandetto Esdras of Granado. O, so I was tickled in the spleen with that word; my heart hopped and danced, my elbows itched, my fingers frisked, I wist not what should become of my feet, nor knew what I did for joy. The fray parted. I thought it not convenient to single him out (being a sturdy knave) in the street, but to stay till I had got him at more advantage. To his lodging I dogged him, lay at the door all night where he entered for fear he should give me the slip any way. Betimes in the morning I rung the bell and craved to speak with him. Up to his chamber door I was brought, where knocking, he rose in his shirt and let me in and, when I was entered, bade me lock the door and declare my errand, and so he slipped to bed again.

'"Marry this", quoth I, "is my errand. Thy name is Esdras of Granado, is it not? Most treacherously thou slewest my brother Bartol about two years ago in the streets of Rome. His death am I come to revenge. In quest of thee ever since, above three thousand miles have I travelled. I have begged to maintain me the better part of the way only because I would intermit no time from my pursuit in going back for money. Now have I got thee naked in my power; die thou shalt, though my mother and my grandmother dying did entreat for thee. I have promised the devil thy soul within this hour; break my word I will not. In thy breast I intend to bury a bullet. Stir not, quinch not, make no noise, for if thou dost it will be worse for thee."

'Quoth Esdras, "Whatever thou be at whose mercy I lie, spare me and I will give thee as much gold as thou wilt ask. Put me to any pains, my life reserved, and I willingly will sustain them. Cut off my arms and legs and leave me as a lazar to some loathsome spital, where I may but live a year to pray and repent me. For thy brother's death, the despair of mind that hath ever since haunted me, the guilty gnawing worm of conscience I feel, may be sufficient penance. Thou canst not send me to such a hell as already there is in my heart. To dispatch me presently is no revenge; it will soon be forgotten. Let me die a lingering death; it will be remembered a great deal longer. A lingering death may avail my soul but it is the illest of ills that can befortune my body. For my soul's health I beg my body's torment. Be not thou a devil to torment my soul, and send me to eternal damnation. Thy overhanging sword hides heaven from my sight. I dare not look up lest I embrace my death's wound unawares. I cannot pray to God and plead to thee both at once. Ay me, already I see my life buried in the wrinkles of thy brows. Say but I shall live, though thou meanest to kill me. Nothing confounds like to sudden terror, it thrusts every sense out of office. Poison wrapped up in sugared pills is but half a poison; the fear of death's looks are more terrible than his stroke. The whilst I view death my faith is deaded; where a man's fear is, there his heart is. Fear never engenders hope; how can I hope that heaven's Father will save me from the hell everlasting when He gives me over to the hell of thy fury.

'"Heraclide, now think I on thy tears sown in the dust; thy tears that my bloody mind made barren. In revenge of thee God hardens this man's heart against me. Yet I did not slaughter thee, though hundreds else my hand hath brought to the shambles. Gentle sir, learn of me what it is to clog your conscience with murder, to have your dreams, your sleeps, your solitary walks, troubled and disquieted with murder. Your shadow by day will affright you; you will not see a weapon unsheathed but immediately you will imagine it is predestinate for your destruction.

'"This murder is a house divided within itself; it suborns a man's own soul to inform against him. His soul, being his accuser, brings forth his two eyes as witnesses against him, and the least eyewitness is unrefutable. Pluck out my eyes if thou wilt, and deprive my traitorous soul of her two best witnesses. Dig out my blasphemous tongue with thy dagger. Both tongue and eyes will I gladly forgo to have a little more time to think on my journey to heaven.

'"Defer a while thy resolution. I am not at peace with the world, for even but yesterday I fought and in my fury threatened further vengeance. Had I face to face asked forgiveness, I should think half my sins were forgiven. A hundred devils haunt me daily for my horrible murders. The devils when I die will be loath to go to hell with me, for they desired of Christ he would not send them to hell before their time. If they go not to hell, into thee they will go, and hideously vex thee for turning them out of their habitation. Wounds I contemn, life I prize light, it is another world's tranquillity which makes me so timorous: everlasting damnation, everlasting howling and lamentation. It is not from death I request thee to deliver me, but from this terror of torment's eternity. Thy brother's body only I pierced unadvisedly, his soul meant I no harm to at all. My body and soul both shalt thou cast away quite if thou dost at this instant what thou mayest. Spare me, spare me I beseech thee! By thy own soul's salvation, I desire thee, seek not my soul's utter perdition. In destroying me thou destroyest thyself and me."

'Eagerly I replied after his long suppliant oration. "Though I knew God would never have mercy on me except I had mercy on thee, yet of thee no mercy would I have. Revenge in our tragedies continually is raised from hell; of hell do I esteem better than heaven if it afford me revenge. There is no heaven but revenge. I tell thee, I would not have undertook so much toil to gain heaven as I have done in pursuing thee for revenge. Divine revenge, of which (as of the joys above) there is no fullness or satiety! Look how my feet are blistered with following thee from place to place. I have riven my throat with overstraining it to curse thee. I have ground my teeth to powder with grating and grinding them together for anger when any hath named thee. My tongue with vain threats is bollen and waxen too big for my mouth. My eyes have broken their strings with staring and looking ghastly as I stood devising how to frame or set my countenance when I met thee. I have near spent my strength in imaginary acting on stone walls what I determined to execute on thee. Entreat not; a miracle may not reprieve thee. Villain, thus march I with my blade into thy bowels!"

'"Stay, stay," exclaimed Esdras, "and hear me but one word further. Though neither for God nor man thou carest, but placest thy whole felicity in murder, yet of thy felicity learn how to make a greater felicity. Respite me a little from thy sword's point, and set me about some execrable enterprise that may subvert the whole state of Christendom and make all men's ears tingle that hear of it. Command me to cut all my kindred's throats, to burn men, women, and children in their beds in millions by firing their cities at midnight. Be it Pope, Emperor, or Turk that displeaseth thee, he shall not breathe on the earth. For thy sake will I swear and forswear, renounce my baptism and all the interest I have in any other sacrament. Only let me live, how miserable soever, be it in a dungeon amongst toads, serpents, and adders, or set up to the neck in dung. No pains I will refuse, however prorogued, to have a little respite to purify my spirit. Oh, hear me, hear me, and thou canst not be hardened against me!"

'At this his importunity I paused a little, not as retiring from my wreakful resolution, but going back to gather more forces of vengeance. With myself I devised how to plague him double for his base mind. My thoughts travelled in quest of some notable new Italianism, whose murderous platform might not only extend on his body, but his soul also. The groundwork of it was this. That whereas he had promised for my sake to swear and forswear, and commit Julian-like violence on the highest scales of religion, if he would but thus far satisfy me he should be dismissed from my fury. First and foremost he should renounce God and his laws, and utterly disclaim the whole title or interest he had in any covenant of salvation. Next he should curse Him to His face, as Job was willed by his wife, and write an absolute firm obligation of his soul to the devil, without condition or exception. Thirdly and lastly, having done this, he should pray to God fervently never to have mercy upon him or pardon him.

'Scarce had I propounded these articles unto him but he was beginning his blasphemous abjurations. I wonder the earth opened not and swallowed us both, hearing the bold terms he blasted forth in contempt of Christianity. Heaven hath thundered when half less contumelies against it hath been uttered. Able they were to raise saints and martyrs from their graves, and pluck Christ himself from the right hand of his Father. My joints trembled and quaked with attending them; my hair stood upright, and my heart was turned wholly to fire. So affectionately and jealously did he give himself over to infidelity as if Satan had gotten the upper hand of our high Maker. The vein in his left hand, that is derived from his heart, with no faint blow he pierced, and with the blood that flowed from it writ a full obligation of his soul to the devil. Yea, more earnestly he prayed unto God never to forgive his soul than many Christians do to save their souls.

'These fearful ceremonies brought to an end, I bade him open his mouth and gape wide. He did so (as what will not slaves do for fear). Therewith made I no more ado, but shot him full into the throat with my pistol. No more spake he after; so did I shoot him that he might never speak after, or repent him. His body, being dead, looked as black as a toad; the devil presently branded it for his own. This is the fault that hath called me hither. No true Italian but will honour me for it. Revenge is the glory of arms and the highest performance of valour. Revenge is whatsoever we call law or justice. The farther we wade in revenge the nearer come we to the throne of the Almighty. To His sceptre it is properly ascribed, His sceptre he lends unto man when He lets one man scourge another. All true Italians imitate me in revenging constantly and dying valiantly. Hangman to thy task, for I am ready for the utmost of thy rigour.'

Herewith all the people (outrageously incensed) with one conjoined outcry yelled mainly 'Away with him, away with him! Executioner torture him, tear him, or we will tear thee in pieces if thou spare him.' The executioner needed no exhortation hereunto, for of his own nature was he hackster good enough. Old excellent he was at a bone-ache. At the first chop with his wood-knife would he fish for a man's heart and fetch it out as easily as a plum from the bottom of a porridge pot. He would crack necks as fast as a cook cracks eggs. A fiddler cannot turn his pin so soon as he would turn a man off the ladder. Bravely did he drum on this Cutwolf's bones, not breaking them outright but, like a saddler knocking in of tacks, jarring on them quaveringly with his hammer a great while together. No joint about him but with a hatchet he had for the nonce he disjointed half, and then with boiling lead soldered up the wound from bleeding. His tongue he pulled out, lest he should blaspheme in his torment. Venomous stinging worms he thrust into his ears to keep his head ravingly occupied. With cankers scruzed to pieces he rubbed his mouth and his gums. No limb of his but was lingeringly splintered in shivers. In this horror left they him on the wheel as in hell; where yet living he might behold his flesh legacied amongst the souls of the air.

Unsearchable is the book of our destinies. One murder begetteth another; was never yet bloodshed barren from the beginning of the world to this day. Mortifiedly abjected and danted was I with this truculent tragedy of Cutwolf and Esdras. To such straight life did it thenceforward incite me that, ere I went out of Bologna, I married my courtesan, performed many almsdeeds, and hasted so fast out of the Sodom of Italy that within forty days I arrived at the King of England's camp 'twixt Ardes and Guines* in France, where he with great triumphs met and entertained the Emperor and the French King and feasted many days.

And so as my story began with the King at Turney and Turwin, I think meet here to end it with the King at Ardes and Guines. All the conclusive epilogue I will make is this: that if herein I have pleased any, it shall animate me to more pains in this kind. Otherwise I will swear upon an English chronicle never to be outlandish chronicler more while I live. Farewell as many as wish me well. June 27, 1593.

THOMAS DELONEY

Jack of Newbury
(*c.*1597)

The Pleasant History of John Winchcomb,* in his younger years called Jack of Newbury, the famous and worthy clothier of England; declaring his life and love together with his charitable deeds and great hospitality. And how he set continually five hundred poor people at work to the great benefit of the commonwealth. Worthy to be read and regarded.

To All Famous Cloth Workers in England,
I wish all happiness of life, prosperity, and brotherly affection.

Among all manual arts used in this land, none is more famous for desert or more beneficial to the commonwealth than is the most necessary art of clothing; and therefore as the benefit thereof is great, so are the professors of the same to be both loved and maintained. Many wise men therefore having deeply considered the same, most bountifully have bestowed their gifts for upholding of so excellent a commodity which hath been and yet is the nourishing of many thousands of poor people. Wherefore to you, most worthy clothiers, do I dedicate this my rude work, which hath raised out of the dust of forgetfulness a most famous and worthy man, whose name was John Winchcomb, alias Jack of Newbury, of whose life and love I have briefly written, and in a plain and humble manner that it may be the better understood of those for whose sake I take pains to compile it. That is, for the well-minded clothiers, that herein they may behold the great worship and credit which men of this trade have in former time come unto. If therefore it be of you kindly accepted, I have the end of my desire, and think my pains well recompensed; and finding your gentleness answering my hope, it shall move me shortly to set to your sight the long-hidden history of Thomas of Reading,* George of Gloucester, Richard of Worcester, and William of Salisbury, with diverse others who were all most notable members in the commonwealth of this land, and men of great fame and dignity. In the mean space I commend you all to the most high God, who ever increase in all perfection and prosperous estate the long-honoured trade of English clothiers.

Yours in all humble service,
T.D.

CHAPTER 1

IN the days of King Henry VIII, that most noble and victorious prince, in the beginning of his reign, John Winchcomb, a broadcloth weaver, dwelt in Newbury, a town in Berkshire; who for that he was a man of a merry disposition and honest conversation was wondrous well-beloved of rich and poor, especially because in every place where he came he would spend his money with the best, and was not at any time found a churl of his purse. Wherefore, being so good a companion, he was called of old and young Jack of Newbury; a man so generally well known in all his country for his good fellowship that he could go in no place but he found acquaintance, by means whereof Jack could no sooner get a crown but straight he found means to spend it. Yet had he ever this care: that he would always keep himself in comely and decent apparel. Neither at any time would he be overcome in drink, but so discreetly behave himself with honest mirth and pleasant conceits that he was every gentleman's companion.

After that Jack had long led this pleasant life, being (though he were but poor) in good estimation, it was his master's chance to die and his dame to be a widow, who was a very comely ancient woman, and of reasonable wealth. Wherefore she, having a good opinion of her man John, committed unto his government the guiding of all her workfolks for the space of three years together. In which time she found him so careful and diligent that all things came forward and prospered wondrous well. No man could entice him from his business all the week by all the entreaty they could use, insomuch that in the end some of the wild youths of the town began to deride and scoff at him.

'Doubtless', quoth one, 'I doubt some female spirit hath enchanted Jack to her treadles, and conjured him within the compass of his loom that he can stir no further.' 'You say truth,' quoth Jack, 'and if you have the leisure to stay till the charm be done, the space of six days and five nights, you shall find me ready to put on my holiday apparel, and on Sunday morning for your pains I will give you a pot of ale over against the maypole.'

'Nay,' quoth another, 'I'll lay my life that as the salamander cannot live without the fire, so Jack cannot live without the smell of his dame's smoke.' 'And I marvel', quoth Jack, 'that you, being of the nature of the herring (which so soon as he is taken out of the sea straight dies), can live so long with your nose out of the pot.' 'Nay Jack, leave thy jesting,' quoth another, 'and go along with us. Thou shalt not stay a jot.' 'And because I will not stay, nor make you a liar,' quoth Jack, 'I'll keep me here still, and so farewell.'

Thus then they departed, and after they had for half a score times tried him to this intent, and saw he would not be led by their lure, they left him to his own will. Nevertheless, every Sunday in the afternoon, and every holiday, Jack would keep them company and be as merry as a pie; and having still good store of money in his purse, one or other would ever be borrowing of him, but never could he get penny of it again; which when Jack perceived he would never after carry above twelve pence at once in his purse, and that being spent he would straight return home merrily taking his leave of the company in this sort.

> My masters I thank you, it's time to pack home,
> For he that wants money is counted a mome,
> And twelve pence a Sunday being spent in good cheer
> To fifty-two shillings amounts in the year—
> Enough for a craftsman that lives by his hands,
> And he that exceeds it shall purchase no lands.
> For that I spend this day I'll work hard tomorrow,
> For woe is that party that seeketh to borrow.
> My money doth make me full merry to be,
> And without my money none careth for me.
> Therefore, wanting money, what should I do here
> But haste home, and thank-you for all my good cheer.

Thus was Jack's good government and discretion noted of the best and substantialest men of the town, so that it wrought his great commendations, and his dame thought herself not a little blessed to have such a servant that was so obedient unto her, and so careful for her profit; for she had never a prentice that yielded her more obedience than he did or was more dutiful. So that by his good example he did as much good as by his diligent labour and travail, which his singular virtue being noted by the widow, she began to cast very good countenance to her man John, and to use very much talk with him in private. And first, by way of communication, she would tell unto him what suitors she had, and the great offers they made her; what gifts they sent her and the great affection they bare her, craving his opinion in the matter.

When Jack found the favour to be his dame's secretary, he thought it an extraordinary kindness, and guessing by the yarn it would prove a good web, began to question with his dame in this sort. 'Although it becometh not me, your servant, to pry into your secrets, nor to be busy about matters of your love, yet for so much as it hath pleased you to use conference with me in those causes, I pray you let me entreat you to know their names that be your suitors, and of what profession they be.'

'Marry John,' saith she, 'that you shall, and I pray thee take a cushion and sit down by me.' 'Dame,' quoth he, 'I thank you, but there is no reason I should sit on a cushion till I have deserved it.' 'If thou hast not thou mightest have done,' said she, 'but faint soldiers never find favour.' John replied 'That makes me indeed to want favour, for I durst not try maidens because they seem coy, nor wives for fear of their husbands, nor widows doubting their disdainfulness.' 'Tush John,' quoth she, 'he that fears and doubts womankind cannot be counted mankind, and take this for a principle: all things are not as they seem. But let us leave this and proceed to our former matter. My first suitor dwells at Wallingford, by trade a tanner, a man of good wealth, and his name is Crafts; of comely personage and very good behaviour; a widower, well thought of amongst his neighbours. He hath proper land, a fair house and well furnished, and never a child in the world, and he loves me passing well.'

'Why then, dame,' quoth John, 'you were best to have him.' 'Is that your opinion?' quoth she. 'Now trust me, so it is not mine, for I find two special reasons to the contrary. The one is that he being overworn in years makes me overloath to love him, and the other that I know one nearer hand.' 'Believe me dame,' quoth Jack, 'I perceive store is no sore, and proffered ware is worse by ten in the hundred than that which is sought. But I pray ye, who is your second suitor?'

'John,' quoth she, 'it may seem immodesty in me to bewray my love secrets, yet seeing thy discretion, and being persuaded of thy secrecy, I will show thee. The other is a man of middle years but yet a bachelor; by occupation a tailor, dwelling at Hungerford; by report a very good husband, such a one as hath crowns good store, and to me he professes much good will. For his person, he may please any woman.' 'Aye dame,' quoth John, 'because he pleaseth you.' 'Not so,' said she, 'for my eyes are unpartial judges in that case, and albeit my opinion may be contrary to others, if his art deceive not my eyesight he is worthy of a good wife both for his person and conditions.'

'Then trust me dame,' quoth John, 'for so much as you are without doubt of yourself that you will prove a good wife, and so well persuaded of him, I should think you could make no better a choice.' 'Truly John,' quoth she, 'there be also two reasons that move me not to like of him. The one, that being so long a ranger he would at home be a stranger; and the other, that I like better of one nearer hand.' 'Who is that?' quoth Jack.

Saith she, 'The third suitor is the parson of Speenhamland, who hath a proper living. He is of holy conversation and good estimation, whose affection to me is great.' 'No doubt dame,' quoth John, 'you may do wondrous well with him, where you shall have no care but to serve God, and to make ready his meat.' 'O John,' quoth she, 'the flesh and the spirit agrees not, for he will be so bent to his books that he will have little mind of his bed, for one month's studying for a sermon will make him forget his wife a whole year.' 'Truly dame,' quoth John, 'I must needs speak in his behalf, and the rather for that he is a man of the church and your near neighbour, to whom (as I guess) you bear the best affection. I do not think that he will be so much bound to his book, or subject to the spirit, but that he will remember a woman at home or abroad.'

'Well John,' quoth she, 'I wis my mind is not that way, for I like better of one nearer hand.' 'No marvel,' quoth Jack, 'you are so peremptory, seeing you have so much choice. But I pray ye dame,' quoth he, 'let me know this fortunate man that is so highly placed in your favour.' 'John,' quoth she, 'they are worthy to know nothing that cannot keep something. That man, I tell thee, must go nameless, for he is lord of my love and king of my desires. There is neither tanner, tailor, nor parson may compare with him. His presence is a preservative to my health, his sweet smiles my heart's solace, and his words heavenly music to my ears.'

'Why then, dame,' quoth John, 'for your body's health, your heart's joy, and your ears' delight, delay not the time but entertain him with a kiss, make his bed next yours, and chop up the match in the morning.' 'Well,' quoth she, 'I perceive thy consent is quickly got to any, having no care how I am matched so I be matched. I wis, I wis I could not let thee go so lightly, being loath that anyone should have thee, except I could love her as well as myself.' 'I thank you for your kindness and good will, good dame,' quoth he, 'but it is not wisdom for a young man that can scantly keep himself to take a wife. Therefore I hold it the best way to lead a single life, for I have heard say that many sorrows follow marriage, especially where want remains. And beside, it is a hard matter to find a constant woman, for as young maids are fickle, so are old women jealous; the one a grief too common, the other a torment intolerable.'

'What John,' quoth she, 'consider that maidens' fickleness proceeds of vain fancies, but old women's jealousy of superabounding love, and therefore the more to be borne withal.' 'But dame,' quoth he, 'many are jealous without cause, for is it sufficient for their mistrusting natures to take exceptions at a shadow, at a word, at a look, at a smile—nay, at the twinkle of an eye, which neither man nor woman is able to expel? I knew a woman that was ready to hang herself for seeing but her husband's shirt hang on a hedge with her maid's smock.' 'I grant that this fury may haunt some,' quoth she, 'yet there be many other that complain not without great cause.' 'Why, is there any cause that should move jealousy?' quoth John.

'Aye, by St Mary is there,' quoth she, 'for would it not grieve a woman (being one every way able to delight her husband) to see him forsake her, despise and contemn her, being never so merry as when he is in other company, sporting abroad from morning till noon, from noon till night, and when he comes to bed, if he turn to his wife, it is in such solemness and wearisome, drowsy lameness, that it brings rather loathsomeness than any delight. Can you then blame a woman in this case to be angry and displeased? I'll tell you what, among brute beasts it is a grief intolerable, for I heard my grandame tell that the bell wether of her flock, fancying one of the ewes above the rest, and seeing Gratis the shepherd abusing her in abominable sort (subverting the law of nature) could by no means bear that abuse, but watching opportunity for revenge, on a time found the said shepherd sleeping in the field, and suddenly ran against him in such violent sort that by the force of his wreathen horns he beat the brains out of the shepherd's head and slew him. If then a sheep could not endure that injury, think not that women are so sheepish to suffer it.'

'Believe me,' quoth John, 'if every horn-maker should be so plagued by a horned beast there should be less horns made in Newbury by many in a year. But dame,' quoth he, 'to make an end of this prattle, because it is an argument too deep to be discussed between you and I, you shall hear me sing an old song, and so we will depart to supper.

> A maiden fair I dare not wed
> For fear to have Actaeon's head.*
> A maiden black is often proud,
> A maiden little will be loud.
> A maiden that is high of growth
> They say is subject unto sloth.
> Thus fair or foul, little or tall,
> Some faults remain among them all.
> But of all the faults that be
> None is so bad as jealousy.
> For jealousy is fierce and fell,
> And burns as hot as fire in hell,
> It breeds suspicion without cause
> And breaks the bonds of reason's laws.

> To none it is a greater foe
> Than unto those where it doth grow,
> And God keep me both day and night
> From that fell, fond, and ugly sprite.
> For why? Of all the plagues that be
> The secret plague is jealousy.
> Therefore I wish all womenkind
> Never to bear a jealous mind.

'Well said John,' quoth she, 'thy song is not so sure but thy voice is as sweet. But seeing the time agrees with our stomachs, though loath, yet will we give over for this time and betake ourselves to our suppers.'

Then, calling the rest of her servants, they fell to their meat merrily, and after supper the goodwife went abroad for her recreation, to walk a while with one of her neighbours. And in the mean space, John got him up into his chamber and there began to meditate on this matter, bethinking with himself what he were best to do; for well he perceived that his dame's affection was great toward him. Knowing therefore the woman's disposition, and withal that her estate was reasonable good, and considering beside that he should find a house ready furnished, servants ready taught, and all other things for his trade necessary, he thought it best not to let slip that good occasion, lest he should never come to the like. But again, when he considered her years to be unfitting to his youth, and that she that sometime had been his dame would (perhaps) disdain to be governed by him that had been her poor servant, that it would prove but a bad bargain, doubting many inconveniences that might grow thereby, he therefore resolved to be silent rather than to proceed further. Wherefore he got him straight to bed, and the next morning settled himself close to his business.

His dame coming home and hearing that her man was gone to bed, took that night but small rest, and early in the morning, hearing him up at his work merrily singing, she by and by arose and in seemly sort attiring herself, she came into the workshop, and sat her down to make quills. Quoth John, 'Good morrow dame, how do you today?' 'God a mercy John,' quoth she, 'even as well as I may, for I was sore troubled in my dreams. Methought two doves walked together in a corn field, the one (as it were) in communication with the other, without regard of pecking up anything to sustain themselves. And after they had, with many nods, spent some time to their content, they both fell hard with their pretty bills to peck up the scattered corn left by the weary reaper's hand. At length (finding themselves satisfied) it chanced another pigeon to light in that place, with whom one of the first pigeons at length kept company, and after, returning to the place where she left her first companion, perceived he was not there. She, kindly searching up and down the high stubble to find him, lighted at length on a hog fast asleep, wherewith methought the poor dove was so dismayed that presently she fell down in a trance. I, seeing her legs fail and her wings quiver, yielding herself to death, moved with pity ran unto her, and thinking to take up the pigeon methought I had in my hands my own heart, wherein methought an arrow stuck so deep that the blood trickled down the shaft and lay upon the feathers like the silver pearled dew on the green grass; which made me to weep most bitterly. But presently methought there came one to me crowned like a queen, who told me my heart would die except in time I got some of that sleeping hog's grease to heal the wounds thereof. Whereupon I ran in all haste to the hog with my heart bleeding in my hand, who (methought) grunted at me in most churlish sort, and vanished out of my sight. Whereupon coming straight home, methought I found this hog rustling among my looms, wherewith I presently awaked suddenly after midnight, being all in a sweat and very ill, and I am sure you could not choose but hear me groan.'

'Trust me dame, I heard you not,' quoth John, 'I was so sound asleep.' 'And thus', quoth she, 'a woman may die in the night before you will have the care to see what she ails, or ask what she lacks. But truly John,' quoth she, 'all is one, for if thou shouldst have come thou couldst not have got in because my chamber door was locked. But while I live this shall teach me wit, for henceforth I will have no other lock but a latch till I am married.'

'Then dame,' quoth he, 'I perceive though you be curious in your choice, yet at length you will marry.' 'Aye, truly,' quoth she, 'so thou wilt not hinder me.' 'Who I?' quoth John, 'on my faith dame, not for a hundred pounds, but rather will further you to the uttermost of my power.' 'Indeed,' quoth she, 'thou hast no reason to show any discourtesy to me in that matter, although some of our neighbours do not stick to say that I am sure to thee already.' 'If it were so,' quoth John, 'there is no cause to deny it, or to be ashamed thereof, knowing myself far unworthy of so high a favour.' 'Well, let this talk rest,' quoth she, 'and take there thy quills, for it is time for me to go to market.'

Thus the matter rested for two or three days, in which space she daily devised which way she might obtain her desire, which was to marry her man. Many things came in her head, and sundry sleights in her mind, but none of them did fit her fancy, so that she became wondrous sad, and as civil* as the nine sibyls. And in this melancholy humour continued three weeks or a month, till at last it was her luck upon a Bartholomew day (having a fair in the town) to spy her man John give a pair of gloves to a proper maid for a fairing, which the maiden with a bashful modesty kindly acepted and requited it with a kiss, which kindled in her an inward jealousy. But notwithstanding, very discreetly she covered it, and closely passed along unspied of her man or the maid.

She had not gone far but she met with one of her suitors, namely the tailor, who was very fine and brisk in his apparel, and needs he would bestow the wine upon the widow. And after some faint denial, meeting with a gossip of hers, to the tavern they went, which was more courtesy than the tailor could ever get of her before, showing herself very pleasant and merry. And finding her in such a pleasing humour, the tailor after a new quart of wine renewed his old suit. The widow with patience heard him, and gently answered that in respect of his great good will long time borne unto her, as also in regard of his gentleness, cost, and courtesy at that present bestowed, she would not flatly deny him. 'Therefore', quoth she, 'seeing this is not a place to conclude of such matters, if I may entreat you to come to my poor house on Thursday next, you shall be heartily welcome and be further satisfied of my mind'; and thus preferred to a touch of her lips, he payed the shot and departed.

The tailor was scant out of sight when she met with the tanner who, albeit he was aged, yet lustily he saluted her, and to the wine she must, there was no nay. The widow, seeing his importunacy, calls her gossip and along they walked together. The old man called for wine plenty, and the best cheer in the house, and in hearty manner he bids the widow welcome. They had not sitten long but in comes a noise of musicians in tawny coats who (putting off their caps) asked if they would have any music. The widow answered no, they were merry enough. 'Tut,' quoth the old man, 'let us hear, good fellows, what you can do, and play me *The Beginning of the World*.'*

'Alas,' quoth the widow, 'you had more need to hearken to the ending of the world.' 'Why widow,' quoth he, 'I tell thee the beginning of the world was the begetting of children, and if you find me faulty in that occupation turn me out of thy bed for a bungler and then send for the sexton.'

He had no sooner spoke the word but the parson of Speen, with his corner cap, popped in at the door, who, seeing the widow sitting at the table, craved pardon and came in. Quoth she, 'For want of the sexton, here is the priest if you need him.' 'Marry,' quoth the tanner, 'in good time, for by this means we need not go far to be married.' 'Sir,' quoth the parson, 'I shall do my best in convenient place.' 'Wherein?' quoth the tanner. 'To wed her myself,' quoth the parson. 'Nay soft,' said the widow, 'one swallow makes not a summer, nor one meeting a marriage. As I lighted on you unlooked for, so came I hither unprovided for the purpose.'

'I trust', quoth the tanner, 'you came not without your eyes to see, your tongue to speak, your ears to hear, your hands to feel, nor your legs to go.' 'I brought my eyes', quoth she, 'to discern colours, my tongue to say no to questions I like not, my hands to thrust from me the things that I love not, my ears to judge betwixt flattery and friendship, and my feet to run from such as would wrong me.' 'Why then,' quoth the parson, 'by your gentle abiding in this place it is evident that here are none but those you like and love.' 'God forbid I should hate my friends', quoth the widow, 'whom I take all these in this place to be.' 'But there be diverse sorts of loves,' quoth the parson. 'You say truth,' quoth the widow, 'I love yourself for your profession, and my friend the tanner for his courtesy and kindness; and the rest for their good company.'

'Yet', quoth the parson, 'for the explaining of your love, I pray you drink to them you love best in the company.' 'Why,' quoth the tanner, 'have you any hope in her love?' 'Believe me,' saith the parson, 'as much as another.' 'Why then parson, sit down,' said the tanner, 'for you that are equal with me in desire shall surely be half with me in the shot, and so widow, on God's name fulfil the parson's request.'

'Seeing', quoth the widow, 'you are so pleasantly bent, if my courtesy might not breed contention between you, and that I may have your favour to show my fancy, I will fulfil your request.' Quoth the parson, 'I am pleased howsoever it be.' 'And I,' quoth the tanner. 'Why then,' quoth she, 'with this cup of claret wine and sugar I heartily drink to the minstrel's boy.'

'Why, is it he you love best?' quoth the parson. 'I have reason', said she, 'to like and love them best that will be least offended with my doings.' 'Nay widow,' quoth they, 'we meant you should drink to him whom you loved best in the way of marriage.' Quoth the widow, 'You should have said so at first; but, to tell you my opinion, it is small discretion for a woman to disclose her secret affection in an open assembly. Therefore, if to that purpose you spake, let me entreat you both to come home to my house on Thursday next, where you shall be heartily welcome, and there be fully resolved of my mind, and so with thanks at this time I'll take my leave.'

The shot being payed, and the musicians pleased, they all departed; the tanner to Wallingford, the parson to Speen, and the widow to her own house, where in her wonted solemness she settled herself to her business.

Against Thursday she dressed her house fine and brave, and set herself in her best apparel. The tailor, nothing forgetting his promise, sent to the widow a good fat pig and a goose. The parson, being as mindful as he, sent to her house a couple of fat rabbits and a capon; and the tanner came himself and brought a good shoulder of mutton and half a dozen chickens, beside he brought a good gallon of sack and half a pound of the best sugar. The widow, receiving this good meat, set her maid to dress it incontinent, and when dinner time drew near, the table was covered, and every other thing provided in convenient and comely sort.

At length, the guests being come, the widow bade them all heartily welcome. The priest and the tanner, seeing the tailor, mused what he made there; the tailor, on the other side, marvelled as much at their presence. Thus looking strangely one at another, at length the widow came out of the kitchen in a fair train gown stuck full of silver pins, a fine white cap on her head, with cuts of curious needle-work under the same, and an apron before her as white as the driven snow. Then, very modestly making curtsy to them all, she requested them to sit down. But they straining courtesy the one with the other, the widow, with a smiling countenance, took the parson by the hand saying 'Sir, as you stand highest in the church, so is it meet you should sit highest at the table, and therefore I pray you sit down there on the bench side. And sir,' said she to the tanner, 'as age is to be honoured before youth for their experience, so are they to sit above bachelors for their gravity,' and so she set him down on this side the table, over against the parson. Then, coming to the tailor, she said 'Bachelor, though your lot be the last, your welcome is equal with the first, and seeing your place points out itself, I pray you take a cushion and sit down. And now,' quoth she, 'to make the board equal, and because it hath been an old saying that three things are to small purpose if the fourth be away, if so it may stand with your favours, I will call in a gossip of mine to supply this void place.' 'With a good will,' quoth they.

With that she brought in an old woman with scant ever a good tooth in her head, and placed her right against the bachelor. Then was the meat brought to the board in due order by the widow's servants, her man John being chief servitor. The widow sat down at the table's end between the parson and the tanner, who in very good sort carved meat for them all, her man John waiting on the table.

After they had sitten a while, and well refreshed themselves, the widow, taking a crystal glass filled with claret wine, drunk unto the whole company and bade them welcome. The parson pledged her, and so did all the rest in due order; but still in their company the cup passed over the poor old woman's nose, insomuch that at length the old woman (in a merry vein) spake thus unto the company. 'I have had much good meat among you, but as for the drink, I can nothing commend it.' 'Alas good gossip,' quoth the widow, 'I perceive no man hath drunk to thee yet.'

'No truly,' quoth the old woman, 'for churchmen have so much mind of young rabbits, old men such joy in young chickens, and bachelors in pig's flesh take such delight, that an old sow, a tough hen, or a grey cony are not accepted; and so it is seen by me, else I should have been better remembered.' 'Well old woman,' quoth the parson, 'take here the leg of a capon to stop thy mouth.' 'Now by St Anne I dare not,' quoth she. 'No? Wherefore?' said the parson. 'Marry, for fear lest you should go home with a crutch,' quoth she.

The tailor said 'Then taste here a piece of goose.' 'Now God forbid,' said the old woman, 'let goose go to his kind; you have a young stomach, eat it yourself and much good may it do your heart, sweet young man.' 'The old woman lacks most of her teeth,' quoth the tanner, 'and therefore a piece of tender chick is fittest for her.' 'If I did lack as many of my teeth', quoth the old woman, 'as you lack points of good husbandry, I doubt I should starve before it were long.'

At this the widow laughed heartily, and the men were stricken into such a dump that they had not a word to say. Dinner being ended, the widow with the rest rose from the table, and after they had sitten a pretty while merrily talking, the widow called her man John to bring her a bowl of fresh ale, which he did. Then said the widow 'My masters, now for your courtesy and cost I heartily thank you all, and in requital of all your favour, love, and good will, I drink to you, giving you free liberty when you please to depart.'

At these words, her suitors looked so sourly one upon another, as if they had been newly champing of crabs. Which when the tailor heard, shaking up himself in his new russet jerkin, and setting his hat on one side, he began to speak thus.

'I trust sweet widow,' quoth he, 'you remember to what end my coming was hither today. I have long time been a suitor unto you, and this day you promised to give me a direct answer.' ''Tis true,' quoth she, 'and so I have. For your love I give you thanks, and when you please you may depart.' 'Shall I not have you?' said the tailor. 'Alas,' quoth the widow, 'you come too late.'

'Good friend,' quoth the tanner, 'it is manners for young men to let their elders be served before them. To what end should I be here if the widow should have thee? A flat denial is meet for a saucy suitor; but what sayest thou to me, fair widow?' quoth the tanner. 'Sir,' said she, 'because you are so sharp set, I would wish you as soon as you can to wed.' 'Appoint the time yourself,' quoth the tanner. 'Even as soon', quoth she, 'as you can get a wife, and hope not after me for I am already promised.'

'Now tanner, you may take your place with the tailor,' quoth the parson, 'for indeed the widow is for no man but myself.' 'Master parson,' quoth she, 'many have run near the goal and yet lost the game, and I cannot help it though your hope be in vain. Besides, parsons are but newly suffered to have wives,* and for my part, I will have none of the first head.'

'What,' quoth the tailor, 'is our merriment grown to this reckoning? I never spent a pig and a goose to so bad purpose before. I promise you, when I came in I verily thought that you were invited by the widow to make her and me sure together, and that the jolly tanner was brought to be a witness to the contract, and the old woman fetched in for the same purpose, else I would never have put up so many dry bobs at her hands.' 'And surely,' quoth the tanner, 'I, knowing thee to be a tailor, did assuredly think that thou wast appointed to come and take measure for our wedding apparel.' 'But now we are all deceived,' quoth the parson, 'and therefore as we came fools, so we may depart hence like asses.'

'That is as you interpret the matter,' said the widow, 'for I, ever doubting that a concluding answer would breed a jar in the end among you every one, I thought it better to be done at one instant and in mine own house, than at sundry times and in common taverns. And as for the meat you sent, as it was unrequested of me, so had you your part thereof, and if you think good to take home the remainder, prepare your wallets and you shall have it.' 'Nay widow,' quoth they, 'although we have lost our labours we have not altogether lost our manners; that which you have, keep, and God send to us better luck, and to you your heart's desire,' and with that they departed.

The widow, being glad she was thus rid of her guests, when her man John with all the rest sat at supper she, sitting in a chair by, spake thus unto them. 'Well my masters, you saw that this day your poor dame had her choice of husbands if she had listed to marry, and such as would have loved and maintained her like a woman.' ''Tis true,' quoth John, 'and I pray God you have not withstood your best fortune.' 'Trust me,' quoth she, 'I know not, but if I have I may thank mine own foolish fancy.'

Thus it passed on from Bartholomewtide till it was near Christmas, at what time the weather was so wonderful cold that all the running rivers round about the town were frozen very thick. The widow, being very loath any longer to lie without company in a cold winter's night, made a great fire and sent for her man John. Having also prepared a chair and a cushion, she made him sit down therein and, sending for a pint of good sack, they both went to supper.

In the end, bed time coming on, she caused her maid in a merriment to pluck off his hose and shoes, and caused him to be layed in his master's best bed standing in the best chamber, hung round about with very fair curtains. John being thus preferred thought himself a gentleman and lying soft after his hard labour and a good supper, quickly fell asleep. About midnight the widow, being cold on her feet, crept into her man's bed to warm them. John, feeling one lift up the clothes, asked who was there. 'O good John it is I,' quoth the widow, 'the night is so extreme cold, and my chamber walls so thin, that I am like to be starved in my bed, wherefore rather than I would any way hazard my health I thought it much better to come hither and try your courtesy to have a little room beside you.'

John, being a kind young man, would not say her nay, and so they spent the rest of the night both together in one bed. In the morning betime she rose up and made herself ready, and willed her man John to run and fetch her a link with all speed. 'For', quoth she, 'I have earnest business to do this morning.' Her man did so, which done, she made him to carry the link before her until she came to St Bartholomew's chapel, where Sir John, the priest, and his clerk and sexton stood waiting for her.

'John,' quoth she, 'turn into the chapel, for before I go further I will make my prayers to St Bartholomew, so shall I speed the better in my business.' When they were come in the priest, according to his order, came to her and asked where the bridegroom was. Quoth she, 'I thought he had been here before me. Sir,' quoth she, 'I will sit down and say over my beads, and by that time he will come.'

John mused at this matter, to see that his dame should so suddenly be married, and he hearing nothing thereof before. The widow rising from her prayers, the priest told her that the bridegroom was not yet come. 'Is it true?' quoth the widow. 'I promise you I will stay no longer for him if he were as good as George a Green,* and therefore dispatch', quoth she, 'and marry me to my man John.' 'Why dame,' quoth he, 'you do but jest I trow.' 'John,' quoth she, 'I jest not, for so I mean it shall be, and stand not strangely, but remember that you did promise me on your faith not to hinder me when I came to the church to be married, but rather to set it forward. Therefore set your link aside and give me your hand, for none but you shall be my husband.'

John, seeing no remedy, consented because he saw the matter could not otherwise be amended, and married they were presently. When they were come home, John entertained his dame with a kiss, which the other servants seeing thought him something saucy. The widow caused the best cheer in the house to be set on the table, and to breakfast they went, causing her new husband to be set in a chair at the table's end with a fair napkin laid on his trencher. Then she called out the rest of her servants, willing them to sit down and take part of their good cheer. They, wondering to see their fellow John sit at the table's end in their old master's chair, began heartily to smile and openly to laugh at the matter, especially because their dame so kindly sat by his side. Which she perceiving asked if they were all the manners they could show before their master. 'I tell you,' quoth she, 'he is my husband, for this morning we were married, and therefore henceforward look you acknowledge your duty towards him.'

The folks looked one upon another, marvelling at this strange news. Which when John perceived he said 'My masters muse not at all, for although by God's providence and your dame's favour I am preferred from being your fellow to be your master, I am not thereby so much puffed up in pride that any way I will forget my former estate. Notwithstanding, seeing I am now to hold the place of a master, it shall be wisdom in you to forget what I was and to take me as I am; and in doing your diligence you shall have no cause to repent that God made me your master.' The servants hearing this, as also knowing his good government before time, passed their years with him in dutiful manner.

The next day the report was over all the town that Jack of Newbury had married his dame, so that when the woman walked abroad everyone bade God give her joy. Some said that she was matched to her sorrow, saying that so lusty a young man as he would never love her, being so ancient. Whereupon the woman made answer that she would take him down in his wedding shoes and would try his patience in the prime of his lustiness, whereunto many of her gossips did likewise encourage her. Every day, therefore, for the space of a month after she was married, it was her ordinary custom to go forth in the morning among her gossips and acquaintance to make merry, and not to return home till night, without any regard of her household. Of which, at her coming home, her husband did very oftentimes admonish her in very gentle sort, showing what great inconvenience would grow thereby; the which sometime she would take in gentle part, and sometime in disdain, saying:

'I am now in very good case, that he which was my servant but the other day will now be my master. This it is for a woman to make her foot her head. The day hath been when

I might have gone forth when I would and come in again when it had pleased me without controlment, and now I must be subject to every Jack's check. I am sure', quoth she, 'that by my gadding abroad and careless spending I waste no goods of thine. I, pitying thy poverty, made thee a man and master of the house, but not to the end I would become thy slave. I scorn, I tell thee true, that such a youngling as thyself should correct my conceit, and give me instructions as if I were not able to guide myself. But ifaith, ifaith, you shall not use me like a babe, nor bridle me like an ass, and seeing my going abroad grieves thee, where I have gone forth one day I will go abroad three, and for one hour I will stay five.'

'Well,' quoth her husband, 'I trust you will be better advised,' and with that he went from her about his business, leaving her swearing in her fustian furies. Thus the time passed on, till on a certain day she had been abroad in her wonted manner and staying forth very late, he shut the doors and went to bed. About midnight she comes to the door and knocks to come in, to whom he, looking out of the window, answered in this sort. 'What, is it you that keeps such a knocking? I pray you get hence and request the constable to provide you a bed, for this night you shall have no lodging here.'

'I hope', quoth she, 'you will not shut me out of doors like a dog, or let me lie in the streets like a strumpet.' 'Whether like a dog or drab', quoth he, 'all is one to me, knowing no reason but that as you have stayed out all day for your delight, so you may lie forth all night for my pleasure. Both birds and beasts at the night's approach prepare to their rest, and observe a convenient time to return to their habitation. Look but upon the poor spider, the frog, the fly, and every other silly worm, and you shall see all these observe time to return to their home; and if you being a woman will not do the like, content yourself to bear the brunt of your own folly, and so farewell.'

The woman, hearing this, made piteous moan, and in very humble sort entreated him to let her in, and to pardon this offence, and while she lived vowed never to do the like. Her husband at length, being moved with pity towards her, slipped on his shoes and came down in his shirt. The door being opened, in she went quaking, and as he was about to lock it again, in very sorrowful manner she said 'Alack husband, what hap have I? My wedding ring was even now in my hand and I have let it fall about the door. Good sweet John, come forth with the candle and help me to seek it.'

The man incontinent did so, and while he sought for that which was not there to be found, she whipped into the house and, quickly clapping to the door, she locked her husband out. He stood calling with the candle in his hand to come in, but she made as if she heard not. Anon she went up into her chamber and carried the key with her. But when he saw she would not answer, he presently began to knock as loud as he could at the door. At last she thrust her head out at the window, saying 'Who is there?'

''Tis I,' quoth John, 'what mean you by this? I pray you, come down and open the door that I may come in.' 'What sir,' quoth she, 'is it you? Have you nothing to do but dance about the streets at this time of night, and like a spirit of the buttery, hunt after crickets? Are you so hot that the house cannot hold you?' 'Nay I pray thee sweetheart,' quoth he, 'do not gibe any longer, but let me in.'

'O sir remember', quoth she, 'how you stood even now at the window like a judge on the bench and in taunting sort kept me out of my own house. How now Jack, am I even with you? What John my man, were you so lusty to lock your dame out of doors? Sirra, remember you bade me go to the constable to get lodging; now you have leisure to try if his wife will prefer you to a bed. You, sir sauce, that made me stand in the cold till my feet did freeze and my teeth chatter while you stood preaching of birds and beasts, telling me a tale of spiders, flies, and frogs. Go try now if any of them will be so friendly to let thee have lodging. Why go you not man? Fear not to speak with them, for I am sure you shall find them at home. Think not they are such ill husbands as you, to be abroad at this time of night.'

With this John's patience was greatly moved, insomuch that he deeply swore that if she would not let him in he would break down the door. 'Why John,' quoth she, 'you need not be so hot, your clothing is not so warm; and, because I think this will be a warning unto ye against another time how you shut me out of my house, catch, there is the key, come in at thy pleasure, and look you go to bed to your fellows, for with me thou shalt not lie tonight.'

With that she clapped to the casement and got her to bed, locking the chamber door fast. Her husband knew that* it was in vain to seek to come into her chamber, and being no longer able to endure the cold, got him a place among his prentices and there slept soundly. In the morning his wife rose betime, and merrily made him a caudle, and bringing it up to his bed, asked him how he did.

Quoth John: 'Troubled with a shrew, who the longer she lives the worse she is; and as the people of Illyris kill men with their looks, so she kills her husband's heart with untoward conditions. But trust me wife,' quoth he, 'seeing I find you of such crooked qualities that (like the spider) ye turn the sweet flowers of good counsel into venomous poison, from henceforth I will leave you to your own wilfulness, and neither vex my mind nor trouble myself to restrain you, the which if I had wisely done last night I had kept the house in quiet and myself from cold.'

'Husband,' quoth she, 'think that women are like starlings, that will burst their gall before they will yield to the fowler; or like the fish scolopendra, that cannot be touched without danger. Notwithstanding, as the hard steel doth yield to the hammer's stroke, being used to his kind, so will women to their husbands where they are not too much crossed. And seeing ye have sworn to give me my will, I vow likewise that my wilfulness shall not offend you. I tell you husband, the noble nature of a woman is such that for their loving friends they will not stick (like the pelican) to pierce their own hearts to do them good. And therefore, forgiving each other all injuries past, having also tried one another's patience, let us quench these burning coals of contention with the sweet juice of a faithful kiss and, shaking hands, bequeath all our anger to the eating up of this caudle.'

Her husband courteously consented, and after this time they lived long together in most godly, loving, and kind sort, till in the end she died, leaving her husband wondrous wealthy.

CHAPTER 2

Of Jack of Newbury his great wealth and number of servants, and also how he brought the Queen Katherine one hundred and fifty men prepared for the war at his own cost against the King of Scots at Flodden Field.

NOW Jack of Newbury, being a widower, had the choice of many wives: men's daughters of good credit and widows of great wealth. Notwithstanding, he bent his only like to one of his own servants, whom he had tried in the guiding of his house a year or two; and knowing her careful in her business, faithful in her dealing, and an excellent good housewife, thought it better to have her with nothing than some other with much treasure. And besides, as her qualities were good, so was she of very comely personage, of a sweet favour and fair complexion. In the end he opened his mind unto her and craved her good will.

The maid (though she took this motion kindly) said she would do nothing without consent of her parents. Whereupon a letter was writ to her father, being a poor man dwelling at Aylesbury in Buckinghamshire; who, being joyful of his daughter's good fortune, speedily came to Newbury, where of her master he was friendly entertained, who after he had made him good cheer, showed him all his servants at work and every office in his house.

Within one room, being large and long,
There stood two hundred looms full strong;
Two hundred men, the truth is so,
Wrought in these looms all in a row.
By every one a pretty boy
Sat making quills with mickle joy.
And in another place hard by
A hundred women merrily
Were carding hard with joyful cheer,
Who singing sat with voices clear.
And in a chamber close beside
Two hundred maidens did abide,

In petticoats of stammel red,
And milk-white kerchers on their head;
Their smock sleeves like to winter snow
That on the Western mountains flow,
And each sleeve with a silken band
Was featly tied at the hand.
These pretty maids did never lin
But in that place all day did spin,
And spinning so with voices meet
Like nightingales they sung full sweet.
Then to another room came they
Where children were in poor array,
And every one sat picking wool
The finest from the coarse to cull;
The number was seven score and ten,
The children of poor, silly men,
And these, their labours to requite,
Had every one a penny at night
Beside their meat and drink all day,
Which was to them a wondrous stay.
Within another place likewise
Full fifty proper men he spies,
And these were shearmen every one
Whose skill and cunning there was shown;
And hard by them there did remain
Full four score rowers taking pain.
A dye-house likewise had he then,
Wherein he kept full forty men,
And likewise in his fulling mill
Full twenty persons kept he still.
Each week ten good fat oxen he
Spent in his house for certainty,
Beside good butter, cheese, and fish,
And many another wholesome dish.
He kept a butcher all the year,
A brewer eke for ale and beer,
A baker for to bake his bread,
Which stood his household in good stead.
Five cooks within his kitchen great
Were all the year to dress his meat.
Six scullion boys unto their hands
To make clean dishes, pots, and pans,
Beside poor children that did stay

To turn the broaches every day.
The old man that did see this sight
Was much amazed, as well he might.
This was a gallant clothier sure,
Whose fame for ever shall endure.

When the old man had seen this great household and family,
then he was brought into the warehouses, some being filled
with wool, some with flocks, some with woad and madder,*
and some with broadcloths and kersies* ready dyed and
dressed, beside a great number of others; some stretched on
the tenters, some hanging on poles, and a great many more
lying wet in other places.

'Sir,'* quoth the old man, 'Iwis che zee you be bominable
rich, and cham content you shall have my daughter, and
God's blessing and mine light on you both.' 'But father,'
quoth Jack of Newbury, 'what will you bestow with her?'
'Marry hear you,' quoth the old man, 'ivaith cham but a poor
man, but I thong God cham of good exclamation among my
neighbours, and they will as zoon take my vice for anything
as a richer man's. Thick I will bestow, you shall have with a
good will, because che hear very good condemnation of you
in every place, therefore chill give you twenty nobles and a
weaning calf, and when I die and my wife you shall have the
revelation of all my goods.'

When Jack heard his offer he was straight content, making
more reckoning of the woman's modesty than her father's
money. So the marriage day being appointed, all things were
prepared meet for the wedding, and royal cheer ordained.
Most of the lords, knights, and gentlemen thereabout were
invited thereunto; the bride being attired in a gown of sheep's
russet and a kirtle of fine worsted, her head attired with a
billiment of gold, and her hair as yellow as gold hanging
down behind her, which was curiously combed and pleated,
according to the manner in those days. She was led to church
between two sweet boys, with bride laces and rosemary tied
about their silken sleeves. The one of them was son to Sir
Thomas Parry, the other to Sir Francis Hungerford.* Then
was there a fair bridecup of silver and gilt carried before her,
wherein was a goodly branch of rosemary gilded very fair,

hung about with silken ribbons of all colours. Next was there a noise of musicians that played all the way before her. After her came all the chiefest maidens of the country, some bearing great bride-cakes, and some garlands of wheat finely gilded, and so she passed into the church.

It is needless for me to make any mention here of the bridegroom who, being a man so well-beloved, wanted no company, and those of the best sort, beside diverse merchant strangers of the Stillyard* that came from London to the wedding. The marriage being solemnized, home they came in order as before, and to dinner they went, where was no want of good cheer, no lack of melody. Rhenish wine at this wedding was as plentiful as beer or ale, for the merchants had sent thither ten tons of the best in the Stillyard.

This wedding endured ten days, to the great relief of the poor that dwelt all about; and in the end the bride's father and mother came to pay their daughter's portion, which when the bridegroom had received he gave them great thanks. Notwithstanding, he would not suffer them yet to depart, and against they should go home, their son-in-law came unto them saying 'Father and mother, all the thanks that my poor heart can yield I give you for your good will, cost, and courtesy, and while I live make bold to use me in anything that I am able; and in requital of the gift you gave me with your daughter, I give you here twenty pound to bestow as you find occasion, and for your loss of time and charges riding up and down, I give you here as much broadcloth as shall make you a cloak and my mother a holiday gown, and when this is worn out, come to me and fetch more.'

'O my good zon,' quoth the old woman, 'Christ's benizon be with thee evermore, for to tell thee true, we had zold all our kine to make money for my daughter's marriage, and this zeven year we should not have been able to buy more. Notwithstanding, we should have zold all that ever we had before my poor wench should have lost her marriage.' 'Aye,' quoth the old man, 'chud have zold my coat from my back and my bed from under me before my girl should have gone without you.' 'I thank you good father and mother,' said the bride, 'and I pray God long to keep you in health.' Then the bride kneeled down and did her duty to her parents who, weeping for very joy, departed.

Not long after this it chanced, while our noble King was making war in France, that James, King of Scotland, falsely breaking his oath invaded England with a great army and did much hurt upon the borders; whereupon on the sudden every man was appointed according to his ability to be ready with his men and furniture at an hour's warning, on pain of death. Jack of Newbury was commanded by the justices to set out six men, four armed with pikes and two calivers, and to meet the Queen in Buckinghamshire, who was there raising a great power to go against the faithless King of the Scots.

When Jack had received this charge he came home in all haste and cut out a whole broadcloth for horsemen's coats, and so much more as would make up coats for the number of a hundred men. In short time he had made ready fifty tall men well mounted in white coats and red caps with yellow feathers, demi-lances in their hands, and fifty armed men on foot with pikes, and fifty shot in white coats also, every man so expert in the handling of his weapon as few better were found in the field. Himself likewise, in complete armour on a goodly barbed horse, rode foremost of the company with a lance in his hand and a fair plume of yellow feathers in his crest; and in this sort he came before the justices, who at the first approach did not a little wonder what he should be.

At length when he had discovered what he was, the justices and most of the gentlemen gave him great commendations for this his good and forward mind showed in this action; but some other, envying hereat, gave out words that he showed himself more prodigal than prudent, and more vainglorious than well-advised, seeing that the best nobleman in the country would scarce have done so much. 'And no marvel', quoth they, 'for such a one would call to his remembrance that the King had often occasions to urge his subjects to such charges, and therefore would do at one time as they might be able to do at another; but Jack of Newbury, like the stork in the Spring time, thinks the highest cedar too low for him to build his nest in, and ere the year be half done may be glad to have his bed in a bush.'

These disdainful speeches being at last brought to Jack of Newbury's ear, though it grieved him much, yet patiently

put them up till time convenient. Within a while after, all
the soldiers in Berkshire, Hampshire, and Wiltshire were
commanded to show themselves before the Queen at Stony
Stratford, where her Grace with many lords, knights, and
gentlemen were assembled with ten thousand men. Against
Jack should go to the Queen, he caused his face to be smeared
with blood, and his white coat in like manner.

When they were come before her Highness, she demanded
(above all the rest) what those white coats were. Whereupon
Sir Henry Englefield* (who had the leading of the Berkshire
men) made answer 'May it please your Majesty to understand
that he which rideth foremost there is called Jack of Newbury,
and all those gallant men in white are his own servants who
are maintained all the year by him, whom he at his own cost
hath set out in this time of extremity to serve the King against
his vaunting foe; and I assure your Majesty there is not, for
the number, better soldiers in the field.'

'Good Sir Henry,' quoth the Queen, 'bring the man to me
that I may see him,' which was done accordingly. Then Jack
with all his men alighted, and humbly on their knees fell
before the Queen. Her Grace said 'Gentlemen arise,' and
putting forth her lily white hand, gave it him to kiss. 'Most
gracious Queen,' quoth he, 'gentleman I am none, nor the son
of a gentleman, but a poor clothier, whose lands are his looms,
having no other rents but what I get from the backs of little
sheep, nor can I claim any cognizance but a wooden shuttle.
Nevertheless, most gracious Queen, these my poor servants
and myself with life and goods are ready at your Majesty's
command not only to spend our bloods but also to lose our
lives in defence of our King and country.'

'Welcome to me, Jack of Newbury,' said the Queen, 'though
a clothier by trade yet a gentleman by condition, and a faithful
subject in heart; and if thou chance to have any suit in court
make account the Queen will be thy friend, and would to God
the King had many such clothiers. But tell me, how came thy
white coat besmeared with blood, and thy face so bescratched?'

'May it please your Grace', quoth he, 'to understand that it
was my chance to meet with a monster who, like the people
Cynomolgy,* had the proportion of a man but headed like a

dog, the biting of whose teeth was like the poisoned teeth of a crocodile, his breath like the basilisk's, killing afar off. I understand his name was Envy, who assailed me invisibly like the wicked spirit of Mogunce* who flung stones at men and could not be seen; and so I come by my scratched face, not knowing when it was done.'

'What was the cause this monster should afflict thee above the rest of thy company or other men in the field?'

'Although, most sovereign Queen,' quoth he, 'this poisoned cur snarleth at many, and that few can escape the hurt of his wounding breath, yet at this time he bent his force against me not for any hurt I did him, but because I surpassed him in hearty affection to my sovereign Lord, and with the poor widow offered all I had to serve my prince and country.' 'It were happy for England', said the Queen, 'if in every market town there were a gibbet to hang up curs of that kind, who like Aesop's dog lying in the manger will do no good himself, nor suffer such as would to do any.'

This speech being ended, the Queen caused her army to be set in order, and in warlike manner to march toward Flodden,* where King James had pitched his field. But as they passed along with drum and trumpet, there came a post from the valiant Earl of Surrey, with tidings to her Grace that now she might dismiss her army, for that it had pleased God to grant the noble Earl victory over the Scots, whom he had by his wisdom and valiancy vanquished in fight and slain their King in battle. Upon which news her Majesty discharged her forces and joyfully took her journey to London with a pleasant countenance, praising God for her famous victory and yielding thanks to all the noble gentlemen and soldiers for their readiness in the action, giving many gifts to the nobility and great rewards to the soldiers, among whom she nothing forgot Jack of Newbury, about whose neck she put a rich chain of gold, at what time he, with all the rest, gave a great shout, saying 'God save Katherine, the noble Queen of England!'

Many noblemen of Scotland were taken prisoners at this battle, and many more slain, so that there never came a greater foil to Scotland than this, for you shall understand that the Scottish King made full account to be lord of this land, watching opportunity to bring to pass his faithless and traitorous practice, which was when our King was in France at Turney and Turwin,* in regard of which wars the Scots vaunted there was none left in England but shepherds and ploughmen who were not able to lead an army, having no skill in martial affairs. In consideration of which advantage he invaded the country, boasting of victory before he had won, which was no small grief to Queen Margaret his wife, who was eldest sister to our noble King. Wherefore, in disgrace of the Scots, and in remembrance of the famous achieved victory, the commons of England made this song, which to this day is not forgotten of many.

THE SONG*

King Jamie had made a vow,
   Keep it well if he may,
That he will be at lovely London
   Upon St James his day.

'Upon St James' day at noon,
   At fair London will I be,
And all the lords in merry Scotland,
   They shall dine there with me.'

Then bespoke good Queen Margaret,
   The tears fell from her eye,
'Leave off these wars, most noble king,
   Keep your fidelity.

'The water runs swift and wondrous deep
   From bottom unto the brim,
My brother Henry hath men good enough,
   England is hard to win.'

'Away', quoth he, 'with this silly fool,
   In prison fast let her lie,
For she is come of the English blood,
   And for these words she shall die.'

With that bespake Lord Thomas Howard,
   The Queen's chamberlain that day,
'If that you put Queen Margaret to death
   Scotland shall rue it alway.'

Then in a rage King Jamie did say
    'Away with this foolish mome,
He shall be hanged and the other be burned
    So soon as I come home.'

At Flodden Field the Scots came in
    Which made our Englishmen fain,
At Bramston Green this battle was seen,
    There was King Jamie slain.

Then presently the Scots did fly,
    Their cannons they left behind,
Their ensigns gay were won all away,
    Our soldiers did beat them blind.

To tell you plain, twelve thousand were slain,
    That to the fight did stand,
And many prisoners took that day,
    The best in all Scotland.

That day made many a fatherless child,
    And many a widow poor,
And many a Scottish gay lady
    Sat weeping in her bower.

Jack with a feather was lapped all in leather,
    His boastings were all in vain,
He had such a chance with a new morris dance
    He never went home again.

FINIS

CHAPTER 3

How Jack of Newbury went to receive the King as he went a progress into Berkshire, and how he made him a banquet in his own house.

ABOUT the tenth year of the King's reign, his Grace made his progress into Berkshire, against which time Jack of Newbury clothed thirty tall fellows, being his household servants, in blue coats faced with sarsenet, every one having a good sword and buckler on his shoulder; himself in a plain russet coat, a pair of white kersey breeches without welt or guard,* and stockings of the same piece sewed to his slops, which had a great codpiece whereon he stuck his pins; who, knowing the King would come over a certain meadow near adjoining to the town, got himself thither with all his men and, repairing to a certain ant-hill which was in the field, took up his seat there, causing his men to stand round about the same with their swords drawn.

The King coming near the place with the rest of his nobility, and seeing them stand with their drawn weapons, sent to know the cause. Garter* king at arms was the messenger, who spake in this sort. 'Good fellows, the King's Majesty would know to what end you stand here with your swords and bucklers prepared to fight.'

With that, Jack of Newbury started up and made this answer. 'Herald,' quoth he, 'return to his Highness it is poor Jack of Newbury who, being scant Marquis of a mole-hill, is chosen prince of ants, and here I stand with my weapons and guard about me to defend and keep these my poor and painful subjects from the force of the idle butterflies, their sworn enemies, lest they should disturb this quiet commonwealth who this summer season are making their winter's provision.'

The messenger returning told his Grace that it was one Jack of Newbury that stood there with his men about him to guard (as they say) a company of ants from the furious wrath of the prince of butterflies. With this news the King heartily laughed, saying 'Indeed it is no marvel he stand so well prepared, considering what a terrible tyrant he hath to deal withal. Certainly my lords,' quoth he, 'this seems to be a pleasant fellow, and therefore we will send to talk with him.'

The messenger, being sent, told Jack he must come speak with the King. Quoth he, 'His Grace hath a horse, and I am on foot, therefore will him to come to me. Beside that, while I am away our enemies might come and put my people in hazard as the Scots did England while our King was in France.'

'How dares the lamb be so bold with the lion?' quoth the herald. 'Why,' quoth he, 'if there be a lion in the field, here is never a cock to fear him; and tell his Majesty he might think me a very bad governor that would walk aside upon pleasure and leave my people in peril. Herald,' quoth he, 'it is written "He that hath a charge must look to it", and so tell thy Lord my King.'

The message being done, the King said 'My lords, seeing it will be no other, we will ride up to the emperor of ants that is so careful in his government.' At the King's approach, Jack of Newbury and his servants put up all their weapons and with a joyful cry flung up their caps in token of victory. 'Why, how now my masters,' quoth the King, 'is your wars ended? Let me see where is the lord general of this great camp?' With that, Jack of Newbury with all his servants fell on their knees saying 'God save the King of England, whose sight hath put our foes to flight, and brought great peace to the poor labouring people.' 'Trust me,' quoth our King, 'here be pretty fellows to fight against butterflies. I must commend your courage that dares withstand such mighty giants.'

'Most dread sovereign,' quoth Jack, 'not long ago, in my conceit I saw the most provident nation of the ants* summoned their chief peers to a parliament which was held in the famous city Dry Dusty, the one and thirtieth day of September, whereas by their wisdoms I was chosen their King; at what time also many bills of complaint were brought in against diverse ill members in the commonwealth, among whom the mole was attainted of high treason to their state and therefore was banished forever from their quiet kingdom. So was the grasshopper and the caterpillar, because they were not only idle but also lived upon the labours of other men. Amongst the rest the butterfly was very much misliked, but few durst say anything to him because of his golden apparel, who through sufferance grew so ambitious and malapert that the poor ant could no sooner get an egg into her nest but he would have it away, and especially against Easter, which at length was misliked. This painted ass took snuff in the nose and assembled a great many other of his own coat, by windy wars to root these painful people out of the land, that he himself might be seated above them all.' ('These were proud butterflies,' quoth the King.) 'Whereupon I with my men', quoth Jack, 'prepared ourselves to withstand them till such time as your Majesty's royal presence put them to flight.'

'Tush,' said the King, 'thou must think that the force of flies is not great.' 'Notwithstanding,' quoth Jack, 'their gay gowns make poor men afraid.' 'I perceive', quoth Cardinal Wolsey, 'that you, being king of ants, do carry a great grudge to the butterflies.'

'Aye,' quoth Jack, 'we be as great foes as the fox and the snake are friends; for the one of them, being subtle, loves the other for his craft. But now I intend to be no longer a prince, because the majesty of a King hath eclipsed my glory, so that looking, like the peacock, on my black feet makes me abase my vainglorious feathers, and humbly I yield unto his Majesty all my sovereign rule and dignity, both of life and goods, casting my weapons at his feet to do any service wherein his Grace shall command me.'

'God a mercy good Jack,' quoth the King, 'I have often heard of thee, and this morning I mean to visit thy house.' Thus the King with great delight rode along until he came to the town's end, where a great multitude of people attended to see his Majesty, where also Queen Katherine with all her train met him. Thus, with great rejoicing of the commons, the King and Queen passed along to this jolly clothier's house, where the good wife of the house, with three score maidens attending on her, presented the King with a bee hive most richly gilt with gold, and all the bees therein were also of gold curiously made by art, and out of the top of the same hive sprung a flourishing green tree which bore golden apples, and at the root thereof lay diverse serpents seeking to destroy it, whom Prudence and Fortitude trod under their feet, holding this inscription in their hands:

> Lo here presented to your royal sight,
> The figure of a flourishing commonwealth,
> Where virtuous subjects labour with delight,
> And beat the drones to death which live by stealth.
> Ambition, envy, treason, loathsome serpents be,
> Which seek the downfall of this fruitful tree.
>
> But Lady Prudence with deep searching eye
> Their ill-intended purpose doth prevent,

And noble fortitude standing always nigh
Dispersed their power prepared with bad intent.
Thus are they foiled that mount by means unmeet,
And so like slaves are trodden under feet.

The King favourably accepted this emblem, and receiving it at the woman's hands, willed Cardinal Wolsey to look thereon, commanding it should be sent to Windsor castle. This Cardinal was at that time Lord Chancellor of England, and a wonderful proud prelate, by whose means great variance was set betwixt the King of England and the French King, the Emperor of Almaine, and diverse other princes of Christendom, whereby the traffic of those merchants was utterly forbidden, which bred a general woe through England, especially among clothiers, insomuch that, having no sale for their cloth, they were fain to put away many of their people which wrought for them, as hereafter more at large shall be declared.

Then was his Majesty brought into a great hall, where four long tables stood ready covered, and passing through that place, the King and Queen came into a fair and large parlour hung about with goodly tapestry, where was a table prepared for his Highness and the Queen's Grace. All the floor where the King sat was covered with broadcloths instead of green rushes; these were choice pieces of the finest wool of an azure colour, valued at an hundred pound a cloth, which afterward was given to his Majesty.

The King being set with the chiefest of his council about him, after a delicate dinner, a sumptuous banquet was brought in, served all in glass, the description whereof were too long for me to write and you to read. The great hall was also filled with lords, knights, and gentlemen who were attended by no other but the servants of the house. The ladies of honour and gentlewomen of the court were all seated in another parlour by themselves, at whose table the maidens of the house did wait in decent sort. The servingmen by themselves and the pages and footmen by themselves, upon whom the prentices did attend most diligently. During the King's abiding in this place there was no want of delicates; Rhenish wine, claret wine, and sack was as plentiful as small ale. Then, from the highest to the lowest, they were served in such sort as no discontent was found any way, so that great commendations redounded unto the good man of the house.

The Lord Cardinal, that of late found himself galled by the allegory of the ants, spoke in this wise to the King. 'If it would please your Highness', quoth he, 'but to note the vainglory of these artificers, you should find no small cause of dislike in many of their actions. For an instance, the fellow of this house, he hath not stuck this day to undo himself only to become famous by receiving of your Majesty, like Herostratus the shoemaker, that burned the Temple of Diana only to get himself a name, more than for any affection he bears to your Grace, as may well be proved by this. Let there be but a simple subsidy levied upon them for the assistance of your Highness' wars, or any other weighty affairs of the commonwealth and state of the realm, though it be not the twentieth part of their substance, they will so grudge and repine that it is wonderful, and like people desperate cry out they be quite undone.'

'My Lord Cardinal,' quoth the Queen, 'under correction of my Lord the King, I durst lay an hundred pound Jack of Newbury was never of that mind, nor is not at this instant; if ye ask him I warrant he will say so. Myself also had a proof thereof at the Scottish invasion, at what time this man, being seased but at six men, brought at his own cost an hundred and fifty into the field.'

'I would I had mo such subjects', said the King, 'and many of so good a mind.' 'Ho, ho Harry,' quoth Will Summers,* 'then had not Empson and Dudley* been chronicled for knaves, or sent to the tower for treason.' 'But then they had not known the pain of imprisonment', quoth our King, 'who with their subtlety grieved many others.' 'But their subtlety was such that it broke their necks,' quoth Will Summers.

Whereat the King and Queen, laughing heartily, rose from the table, by which time Jack of Newbury had caused all his folks to go to their work, that his Grace and all the nobility might see it; so indeed the Queen had requested. Then came his Highness where he saw an hundred looms standing in one

room, and two men working in every one, who pleasantly
sung in this sort.

THE WEAVERS' SONG

When Hercules did use to spin,
    And Pallas wrought upon the loom,
Our trade to flourish did begin,
    While conscience went not selling broom.*
      Then love and friendship did agree
      To keep the band of amity.

When princes' sons kept sheep in field,
    And queens made cakes of wheaten flour,
Then men to lucre did not yield,
    Which brought good cheer in every bower.
      Then love and friendship did agree
      To hold the bands of amity.

But when that giants huge and high
    Did fight with spears like weavers' beams,
Then they in iron beds did lie
    And brought poor men to hard extremes.
      Yet love and friendship did agree
      To hold the bands of amity.

Then David took his sling and stone,
    Not fearing great Golia's* strength,
He pierced his brains and broke the bone,
    Though he were fifty foot of length.
      For love and friendship, etc.

But while the Greeks besieged Troy
    Penelope apace did spin,
And weavers wrought with mickle joy,
    Though little gains were coming in.
      For love and friendship, etc.

Had Helen then sat carding wool
    (Whose beauteous face did breed such strife)
She had not been Sir Paris' trull,
    Nor caused so many lose their life.
      Yet we by love did still agree, etc.

Or had King Priam's wanton son
　Been making quills with sweet content,
He had not then his friends undone
　When he to Greece a gadding went.
　　For love and friendship did agree, etc.

The cedar trees endure more storms
　Than little shrubs that sprout on high,
The weavers live more void of harms
　Than princes of great dignity,
　　While love and friendship doth agree, etc.

The shepherd sitting in the field
　Doth tune his pipe with heart's delight,
When princes watch with spear and shield
　The poor man soundly sleeps all night.
　　While love and friendship doth agree, etc.

Yet this by proof is daily tried,
　For God's good gifts we are ingrate,
And no man through the world so wide
　Lives well contented with his state.
　　No love and friendship we can see
　　To hold the bands of amity.

'Well sung good fellows,' said our King, 'light hearts and merry minds live long without grey hairs.' 'But', quoth Will Summers, 'seldom without red noses.' 'Well,' said the King, 'there is a hundred angels to make good cheer withal, and look that every year once you make a feast among yourselves and frankly, every year, I give you leave to fetch four bucks out of Dunnington Park without any man's let or controlment.'

'O, I beseech your Grace,' quoth Will Summers, 'let it be with a condition.' 'What is that?' said our King. 'My liege,' quoth he, 'that although the keeper will have the skins, that they may give their wives the horns.' 'Go to,' said the Queen, 'thy head is fuller of knavery than thy purse is of crowns.'

The poor workmen humbly thanked his Majesty for his bountiful liberality, and ever since it hath been a custom among the weavers every year presently after Bartholomewtide, in remembrance of the King's favour, to meet together and make a merry feast. His Majesty came next among the spinners and carders, who were merrily a working, whereat Will Summers fell into a great laughter. 'What ails the fool to laugh?' said the King. 'Marry,' quoth Will Summers, 'to see these maidens get their living as bulls do eat their meat.' 'How is that?' said the Queen. 'By going still backward,' quoth Will Summers, 'and I will lay a wager that they that practise so well being maids to go backward will quickly learn ere long to fall backward.' 'But sirra,' said the Cardinal, 'thou didst fall forward when thou brokest thy face in master Kingsmill's cellar.' 'But you, my lord, sat forward', quoth Will Summers, 'when you sat in the stocks at Sir Amias Paulet's.'* Whereat there was greater laughing than before.

The King and Queen and all the nobility heedfully beheld these women, who for the most part were very fair and comely creatures, and were all attired alike from top to toe. Then, after due reverence, the maidens in dulcet manner chanted out this song, two of them singing the ditty, and all the rest bearing the burden.

THE MAIDENS' SONG*

It was a knight in Scotland born,
    Follow my love, leap over the strand,
Was taken prisoner and left forlorn,
    Even by the good Earl of Northumberland.

Then was he cast in prison strong,
    Follow my love, leap over the strand,
Where he could not walk nor lie along,
    Even by the good Earl of Northumberland.

And as in sorrow thus he lay,
    Follow my love, come over the strand,
The earl's sweet daughter walked that way,
    And she the fair flower of Northumberland.

And passing by like an angel bright,
    Follow my love, come over the strand,
This prisoner had of her a sight,
    And she the fair flower of Northumberland.

And loud to her this knight did cry,
    Follow my love, come over the strand,
The salt tears standing in his eye,
    And she the fair flower of Northumberland.

'Fair lady,' he said, 'take pity on me,'
  Follow my love, come over the strand,
'And let me not in prison die,
  And you the fair flower of Northumberland.'

'Fair sir how should I take pity on thee,'
  Follow my love, come over the strand:
'Thou being a foe to our country,
  And I the fair flower of Northumberland?'

'Fair lady I am no foe,' he said,
  Follow my love, come over the strand,
'Through thy sweet love here was I stayed,
  For thee, the fair flower of Northumberland.'

'Why shouldst thou come here for love of me,'
  Follow my love, come over the strand,
'Having wife and children in thy country,
  And I the fair flower of Northumberland?'

'I swear by the blessed Trinity',
  Follow my love, come over the strand,
'I have no wife nor children I,
  Nor dwelling at home in merry Scotland.

'If courteously you will set me free,'
  Follow my love, come over the strand,
'I vow that I will marry thee,
  So soon as I come in fair Scotland.

'Thou shalt be a lady of castles and towers,'
  Follow my love, come over the strand,
'And sit like a queen in princely bowers,
  When I am at home in fair Scotland.'

Then parted hence this lady gay,
  Follow my love, come over the strand,
And got her father's ring away,
  To help this sad knight into fair Scotland.

Likewise much gold she got by sleight,
  Follow my love, come over the strand,
And all to help this forlorn knight
  To wend from her father to fair Scotland.

Two gallant steeds both good and able,
  Follow my love, come over the strand,
She likewise took out of the stable,
  To ride with this knight into fair Scotland.

And to the jailor she sent this ring,
   Follow my love, come over the strand,
The knight from prison forth to bring,
   To wend with her into fair Scotland.

This token set the prisoner free,
   Follow my love, come over the strand,
Who straight went to this fair lady,
   To wend with her into fair Scotland.

A gallant steed he did bestride,
   Follow my love, come over the strand,
And with the lady away did ride,
   And she the fair flower of Northumberland.

They rode till they came to a water clear,
   Follow my love, come over the strand,
'Good Sir, how should I follow you here,
   And I the fair flower of Northumberland?

'The water is rough and wonderful deep,'
   Follow my love, come over the strand,
'And on my saddle I shall not keep,
   And I the fair flower of Northumberland.'

'Fear not the ford, fair lady,' quoth he,
   Follow my love, come over the strand,
'For long I cannot stay for thee,
   And thou the fair flower of Northumberland.'

The lady pricked her wanton steed,
   Follow my love, come over the strand,
And over the river swum with speed,
   And she the fair flower of Northumberland.

From top to toe all wet was she,
   Follow my love, come over the strand,
'This have I done for love of thee,
   And I the fair flower of Northumberland.'

Thus rode she all one winter's night,
   Follow my love, come over the strand,
Till Edinburgh they saw in sight,
   The chiefest town in all Scotland.

'Now choose,' quoth he, 'thou wanton flower,'
   Follow my love, come over the strand,
'Whether* thou wilt be my paramour,
Or get thee home to Northumberland.

'For I have wife and children five,'
  Follow my love, come over the strand,
'In Edinburgh they be alive,
  Then get thee home to fair England.

'This favour shalt thou have to boot,'
  Follow my love, come over the strand,
'I'll have thy horse, go thou on foot;
  Go, get thee home to Northumberland!'

'O false and faithless knight!' quoth she,
  Follow my love, come over the strand,
'And canst thou deal so bad with me,
  And I the fair flower of Northumberland?

'Dishonour not a lady's name,'
  Follow my love, come over the strand,
'But draw thy sword and end my shame,
  And I the fair flower of Northumberland.'

He took her from her stately steed,
  Follow my love, come over the strand,
And left her there in extreme need,
  And she the fair flower of Northumberland.

Then sat she down full heavily,
  Follow my love, come over the strand,
At length two knights came riding by,
  Two gallant knights of fair England.

She fell down humbly on her knee,
  Follow my love, come over the strand,
Saying 'Courteous knights, take pity on me,
  And I the fair flower of Northumberland.

'I have offended my father dear,'
  Follow my love, come over the strand,
'And by a false knight that brought me here
  From the good Earl of Northumberland.'

They took her up behind them then,
  Follow my love, come over the strand,
And brought her to her father's again,
  And he the good Earl of Northumberland.

All you fair maidens be warned by me,
    Follow my love, come over the strand,
Scots were never true, nor never will be,
    To lord, to lady, nor fair England.

FINIS

After the King's Majesty and the Queen had heard this song sweetly sung by them, he cast them a great reward, and so departing thence, went to the fulling mills and dyehouse where a great many also were hard at work; and his Majesty, perceiving what a great number of people were by this one man set on work, both admired and commended him, saying further that no trade in all the land was so much to be cherished and maintained as this, 'Which', quoth he, 'may well be called the life of the poor'. And as the King returned from this place with intent to take horse and depart, there met him a great many of children in garments of white silk fringed with gold, their heads crowned with golden bays and about their arms each one had a scarf of green sarsenet fast tied; in their hands they bore silver bows, and under their girdles golden arrows.

The foremost of them represented Diana, goddess of chastity, who was attended upon by a train of beautiful nymphs, and they presented to the King four prisoners. The first was a stern and grisly woman, carrying a frowning countenance, and her forehead full of wrinkles; her hair black as pitch, and her garments all bloody. A great sword she had in her hand all stained with purple gore. They called her name Bellona, goddess of wars, who had three daughters. The first of them was a tall woman, so lean and ill-favoured that her cheek bones were ready to start out of the skin, of a pale and deadly colour; her eyes sunk into her head; her legs so feeble that they could scantly carry the body. All along her arms and hands through the skin you might tell the sinews, joints, and bones. Her teeth were very strong and sharp withal; she was so greedy that she was ready with her teeth to tear the skin from her own arms. Her attire was black and all torn and ragged; she went bare-footed and her name was Famine.

The second was a strong and lusty woman, with a look pitiless and unmerciful countenance. Her garments were all made of iron and steel, and she carried in her hand a naked weapon, and she was called the Sword. The third was also a cruel creature; her eyes did sparkle like burning coals, her hair was like a flame, and her garments like burning brass. She was so hot that none could stand near her, and they called her name Fire.

After this they retired again, and brought unto his Highness two other personages; their countenance was princely and amiable, their attire most rich and sumptuous. The one carried in his hand a golden trumpet, and the other a palm tree, and these were called Fame and Victory, whom the goddess of chastity charged to wait upon this famous prince forever. This done, each child after other with due reverence gave unto his Majesty a sweet-smelling gillyflower, after the manner of the Persians offering something in token of loyalty and obedience. The King and Queen beholding the sweet favour and countenance of these children, demanded of Jack of Newbury whose children they were, who answered 'It shall please your Highness to understand that these are the children of poor people that do get their living by picking of wool, having scant a good meal once in a week'.

With that the King began to tell his gillyflowers, whereby he found that there was ninety-six children. 'Certainly', said the Queen, 'I perceive God gives as fair children to the poor as to the rich, and fairer many times, and though their diet and keeping be but simple, the blessing of God doth cherish them. Therefore', said the Queen, 'I will request to have two of them to wait in my chamber.'

'Fair Katherine,' said the King, 'thou and I have jumped in one opinion, thinking these children fitter for the court than the country.' Whereupon he made choice of a dozen more. Four he ordained to be pages to his royal person, and the rest he sent to universities, allotting to every one a gentleman's living. Diverse of the noblemen did in like sort entertain some of those children into their services, so that in the end not one was left to pick wool, but were all so provided for that their parents never needed to care for them, and God so blessed them that each of them came to be men of great account and authority in the land, whose posterities remain to this day worshipful and famous.

The King, Queen, and nobles being ready to depart, after great thanks and gifts given to Jack of Newbury, his Majesty would have made him knight, but he meekly refused it, saying 'I beseech your Grace, let me live a poor clothier among my people, in whose maintenance I take more felicity than in all the vain titles of gentility, for these are the labouring ants whom I seek to defend, and these be the bees which I keep, who labour in this life not for ourselves but for the glory of God, and to do service to our dread sovereign.'

'Thy knighthood need be no hindrance of thy faculty,' quoth the King. 'O my dread sovereign,' said Jack, 'honour and worship may be compared to the lake of Lethe, which makes men forget themselves that taste thereof; and to the end I may still keep in mind from whence I came, and what I am, I beseech your Grace let me rest in my russet coat a poor clothier to my dying day.' 'Seeing then', said the King, 'that a man's mind is a kingdom to himself, I will leave thee to the riches of thy own content, and so farewell.'

The Queen's Majesty taking her leave of the good wife with a princely kiss, gave her in token of remembrance a most precious and rich diamond set in gold, about the which was also curiously set six rubies and six emeralds in one piece, valued at nine hundred marks; and so her Grace departed.

But in this mean space, Will Summers kept company among the maids, and betook himself to spinning as they did, which among them was held as a forfeit of a gallon of wine, but William by no means would pay it except they would take it out in kisses, rating every kiss at a farthing. 'This payment we refuse for two causes,' quoth the maidens, 'the one for that we esteem not kisses at so base a rate, and the other because in so doing we should give as much as you.'

CHAPTER 4

How the maidens served Will Summers for his sauciness.

THE maidens consented together, seeing Will Summers was so busy both with their work and in his words, and would not pay his forfeiture, to serve him as he served. First, therefore, they bound him hand and foot, and set him upright against a post, tying him thereto—which he took in ill part, notwithstanding he could not resist them; and because he let his tongue run at random, they set a fair gag in his mouth, such a one as he could not for his life put away, so that he stood as one gaping for wind. Then one of them got a couple of dog's droppings and, putting them in a bag, laid them in soak in a basin of water, while the rest turned down the collar of his jerkin and put an host cloth* about his neck instead of a fine towel. Then came the other maid with a basin and water in the same, and with the perfume in her pudding bag flapped him about the face and lips till he looked like a tawny moor, and with her hand washed him very orderly. The smell being somewhat strong, Will could by no means abide it, and for want of other language cried 'Ah ha ha ha!' Fain he would have spit and could not, so that he was fain to swallow down such liquor as he never tasted the like.

When he had a pretty while been washed in this sort, at the length he crouched down upon his knees, yielding himself to their favour; which the maidens perceiving pulled the gag out of his mouth. He had no sooner the liberty of his tongue but that he cursed and swore like a devil. The maids, that could scant stand for laughing, at last asked how he liked his washing. 'Washing,' quoth he, 'I was never thus washed, nor ever met with such barbers since I was born. Let me go', quoth he, 'and I will give you whatsoever you will demand,' wherewith he cast them an English crown.

'Nay,' quoth one of the maids, 'you are yet but washed, but we will shave you ere ye go.' 'Sweet maids,' quoth he, 'pardon my shaving, let it suffice that you have washed me. If I have done a trespass to your trade, forgive it me, and I will never hereafter offend you.' 'Tush,' said the maids, 'you have made our wheels cast their bands and bruised the teeth of our cards in such sort as the offence may not be remitted without great penance. As for your gold, we regard it not. Therefore, as you are perfumed fit for the dogs, so we enjoin you this night to serve all our hogs, which penance if you will swear with all speed to perform we will let you loose.'

'O,' quoth Will, 'the huge elephant was never more fearful of the silly sheep than I am of your displeasures. Therefore let me loose, and I will do it with all diligence.' Then they unbound him and brought him among a great company of swine, which when Will had well viewed over he drave out of the yard all the sows. 'Why, how now,' quoth the maids, 'what mean you by this?' 'Marry,' quoth Will, 'these be all sows, and my penance is but to serve the hogs.' 'It is true,' quoth they, 'have you overtaken us in this sort? Well, look there be not one hog unserved, we would advise you.'

Will Summers stripped up his sleeves very orderly, and clapped an apron about his motley hosen, and taking a pail, served the hogs handsomely. When he had given them all meat, he said thus:

> My task is duly done,
> My liberty is won.
> The hogs have eat their crabs,
> Therefore, farewell ye drabs.

'Nay soft, friend,' quoth they, 'the veriest hog of all hath yet had nothing.' 'Where the devil is he', said Will, 'that I see him not?' 'Wrapped in a motley jerkin,' quoth they, 'take thyself by the nose, and thou shalt catch him by the snout.' 'I was never so very a hog', quoth he, 'but that I would always spare from my own belly to give to a woman.' 'If thou do not', say they, 'eat like the prodigal child with thy fellow hogs, we will so shave thee as thou shalt dearly repent thy disobedience.'

He, seeing no remedy, committed himself to their mercy, and so they let him go. When he came to the court, he showed to the King all his adventure among the weaver's maidens, whereat the King and Queen laughed heartily.

CHAPTER 5

Of the pictures which Jack of Newbury had in his house, whereby he encouraged his servants to seek for fame and dignity.

IN a fair, large parlour which was wainscotted about, Jack of Newbury had fifteen fair pictures hanging, which were covered with curtains of green silk fringed with gold, which he would often show to his friends and servants. In the first was the picture of a shepherd, before whom kneeled a great king named Viriat,* who sometime governed the people of Portugal. 'See here,' quoth Jack, 'the father a shepherd, the son a sovereign. This man ruled in Portugal, and made great wars against the Romans, and after that invaded Spain, yet in the end was traitorously slain.'

The next was the portraiture of Agathocles, which for his surpassing wisdom and manhood was created King of Sicilia, and maintained battle against the people of Carthage. His father was a poor potter, before whom he also kneeled. And it was the use of this king that, whensoever he made a banquet, he would have as well vessels of earth as of gold set upon the table, to the intent he might always bear in mind the place of his beginning: his father's house and family.

The third was the picture of Iphicrates, an Athenian born, who vanquished the Lacedemonians in plain and open battle. This man was captain general to Artaxerxes, King of Persia, whose father was notwithstanding a cobbler, and there likewise pictured. Eumenes was also a famous captain to Alexander the Great, whose father was no other than a carter.

The fourth was the similitude of Aelius Pertinax, sometime Emperor of Rome, yet was his father but a weaver; and afterward, to give example to others of low condition to bear minds of worthy men, he caused the shop to be beautified with marble curiously cut, wherein his father before him was wont to get his living.

The fifth was the picture of Diocletian, that so much

adorned Rome with his magnifical and triumphant victories. This was a most famous emperor, although no other than the son of a bookbinder.

Valentinian stood the next, painted most artificially, who also was crowned emperor, and was but the son of a poor ropemaker, as in the same picture was expressed, where his father was painted by him, using his trade.

The seventh was the Emperor Probus, whose father being a gardener was pictured by him holding a spade.

The eighth picture was of Marcus Aurelius, whom every age honoureth, he was so wise and prudent an emperor. Yet was he but a cloth-weaver's son.

The ninth was the portraiture of the valiant Emperor Maximinus, the son of a blacksmith, who was there painted as he was wont to work at the anvil.

In the tenth table was painted the Emperor Gabienus,* who at the first was but a poor shepherd.

Next to this picture was placed the pictures of two Popes of Rome, whose wisdom and learning advanced them to that dignity. The first was the lively counterfeit of Pope John XXII, whose father was a shoemaker. He, being elected Pope, increased their rents and patrimony greatly. The other was the picture of Pope Sextus the fourth of that name, being a poor mariner's son.

The thirteenth picture was of Lamusius, King of Lombardy, who was no better than the son of a common strumpet, being painted like a naked child walking in water, and taking hold of the point of a lance, by the which he hung fast and saved himself. The reason whereof is this: after his lewd mother was delivered of him, she unnaturally threw him into a deep stinking ditch wherein was some water. By hap, King Agilmond passed that way and found this child almost drowned, who, moving him somewhat with the point of his lance the better to perceive what he was, the child (though newly born) took hold thereof with one of his pretty hands, not suffering it to slide or slip away again. Which thing the King considering, being amazed at the strange force of this young little infant, caused it to be taken up and carefully to be fostered. And because the place where he found it was called Lama, he named the child Lamusius, who after grew to be so brave a man, and so much honoured of fortune, that in the end he was crowned King of the Lombards, who lived there in honour and in his succession after him, even unto the time of the unfortunate King Albovina, when all came to ruin, subversion, and destruction.

In the fourteenth picture, Primislas, King of Bohemia, was most artificially drawn, before whom there stood an horse without bridle or saddle in a field where husbandmen were at plough. 'The cause why this King was thus painted', quoth Jack, 'was this. At that time the King of the Bohemians died without issue, and great strife being among the nobility for a new king, at length they all consented that a horse should be let into the field without bridle or saddle, having all determined with a most assured purpose to make him their king before whom this horse rested. At what time it came to pass that the horse first stayed himself before this Primislas, being a simple creature, who was then busy driving the plough. They presently made him their sovereign, who ordered himself and his kingdom very wisely. He ordained many good laws, he compassed the city of Prague with strong walls, besides many other things meriting perpetual laud and commendations.

The fifteenth was the picture of Theophrastus, a philosopher, a counsellor of kings and companion of nobles, who was but son of a tailor.

'Seeing then, my good servants, that these men have been advanced to high estate and princely dignities by wisdom, learning, and diligence, I would wish you to imitate the like virtues, that you might attain the like honours, for which of you doth know what good fortune God hath in store for you? There is none of you so poorly born but that men of baser birth have come to great honours. The idle hand shall ever go in a ragged garment, and the slothful live in reproach, but such as do lead a virtuous life and govern themselves discreetly shall of the best be esteemed, and spend their days in credit.'

CHAPTER 6

How all the clothiers in England joined together and with one consent complained to the King of their great hindrance sustained for want of traffic into other countries, whereupon they could get no sale for their cloth.

BY means of the wars our King had with other countries, many merchant strangers were prohibited for coming to England, and also our own merchants (in like sort) were forbidden to have dealing with France or the low countries. By means whereof the clothiers had most of their cloth lying on their hands, and that which they sold was at so low a rate that money scarcely paid for the wool and workmanship. Whereupon they thought to ease themselves by abating the poor workmen's wages, and when that did not prevail they turned away their people—weavers, shearmen, spinners, and carders—so that where there was a hundred looms kept in one town there was scant fifty, and he that kept twenty put down ten. Many a poor man for want of work was hereby undone with his wife and children, and it made many a poor widow to sit with an hungry belly. This bred great woe in most places in England. In the end, Jack of Newbury intended, in the behalf of the poor, to make a supplication to the King, and to the end he might do it the more effectually, he sent letters to all the chief clothing towns in England to this effect.

THE LETTER

Well-beloved friends and brethren, having a taste of the general grief, and feeling in some measure the extremity of these times, I fell into consideration by what means we might best expel these sorrows and recover our former commodity. When I had well thought thereon, I found that nothing was more needful herein than a faithful unity among ourselves. This sore of necessity can no way be cured but by concord, for like as the flame consumes the candle, so men through discord waste themselves. The poor hate the rich because they will not set them on work, and the rich hate the poor because they seem

burdenous; so both are offended for want of gain. When Belinus and
Brennus* were at strife, the Queen their mother in their greatest fury
persuaded them to peace by urging her conception of them in one
womb, and mutual cherishing of them from their tender years. So let
our art of clothing, which like a kind mother hath cherished us with
the excellency of her secrets, persuade us to an unity. Though our
occupation be decayed, let us not deal with it as men do by their old
shoes, which after they have long born them out of the mire do in
the end fling them on the dunghill, or as the husbandman doth by
his bees, who for their honey burns them. Dear friends, consider that
our trade will maintain us if we will uphold it, and there is nothing
base but that which is basely used. Assemble therefore yourselves
together, and in every town tell the number of those that have their
living by means of this trade. Note it in a bill and send it to me, and
because suits in court are, like winter nights, long and wearisome, let
there be in each place a weekly collection made to defray charges. For
I tell you, noblemen's secretaries and cunning lawyers have slow
tongues and deaf ears, which must daily be nointed with the sweet
oil of angels. Then let two honest, discreet men be chosen and sent
out of every town to meet me at Blackwell Hall* in London on All
Saint's Eve, and then we will present our humble petition to the
King. Thus I bid you heartily farewell.

Copies of this letter being sealed, they were sent to all the
clothing towns of England, and weavers, both of linen and
woollen, gladly received them; so that, when all the bills
were brought together, there were found of the clothiers and
those they maintained threescore thousand and six hundred
persons. Moreover, every clothing town sending up two men
to London, they were found to be an hundred and twelve
persons, who in very humble sort fell down before his
Majesty, walking in St James his park, and delivered unto him
their petition. The King presently perusing it asked if they
were all clothiers, who answered (as it were one man) in this
sort: 'We are, most gracious King, all poor clothiers and your
Majesty's faithful subjects.'

'My lords,' quoth the King, 'let these men's complaint be
thoroughly looked unto, and their grief redressed, for I
account them in the number of the best commonwealth's men.
As the clergy for the soul, the soldier for defence of his
country, the lawyer to execute justice, the husbandman to feed

the belly, so is the skilful clothier no less necessary for the clothing of the back, whom we may reckon among the chief yeomen of our land; and as the crystal sight of the eye is tenderly to be kept from harms because it gives to the whole body light, so is the clothier,* whose cunning hand provides garments to defend our naked parts from the winter's nipping frost. Many more reasons there are which may move us to redress their griefs, but let it suffice that I command to have it done.'

With that his Grace delivered the petition to the lord chancellor, and all the clothiers cried 'God save the King!' But as the King was ready to depart, he suddenly turned about saying 'I remember there is one Jack of Newbury, I muse he had not his hand in this business, who professed himself to be a defender of true labourers.' Then said the Duke of Somerset 'It may be his purse is answerable for his person.' 'Nay,' quoth the Lord Cardinal, 'all his treasure is little enough to maintain wars against the butterflies.'

With that Jack showed himself unto the King, and privately told his Grace of their grief anew, to whom his Majesty said 'Give thy attendance at the council chamber, where thou shalt receive an answer to thy content.' And so his Highness departed.

Finally it was agreed that the merchants should freely traffic one with another, and that proclamation thereof should be made as well on the other side of the sea as in our land. But it was long before this was effected, by reason the Cardinal, being Lord Chancellor, put off the matter from time to time. And because the clothiers thought it best not to depart before it was ended, they gave their daily attendance at the Cardinal's house, but spent many days to no purpose. Sometimes they were answered my lord was busy, and could not be spoke withal; or else he was asleep, and they durst not wake him; or at his study, and they would not disturb him; or at his prayers, and they durst not displease him; and still one thing or other stood in the way to hinder them.

At last Patch,* the Cardinal's Fool, being (by their often repair thither) well acquainted with the clothiers, came unto them and said 'What, have you not spoken with my Lord yet?'

'No truly,' quoth they, 'we hear say he is busy, and we stay till his Grace be at leisure.' 'It is true,'* said Patch, and with that in all haste he went out of the hall, and at last came in again with a great bundle of straw on his back. 'Why how now Patch,' quoth the gentlemen, 'what wilt thou do with that straw?' 'Marry,' quoth he, 'I will put it under these honest men's feet, lest they should freeze ere they find my lord at leisure.' This made them all to laugh, and caused Patch to carry away his straw again. 'Well, well,' quoth he, 'if it cost you a groat's worth of faggots at night, blame not me.'

'Trust me,' said Jack of Newbury, 'if my Lord Cardinal's father had been no hastier in killing of calves* than he is in dispatching of poor men's suits, I doubt he had never worn a mitre.' Thus he spake betwixt themselves softly, but yet not so softly but that he was overheard by a flattering fellow that stood by, who made it known to some of the gentlemen, and they straight certified the Cardinal thereof.

The Cardinal, who was of a very high spirit, and a lofty aspiring mind, was marvellously displeased at Jack of Newbury, wherefore in his rage he commanded and sent the clothiers all to prison, because the one of them should not sue for the others' releasement. Four days lay these men in the Marshalsea, till at last they made their humble petition to the King for their release. But some of the Cardinal's friends kept it from the King's sight. Notwithstanding, the Duke of Somerset, knowing thereof, spake with the Lord Cardinal about the matter, wishing he should speedily release them, lest it bred him some displeasure. 'For you may perceive', quoth the Duke, 'how highly the King esteems men of that faculty.'

'Sir,' quoth the Cardinal, 'I doubt not but to answer their imprisonment well enough, being persuaded that none would have given me such a quip but an heretic, and I dare warrant you, were this Jack of Newbury well examined he would be found to be infected with Luther's spirit, against whom our King hath of late written a most learned book, in respect whereof the Pope's Holiness hath entitled his Majesty, Defender of the Faith. Therefore, I tell you such fellows are fitter to be faggots for fire than fathers of families. Notwithstanding, at your Grace's request, I will release them.'

Accordingly, the Cardinal sent for the clothiers before him
to Whitehall, his new-built house by Westminster, and there
bestowing his blessing upon them said 'Though you have
offended me, I pardon you; for as Steven forgave his enemies
that stoned him, and our Saviour those sinful men that
crucified him, so do I forgive you that high trespass committed in disgrace of my birth. For herein do men come
nearest unto God, in showing mercy and compassion. But see
hereafter you offend no more. Touching your suit, it is
granted, and tomorrow shall be published through London.'

This being said, they departed, and according to the
Cardinal's words, their business was ended. The Stillyard
merchants, joyful thereof, made the clothiers a great banquet,
after which each man departed home, carrying tidings of their
good success; so that in short space clothing again was very
good, and poor men as well set on work as before.

CHAPTER 7

*How a young Italian merchant, coming to Jack of Newbury's house, was
greatly enamoured of one of his maidens, and how he was served.*

AMONG other servants which Jack of Newbury kept, there
were in his house threescore maidens which every Sunday
waited on his wife to church and home again, who had diverse
offices. Among other, two were appointed to keep the beams
and weights, to weigh out wool to the carders and spinners, and
to receive it in again by weight. One of them was a comely
maiden, fair and lovely, born of wealthy parents and brought up
in good qualities. Her name was Joan. So it was* that a young,
wealthy Italian merchant, coming oft from London thither to
bargain for cloth (for at that time clothiers most commonly had
their cloth bespoken, and half paid for aforehand).

This Master Benedick fell greatly enamoured of this
maiden, and therefore offered much courtesy to her, bestowing many gifts on her, which she received thankfully;
and albeit his outward countenance showed his inward

affection, yet Joan would take no knowledge thereof. Half the day sometime would he sit by her as she was weighing wool, often sighing and sobbing to himself yet saying nothing, as if he had been tongueless like the men of Coromandae,* and the loather to speak for that he could speak but bad English. Joan on the other side, that well perceived his passions, did as it were triumph over him as one that were bondslave to her beauty; and although she knew well enough before that she was fair, yet did she never so highly esteem of herself as at this present, so that when she heard him either sigh, sob, or groan, she would turn her face in a careless sort as if she had been born (like the women of Taprobana)* without ears.

When Master Benedick saw she made no reckoning of his sorrows, at length he blabbered out this broken English, and spoke to her in this sort: 'Metressa Joan, be me tra and fa, me love you wod all mine heart, and if you no shall love me again, me know me shall die. Sweet metressa love a me, and by my fa and tra you shall lack nothing. First me will give you de silk for make you a frog. Second de fin camree for make you ruffles, and de turd shall be for make fin hankercher for wipe your nose.'

She, mistaking his speech, began to be choleric, wishing him to keep that bodkin to pick his teeth. 'Ho ho, metressa Joan,' quoth he, 'be Got, you are angry. Oh metressa Joan, be not chafe with your frien' for noting.' 'Good sir,' quoth she, 'keep your friendship for them that care for it, and fix your love on those that can like you; as for me, I tell you plain, I am not minded to marry.'

'O, 'tis no matter for marry if you will come to my chamber, beshit my bed, and let me kiss you.' The maid, though she were very much displeased, yet at these words she could not forbear laughing for her life. 'Aha! Metressa Joan, me is very glad to see you merry. Hold, metressa Joan, hold you hand I say, and there is four crown because you laugh on me.' 'I pray you sir, keep your crowns, for I need them not.' 'Yes, be Got, you shall have them metressa Joan, to keep in box for you.'

She, that could not well understand his broken language, mistook his meaning in many things, and therefore willed him not to trouble her any more. Notwithstanding, such was his love toward her that he could not forbear her company, but made many journeys thither for her sake; and as a certain spring in Arcadia makes men to starve that drink of it, so did poor Benedick, feeding his fancy on her beauty, for when he was in London he did nothing but sorrow, wishing he had wings like the monsters of Tartaria that he might fly to and fro at his pleasure.

When any of his friends did tell her of his ardent affection toward her, she wished them to rub him with the sweat of a mule to assuage his amorous passion, or to fetch him some of the water in Boetia to cool and extinguish the heat of his affection. 'For', quoth she, 'let him never hope to be helped by me.' 'Well,' quoth they, 'before he saw thy alluring face he was a man reasonable and wise, but is now a stark fool, being by thy beauty bereft of wit as if he had drunk of the river Cea, and like bewitching Circes thou hast certainly transformed him from a man to an ass. There are stones in Pontus', quoth they, 'that the deeper they be laid in water the fiercer they burn, unto the which fond lovers may fitly be compared, who the more they are denied the hotter is their desire. But seeing it is so, that he can find no favour at your hands, we will show him what you have said and either draw him from his dumps or leave him to his own will.'

Then spake one of the weavers that dwelt in the town, and was a kinsman to this maid. 'I muse', quoth he, 'that Master Benedick will not be persuaded, but like the moth will play with the flame that will scorch his wings. Methinks he should forbear to love, or learn to speak, or else woo such as can answer him in his language, for I tell you that Joan my kinswoman is no taste for an Italian.'

These speeches were told to Benedick with no small addition. When our young merchant heard the matter so plain he vowed to be revenged of the weaver, and to see if he could find any more friendship of his wife. Therefore, dissembling his sorrow, and covering his grief, with speed he took his journey to Newbury, and pleasantly saluted Mistress Joan, and having his purse full of crowns, he was very liberal to the workfolks, especially to Joan's kinsman, insomuch that he got his favour many times to go forth with him, promising him very largely to do great matters and to lend him a hundred pound, willing him to be a servant no longer. Beside, he liberally bestowed on his wife many gifts, and if she washed him but a band he would give her an angel; if he did but send her child for a quart of wine he would give him a shilling for his pains. The which his courtesy changed the weaver's mind, saying he was a very honest gentleman and worthy to have one far better than his kinswoman.

This pleased Master Benedick well to hear him say so; notwithstanding he made light of the matter, and many times when the weaver was at his master's at work, the merchant would be at home with his wife, drinking and making merry. At length, time bringing acquaintance, and often conference breeding familiarity, Master Benedick began somewhat boldly to jest with Gillian, saying that her sight and sweet countenance had quite reclaimed his love from Joan, and that she only was the mistress of his heart; and if she would lend him her love, he would give her gold from Arabia, orient pearls from India, and make her bracelets of precious diamonds. 'Thy garments shall be of the finest silk that is made in Venice, and thy purse shall still be stuffed with angels. Tell me thy mind, my love, and kill me not with unkindness as did thy scornful kinswoman, whose disdain had almost cost me my life.'

'O Master Benedick, think not the wives of England can be won by rewards, or enticed with fair words, as children are with plums. It may be that you, being merrily disposed, do speak this to try my constancy. Know then that I esteem more the honour of my good name, than the sliding wealth of the world.' Master Benedick, hearing her say so, desired her that, considering it was love which forced his tongue to bewray his heart's affection, that yet she would be secret, and so for that time took his leave.

When he was gone, the woman began to call her wits together and to consider of her poor estate, and withal the better to note the comeliness of her person and the sweet favour of her face, which when she had well thought upon, she began to harbour new thoughts, and to entertain contrary affections, saying 'Shall I content myself to be wrapped in sheep's russet that may swim in silks, and sit all day carding for a groat that may have crowns at my command? No,' quoth she, 'I will no more bear so base a mind, but take fortune's favours while they are to be had. The sweet rose doth flourish but one month, nor women's beauties but in young years; as the winter's frost consumes the summer flowers, so doth old age banish pleasant delight. O glorious gold,' quoth she, 'how sweet is thy smell, how pleasing is thy sight! Thou subduest princes and overthrowest kingdoms; then how should a silly woman withstand thy strength?' Thus she rested meditating on preferment, minding to hazard her honesty to maintain herself in bravery, even as occupiers corrupt their consciences to gather riches.

Within a day or two, Master Benedick came to her again, on whom she cast a smiling countenance. He, perceiving that, according to his old custom sent for wine, and very merry they were. At last in the midst of their cups he cast out his former question, and after farther conference she yielded, and appointed a time when he should come to her, for which favour he gave her half a dozen portigues. Within an hour or two after, entering into her own conscience, bethinking how sinfully she had sold herself to folly, began thus to expostulate.

'Good Lord,' quoth she, 'shall I break that holy vow which I made in marriage, and pollute my body which the Lord hath sanctified? Can I break the commandment of my God, and not rest accursed? Or be a traitor to my husband, and suffer no shame? I heard once my brother read in a book that Bucephalus, Alexander's steed, being a beast, would not be backed by any but the emperor, and shall I consent to any but my husband? Artemisia, being a heathen lady, loved her husband so well that she drunk up his ashes and buried him in her own bowels, and should I, being a Christian, cast my husband out of my heart? The women of Rome were wont to crown their husbands' heads with bays in token of victory, and shall I give my husband horns in token of infamy? An harlot is hated of all virtuous people, and shall I make myself a whore? O my God, forgive my sin', quoth she, 'and cleanse my heart from these wicked imaginations.'

And as she was thus lamenting, her husband came home,

at whose sight her tears were doubled, like a river whose stream is increased by showers of rain. Her husband, seeing this, would needs know the cause of her sorrow, but a great while she would not show him, casting many a piteous look upon him and shaking her head. At last she said 'O my dear husband, I have offended against God and thee, and made such a trespass by my tongue as hath cut a deep scar in my conscience, and wounded my heart with grief like a sword. Like Penelope so have I been wooed, but like Penelope I have not answered.'

'Why woman,' quoth he, 'what is the matter? If it be but the bare offence of the tongue why shouldst thou so grieve, considering that women's tongues are like lambs' tails, which seldom stand still? And the wise man saith, where much talk is, must needs be some offence. Women's beauties are fair marks for wandering eyes to shoot at, but as every archer hits not the white, so every wooer wins not his mistress' favour. All cities that are besieged are not sacked, nor all women to be misliked that are loved. Why wife, I am persuaded thy faith is more firm and thy constancy greater to withstand lovers' alarms than that any other but myself should obtain the fortress of thy heart.'

'O sweet husband,' quoth she, 'we see the strongest tower at length falleth down by the cannon's force, though the bullets be but iron. Then how can the weak bulwark of a woman's breast make resistance when the hot cannons of deep persuading words are shot off with golden bullets, and every one as big as a portigue?'

'If it be so wife, I may think myself in a good case, and you to be a very honest woman. As Mars and Venus danced naked together in a net, so I doubt you and some knave have played naked together in a bed. But in faith, you quean, I will send thee to salute thy friends without a nose, and as thou hast sold thy honesty, so will I sell thy company.'

'Sweet husband, though I have promised I have performed nothing. Every bargain is not effected, and therefore as Judas brought again the thirty silver plates for the which he betrayed his master, so repenting my folly, I'll cast him again his gold, for which I should have wronged my husband.' 'Tell me', quoth her husband, 'what he is.' 'It is Master Benedick,' quoth she, 'which for my love hath left the love of our kinswoman, and hath vowed himself forever to live my servant.' 'O dissembling Italian,' quoth he, 'I will be revenged on him for this wrong. I know that any favour from Joan my kinswoman will make him run like a man bitten with a mad dog. Therefore, be ruled by me, and thou shalt see me dress him in his kind.' The woman was very well pleased, saying he would be there that night. 'All this works well with me,' quoth her husband, 'and to supper will I invite Joan my kinswoman, and in the mean space make up the bed in the parlour very decently.'

So the good man went forth, and got a sleepy drench from the pothecary's, the which he gave to a young sow which he had in his yard, and in that evening laid her down in the bed in the parlour, drawing the curtains round about. Supper time being come, Master Benedick gave his attendance, looking for no other company but the good wife. Notwithstanding, at the last Mistress Joan came in with her kinsman and sat down to supper with them. Master Benedick, musing at their sudden approach, yet nevertheless glad of Mistress Joan's company, passed the supper time with many pleasant conceits, Joan showing herself that night more pleasant in his company than at any time before. Therefore he gave the good man great thanks.

'Good Master Benedick, little do you think how I have travailed in your behalf to my kinswoman, and much ado I had to bring the peevish wench into any good liking of your love. Notwithstanding, by my great diligence and persuasions I did at length win her good will to come hither, little thinking to find you here, or any such good cheer to entertain her, all which I see is fallen out for your profit. But trust me, all the world cannot alter her mind, nor turn her love from you. In regard whereof, she hath promised me to lie this night in my house for the great desire she hath of your good company, and in requital of all your great courtesies showed to me, I am very well content to bring you to her bed. Marry this you must consider, and so she bade me tell you: that you should come to bed with as little noise as you could, and tumble nothing that you find, for fear of her best gown and her hat, which she will lay hard by the bedside next her best partlet, and in so doing you may have company with her all night, but say nothing in any case till you be abed.'

'O,' quoth he, 'Mater Jan, be Got Mater Jan, me will not spoil her clothes for a tousand pound. Ah, me love Matress Joan more then my wife!'

Well, supper being done, they rose from the table. Master Benedick, embracing Mistress Joan, thanked her for her great courtesy and company, and then the good man and he walked into the town, and Joan hied her home to her master's, knowing nothing of the intended jest. Master Benedick thought every hour twain till the sun was down, and that he were abed with his beloved. At last he had his wish, and home he came to his friend's house.

Then said John, 'Master Benedick, you must not in any case have a candle when you go into the chamber, for then my kinswoman will be angry, and dark places fit best lovers' desires.' 'O Master Jan,' quoth he, ''tis no such matter for light; me shall find Metress Joan will enough in the dark.' And entering in the parlour, groping about, he felt a gown and hat. 'O Metress Joan,' quoth he, 'here is your gown and hat. Me shall no hurt for a tousand pound.' Then, kneeling down by the bed's side, instead of Mistress Joan he saluted the sow in this sort.

'O my love and my delight, it is thy fair face that hath wounded my heart; thy grey sparkling eyes and thy lily-white hands, with the comely proportion of thy pretty body, that made me in seeking thee to forget myself and, to find thy favour, lose my own freedom. But now is the time come wherein I shall reap the fruits of a plentiful harvest. Now my dear, from thy sweet mouth let me suck the honey balm of thy breath, and with my hand stroke those rosy cheeks of thine wherein I have took such pleasure. Come with thy pretty lips and entertain me into thy bed with one gentle kiss (why speakest thou not, my sweetheart?) and stretch out thy alabaster arms to enfold thy faithful friend. Why should ill-pleasing sleep close up the crystal windows of thy body so fast and bereave thee of thy fine, lordly attendants wherewith thou was wont to salute thy friends? Let it not offend thy gentle ears that I thus talk to thee. If thou hast vowed not to speak I will not break it, and if thou wilt command me to be silent I will be dumb. But thou needest not fear to speak thy mind, seeing the cloudy night concealeth everything.'

By this time Master Benedick was unready, and slipped into bed, where the sow lay swathed in a sheet and her head bound in a great linen cloth. As soon as he was laid, he began to embrace his new bedfellow, and laying his lips somewhat near her snout, he felt her draw her breath very short. 'Why, how now love,' quoth he, 'be you sick? Mistress Joan, your breath be very strong; have you no cack* abed?'

The sow, feeling herself disturbed, began to grunt and keep a great stir, whereat Master Benedick, like a madman, ran out of bed crying 'De divel, de divel!' The good man of the house, being purposely provided, came rushing in with half a dozen of his neighbours, asking what was the matter. 'Poh me,' quoth Benedick, 'here be the great divel, cry "hoh, hoh, hoh"; be gossen I tink dee play the knave vid me, and me will be revenged on you.'

'Sir,' quoth he, 'I, knowing you love mutton, thought pork nothing unfit, and therefore provided you a whole sow, and as you like this entertainment, spend portigues. Walk, walk! Berkshire maids will be no Italian's strumpets, nor the wives of Newbury their bawds.' 'Berkshire dog,' quoth Benedick, 'owlface shack!* Hang dou and dy wife. Have it not be for me love to sweet Metress Joan, I will no come in your houze. But farewell till I cash you;* I shall make your hog nose bud.'*

The good man and his neighbours laughed aloud; away went Master Benedick, and for very shame departed from Newbury before day.

CHAPTER 8

How Jack of Newbury, keeping a very good house both for his servants and relief of the poor, won great credit thereby, and how one of his wife's gossips found fault therewith.

'GOOD morrow gossip, now by my truly, I am glad to see you in health. I pray you, how doth Master Winchcomb? What, never a great belly yet? Now fie, by my fa your husband is waxed idle!' 'Trust me gossip,' saith Mistress Winchcomb, 'a great belly comes sooner than a new coat, but you must consider we have not been long married. But truly gossip, you are welcome. I pray you sit down, and we will have a morsel of something by and by.' 'Nay truly gossip, I cannot stay,' quoth she, 'indeed I must be gone, for I did but even step in to see how you did.' 'You shall not choose but stay a while,' quoth Mistress Winchcomb, and with that a fair napkin was laid upon the little table in the parlour, hard by the fireside, whereon was set a fine cold capon, with a great deal of other good cheer, with ale and wine plenty.

'I pray you gossip, eat, and I beshrew you if you spare,' quoth the one. 'I thank you heartily gossip,' saith the other. 'But hear you gossip, I pray you tell me. Doth your husband love you well and make much of you?' 'Yes truly, I thank God,' quoth she. 'Now by my troth,' said the other, 'it were a shame for him if he should not, for though I say it before your face, though he had little with you, yet you were worthy to be as good a man's wife as his.'

'Trust me, I would not change my John for my lord marquess,' quoth she, 'a woman can be but well, for I live at heart's ease, and have all things at will, and truly he will not see me lack anything.' 'God's blessing on his heart,' quoth her gossip, 'it is a good hearing. But I pray you tell me, I heard say your husband is chosen for our burgess in the parliament house, is it true?' 'Yes verily,' quoth his wife, 'iwis it is against his will, for it will be no small charges unto him.' 'Tush woman, what talk you of that? Thanks be to God, there is never a gentleman in all Berkshire that is better able to bear it. But hear you gossip, shall I be so bold to ask you one question more?' 'Yes, with all my heart,' quoth she. 'I heard say that your husband would now put you in your hood and silk gown—I pray you, is it true?'

'Yes, in truth,' quoth Mistress Winchcomb, 'but far against my mind, gossip. My French hood is bought already, and my silk gown is a making; likewise the goldsmith hath brought home my chain and bracelets. But I assure you gossip, if you will believe me, I had rather go an hundred miles than wear them, for I shall be so ashamed that I shall not look upon any of my neighbours for blushing.' 'And why, I pray you?' quoth her gossip. 'I tell you, dear woman, you need not be anything abashed or blush at the matter, especially seeing your husband's estate is able to maintain it. Now trust me truly, I am of opinion you will become it singular well.'

'Alas,' quoth Mistress Winchcomb, 'having never been used to such attire, I shall not know where I am, nor how to behave myself in it; and beside, my complexion is so black that I shall carry but an ill-favoured countenance under a hood.' 'Now without doubt', quoth her gossip, 'you are to blame to say so. Beshrew my heart if I speak it to flatter: you are a very fair and well-favoured young woman as any is in Newbury. And never fear your behaviour in your hood, for I tell you true, as old and withered as I am myself, I could become a hood well enough and behave myself as well in such attire as any other whatsoever, and I would not learn of never a one of them all. What woman, I have been a pretty wench in my days, and seen some fashions. Therefore you need not to fear, seeing both your beauty and comely personage deserves no less than a French hood, and be of good comfort. At the first, (possible) folks will gaze something at you, but be not you abashed for that—it is better they should wonder at your good fortune than lament at your misery. But when they have seen you two or three times in that attire they will afterward little respect it, for every new thing at the first seems rare, but being once a little used it grows common.'

'Surely gossip you say true,' quoth she, 'and I am but a fool to be so bashful. It is no shame to use God's gifts for our credits, and well might my husband think me unworthy to have them if I would not wear them. And though I say it, my hood is a fair one as any woman wears in this country, and my gold chain and bracelets are none of the worst sort, and I will show them you because you shall give me your opinion upon them.' And therewithal she stepped into her chamber and fetched them forth.

When her gossip saw them she said 'Now beshrew my

fingers, but these are fair ones indeed. And when do you mean to wear them, gossip?' 'At Whitsuntide,' quoth she, 'if God spare me life.' 'I wish that well you may wear them,' said her gossip, 'and I would I were worthy to be with you when you dress yourself. I should be never the worse for you; I would order the matter so that you should set everything about you in such sort as never a gentlewoman of them all should stain you.' Mistress Winchcomb gave her great thanks for her favour, saying that if she needed her help she would be bold to send for her.

Then began her gossip to turn her tongue to another tune, and now to blame her for her great house-keeping. And thus she began: 'Gossip, you are but a young woman, and one that hath had no great experience of the world. In my opinion, you are something too lavish in expenses. Pardon me, good gossip, I speak but for good will, and because I love you I am the more bold to admonish you. I tell you plain, were I the mistress of such a house, having such large allowance as you have, I would save twenty pound a year that you spend to no purpose.'

'Which way might that be?' quoth Mistress Winchcomb. 'Indeed, I confess I am but a green housewife, and one that hath but small trial in the world. Therefore I should be very glad to learn anything that were for my husband's profit and my commodity.' 'Then listen to me,' quoth she, 'you feed your folks with the best of the beef and the finest of the wheat, which in my opinion is a great oversight. Neither do I hear of any knight in this country that doth it. And to say the truth, how were they able to bear that port which they do if they saved it not by some means? Come thither, and I warrant you that you shall see but brown bread on the board; if it be wheat and rye mingled together it is a great matter, and the bread highly commended, but most commonly they eat either barley bread or rye mingled with pease and such like coarse grain, which is doubtless but of small price, and there is no other bread allowed except at their own board. And in like manner for their meat: it is well known that necks and points of beef is their ordinary fare, which because it is commonly lean, they seethe therewith now and then a piece of bacon or pork, whereby they make their pottage fat, and therewith drives out the rest with more content—and thus must you learn to do. And beside that, the midriffs of the oxen and the cheeks, the sheeps' heads, and the gathers, which you give away at your gate, might serve them well enough, which would be a great sparing to your other meat, and by this means you would save in the year much money, whereby you might the better maintain your hood and silk gown. Again, you serve your folks with such superfluities that they spoil in manner as much as they eat; believe me, were I their dame they would have things more sparingly, and then they would think it more dainty.'

'Trust me gossip,' quoth Mistress Winchcomb, 'I know your words in many things to be true, for my folks are so corn-fed that we have much ado to please them in their diet. One doth say this is too salt, and another saith this is too gross; this is too fresh and that too fat, and twenty faults they will find at their meals. I warrant you they make such parings of their cheese, and keep such chipping of their bread, that their very orts would serve two or three honest folks to their dinner.'

'And from whence, I pray you, proceeds that', quoth her gossip, 'but of too much plenty? But i'faith, were they my servants, I would make them glad of the worst crumb they cast away, and thereupon I drink to you, and I thank you for my good cheer with all my heart.' 'Much good may it do you, good gossip,' said Mistress Winchcomb, 'and I pray you, when you come this way, let us see you.' 'That you shall verily,' quoth she, and so away she went.

After this, Mistress Winchcomb took occasion to give her folks shorter commons and coarser meat than they were wont to have, which at length being come to the good man's ear, he was very much offended therewith, saying 'I will not have my people thus pinched of their victuals. Empty platters make greedy stomachs, and where scarcity is kept, hunger is nourished, and therefore wife, as you love me, let me have no more of this doings.'

'Husband,' quoth she, 'I would they should have enough, but it is a sin to suffer and a shame to see the spoil they make. I could be very well content to give them their bellies' full and that which is sufficient, but it grieves me, to tell you true, to see how coy they are, and the small care they have in wasting of things. And I assure you, the whole town cries shame of it, and it hath bred me no small discredit for looking no better to it. Trust me no more, if I was not checked in my own house about this matter, when my ears did burn to hear what was spoken.'

'Who was it that checked thee, I pray thee tell me? Was it not your old gossip, Dame Dainty, Mistress Trip and Go? I believe it was.' 'Why man, if it were she, you know she hath been an old housekeeper and one that hath known the world, and that she told me was for good will.' 'Wife,' quoth he, 'I would not have thee to meddle with such light-brained housewives, and so I have told thee a good many times; and yet I cannot get you to leave her company.'

'Leave her company! Why husband, so long as she is an honest woman, why should I leave her company? She never gave me hurtful counsel in all her life, but hath always been ready to tell me things for my profit, though you take it not so. Leave her company! I am no girl, I would you should well know, to be taught what company I should keep. I keep none but honest company I warrant you. Leave her company, ketha! Alas, poor soul, this reward she hath for her good will. I wis, I wis, she is more your friend than you are your own.'

'Well, let her be what she will,' said her husband, 'but if she come any more in my house she were as good no. And therefore take this for a warning, I would advise you.' And so away he went.

CHAPTER 9

How a draper in London, who owed Jack of Newbury much money, became bankrout, whom Jack of Newbury found carrying a porter's basket on his neck, and how he set him up again at his own cost; which draper afterward became an alderman of London.

THERE was one Randoll Pert, a draper, dwelling in Watling Street, that owed Jack of Newbury five hundred pounds at one time, who in the end fell greatly to decay, in so much that he was cast in prison and his wife with her poor children turned out of doors. All his creditors except Winchcomb had a share of his goods, never releasing him out of prison so long as he had one penny to satisfy them. But when this tidings was brought to Jack of Newbury's ear, his friends counselled him to lay his action against him.

'Nay,' quoth he, 'if he be not able to pay me when he is at liberty, he will never be able to pay me in prison, and therefore it were as good for me to forbear my money without troubling him as to add more sorrow to his grieved heart and be never the nearer. Misery is trodden down by many,* and once brought low they are seldom or never relieved; therefore he shall rest for me untouched, and I would to God he were clear of all other men's debts, so that I gave him mine to begin the world again.'

Thus lay the poor draper a long time in prison, in which space his wife, which before for daintiness would not foul her fingers, nor turn her head aside for fear of hurting the set of her neckenger, was glad to go about and wash bucks at the Thames' side, and to be a charwoman in rich men's houses. Her soft hand was now hardened with scouring, and instead of gold rings upon her lily fingers, they were now filled with chaps provoked by the sharp lee and other drudgeries.

At last, Master Winchcomb being (as you heard) chosen against the parliament a burgess for the town of Newbury, and coming up to London for the same purpose, when he was alighted at his inn, he left one of his men there to get a porter to bring his trunk up to the place of his lodging. Poor Randoll Pert, which lately before was come out of prison, having no other means of maintenance, became a porter to carry burthens from one place to another, having an old, ragged doublet and a torn pair of breeches with his hose out at the heels and a pair of old, broken slip shoes on his feet, a rope about his middle instead of a girdle, and on his head an old, greasy cap, which had so many holes in it that his hair started through it; who, as soon as he heard one call for a porter made answer straight 'Here master, what is it that you would have carried?'

'Marry,' quoth he, 'I would have this trunk borne to the Spread Eagle at Ivybridge.' 'You shall, master,' quoth he, 'but what will you give me for my pains?' 'I will give thee two pence.' 'A penny more and I will carry it,' said the porter; and so being agreed, away he went with his burthen till he came to the Spread Eagle door, where on a sudden espying Master Winchcomb standing, he cast down the trunk and ran away as hard as ever he could.

Master Winchcomb, wondering what he meant thereby, caused his man to run after him and to fetch him again. But when he saw one pursue him, he ran then the faster, and in running, here he lost one of his slip shoes, and there another, ever looking behind him like a man pursued with a deadly weapon, fearing every twinkling of an eye to be thrust through. At last, his breech being tied but with one point, what with the haste he made and the weakness of the thong, fell about his heels, which so shackled him that down he fell in the street all along, sweating and blowing, being quite worn out of breath. And so by this means the servingman overtook him, and taking him by the sleeve, being as windless as the other, stood blowing and puffing a great while ere they could speak one to another.

'Sirra,' quoth the servingman, 'you must come to my master; you have broken his trunk all to pieces by letting it fall.' 'O for God's sake,' quoth he, 'let me go, for Christ's sake let me go, or else Master Winchcomb of Newbury will arrest me, and then I am undone forever!'

Now by this time Jack of Newbury had caused his trunk to be carried into the house, and then he walked along to know what the matter was. But when he heard the porter say that he would arrest him, he wondered greatly, and having quite forgot Pert's favour, being so greatly changed by imprisonment and poverty, he said 'Wherefore should I arrest thee? Tell me good fellow; for mine own part I know no reason for it.' 'O sir,' quoth he, 'I would to God I knew none neither.'

Then, asking him what his name was, the poor man, falling down on his knees, said 'Good Master Winchcomb, bear with me and cast me not into prison. My name is Pert, and I do

not deny but I owe you five hundred pound, yet for the love
of God take pity upon me!'

When Master Winchcomb heard this he wondered greatly
at the man, and did as much pity his misery, though as yet he
made it not known, saying 'Passion of my heart man, thou wilt
never pay me thus! Never think, being a porter, to pay five
hundred pound debt. But this hath your prodigality brought
you to, your thriftless neglecting of your business, that set
more by your pleasure than your profit.' Then, looking better
upon him, he said 'What, never a shoe to thy foot, hose to thy
leg, band to thy neck, nor cap to thy head? O Pert, this is
strange! But wilt thou be an honest man, and give me a bill
of thy hand for my money?' 'Yes sir, with all my heart,' quoth
Pert. 'Then come to the scrivener's,' quoth he, 'and dispatch
it, and I will not trouble thee.'

Now when they were come thither, with a great many
following them at their heels, Master Winchcomb said
'Hearest thou scrivener, this fellow must give me a bill of his
hand for five hundred pounds. I pray thee, make it as it should
be.' The scrivener, looking upon the poor man and seeing him
in that case, said to Master Winchcomb 'Sir, you were better
to let it be a bond, and have some sureties bound with him.'
'Why scrivener,' quoth he, 'dost thou think this is not a
sufficient man of himself for five hundred pound?' 'Truly sir,'
said the scrivener, 'if you think him so, you and I are of two
minds.'

'I'll tell thee what,' quoth Master Winchcomb, 'were it not
that we are all mortal, I would take his word as soon as his
bill or bond; the honesty of a man is all.' 'And we in London',
quoth the scrivener, 'do trust bonds far better than honesty.
But sir, when must this money be paid?' 'Marry scrivener,
when this man is sheriff of London.' At that word the
scrivener and the people standing by laughed heartily, saying
'In truth sir, make no more ado but forgive it him, as good to
do the one as the other.' 'Nay, believe me,' quoth he, 'not so;
therefore do as I bid you.'

Whereupon the scrivener made the bill to be paid when
Randoll Pert was sheriff of London, and thereunto set his own
hand for a witness, and twenty persons more that stood by set

to their hands likewise. Then he asked Pert what he should have for carrying his trunk. 'Sir,' quoth he, 'I should have three pence, but seeing I find you so kind, I will take but two pence at this time.' 'Thanks, good Pert,' quoth he, 'but for thy three pence there is three shillings, and look thou come to me tomorrow morning betimes.'

The poor man did so, at what time Master Winchcomb had provided him out of Birchin Lane a fair suit of apparel, merchantlike, with a fair black cloak and all other things fit to the same. Then he took him a shop in Canweek Street and furnished the same shop with a thousand pounds worth of cloth, by which means, and other favours that Master Winchcomb did him, he grew again into great credit, and in the end became so wealthy that while Master Winchcomb lived he was chosen sheriff, at what time he payed five hundred pounds every penny, and after died an alderman of the city.

CHAPTER 10

How Jack of Newbury's servants were revenged of their dame's tattling gossip.

UPON a time it came to pass, when Master Winchcomb was far from home and his wife gone abroad, that Mistress Many-Better, Dame Tittle Tattle, Gossip Pint-Pot, according to her old custom came to Mistress Winchcomb's house, perfectly knowing of the good man's absence, and little thinking the good wife was from home. Where, knocking at the gate, Tweedle stepped out and asked who was there, where hastily opening the wicket he suddenly discovered the full proportion of this foul beast, who demanded if their mistress were within.

'What, Mistress Frank?' quoth he, 'in faith welcome. How have you done a great while? I pray you, come in.' 'Nay, I cannot stay,' quoth she. 'Notwithstanding, I did call to speak a word or two with your mistress. I pray you, tell her that I am here.' 'So I will,' quoth he, 'so soon as she comes in.' Then said the woman 'What, is she abroad? Why then, farewell good Tweedle.'

'Why, what haste, what haste Mistress Frank,' quoth he, 'I pray you, stay and drink ere you go. I hope a cup of new sack will do your old belly no hurt.' 'What,' quoth she, 'have you new sack already? Now by my honesty, I drunk none this year, and therefore I do not greatly care if I take a taste before I go.' And with that she went into the wine cellar with Tweedle, where first he set before her a piece of powdered beef as green as a leek, and then going into the kitchen he brought her a piece of roasted beef hot from the spit.

Now, certain of the maidens of the house and some of the young men, who had long before determined to be revenged of this prattling housewife, came into the cellar one after another, one of them bringing a great piece of a gambon of bacon in his hand, and everyone bade Mistress Frank welcome. And first one drank to her, and then another, and so the third, the fourth, and the fifth, so that Mistress Frank's brains waxed as mellow as a pippin at Michaelmas, and so light that, sitting in the cellar, she thought the world ran round. They, seeing her to fall into merry humours, whetted her on in merriment as much as they could, saying 'Mistress Frank, spare not I pray you, but think yourself as welcome as any woman in Newbury, for we have cause to love you because you love our mistress so well.'

'Now, assure you,' quoth she, lisping in her speech, her tongue waxing somewhat too big for her mouth, 'I love your mistress well indeed, as if she were my own daughter.' 'Nay, but hear you,' quoth they, 'she begins not to deal well with us now.' 'No, my lamb,' quoth she, 'why so?' 'Because', quoth they, 'she seeks to bar us of our allowance, telling our master that he spends too much in housekeeping.'

'Nay then,' quoth she, 'your mistress is an ass and a fool, and though she go in her hood, what care I? She is but a girl to me. Twittle twattle, I know what I know. Go to, drink to me! Well, Tweedle, I drink to thee with all my heart; why, thou whoreson, when wilt thou be married? O that I were a young wench for thy sake! But 'tis no matter, though I be but a poor woman, I am a true woman. Hang dogs, I have dwelt in this town these thirty winters.'

'Why then,' quoth they, 'you have dwelt here longer than our master.' 'Your master!' quoth she. 'I knew your master a boy, when he was called Jack of Newbury; aye Jack, I knew him called plain Jack—and your mistress, now she is rich and I am poor, but 'tis no matter, I knew her a draggle-tail girl, mark ye!' 'But now', quoth they, 'she takes upon her lustily, and hath forgot what she was.'

'Tush, what will you have of a green thing,' quoth she. 'Here, I drink to you. So long as she goes where she list a-gossiping; and 'tis no matter, little said is soon amended. But hear you my masters, though Mistress Winchcomb go in her hood, I am as good as she, I care not who tell it her. I spend not my husband's money in cherries and coddlings. Go to, go to, I know what I say well enough! I am sure I am not drunk. Mistress Winchcomb—Mistress? No, Nan Winchcomb I will call her name, plain Nan. What, I was a woman when she was, se-reverence, a paltry girl, though now she goes in her hood and chain of gold. What care I for her? I am her elder, and I know more of her tricks. Nay, I warrant you I know what I say, 'tis no matter, laugh at me and spare not. I am not drunk, I warrant.'

And with that, being scant able to hold open her eyes, she began to nod and to spill the wine out of the glass, which they perceiving let her alone, going out of the cellar till she was sound asleep, and in the mean space they devised how to finish this piece of knavery. At last they consented to lay her forth at the back side of the house, half a mile off, even at the foot of a stile, that whosoever came next over might find her. Notwithstanding, Tweedle stayed hard by to see the end of this action.

At last comes a notable clown from Greenham taking his way to Newbury who, coming hastily over the stile, stumbled at the woman and fell down clean over her. But in the starting up, seeing it was a woman, cried out 'Alas, alas!' 'How now, what is the matter?' quoth Tweedle. 'O,' quoth he, 'here lies a dead woman.' 'A dead woman,' quoth Tweedle, 'that's not so I trow,' and with that he tumbled her about. 'Bones of me,' quoth Tweedle, 'it's a drunken woman, and one of the town undoubtedly. Surely it is great pity she should lie here.' 'Why, do you know her?' quoth the clown. 'No, not I,' quoth Tweedle, 'nevertheless, I will give thee half a groat, and take her in thy basket and carry her throughout the town, and see if anybody know her.'

Then said th'other 'Let me see the money and I will, for by the mass, che earned not half a groat this great while.' 'There it is,' quoth Tweedle. Then the fellow put her in his basket and so lifted her upon his back. 'Now by the mass, she stinks vilely of drink or wine or something. But tell me, what shall I say when I come into the town?' quoth he.

'First', quoth Tweedle, 'I would have thee, so soon as ever thou canst, go to the town's end with a lusty voice to cry "O yes!", and then say "Who knows this woman, who?" And though possible some will say "I know her" and "I know her", yet do not thou set her down till thou comest to the market cross, and there use the like words; and if any be so friendly to tell thee where she dwells, then just before her door cry so again, and if thou perform this bravely I will give thee half a groat more.'

'Master Tweedle,' quoth he, 'I know you well enough. You dwell with Master Winchcomb, do you not? Well, if I do it not in the nick, give me never a penny.' And so away he went till he came to the town's end, and there he cries out as boldly as any bailiff's man 'O yes, who knows this woman, who?' Then said the drunken woman in the basket, her head falling first on one side and then on the other side 'Who co me, who?' Then said he again 'Who knows this woman, who?' 'Who co me, who?' quoth she. And look, how oft he spake the one, she spake the other, saying still 'Who co me, who co me, who?', whereat all the people in the street fell into such a laughing that the tears ran down again.

At last one made answer, saying 'Good fellow, she dwells in the North Brook Street, a little beyond Master Winchcomb's.' The fellow, hearing that, goes down thither in all haste, and there in the hearing of a hundred people cries 'Who knows this woman, who?', whereat her husband comes out saying 'Marry, that do I too well, God help me'. 'Then', said the

clown, 'if you know her, take her, for I know her not but for
a drunken beast.' And as her husband took her out of the
basket, she gave him a sound box on the ear, saying 'What,
you queans, do you mock me?', and so was carried in.

But the next day, when her brains were quiet and her head
cleared of these foggy vapours, she was so ashamed of herself
that she went not forth of her doors a long time after, and if
anybody did say unto her 'Who co me, who?', she would be
so mad and furious that she would be ready to draw her knife
and to stick them, and scold as if she strove for the best game
at the cucking stools. Moreover, her prattling to Mistress
Winchcomb's folks of their mistress made her, on the other
side, to fall out with her in such sort that she troubled them
no more, either with her company or her counsel.

CHAPTER 11

How one of Jack of Newbury's maidens became a lady.

AT the winning of Morlesse* in France, the noble Earl of
Surrey, being at that time Lord High Admiral of England,
made many knights. Among the rest was Sir George Rigley,*
brother to Sir Edward Rigley, and sundry other whose valours
far surpassed their wealth. So that when peace bred a scarcity
in their purses that their credits grew weak in the city, they
were enforced to ride into the country, where at their friends'
houses they might have favourable welcome without coin or
grudging. Among the rest, Jack of Newbury that kept a table
for all comers was never lightly without many such guests,
where they were sure to have both welcome and good cheer,
and their mirth no less pleasing than their meat was plenty.

Sir George, having lien long at board in this brave yeoman's
house, at length fell in liking of one of his maidens, who was
as fair as she was fond. This lusty wench he so allured with
hope of marriage that at length she yielded him her love, and
therewithal bent her whole study to work his content. But in
the end she so much contented him that it wrought altogether

her own discontent. To become high, she laid herself so low that the knight suddenly fell over her, which fall became the rising of her belly. But when this wanton perceived herself to be with child, she made her moan unto the knight, saying 'Ah, Sir George, now is the time to perform your promise, or to make me a spectacle of infamy to the whole world forever. In the one you shall discharge the duty of a true knight, but in the other show yourself a most perjured person. Small honour will it be to boast in the spoil of poor maidens, whose innocency all good knights ought to defend.'

'Why thou lewd, paltry thing,' quoth he, 'comest thou to father thy bastard upon me? Away, ye dunghill carrion, away! Hear you, good huswife, get you among your companions, and lay your litter where you list, but if you trouble me any more, trust me thou shalt dearly aby it.' And so, bending his brows like the angry god of war, he went his ways, leaving the child-breeding wench to the hazard of her fortune, either good or bad.

The poor maiden, seeing herself for her kindness thus cast off, shed many tears of sorrow for her sin, inveighing with many bitter groans against the unconstancy of love-alluring men. And in the end, when she saw no other remedy, she made her case known unto her mistress, who after she had given her many checks and taunts, threatening to turn her out of doors, she opened the matter to her husband.

So soon as he heard thereof he made no more to do but presently posted to London after Sir George, and found him at my Lord Admiral's. 'What Master Winchcomb,' quoth he, 'you are heartily welcome to London, and I thank you for my good cheer. I pray you, how doth your good wife, and all our friends in Berkshire?'

'All well and merry, I thank you good Sir George,' quoth he, 'I left them in good health, and I hope they do so continue. And trust me Sir,' quoth he, 'having earnest occasion to come up to talk with a bad debtor, in my journey it was my chance to light in company of a gallant widow. A gentlewoman she is of wondrous good wealth, whom grisly death hath bereft of a kind husband, making her a widow ere she had been half a year a wife. Her land, Sir George, is as well worth a hundred pound a year as one penny, being as fair and comely a creature as any of her degree in our whole country. Now Sir, this is the worst: by the reason that she doubts herself to be with child, she hath vowed not to marry these 12 months, but because I wish you well, and the gentlewoman no hurt, I came of purpose from my business to tell you thereof. Now, Sir George, if you think her a fit wife for you, ride to her, woo her, win her, and wed her.'

'I thank you, good Master Winchcomb,' quoth he, 'for your favour ever toward me, and gladly would I see this young widow if I wist where.' 'She dwells not half a mile from my house,' quoth Master Winchcomb, 'and I can send for her at any time, if you please.'

Sir George, hearing this, thought it was not best to come there, fearing Joan would father a child upon him, and therefore said he had no leisure to come from my Lord. 'But', quoth he, 'would I might see her in London, on the condition it cost me twenty nobles.' 'Tush Sir George,' quoth Master Winchcomb, 'delay in love is dangerous, and he that will woo a widow must take time by the forelock, and suffer none other to step* before him lest he leap without the widow's love. Notwithstanding, seeing now I have told you of it, I will take my gelding and get me home. If I hear of her coming to London I will send you word, or perhaps come myself; till when adieu, good Sir George.'

Thus parted Master Winchcomb from the knight, and being come home, in short time he got a fair taffety gown and a French hood for his maid, saying 'Come ye drab, I must be fain to cover a foul fault with a fair garment, yet all will not hide your great belly. But if I find means to make you a lady, what wilt thou say then?' 'O master,' quoth she, 'I shall be bound while I live to pray for you.' 'Come then minion,' quoth her mistress, 'and put you on this gown and French hood, for seeing you have lien with a knight, you must needs be a gentlewoman.'

The maid did so, and being thus attired, she was set on a fair gelding, and a couple of men sent with her up to London. And being well instructed by her master and dame what she should do, she took her journey to the city in the term time, and lodged at the Bell in the Strand; and Mistress Loveless must be her name, for so her master had warned her to call herself. Neither did the men that waited on her know the contrary, for Master Winchcomb had borrowed them of their master to wait upon a friend of his to London because he* could not spare any of his own servants at that time. Notwithstanding, they were appointed, for the gentlewoman's credit, to say they were her own men.

This being done, Master Winchcomb sent Sir George a letter, that the gentlewoman which he told him of was now in London, lying at the Bell in the Strand, having great business at the Term. With which news Sir George's heart was on fire till such time as he might speak with her. Three or four times went he thither, and still she would not be spoken withal, the which close keeping of herself made him the more earnest in his suit.

At length he watched her so narrowly that, finding her going forth in an evening, he followed her, she having one man before and another behind, carrying a very stately gait in the street, it drave him into the greater liking of her, being the more urged to utter his mind. And suddenly stepping before her, he thus saluted her: 'Gentlewoman, God save you; I have often been at your lodging and could never find you at leisure.' 'Why sir,' quoth she, counterfeiting her natural speech, 'have you any business with me?'

'Yes, fair widow,' quoth he, 'as you are a client to the law, so am I a suitor for your love, and may I find you so favourable to let me plead my own case at the bar of your beauty, I doubt not but to unfold so true a tale as I trust will cause you to give sentence on my side.' 'You are a merry gentleman,' quoth she, 'but for my own part I know you not. Nevertheless, in a case of love I will be no let to your suit, though perhaps I help you little therein. And therefore sir, if it please you to give attendance at my lodging, upon my return from the Temple* you shall know more of my mind.' And so they parted.

Sir George, receiving hereby some hope of good hap, stayed for his dear at her lodging door, whom at her coming she friendly greeted, saying 'Surely sir, your diligence is more than the profit you shall get thereby. But, I pray you, how shall I call your name?' 'George Rigley', quoth he, 'I am called, and for some small deserts I was knighted in France.' 'Why then, Sir George,' quoth she, 'I have done you too much wrong to make you thus dance attendance on my worthless person. But let me be so bold to request you to tell me how you came to know me. For my own part, I cannot remember that ever I saw you before.'

'Mistress Loveless,' said Sir George, 'I am well acquainted with a good neighbour of yours called Master Winchcomb, who is my very good friend; and to say the truth, you were commended unto me by him.' 'Truly Sir George,' said she, 'you are so much the better welcome. Nevertheless, I have made a vow not to love any man for this twelvemonth's space. And therefore sir, till then I would wish you to trouble yourself no further in this matter till that time be expired, and then if I find you be not entangled to any other, and that by trial I find out the truth of your love, for Master Winchcomb's sake your welcome shall be as good as any other gentleman's whatsoever.'

Sir George, having received this answer, was wondrous woe, cursing the day that ever he meddled with Joan, whose time of deliverance would come long before a twelvemonth were expired, to his utter shame and overthrow of his good fortune; for by that means should he have Master Winchcomb his enemy, and therewithal the loss of this fair gentlewoman. Wherefore, to prevent this mischief, he sent a letter in all haste to Master Winchcomb, requesting him most earnestly to come up to London, by whose persuasion he hoped straight to finish the marriage.

Master Winchcomb fulfilled his request, and then presently was the marriage solemnized at the Tower of London, in presence of many gentlemen of Sir George's friends. But when he found it was Joan, whom he had gotten with child, he fretted and fumed, stamped, and stared like a devil. 'Why,' quoth Master Winchcomb, 'what needs all this? Came you to my table to make my maid your strumpet? Had you no man's house to dishonour but mine? Sir, I would you should well know that I account the poorest wench in my house too good to be your whore, were you ten knights. And seeing you took pleasure in making her your wanton, take it no scorn to make her your wife; and use her well too, or you shall hear of it. And hold thee Joan,' quoth he, 'there is a hundred pounds for thee, and let him not say thou comest to him a beggar.'

Sir George seeing this, and withal casting in his mind what friend Master Winchcomb might be to him, taking his wife by the hand gave her a loving kiss, and Master Winchcomb great thanks. Whereupon he willed him for two years' space to take his diet and his lady's at his house; which the knight accepting rode straight with his wife to Newbury. Then did the mistress make curtsy to the maid, saying 'You are welcome Madam', giving her the upper hand in all places. And thus they lived afterward in great joy; and our King, hearing how Jack had matched Sir George, laughing heartily thereat, gave him a living forever, the better to maintain my Lady his wife.

EXPLANATORY NOTES

THE ADVENTURES OF MASTER F. J.

2 *humoral*: in this context, moody, capricious.

5 *opere precium*: a work of value.

6 *aliquid salis*: some wit.

7 *etc.*: used by 'G.T.' a number of times rhetorically, with either, as here, a weary shrug, or a lascivious leer, as on page 61.

8 *work*: her needlework, cf. F.J.'s letter which he offers as a 'bottom to wind your sewing silk'.

11 *her*: emended, following Lawlis, from 'his', both edns.

   bezo las manos: kiss of the hands.

   zuccado dez labros: pseudo-Spanish (?) = kiss on the lips.

   Terza sequenza: sequence of three.

13 *bleeding at the nose*: taken to be a sign of love, or desire.

   had: 1575 edn., 'hath' in 1573.

14 *made semblant*: made a pretence of.

16 *questions*: here and elsewhere the characters play the fashionable courtly game of *questioni d'amore*—questions concerning love.

   your hand on your halfpenny: M. P. Tilley, *A Dictionary of the Proverbs in England in the Sixteenth and Seventeenth Centuries* (Ann Arbor, 1966)—hereafter referred to as Tilley—H315 having a selfish object in view.

   day nor night: neither day nor night.

17 *Cocklorell's music*: cockerel's music = foolish, also a young man's.

   pocket: 1575 edn., packet in 1573.

18 *borrowed the invention of an Italian*: probably Petrarch, *Rime*, CXXIV, trans. by Wyatt, 'Love and fortune and my mind remember'.

   I: 1575 edn., not in 1573.

19 *askances*: note in 1575 edn. 'as who sayeth'.

20 *run for the bell*: cf. Tilley B275, to bear away the bell = win the prize.

23 *continua oratio*: unbroken account.

26 *parts*: emended from 'parties'; 'countries' in 1575 edn.

27 *per misericordiam*: compassionate, chastened.

   lap: lower part of the garment.

28 *supersedias*: legal writ staying proceedings.

   Bradamant . . . etc.: From Ludovico Ariosto, *Orlando Furioso* (1516), XLIV. 61: 'I mean to remain till death just as I have ever been, Ruggiero, and more so if possible', trans. Guido Waldman (Oxford, 1983).

   by whom the same was figured: i.e. who was their subject.

   distained: stained, but also the sense of 'defiled' seems relevant.

29 *at*: emended from 'as' in 1573 and 1575 edns.

31 *travailed*: laboured, perhaps also the sense of 'travelled'.

32 *gaze*: 1575 edn., 'gare' in 1573.

34 *alla Piedmonteze*: in the Piedmont style.

   omnia bene: all went well.

   taking himself in trip: making himself move nimbly.

37 *declaration*: '[the] declaration' perhaps needs to be understood.

38 *jags*: slashes in the surface of a garment to show off the lining underneath; in this context perhaps also rags or tatters.

   slipped: cut to replant.

39 *by her*: about her.

   once: once and for all, in short.

40 *a translation*: Prouty cites analogues by Petrarch, Ronsard, and Du Bellay, and a likely one in *Orlando Furioso*, VII, 11–14.

42 *kept cut*: kept reserved (?)—the exact meaning is unclear.

   [hung]: I think that this emendation helps the sense, but it is not considered necessary by other editors.

   horn: what follows plays upon the Elizabethan notion of the horns worn by a cuckold (husband of an unfaithful wife).

43 *rye*: perhaps punning on 'wry' in its Elizabethan sense of deviate, go astray.

47 *Ariosto*: Prouty notes that ordinarily readers of Ariosto's *Orlando Furioso* would not find the story of Suspicion, which

appeared in a supplement titled *Cinque Canti*. Prouty states that Gascoigne's version is a close translation.

48 *his*: emended from 'this' in both edns.

49 *Ganymede*: carried into heaven by Zeus' command to become the gods' cup-bearer.

Flaminia: Via Appia and Via Flaminia were the major roads of Imperial Rome.

50 *pallet*: emended from 'pallad' in both edns. = straw mattress.

Ariosto's thirty-first song: trans. from *Orlando Furioso* XXXI. 1–5, the last stanza being, as G.T. explains, original.

54 *too broad before, and might not drink of all waters*: too obvious, and might not suit everyone.

proportion: image of something, or perhaps misprint for 'proposition'.

55 *lend him over large thongs of my love*: perhaps the sense here is 'let him have the love that would bind him to me'.

Ardena: in Boiardo's *Orlando Innamorato* (1487) the fountain of Ardenne turned love to hate, in *Orlando Furioso* 1 there is a fountain of love as well as one of hate.

56 *lead apes in hell*: the fate of a spinster.

61 *enrage*: 1575 edn., 'encourage' in 1573.

62 *haggard*: 1575 edn., 'hagger' in 1573 = wild, cross.

eleventh article of her belief: in the Thirty-Nine Articles, issued in 1563, the eleventh concerns justification by faith, not works.

63 *una voce*: in one voice.

married: because 'cuckoo' was associated with cuckold.

66 *a dio*: adieu.

76 *with prick against her breast*: the nightingale, to keep awake, sang with a thorn in her breast, Tilley N183.

77 *allo solito*: according to her custom.

cat out of kind: Tilley C135 and C167.

won with an egg, and lost again with shell: = something like 'easy come, easy go'.

80 *poem*: what follows in 1573 is a series of poems with diverse signatures in initials, but all are presumed to be by Gascoigne.

APPENDIX: in 1575 Gascoigne published a new collection

of his works, *The Posies*, which contained a revised version of *Master F.J.*, possibly in response to accusations that he had depicted real events and people in his narrative. The narrator, G.T., is removed, F.J. renamed Ferdinando Jeronimi in this purported translation from Italian; Frances is named Franceschina at times, but Gascoigne often forgets to rename her.

EUPHUES: THE ANATOMY OF WIT

Owing to the extremely large number of allusions made by Lyly in his lists of exempla, I have only annotated those that seemed to require further explanation.

85 *Euphues*: in Plato, meaning well-endowed with natural gifts, also clever, symmetrical.

augmented: title-page of second edition (1579); the text followed here.

Lord de la Warre: virtually nothing is known of West.

last: in the first edition, the two examples were 'the sweetest rose with his prickles, the finest velvet with his brack', changed because Lyly originally used them twice (see p. 89).

Cyrus . . . Alexander . . . Demonides . . . Damocles: these examples ultimately derive from Plutarch, but Lyly may have relied on later collectors, such as Erasmus.

87 *whitest mouths*: are the most fastidious, derived according to Bond from horses whose mouths were white, not bloody from champing the bit.

88 *Christmas*: The first edition appeared late in December. This image was changed in later editions, the book being bound in midsummer and broken at Christmas.

a thank: pick a thank = curry favour.

Farewell: a preface 'To My Very Good Friends, the Gentlemen Scholars of Oxford', which appears in edns. after 1578, has been omitted, as the remarks in it relate principally to the later sections of *Euphues* not printed in this anthology.

89 *Tully*: Cicero, famous for his oratory.

teenest: unique to Lyly = keenest.

91 *singled his game*: picked one out of the herd.

92 *curious knots*: complex patterned flower-beds.

94 *Symplegades*: Syrtis was a sand-bar off Africa; the Symplegades were floating islands in the Euxine sea.

   lawn: fine linen, marred by a blemish caused by iron (?), or of an iron colour (?).

95 *convince*: convict.

96 *haggardness*: a haggard is a wild, untrainable hawk.

97 *Eubulus*: good or prudent in counsel.

98 *either*: Lyly frequently uses 'either . . . either' for 'either . . . or'.

   ex consequenti: as a result.

   Trochilus: like so many of Lyly's bizarre examples from natural history this one ultimately comes from Pliny the Elder's *Natural History* (AD 77), though they often come to Lyly via other sources, such as Erasmus.

   tabor: drum; the proverb is Tilley H160.

99 *look it*: i.e. look for it.

100 *hard in conceiving*: rigid in comprehending.

   Quae supra nos nihil ad nos: those things above us are nothing to us.

   Sententias loquitur carnifex: the executioner pronounces sentence (i.e. acts as judge and executioner).

101 *stand so on their pantofles*: stand on their dignity; pantofles were shoes or slippers with high cork heels.

   Philautus: a selfish man.

102 *a bushel of salt*: i.e. have many meals.

   whether: which.

103 *that*: in that.

104 *other*: i.e. others.

106 *lust*: list in first edn., has that sense here.

107 *black ox tread on their foot*: Tilley, O103; sign of a calamity or care.

110 *whose*: emended back to 1578 reading from 1579 'most'.

111 *won with a nut . . . lost with an apple*: Tilley, A205; usually won with an apple and lost with a nut.

113 *dictanum*: dittany.

114 *shadow*: first used to mean 'close friend', then 'decoy'.

114 *Gyges cut Candaules*: King Candaules, proud of his wife's beauty, hid Gyges in his room to see his wife naked. Encouraged by the angry Queen, Gyges killed Candaules and married the Queen.

116 *Lucretia*: raped by Tarquinius, Lucretia killed herself, an act leading to a revolt and the foundation of the Roman republic.

take heart at grass: disputed. Either 'take heart at grace' = pluck up courage, or a variant of 'all flesh is grass'.

117 *take thee mate*: punning on 'take the mate' = checkmated. Euphues goes on to say that being mated by a prince (Elizabethan Bishop), i.e. Livia, not a pawn, the loss is lessened.

118 *Propertius' pills*: Ovid, Tibullus, and Propertius all wrote about the pangs of desire.

120 *pinch courtesy*: strain courtesy.

121 *rise*: risen.

without: 1579 has 'with', emended from other edns.

123 *starve*: 'sterve' = die.

sleek-stone: polishing stone—smooth, while the mythical 'cylindrus' is rough.

124 *till time his desire*: 'until the time when his desire'.

125 *to shake hands with*: to farewell.

126 *to Phyllis than Demophon*: Demophon met Phyllis returning from the Trojan war. He promised to return to her from Athens, but she hanged herself in despair owing to his tardiness. The four instances of unfaithful travellers offered by Lucilla were cited frequently, following on from Ovid in *Heroides*.

129 *change your copy*: take a new line of action.

130 *force not*: care not for.

134 *Juno her bed*: Juno is the goddess who attends brides and women in childbirth.

135 *on the parson's side*: in relation to a wedding; usually meant 'save by reducing the Church's tithes'.

136 *Myrrha*: mother of Adonis by her father, changed into a myrtle.

Biblis: changed into a fountain while pursuing her brother.

Phaedra: committed suicide after falling in love with her stepson Hippolytus.

Sinon: persuaded the Trojans to admit the wooden horse.

139 *travail*: perhaps meaning both 'travel' and 'labour' in this context.

140 *Io*: in fact, Io was changed *by* Jupiter into a heifer, while he changed into a bull to beguile Europa.

141 *treacle*: in this context, medicinal syrup, while garlic was called poor man's treacle.

missed the cushion: missed the mark.

144 *openly taken in an iron net*: as Venus and Mars were by Venus' husband Vulcan.

145 *Pasiphaë*: wife of King Minos bore the Minotaur after her encounter with the bull.

146 *Galen*: ancient authority on medicine, as Justinian was on law and Aristotle on moral philosophy.

148 *Danaus*: his fifty daughters married his brother's fifty sons. To revenge previous slights he ordered his daughters to kill their husbands on the wedding night. Hypermnestra disobeyed.

150 *what end came of her*: we learn in the later, didactic part of *Euphues*, not printed here, in a letter from Euphues to Philautus, that Lucilla died suddenly, unrepentant to the last.

farewell: after the narrative section, *Euphues* continues for an equal length, consisting of didactic material such as disquisitions by Euphues on love, education, and religion, and highly didactic letters written to various people by Euphues as virtual manuals of instruction.

PANDOSTO. THE TRIUMPH OF TIME

153 *Temporis filia veritas*: truth is the daughter of time.

Omne tulit punctum qui miscuit utile dulci: Horace, *Ars Poetica*, 'He who has mixed profit and pleasure has won every vote.'

Aphranius: hard to identify, perhaps confused by Greene with a poet who lived 200 years before Trajan.

George Clifford: a buccaneer and gambler, who commanded a ship against the Spanish Armada.

156 *Sicilia*: Sicily.

158 *entered a wrong point in his tables*: a reference to the points on a backgammon board's tables, as well as a sexual *double entendre*.

159 *men*: signature B, missing in the only surviving copy of the first extant edition, is supplied from the second edition of 1592 from this point until page 167.

162 *to straight prison*: directly to prison and/or to a strait prison.

163 *a curst cow hath ofttimes short horns*: curst = savage; Tilley C751, ineffectual rage.

167 *quite*: after this point the first edition resumes on signature c.

nor other: 'method' understood; emended to 'rudder' in 1607 edn.

170 *spiteful*: emended from 'spightfully'.

175 *master went breechless*: i.e. did not wear the pants in the family.

176 *bows*: possibly 'boughs' is intended.

177 *but*: 1592 edn., emended from 'and', 1588 edn.

break with: disclose news to.

179 *at*: of.

Actaeon: the hunter who, as punishment for seeing Diana naked, was changed to a stag and eaten by his own hounds.

180 *with a flea in his ear*: excited, Tilley F534.

maugre his face: in spite of his resistance.

181 *Phoebus liked Sibylla*: exact reference unclear.

183 *which*: 1607 edn., emended from 'with'.

186 *that*: 1592 edn., emended from 1588 'then.'

187 *to become*: became.

therefore not: i.e. therefore ought not.

189 *these news*: i.e. these items of news.

190 *edged tools*: i.e. sharp enough to cut you.

192 *meaning simply*: with an innocent intent.

195 *Trapalonia*: a made-up name.

196 *keep the stuff*: watch over the valuables.

THE UNFORTUNATE TRAVELLER

207 *Qui audiunt audita dicunt*: Plautus, those who hear tell what they have heard.

Baron of Tichfield: the Earl of Southampton, who attended

Nashe's college at Cambridge (St John's). The dedication does not appear in the second edition.

208 *novus, nova, novum*: Latin, news; also a game of dice.

209 *Sic respondeo*: thus I reply.

Acts and Monuments: John Foxe's compendium of Protestant martyrs.

point-trussers: pages; tiers of laces fastening the hose to the doublet.

210 *Turney and Turwin*: Tournai and Terouanne, besieged in 1513.

Coelum petimus stultitia: Horace, in our foolishness we seek the heavens.

Jane Tross: presumably a famous prostitute, but not referred to elsewhere.

Paulo maiora canamus: Virgil, let us sing of rather greater things.

slur a die: cheat by sliding one of the dice.

in grace and virtue to proceed: from the rhyme which began a child's hornbook (first reader).

aliquid latet quod non patet: something is hidden which is not apparent.

211 *the king must lose his right*: Tilley N338.

tendit ad sidera virtus: virtue extends to the stars (sidera = stars/cider).

aqua celestis: heavenly water, a restorative drug.

212 *doit . . . dandiprat . . . half-souse . . . denier*: all coins with a low value.

start: started.

214 *Epimenides*: depending on the classical source he slept for 40 or 57 years.

215 *beaver*: this ingenious beast is described by Pliny in his *Natural History*.

216 *out-brothership of brachet*: care of female dogs? The sense is clearly out of harm's way in a foolish, lowly position.

welfare: good luck to (may it fare well).

thrumming of buttons: ornamenting buttons = wasting time.

fall out: 2nd edn. has fall in, but this does not seem necessary for the sense or the joke.

217 *quarter trey*: either both sides of a die, or one loaded to come up four or three at will.

dead lift: hopeless exigence.

crede mihi res est ingeniosa dare: Ovid, believe me, giving is a matter for good judgement.

nominativo hic asinus: in Latin grammar the declension uses examples like *magister*, not *asinus* (ass).

Jack Drum's entertainment: throw someone out bodily.

high men . . . low men . . . langrets . . . fulhams: all types of loaded dice.

218 *through stitch*: securely, thoroughly.

your staff falls: Tilley W142.

220 *without a bait*: without stopping to eat.

221 *good shipping to Wapping*: good luck on a journey.

three: 2nd edn., 'ten' in 1st.

Gog's Wounds: God's wounds; a common oath.

Quevela?: who goes there?

222 *crosses*: on the reverse side of many coins.

223 *coram nobis*: into our presence.

turned on the toe: hanged (Lawlis) or flogged (McKerrow).

Plura dolor prohibet: grief prevents more.

fly out scuttles: scuttles can be plates, baskets, or portholes—all editors are unclear as to the exact sense.

cue: acting cue, quart pot (q.).

dead pay: the clerks are pocketing the pay of soldiers they have killed (or perhaps simply of men who have died).

224 *at hard meat*: eating fodder = in confinement.

225 *budge*: fur, emended from 2nd edn., 'badge' in 1st.

can pass: 2nd edn., 'compass' in 1st.

226 *sweating sickness*: there was an epidemic in 1517.

Mother Cornelius' tub: used to 'cure' venereal disease.

balls: tennis balls were stuffed with hair.

twelve companies: the great trade guilds.

227 *died up*: i.e. all died.

227 *Plus erat in artifice quam arte*: there was more in the artist than in the art.

brother Banks: had a famous performing horse called Marocco.

fiery facias: fieri facias = execution against property for the settlement of a debt.

diebus illis: in those days.

228 *the King of France and the Switzers*: Francis I's 1515 expedition to recover Milan.

229 *Munster*: Jan Leyden's insurrection took place in 1534.

230 *mittimus*: commital.

Quid plura?: what more?

234 *Ovid*: Nashe uses Marlowe's trans. of the *Amores*.

qui in suas poenas ingeniosus erat: Ovid, who was resourceful in devising his own punishment.

Cnipperdolings and Muncers: Knipperdolinck was a leader of the Munster rebellion; Munzer a founder of Anabaptism.

235 *Deteriora sequunter*: they follow the worse path.

quod petitur poena est: what is sought is punishment.

237 *Henry Howard*: poet and translator, 1517?–45, seems never to have travelled to Italy.

238 *Geraldine*: known only from Surrey's sonnet 'Description and praise of His Love Geraldine', printed in *Tottel's Miscellany*, and thought to be directed at Elizabeth Fitzgerald. The sonnet's opening lines may have suggested to Nashe Surrey's imaginary adventures in Italy: 'From Tuscany came my lady's worthy race, /Fair Florence was sometime her ancient seat.'

239 *Paradise*: the name of a room.

Hinc illae lachrimae: Terence, hence these tears . . .

240 *Erasmus*: Erasmus and More were friends but evidently never met in Rotterdam. Nashe describes (in fiction) the creation of Erasmus' *Praise of Folly* (1511) and More's *Utopia* (1516).

Wittenberg: McKerrow suggests that Nashe might occasionally glance at Cambridge in his satire.

241 *secundum formam statuti*: according to the established decree.

his: i.e. Tully's.

quemadmodums and quapropters: in so far as, wherefore.

241 *esse posse videatur*: it seems that it may be.

dum iuga montis aper: while the boar loves the mountain heights (your name and praises will endure).

dixi: I have spoken.

arms: 2nd edn. adds 'carousing a whole health to the Duke's arms'.

242 *knit*: while the sense of the phrase is clear, this word has defeated all editors.

firking flantado amphibologies: dancing, flaunting quibbles.

243 *Maechi*: adulterers, punning on mechanical and Mecca.

O quantus artifex pereo: O how great an artist is lost in me.

Acolastus the Prodigal Child: by Gulielmus Gnapheus, 1529, trans. into English from the Latin in 1540.

244 *Carolostadius*: Andrew Bodenstein (Carlstadt), a radical Protestant.

Quae supra nos nihil ad nos: those things which are above us are nothing to us.

245 *Nizolius*: Italian compiler of a thesaurus from Cicero's writings.

Cornelius Agrippa: German wide-ranging and colourful scholar, reputed to be a magician.

246 *Cromwell*: was never at the Emperor's court, though he negotiated with him over Henry's divorce from Katherine of Aragon.

249 *but*: absolutely.

251 *Brother Trulies*: feigned friend? McKerrow suggests a name for Puritans.

252 *neck-verse*: usually first verse of psalm 51, beginning 'Miserere', which had to be read in Latin by a felon claiming benefit of clergy, and so avoiding punishment by a secular court.

point in his tables: reference to backgammon, or to a commonplace book.

253 *Ingenium nobis molle Thalia dedit*: Ovid, Thalia has given us a malleable mind; said of all women by Sappho.

255 *Subaudi*: understand.

Mr John Russell: McKerrow cites him as a frequent ambassador and traveller.

255 *Petro Aretino*: an author, when Nashe wrote, much admired especially for his satires. The stories Nashe tells are apocryphal.

Peccavi, confiteor: I have sinned, I confess.

256 *De Tribus Impostoribus Mundi*: much cited in the Renaissance but possibly non-existent attack on the three 'impostors' Moses, Christ, and Mohammed.

257 *Il flagello de principi, Il veritiero, Il divino, and L'unico Aretino*: scourge of princes, truth-teller, the divine, and the rare Aretino.

Beza: Théodore de Bèze, French theologian who wrote *risqué* verses in his youth.

258 *nunc dimittis*: now you are dismissed.

259 *above e-la*: above the highest musical note.

260 *Non veniunt in idem pudor et amor*: shame and love do not come to the same place.

primus motor: the first mover.

261 *dii mundi*: gods of the world.

Dulce puella . . . amari: Ovid, a girl is a sweet evil; I pursue that which flees; love is my cause for following; O unhappy me; why did I see, why have I perished; I love without patience, only let her be patient to be loved.

262 *ex lachrimis lachrimae*: tears produce more tears.

263 *Aculeo alatus*: winged with a spur.

Militat omnis amans: all lovers are fighters.

Sufficit tandem: able to resist.

264 *Ideo mirum quia monstrum*: wonderful because outlandish.

Liberalitas liberalitate perit: the generous spirit perishes through that generosity.

Frontis nulla fides: appearances are not trustworthy.

Cura futuri est: there is a care for the future.

Cani capilli mei compedes: grey hairs are my shackles.

Speramus lucent: we hope, they shine.

Nos quoque florimus: = floruimus.

265 *Spe alor*: fed by hope.

Luctus monumenta manebunt: monuments of grief will remain.

266 *Inopem me copia fecit*: abundance makes me poor.

267 *Quid regna sine usu*: what use are dominions that cannot be enjoyed?

268 *Paschal de Medices*: there was no Medici of this name.

269 *venomous*: emended from 2nd edn., 'venemost' in 1st.

against it: 2nd edn. adds 'The name of the place I remember not, but it is as one goes to Saint Paul's church not far from the jemmes Piazza.' (jemmes = Gems? Jews?)

[*most*] *monstrous*: emended from 'monstrost', both edns.

270 *Gallant Devices*: there was a *Gorgeous Gallery of Gallant Inventions* published in 1578.

271 *over it*: emended from 'it out', both edns.

lineally: McKerrow suggests a misprint for 'lively'.

there: emended by Grosart to 'they'.

273 *Mercator's globe*: he designed a pair of globes of the world in 1541–51.

whilst: emended from 2nd edn., 1st has 'whiles'.

Lanquet's chronicle: the plague is described in the entry for 1522.

274 *zany*: fool, or in this case perhaps simply attendant.

279 *an*: added from 2nd edn.

it: emended by Grosart.

280 *foot spondaeus*: a musical tempo; Nashe took the story from Cornelius Agrippa.

284 *Epicharcus*: Epicharmus, Greek playwright.

Spanish figs: i.e. poisoned.

it: added from 2nd edn.

285 *Vobis . . . credite*: Ovid, *Ars Amatoria*.

286 *misers*: sop made from crumbs, emended from 2nd edn., 1st reads 'misons'.

287 *cum . . . putato*: Ovid, *Tristia*.

290 *shrowd*: Lawlis notes that this spelling puns on shrewd and shroud.

292 *from*: emended McKerrow, 'for' both edns.

293 *yarking the blind bear at Paris Garden*: bull- and bear-baiting

was a popular spectacle; Paris Garden was located in the theatre district on Bankside; yarking = beating.

298 *non est inventus*: he has not been discovered: sherrif's term when an arrest is impossible.

301 *size ace and the dice*: i.e. the whole lot, exact reference unknown.

Tyburn: place of public execution.

the mother: hysteria.

spiritus vini: spirits of wine.

in her grandame's beans: exact reference uncertain = in an impossible spot.

308 *Ardes and Guines*: Ard and Guisnes, where the Field of the Cloth of Gold meeting occurred in 1520.

JACK OF NEWBURY

313 *John Winchcomb*: loosely based on the father and son of that name who were engaged in cloth manufacture in Newbury in the first half of the 16th century.

Thomas of Reading: Deloney published *Thomas of Reading* some time between 1597 and 1600; the earliest extant edition is 1612.

319 *Actaeon's head*: i.e. horns.

322 *civil*: in this context, grave? obliging?

323 *The Beginning of the World*: popular country dance.

327 *parsons . . . wives*: in fact, this happened under Edward VI, not in the reign of Henry VIII, when *Jack of Newbury* is set.

329 *George a Green*: legendary pinder of Wakefield, a popular folk hero.

333 *knew that*: emended from 'that knew', all edns.

336 *woad and madder*: respectively blue and red dyes.

broadcloths and kersies: two standard sizes and weights of cloth.

'Sir': the old man speaks a conventionalized representation of dialect.

Parry . . . Hungerford: well-known Berkshire families in the 16th century.

337 *Stillyard*: trading-hall for foreign merchants in London.

339 *Sir Henry Englefield*: unidentified, but the family was pro-
minent in Berkshire in the 16th century.

the people Cynomolgy: described in Pliny.

340 *Mogunce*: Mainz.

Flodden: Deloney's account of the battle of Flodden Field
(1513) is drawn from contemporary historians (Lawlis).

341 *Turney and Turwin*: cf. the opening of *The Unfortunate
Traveller*.

THE SONG: Child, no. 168; there are other extant versions.

343 *welt or guard*: forms of trimming.

Garter: emended from Q5 following Lawlis, 'Garret' in
preceding edns.

344 *ants*: Jack's story is an attack on Cardinal Wolsey, especially on
his extortionary taxes.

347 *Will Summers*: Henry VIII's jester, looked upon as famous by
the time Deloney wrote.

Empson and Dudley: beheaded in 1510.

348 *selling broom*: the lowest possible trade.

Golia's: Goliath's.

350 *at Sir Amias Paulet's*: according to some early sources this did
occur.

THE MAIDENS' SONG: Child, no. 9, preserved solely by
Deloney.

353 *Whether*: emended from 1626 edn., 1619 has 'Where'.

357 *host cloth*: 'house' in later edns. = cloth used to cover a horse?

359 *Viriat*: the famous men in Jack's paintings were taken by
Deloney from descriptions in Thomas Fortescue's *The Forest*
(1571), a translation from Pedro Mexia (Lawlis; Deloney's
reliance on Fortescue was first explored by H. E. Rollins).

360 *Gabienus*: emended by Lawlis to Galerus, emperor from
AD 305–11, following the source in Fortescue.

363 *Belinus and Brennus*: appear in most Elizabethan chronicles.

Blackwell Hall: the London wool market.

364 *clothier*: emended, following Lawlis, from 'clothiers'.

Patch: was in fact Wolsey's Fool, though, unlike Will
Summers, he achieved little notoriety.

365 *It is true*: emended to 'Is it true?' in later edns.

    killing of calves: Wolsey was the son of an Ipswich butcher.

366 *So it was*: one of Deloney's dangling sentences = 'Thus it happened'.

367 *Coromandae*: reference unknown.

    Taprobana: island off Sri Lanka; possibly the source is Mandeville.

374 *cack*: Benedick's mispronunciation of 'cake', punning on excrete.

    shack: Jack = low fellow.

    you: succeeding edns. add 'be Goz bode'; i.e. by God's bones.

    bud: bleed.

380 *trodden down by many*: i.e. despised by everyone (Lawlis).

387 *Morlesse*: Marlaix, won by Surrey in 1522.

    Sir George Rigley: probably Deloney's creation; his 'brother' Sir Edward did exist and was knighted (Lawlis).

389 *step*: Lawlis reads this as 'stop'.

390 *because he*: emended from later edns. following Lawlis, 1619 reads 'who'.

    Temple: law court.

GLOSSARY

THIS glossary contains words which are unfamiliar to the modern reader and words which sometimes have a dramatically different Elizabethan meaning to their current usage. Some only appear once in the anthology, some many times. They are given in the parts of speech in which they first appear. Non-English words and phrases will be found in the Explanatory Notes.

abeston, asbestos
aby, pay for
accompt, account
addises, adzes
advant, avouch
affects, affections
alla Napolitana, in the Neapolitan style
ambages, roundabout ways
ambassade, message brought by an ambassador
ambs-ace, two aces thrown with the dice, or a particular game
Amphitrio, Amphitrion
ancient, flag or flag-carrier
anciently, as in times past
anita, anise
antepast, i.e. *antipasto*, appetizer
appeach, impeach
apple-squire, whore's attendant
aspis, asp
assuring, betrothal
astonied, astonished
auglet, fringe

baily, bailiff
bankrout, bankrupt
banskin, leather apron
bargynet, a country dance

bark, boat
bavin, kindling
Bergomast, native of Bergamo
Bersabe, Beersheba
besprent, sprinkled
bewrayed, revealed
bill, halberd
billiment, headband
bitter, bittern = small heron-like bird
black sant, black sanctus = burlesque hymn
blist, blessed (blissful)
bollen, puffed up
bona roba, good stuff, sexy woman
boorden, boarded
boot-halers, marauders
boot, advantage
botcher, patcher, cobbler
brack, flaw
brawl, quarrel, but also a dance step
brewer's cow, a brewer's tub (cowl)?
bridal, wedding
broaches, spits
broccing, broken
brocking, stinking
bucks, very dirty clothes
bumbast, cotton-wool padding

calivers, light muskets

camerike, cambric = fine linen

cammock, crooked stick

Camnassado, Spanish = night attack

carterly, like a carter = ill-bred

caudle, warm, soothing drink

caul, obscuring membrane

cauls, netted caps, hairnets

certes, assuredly

chaffer, bargain

chance-medley, mostly accidental

channel, gutter

chipped, chapped

cimeces, bed-bugs

cleanly, ably

cleaving beetle, mallet

clerkly, wisely

cloddered, clotted

clog, wooden leg-iron

cobs, heads

cockering, pampering

cockney, pet, cockered (spoiled) child

cockscomb, fool

coddlings, apples

coif, or quoif = close-fitting cap

coil, noisy disturbance

coistrel, base

collachrymation, weeping

colloquintida, bitter apple, a purgative

compt, count

coney-skins, rabbit skins

confortative, comfortative

congé, pay one's respects on departure

conster, construe

continens, continence (a mythical stone)

contrarieties, balancing of opposites

cookmate, cockmate = chief friend

cool staves, cowl staves: carrying rods for tubs

cool-staff, cowl (tub) staff

cools, cowls

copesmates, companions in business

corrasive, corrosive

corrival, one of several rivals

corses, corpses

countenance, conduct, repute

counterpoint, counterpane

counters, false coins

countervail, equal

courtlike, courtly

crabs, crabapples

crake, crack = boast

crankled, zig-zag

cullises, strong broths

current, modish

cypress, cloth of gold

damask water, rose water

Dan, Master

dangerously, injuriously

danted, daunted

dehortment, dissuasion

delphinical, Delphian (oracular, powerful) and finical?

descant, the melodious accompaniment sung above plainsong

devoir, duty

diddledum, something trifling

discovert, uncovered, at a disadvantage

dissimuled, dissimulated

distrain, grasp

dock, buttocks, tight-fitting stockings

dodkin, diminutive of *doit* = not at all

dole, sorrow
drave, drove
droven, driven
drumbling, wasting time
dry bobs, bitter taunts
dunstable, plain
dunstically, foolishly
eftsoons, shortly, soon
emprise, enterprise
ensamples, examples
entronized, enthroned
erst, first
esprit, mind, cleverness
estridge, ostrich

fa, faith
faburden, the undersong, a kind
  of counterpoint
factotum, with total power
fain, glad, willing
fairing, present bought at a fair
fantasy, imagination
far fet, far-fetched = exotic
fare, bearing, aspect; also
  perhaps fair = unblemished,
  beauty
feat, fit, apt
fere, companion
filed, polished
finigraphical, finical
fizgigging, running about
fleering, mocking, smiling
  obsequiously
fleeting, unfaithfulness,
  inconstancy
fletcher, maker of bows and
  arrows
foist, break wind
fraught, stored
frieze, coarse wool
frisling, frizzling = form hair
  into tight curls
frump, jibe

frushed, crushed, bruised

galded, galled
galliard, a lively dance
gambon, gammon
gan, began
gargarisms, gargles
gathers, heart, liver, and lungs
gear, affair
geason, rare, barren
Gehenna, hell
gelt, slashed
gent, noble
gentils, gentles = people of
  rank
gentry, good breeding
ghostly father, father confessor
gibrige, gibberish
glaze, specious talk, flattery
glazeworm, glow-worm
gleke, taunting jest
glistering, glittering
glozes, flattering speeches
God wot, God knows
goodman, husband
Gramercy, God-a-mercy =
  expression of thanks
grogeran, a coarse fabric
grutch, grudge, blame
guard, trimming
gudgeon, fish
guerdon, reward
guerison, recovery

hackster, prostitute
haled, sailed
halt, limp
hangars, scabbard supports
hap, chance, fortune
hey pass, a magician's call
hight, was named
hobby, small falcon

hoddy-peak, blockhead

honesty, chastity

horseleech, veterinarian

hot-house, brothel

houghs, hofs? = beer houses

huckle, hip

huddles, cranky old people

hugger mugger, secrecy

huswife, housewife

imported, related

in ure, into operation

incarnatives, mixtures to heal wounds

incontinent, at once, immediately

Indian, valuable

inexprimable, inexpressible

infortunate, unfortunate

inkhorn, dull and pedantic

intercommoning, sharing in common

ivy bush, sign of a tavern specifically selling wine

jennet, small horse

jetteth, boasts

ketha, quotha = says he

kirtle, outer-skirt

kitchen-stuff, dripping

kite, bird of prey

lash, lurch

latchet, thong to fasten a shoe

lazar, leper, diseased person

lear and caddis, plain edging or binding

lee, lye used in washing

leese, lose

leman, lover

leno, pander

Lenvoi, sometimes 'envoy', the final section of a poem which directly adresses the reader

level coil, roughly, perhaps from the game *lever le cul*

licorous, lickerous = lustful

lightly, in general

lin, stop

link, torch

liquored, polished

liripoop, long tail on a graduate's hood

lists, strong edges of material

lobcocks, fools

losel, scoundrel

lubeck liquor, strong Lubeck beer

make, mate

manumit, release

mary-bones, marrow-bones = knees

maugre, in spite of

meaning simply, with an innocent intent

meed, reward

mel, honey

memento, brown study

merlin, small European falcon

ming, mix

miniver, ermine, worn on MA hood

minorites, Franciscan friars, persons of minor rank

mithridate, antidote

mo, more

mome, fool, idiot

motley, multi-coloured: the jester's traditional outfit

mushromp, mushroom

neckenger, neckerchief

noddle, head

noise, band
nonce, purpose in hand

occupied, used
occupiers, dishonest merchants
old who, old so and so? A
    person of importance?
ordnance, large guns
orificial, mouth-making =
    bombastic
orlop, lower deck
orts, scraps
ouches, brooches
ought, owed
overlashing, unruly, excessive
overseen, deceived
overthwartness, testiness,
    crossness
overwhart, overthwart =
    indirect

pack needle, large, strong needle
painful, painstaking
palfrey, saddle-horse
pantofles, shoes or slippers with
    high cork heels
pap, nipple
participate, share
partlet, collar, ruff
pavion, pavan = a slow and
    stately type of dance
pentices, overhanging eaves,
    balconies
percase, by chance, it may be
phlebotomy, letting blood
pickerdevant: pique devant =
    Van Dyke beard
pikes, pointed rocks
pile, mole or pier
pillowbere, pillowcase
pin, tuning peg
pinglingly, triflingly

piperly pickthank, paltry
    sycophant
pleated, plaited
plight, plighted
plum, plump, a choice thing
pointed, designed
polt foot, club foot
poniards, daggers
pontificalibus, bishop's robes =
    flash clothes
porpentine's, porcupine's
port coulez, portcullis
portigues, Portuguese gold coins
Portingale, Portuguese
pothecary's, apothecary's =
    dispenser of drugs
pounced, decorated
powdering, pickling
praemunire, awkward
    predicament
pretermitted, overlooked
prick, mark out in musical
    notation
pricking, spurring, urging a
    horse on
princox, saucy youth
purblind, short-sighted, almost
    blind
pursuivant, attendant, herald
puttock, bird of prey, usually
    kite

quatted, overloaded
quean, strumpet
queristers, choristers
quills, bobbins
quinch, flinch
quotidian fit, the daily recurring
    fit of fever

rammishly, foully
rechat, series of notes played to
    call the hounds together
recomfort, console, refresh

recompting, recounting
reduced, brought back
resiance, residence
retchless, reckless
rolls, pads of hair etc. for a head-dress
rooms, positions, situations
rowers, those who smooth down the cloth with rollers
runagate, renegade

sackless, innocent
sarsenet, a fine, silk material
sate, sat
saw, saying, maxim
scruzed, crushed
scuppets, shovels
scutchery, knavery
se-reverence, save your reverence = if you'll excuse me
sea, large swell
seased, assessed
seely, silly = innocent
semblant, demeanour
seventeens, a dance step
shambles, slaughter house
shift, joke
shot, bill
shrubbing, fidgeting
shrucking, shrugging
silly, innocent
sith, since
sithens, since
slaughter budge, lambskin fur from slaughter houses?
sleightly, deftly, slightly
slip shoes, slippers
slip, counterfeit coin
slops, baggy breeches
slut, woman of low character, ill-bred.
snudge, skinflint
soolenest, sullenest

sound play, occupied
sound, swoon, *sounded*, swooned
spital, hospital
squitter-books, diarrhoea-books
stale, decoy
stammel, coarse woollen cloth
start, started = moved
starter, wanderer
steel glass, polished steel mirror
stert, started
stoccado, thrust
straggler, loose woman, wanderer
strait, tight
strakes, streaks
straw, strew
sunonimas, synonyms
surfled, painted
surquedry, arrogance
swath-clouts, swaddling clothes

tainted, tented = protected and allowed to heal
tantara, imitates trumpet sound = loudly and lustily
tentoes, ten toes: on foot
thread-bottom, spool
thripping, snapping
throughly, thoroughly
thurleth, twirl
tickle, capricious
tickled, irritated
toss, handle
train, trickery
travail, labour
trewage, tribute
troup, trope
trulls, drabs, low girls
turned over, executed
twilted, quilted
tympany, swelling like dropsy
tyntarnell, a singing dance tune

uneaths, scarcely
uttered, sold

vilde, vile
violands, violins
vizard, mask, associated with
  prostitutes
vocables, designations, words

walter, roll, toss
wearish, sickly, wizened
weasand, throat
weenest, thinkest

wem, blemish
wheal, pimple
whenas, whereas, while on the
  other hand
whilom, once upon a time
whipperginnie, imaginary place,
  loose woman, card game
whist, silent
wight, person
winch, kick impatiently
wis, know; *wist*, knew

younker, fashionable young
  man

THE WORLD'S CLASSICS

A Select List

HANS ANDERSEN: Fairy Tales
Translated by L. W. Kingsland
Introduction by Naomi Lewis
Illustrated by Vilhelm Pedersen and Lorenz Frølich

ARTHUR J. ARBERRY (Transl.): The Koran

LUDOVICO ARIOSTO: Orlando Furioso
Translated by Guido Waldman

ARISTOTLE: The Nicomachean Ethics
Translated by David Ross

JANE AUSTEN: Emma
Edited by James Kinsley and David Lodge

Mansfield Park
Edited by James Kinsley and John Lucas

Northanger Abbey, Lady Susan, The Watsons,
and Sanditon
Edited by John Davie

HONORÉ DE BALZAC: Père Goriot
Translated and Edited by A. J. Krailsheimer

CHARLES BAUDELAIRE: The Flowers of Evil
Translated by James McGowan
Introduction by Jonathan Culler

WILLIAM BECKFORD: Vathek
Edited by Roger Lonsdale

R. D. BLACKMORE: Lorna Doone
Edited by Sally Shuttleworth

KEITH BOSLEY (Transl.): The Kalevala

JAMES BOSWELL: Life of Johnson
The Hill / Powell edition, revised by David Fleeman
Introduction by Pat Rogers

MARY ELIZABETH BRADDON: Lady Audley's Secret
Edited by David Skilton

ANNE BRONTË: The Tenant of Wildfell Hall
Edited by Herbert Rosengarten and Margaret Smith

CHARLOTTE BRONTË: Jane Eyre
Edited by Margaret Smith

Shirley
Edited by Margaret Smith and Herbert Rosengarten

EMILY BRONTË: Wuthering Heights
Edited by Ian Jack

GEORG BÜCHNER:
Danton's Death, Leonce and Lena, Woyzeck
Translated by Victor Price

JOHN BUNYAN: The Pilgrim's Progress
Edited by N. H. Keeble

EDMUND BURKE: A Philosophical Enquiry into the
Origin of our Ideas of the Sublime and Beautiful
Edited by Adam Phillips

FANNY BURNEY: Camilla
Edited by Edward A. Bloom and Lilian D. Bloom

THOMAS CARLYLE: The French Revolution
Edited by K. J. Fielding and David Sorensen

LEWIS CARROLL: Alice's Adventures in Wonderland
and Through the Looking Glass
Edited by Roger Lancelyn Green
Illustrated by John Tenniel

A London Life *and* The Reverberator
Edited by Philip Horne

The Spoils of Poynton
Edited by Bernard Richards

RUDYARD KIPLING: The Jungle Books
Edited by W. W. Robson

Stalky & Co.
Edited by Isobel Quigly

MADAME DE LAFAYETTE: The Princesse de Clèves
Translated and Edited by Terence Cave

WILLIAM LANGLAND: Piers Plowman
Translated and Edited by A. V. C. Schmidt

J. SHERIDAN LE FANU: Uncle Silas
Edited by W. J. McCormack

CHARLOTTE LENNOX: The Female Quixote
Edited by Margaret Dalziel
Introduction by Margaret Anne Doody

LEONARDO DA VINCI: Notebooks
Edited by Irma A. Richter

MIKHAIL LERMONTOV: A Hero of our Time
Translated by Vladimir Nabokov with Dmitri Nabokov

MATTHEW LEWIS: The Monk
Edited by Howard Anderson

JACK LONDON:
The Call of the Wild, White Fang, and Other Stories
Edited by Earle Labor and Robert C. Leitz III

NICCOLÒ MACHIAVELLI: The Prince
Edited by Peter Bondanella and Mark Musa
Introduction by Peter Bondanella

War and Peace
Translated by Louise and Aylmer Maude
Edited by Henry Gifford

ANTHONY TROLLOPE: The American Senator
Edited by John Halperin

The Belton Estate
Edited by John Halperin

Cousin Henry
Edited by Julian Thompson

The Eustace Diamonds
Edited by W. J. McCormack

The Kellys and the O'Kellys
Edited by W. J. McCormack
Introduction by William Trevor

Orley Farm
Edited by David Skilton

Rachel Ray
Edited by P. D. Edwards

The Warden
Edited by David Skilton

IVAN TURGENEV: First Love and Other Stories
Translated by Richard Freeborn

MARK TWAIN: Pudd'nhead Wilson and Other Tales
Edited by R. D. Gooder

GIORGIO VASARI: The Lives of the Artists
Translated and Edited by Julia Conaway Bondanella and Peter Bondanella

JULES VERNE: Journey to the Centre of the Earth
Translated and Edited by William Butcher

VIRGIL: The Aeneid
Translated by C. Day Lewis
Edited by Jasper Griffin

HORACE WALPOLE : The Castle of Otranto
Edited by W. S. Lewis

IZAAK WALTON and CHARLES COTTON:
The Compleat Angler
Edited by John Buxton
Introduction by John Buchan

OSCAR WILDE: Complete Shorter Fiction
Edited by Isobel Murray

The Picture of Dorian Gray
Edited by Isobel Murray

MARY WOLLSTONECRAFT:
Mary *and* The Wrongs of Woman
Edited by Gary Kelly

VIRGINIA WOOLF: Mrs Dalloway
Edited by Claire Tomalin

Orlando
Edited by Rachel Bowlby

ÉMILE ZOLA:
The Attack on the Mill and Other Stories
Translated by Douglas Parmée

Nana
Translated and Edited by Douglas Parmée

A complete list of Oxford Paperbacks, including The World's Classics, OPUS, Past Masters, Oxford Authors, Oxford Shakespeare, and Oxford Paperback Reference, is available in the UK from the Arts and Reference Publicity Department (BH), Oxford University Press, Walton Street, Oxford OX2 6DP.

In the USA, complete lists are available from the Paperbacks Marketing Manager, Oxford University Press, 200 Madison Avenue, New York, NY 10016.

Oxford Paperbacks are available from all good bookshops. In case of difficulty, customers in the UK can order direct from Oxford University Press Bookshop, Freepost, 116 High Street, Oxford, OX1 4BR, enclosing full payment. Please add 10 per cent of published price for postage and packing.